ord

Peggy Woodford was born and spent her childhood in Assam. She read English at St Anne's College Oxford, spent a postgraduate year in Rome and published her first novel in 1963 at the age of 26. She has since published 14 books in a variety of genres, including biography, history, and teenage fiction, and with *Cupid's Tears* returns after a gap of 32 years to the novel. She is married to a barrister, has three daughters, and lives in South London.

SCEPTRE

Cupid's Tears

PEGGY WOODFORD

SCEPTRE

First published in 1995 by Hodder and Stoughton
First published in paperback in 1996 by Hodder and Stoughton
A division of Hodder Headline PLC
A Sceptre Paperback

British Library Cataloguing in Publication Data

Woodford, Peggy
  Cupid's Tears
  I. Title
  823. 914 [F]

ISBN 0-340-63958-X

Typeset by Hewer Text Composition Services, Edinburgh
Printed and bound in Great Britain by
Cox & Wyman Ltd, Reading, Berkshire

Hodder and Stoughton
A division of Hodder Headline PLC
338 Euston Road
London NW1 3BH

PART ONE

1

Natalie struggled to stay in my womb, Jane burst out of it. Did my mother really say that? The memory neatens and sets family dicta, but the facts remain: I was born two weeks late in breech position, over-big. Jane's rushed arrival took less than two hours and she took her first breath unaided, giving a loud yell as she was lifted away from my mother's thighs. She did everything early – cut her teeth, walked, talked. As I extended the perimeters of my existence ahead of her I became aware of this pushing, hustling force behind me. All elder children feel invaded but I was stormed.

I too was quick, bright, deft – I learned to read, to write, to ride a bike, to swim, as quickly as any of my peers. But Jane was different. Jane wasn't interested in competing with her peers. It was me she matched herself against. She singled me out as soon as her baby eyes could focus.

She is six, I am eight. All morning we play separately on that Devon beach; I build a sand boat and lie in it, staring at the blue sky above me until I have to shut my eyes before they slide into infinity; Jane is over by the rocks trying to catch shrimps in a pool.

Slap. Cold wet brown snakes slither on my skin, tarry squares and weed lie thick on my face, my chest. I scream. I can't sit up, I can't get the filthy old fishing net off me. I can hear Jane laughing, and when I am free at last I run at her, catch her, fall on top of her, dig my nails into her. I want to kill her. She bites my arm, we grab each other's hair. It is the worst of many violent fights.

When I think of my sister I think of nets, of mesh, of toils in its old sense: a netted space into which a quarry is driven and ensnared.

I shouldn't have asked them to the wedding. I needn't have told them anything, after all I'd kept them in the dark up until then. My letters have been so dull and uninformative for years I could have left them thinking that nothing much ever happened to me.

I always choose to write on those pale blue air letters not only because of convenience but because they annihilate real communication – the end is too clearly in sight. You have no space to expand so you don't. My father has used those air letters too, perhaps for the same reasons – I've got no real impression of his life in Sydney beyond the fact his new career is going well and he likes Australia.

On the other hand Jane always uses, on the rare occasions she has written to me, copious sheets of white onion-skin paper and lets her thoughts move freely as she winds through her work, her lovers, her successes. I learn she has got a first at Melbourne University in history, that she works for some tycoon, that she lives with Jack or is it Jake in a lovely flat in Sydney with a view of the harbour, that she has a most agreeable life. She hardly ever mentions Dad, but that means nothing. They were always close. I'm sure nothing has changed.

I also got a good degree – in French and Spanish at UCL – and I did tell Jane about this, but not how hard I worked or how borderline my degree was. A feather of a mark could have slid me down to the next class. I also did not tell her how I'd then read for the Bar, eaten my dinners at Middle Temple, taken a six-month pupillage in the Chambers of Frederick Mentieth QC, done well enough to be kept on for a second six months, and then been offered, to my delight and slight surprise, a place in those same Chambers. I am now a fully fledged barrister with a growing practice and my family know nothing.

I've filled those greyish-blue pages with insipid chatter and hovered often over a possible PS: *By the way, I've been called to the Bar*. Or: *I've successfully defended my first case*. But somehow there has never been quite room for it.

*   *   *

Freddie took me to look at the Stamford Collection the weekend we became engaged. Dunham Massey isn't far from his country hideout; he likes going to look at pictures at weekends. (Anthea was addicted to galleries.)

'That Venus looks like you. I told you she did. The moment I first saw you you reminded me of her.' We stare at Guercino's half-naked Venus, draped in inky blue. I see her massive white stomach and her high tight breasts and am not sure Freddie's flattering me. Then my eyes move to Venus's face and I see exactly what he means. The eyebrows, the bridged nose, the loose line of the mouth – Venus is me.

She is lightly holding a net, a fishing net, in which lies a kicking baby. The baby's left arm and leg are pushing at the net but he doesn't look at all worried at being trapped in mesh. All the same, I shiver.

'That's my favourite Guercino.'

'The poor baby—'

'Cupid. Venus is releasing her son from the net.' Freddie jingles his change in the pockets of his baggy red cotton shorts. He is staring at the picture with the same expression he has for an open bottle of good wine. 'Little does she know what's going to happen.'

'What is going to happen?'

I lean against Freddie, my shivers subsiding. The net isn't cold and rough and tarry, the gull cries of that long-ago beach die in my ears.

'Venus and Vulcan and Mars.'

'Tell me the story, Freddie. You know how ignorant I am.' Freddie beams when he explains things. The first time he noticed me was when I said I'd never heard of a famous judge he was quoting. He stopped in mid-flow and stared at me. I'm sorry, I started to say, but he took my arm and told me how refreshing it was I didn't nod and nod and pretend with a blank look at the back of my smile. How refreshing. Come out to dinner.

So today we stare at the luscious reds and browns and flesh tones of the greatest subtlety and I learn that Venus was married to Vulcan but had a passionate affair with Mars. Vulcan was so angry when he learned about it he constructed a net fine enough to be almost invisible and so strong no one could break out of it which descended on Venus and Mars and pinned them in flagrante on the bed.

'When Vulcan fetched the other gods to witness his triumph they all had a good laugh at the pinned-down pair.' Freddie peers at the picture closely and grunts. 'Look at Cupid and tell me what you think of his position.'

'The net doesn't seem to be bothering him at all. He's very relaxed. In fact, his legs are spread so wide—'

'Quite. Quite. It's a delightful conceit. He's prefiguring his mother's disgrace.' Freddie gives me a look that means bed. We leave soon after and make love for the rest of the afternoon, my brain full of Cupid's sensual limbs, open, avidly pushing against the net.

Dear Jane,
Please don't be too surprised about the enclosed. It's all happened very quickly. Frederick Mentieth is my boss, so to speak. There's so much to tell you I hardly know where to begin. A year or so ago I was called to the Bar, joined a set of Chambers, and somehow found myself involved with the Head of Chambers, i.e. Freddie. (He's a widower, his wife died in an accident.) One thing led to another, as they say, and we decided to get married.

It would be wonderful if you could come. I've sent an invitation to Dad too, but I'm not counting on either of you being able to. Just hoping.

The two letters for Australia sit on the ledge above the radiator along with the postal detritus of a shared flat for two weeks after the rest of the invitations have been posted. They must go air mail, they need a visit to the post office, I keep forgetting to take them with me in the morning and when I do the queue at the post office is too long to endure. Then Freddie notices them one evening when he comes to collect me for a dinner, and pockets them with a frown.

'The clerks' room will post these. You should have handed them in.'

'I don't like to use my clerk for private matters—'

'Don't be ridiculous.'

Freddie is wearing his dinner jacket, and it occurs to me that those letters could stay in his pocket until the next occasion he wears it. Weeks. I smooth out my silk dress as I fold into the Saab, and we head for the Middle Temple. The Saab is new, creamy, smooth, and smells sweetly of money.

Freddie transfers the two envelopes from his pocket to the dashboard compartment, which closes with a deep-toned clunk.

'You're looking very nice, anyway. Is that a new dress?'

'No. I wore it for the opera last week.'

My father cannot come. His homeopathic practice is so busy that he simply can't leave at the moment. Since I knew he wouldn't I feel no particular disappointment or relief. His letter is warm, full of congratulations. I write back at once.

I hear nothing from Jane.

Ten days before the wedding Jane rings me in Chambers. Her accent is so Australian I don't recognise her voice.

'It's Jane.'

'Sorry, Jane who?'

'Your little sister dammit!'

'*Jane!* My God – what a lovely surprise—'

'You don't sound too thrilled.'

'I'm just thrown – I didn't expect a call—'

'Your news had me winded too, I'll admit.'

'You sound so clear and nearby you might be in London.'

'I am in London.'

'How wonderful! You've come! Jane, this is fantastic—'

I hope she didn't notice the swallow, the receiver slipping from my suddenly damp hand. I'm shaking slightly, yet I am pleased too, so pleased I feel tearful.

'Why didn't you tell me you were coming?'

'I like giving people surprises.'

We chat, we arrange to meet that evening (she's staying at a hotel in Queen's Gate) and I stare out of the window through the bare plane trees at the gulls wheeling over the Thames. The branches make a network against the blue sky, punctuated by round seeds like huge black peppercorns dangling from threads.

'It's so cold here, Nat. I'm freezing.'

'You've forgotten what November can be like.'

'What are you looking at?'

'The Thames through the trees.'

'You sound preoccupied. I'm looking at revolting pink velveteen curtains with half the hooks missing. This hotel is certainly not worth the amount they charge you.'

'Jane, I can't really talk now. I've got to hurry.'

'I was hoping you could rearrange your day to mark my arrival.'

'I'm in the middle of a case, and I'm due at the Old Bailey in fifteen minutes.'

'Dear me, how grand.'

It's lucky that all I have to do in Court 14 is listen to the judge's summing-up; my part in the defence of Anthony Obasi, charged with Grievous Bodily Harm with intent – he and his friends half-killed an old lady – is over. I sit watching the jury react and try to ignore the turmoil in my mind. I know I look calm, efficient, businesslike; my black suit, my white shirt and pristine bands, my neat grey wig sitting above my equally neatly tied-back hair, my polished shoes, all convey a reassuring image. My diamond ring is the only unrestrained thing about my attire, and it flashes with jazzy blue fire as I take notes and confer with colleagues. The hushed busyness, the nonstop rustle of papers, the quiet footsteps and lowered voices, the coughing and shuffling of the courtroom slowly reduce the sense of panic Jane's call has induced.

I'm doing what I love doing, I'm a good advocate, I flourish in court, I like thinking on my feet, my practice is growing. Relax, relax, Natalie. Jane is an adult too, with her own life. She's made an effort to come to my wedding, she's my only sister, and my only relative to come. I'm thrilled she's here. I stare at the flashing stone on my finger as it gives off blue and white sparks in the dull light of the court. Freddie holding it out had said:

'This was Anthea's, but she never wore it. She objected to diamonds for some reason. It's a very good South African diamond bought by my father before the last war which I had set for Anthea, but you may feel you'd rather not have something that was hers—'

'It's beautiful.'

'But you'd rather not wear it.'

'No, no, Freddie. I love it. I'd wear it. I'm hesitating because it's so grand . . .'

Grand. Just the word Jane used. My life is grand now, and even though I sometimes panic at the change I can't help rejoicing in it as well, in the visits to the Royal Opera House, to Glyndebourne, to the Garrick Club for supper after a theatre; in the settled acceptance of it all in Freddie's life and now in mine. I love the fact that I eat my lunch in the hall which saw the first production of *Twelfth Night*; I love the elegance of the buildings in the Temple; I love the black cotton gowns of junior counsel and the heavy silk of Queen's Counsel; I even love the sleazy magistrates' courts where I spend most of my time (this is my first appearance at the Old Bailey). The usher calling for silence in court is my muezzin.

My client gets eighteen months and I see the relief flash over him (though by the time he's in the cells he'll no doubt be complaining bitterly: 'It's not my fucking fault they leant so fucking hard on the old bitch.'). I start to collect up my papers and cast an automatic glance at the public gallery. Anthony Obasi's mother is holding her orange and purple turbaned head in her hands. Beyond her is a blonde, tanned woman, faintly familiar. Perhaps one of the girlfriends . . . I freeze. My hands miss the mouth of my briefcase and my notebook, full of loose pages, cascades on to the floor. As I and my leader, Francis Bates, a barrister in my Chambers, fumble about collecting the mess, I snatch another glance. The woman is standing, smiling at me. She makes a familiar gesture of hullo with her left hand. It's my sister Jane.

'I was waiting for you to perform – what a disappointment.'

'How on earth did you find me?'

'You mentioned the Old Bailey.'

'So I did. I hardly recognised you, Jane. You've stretched out. You're miles taller.'

'Well, it has been eight years since we saw each other last. I grew two inches in my first year in Melbourne. No kidding! And I went blonde ages ago – got fed up with the old mouse. You always had the best hair, Nat. You look good. Very soignée.'

'Don't mock—'

'I mean it. And just look at this ring. My God, is he a millionaire or something?'

Her loud Aussie voice carries across Pump Court; Francis Bates is walking ahead of us and I die as he turns his head fractionally, all ears. He collects Spy cartoons and is a vicious gossip.

'Come on, Jane, let's look at Temple Church. It's just here.'

'What?'

'Be a good tourist and go in while I give someone a message for Freddie.'

She goes unwillingly through the door while I chase after Francis.

'He's sitting as a judge this week, so he'll be back about five. Could you tell him my plans have changed for this evening as my sister's arrived unexpectedly from Australia—'

'Wonderful legs she's got. Australians look as if they've been stretched on a painless rack—'

'Sorry to use you as a go-between, Francis, but just tell him I'll pop in as soon as I've given her some tea.'

'I'll give her tea if you've got a problem.' Francis has reddish-brown eyes with blue flecks in them, and never quite meets your gaze. Nor do I ever know quite where he stands on anything.

'It's sweet of you but—'

'Thanks but no thanks, as they say in the movies.'

I smile feebly at him and hurry after Jane.

She is sitting slumped on the stone ledge that runs round the wall of the circular church, staring blankly at the recumbent effigies in the centre of the floor.

'This place feels weird.'

'It was bombed flat and has been reconstructed.'

'Nat, am I jet-lagged. I should have hit the sack this afternoon but I couldn't resist giving you a surprise.' She pats the stone seat beside her. 'Sit down.'

'What about some tea?'

'Sit down, Nat. Is this the church you're getting married in?'

'Yes.'

'I'm surprised you're doing the church bit.'

'Freddie wants it and I don't mind.'

'So tell me about this millionaire of yours.'

'Freddie's not a millionaire. This ring is very misleading. His father bought the diamond in the thirties.' I put my hand in my pocket to stop the ring sending beams through the dimness.

'And he's your boss.'

'Not really. He's Head of Chambers.'

'That sounds like your boss.'

'It doesn't work like that. We're all self-employed, with contracts with the clerks, Freddie too. He's just got the boring unpaid job of keeping us all together, more or less united.' I can see she's not listening.

'How old?'

'Forty-two.'

'Could he be a father figure?'

'Not at *all*.'

'Still Miss Prickly Pear I see.' She hugs me, and I try not to be stiff. She smells overwhelmingly of some scent she's probably bought at the airport; the familiar mole on her neck looks larger. 'But he's fourteen years older than you, Nat. That's a lot.'

'It's totally unimportant. I never think about it.'

'If he's got a young mind—'

'He has. I'm sure you'll like him. And don't be put off by his pompous look – it's just a smokescreen.'

'All Englishmen put up smokescreens. All of them.' There's a pause; out in the distant streets sirens are wailing, but the church is clammily silent.

'How's Jack?'

'Jake. I left him six months ago. Perhaps I didn't tell you.'

'You haven't written for ages.'

'The whole business upset me.' Jane has started shivering.

'Come on, Jane, you need a hot drink. Let's go and have tea.'

'I'm just jet-lagged. I tried to sleep on the plane but there was a baby just across the aisle and it yelled the whole time.' We leave the church and head arm-in-arm for Chancery Lane. It's the first time in our lives that we've walked linked.

'I'm so glad you've come.'

'I was glad to get away. Jake was a slob.'

'You were with him for years.'

'Three bloody wasted years. I always go for the tall good-looking ones and they turn out bastards every time.' Jane's eyes follow a tall blond man as he passes us. 'I sometimes wonder if I'm a nympho.'

'In here. It's nice and warm. You find a table, I'll get the tea.'

When I reach Jane with the tray she is staring at a poster of a muscle-bound man water-skiing off a rocky coast.

'God, I hate water-skiing. Maximum noise and gas consumption just for one person to slide along the surface of the water. Jake loved it. He would. Thanks.'

She takes her cup and cradles it, ignoring the buttered toast.

'So what happened with Jake?'

'I made the mistake of getting pregnant. I didn't mean to, but when I found out I definitely was, do you know, I was happy. I was stupid enough to think Jake might like the idea too.'

'And?'

'He told me to go have an abortion. We discussed it ever so rationally, ever so calmly, and by the time we'd finished I'd forgotten I ever wanted the child. I had the abortion and left Jake a week later.'

'Oh, Jane.'

'Don't listen to anyone who says you can have an abortion without side effects. I came out of it all jaunty, problem solved, on with life, then WHAM. I cried for three days without stopping except to be sick. Jake was useless. All he could say was pull yourself together, it's only an abortion. Eventually I did – enough to pack my stuff and move out then and there.'

Jane is beautiful. Her blue eyes are full of anger, her long hair is soft and untidy, the line of her chin is particularly appealing. Every man in the café is aware of her. I feel tidy and drab.

'In the plane coming over I read a terrible article about what happens to women in China when they have more than the one child they're allowed. They're dragged from their beds at night however pregnant they are and taken to the clinic and dealt with. Rip it out. Hundreds of women, hundreds of foetuses filling rows of bins. I went to the toilet and retched my heart out again. I'm still stiff from it here.' Jane rubs her ribs under her firm, bra-less breasts.

'Horrific.'

'I hate the world sometimes. Do you mind if I come and sit beside you – I'd rather have my back to the poster.'

She joins me and starts to eat the toast voraciously. I persuade her that the best way to spend her evening is to sleep off the effects of her journey, and we arrange to meet for lunch next day.

I'm fractionally late for my five o'clock conference, and when it's over I find a note on my desk from Freddie.

Dearest Nat, my mother isn't very well so I've decided to pop down and see her this evening. Sorry not to see you. Have an early night – you were saying you needed one – and don't forget the do tomorrow night. Love you.

There's no mention of Jane's arrival, so I take it that Francis Bates has not passed on my message.

Why did I buy it? Shrouded in polythene, it hangs on the back of my bedroom door; the thin sheeting moves and breathes in the draught, the dusty cold air sucked into my room by the heat of my gas fire.

Ivory lace, silk cut and curved and stitched by a top couturier, a dream of a wedding dress sold at less than half price because the wedding it was made for was cancelled. The jilted bride had taken it to a second-hand dress shop in Knightsbridge called Dress Sense, and I, passing by chance one day, had seen it in the window. I walked on, walked back, walked on. But the dress drew me, I returned and tried it on. The dress fitted me as if it had been made for me. It smelt of luxury. I looked at the tiny stitches inside the bodice, all hand-done, and was lost.

'It's a wonderful bargain, Madam. I felt so sorry for the young lady who brought it in. She asked me if I'd seen the film of *Great Expectations*.'

'*Great Expectations*?'

'She said she didn't want to be like the lady in it, ruined by a failed wedding. Wearing the dress until it rots in the dust.' The saleswoman was elderly, blue-rinsed, proper, a relic of the past herself. She told me she'd been in ladies' fashion for forty-five years.

'This dress is almost too beautiful.'

'Fit for a princess.'

'That's what worries me.' But I took my cheque book out all the same, and carried the big, softly rustling parcel back in strange trepidation. I had acted right out of character buying it.

That dress is a slowly growing ulcer in my existence. Since its arrival in my room I haven't even tried it on. It gleams richly at me on the rare occasions I sleep the night in the flat. It smells of lavender, of roses, of sweet fantasies. I wish I'd never seen it, never bought it.

I have a phobia about being wrongly dressed. The Bar demands that one should dress in a certain manner; there is no room for an embarrassing mistake. I worry for hours (though I wouldn't admit it) over what I should wear for the formal occasions Freddie takes me to. I have nightmares in which I'm trying to brazen out a banquet in a T-shirt and shorts.

The front door bangs and Sara comes upstairs, sticking her head through my door as she passes.

'Wow. Haven't seen you here on your own at this time for weeks. Have you eaten?'

'Had an omelette.'

'What's wrong, Nat?'

'Nothing. Just tired.'

'Come and talk to me while I eat. I've brought a take-away – there's plenty. Have some. God, I need a vodka!'

'Didn't know we had any.'

'Ta-ra-ra.' Sara produces a bottle with a flourish from her briefcase, pours two big measures and adds tonic. 'I was really afraid I was going to be made redundant this week. Instead, I heard I'd got a rise. So let's celebrate. Cheer up, Nat. Has your Freddie done something to upset you?'

'I'm in a state about that wedding dress.'

'Not again.'

'Plus the fact that my sister Jane has unexpectedly turned up. I'm thrilled to see her, but—'

'But?'

'Jane winds me up. Always has.'

'I could have sworn I'd bought a vegetable biryani, but it doesn't seem to be here. Bugger. Have some rice and a samosa.'

'I won't, thanks, I'm not hungry. But this vodka's just what I need.'

'Have another. Let's get smashed. What happened to your date tonight, anyway?'

'Freddie had to go and see his mother.'

'I'm surprised she's still alive.'

'Cat.'

'I still say he's too old for you.'

'If you get back on that subject I'll take this drink to my room.'

'All right, all right. You're in love with him and he's in love with you. But, Nat, you know as well as I do that's not the end of the story. You're not so naive. What about his friends, for instance – I bet they're all fat and grey-haired and old. I bet they're the kind of people you wouldn't be seen dead with normally.'

I stare at Sara. It's true that Freddie's got a lot of friends who are grey-haired, thick about the waist, and 'old' by our standards. He had a drinks party for me last week and I was the only person under thirty-five.

'I'll dilute the scene with my own friends.'

'You'll end up losing your friends and gaining his. You know why? Because you're moving into his house in Primrose Hill. Even the name is prim and proper. The friends come ready made, they're the neighbours, the locals. If you were the person with the house, you'd have more of a chance. Even then, after a bit his friends would drown you like a grey-suited, grey-haired boring tidal wave.'

'Don't be so bloody depressing. Freddie's not like that.'

'I'm going back to the take-away to fetch that biryani. And some more samosas. For someone who isn't hungry you've done very well.'

The front door crashes as Sara runs out down the street. I go to my room, strip my clothes off and put on the wedding dress. It settles itself round me with satisfying rustles; the silk is soft against my skin. The perfection of the fit and construction again overcome me. I dig out my silver evening shoes and stand in the confusion of my room (every drawer agape, clothes hanging from the picture rail) and stare at my reflection. With my hair still tied low on my neck, I look like a young Queen Victoria. I put some Christmas cracker pearls round my neck as the door crashes again and Sara's footsteps come running up the stairs.

'I'd left it on the counter. I got some more rice and purees and two more veg samosas. My God.'

'Yes.'

I am standing in the hall with the lighted bedroom behind me. Sara's at the inner door of the flat; the corridor between us is full of old letters, bits of paper, even leaves, lying on the floor.

'What a dress.' She is staring at me as if in shock. I twirl in embarrassment; the smell of dust, of unvacuumed carpets, begin to drown the subtle scent of the silk.

'You had it made for you, didn't you? You were lying when you said you got it second-hand.'

'I got it from Dress Sense. I couldn't afford this kind of thing new. Be fair.'

'It's perfect on you. It's utterly amazing.'

'But it's over the top, isn't it? I couldn't possibly wear it at my little low-key wedding.'

'Definitely for the aisle of St Paul's Cathedral and a fleet of bridesmaids trailing behind you.'

'I should never have bought it.'

'It's the most beautiful dress I've ever seen. Really. Just look at these folds and tucks. Did you do *Great Expectations* at school?'

'I know what you're going to say—'

'Miss Havisham's dress. God, that creepy scene, she's sitting there all bonkers in her wedding finery which she's had on for years – I never quite understood why she didn't get married in the first place – anyway, this is exactly the sort of dress she was wearing. A fairytale dress. Another samosa? More vodka?'

'What the hell, why not?'

'Careful – curry down the front would be a disaster.'

'Curry down the front would solve the problem. I wouldn't be able to wear it. End of worries.'

The phone rings, and Sara passes it to me, mouthing Jane.

'Nat? Hi. I can't sleep, I'm fed up with this awful hotel, I'm lonely, and I need cheering up. What are you doing right now?'

'Eating curry with Sara. Come and join us if you like.'

'I didn't think I'd find you in, to be honest.'

'Freddie cancelled. Get a taxi and come here.'

'You're miles out, aren't you?'

'Why does everyone think Clapham is miles out?'

'Is Jane coming?'

'Yes.'

'Take that dress off, Nat. You've spilt some vodka on it already.' Sara dabs at the creamy silk with a grubby teacloth and makes things worse.

'I don't want to take it off. It's doing something wonderful to my psyche.'

'Or the vodka is.'

'I've always said that clothes are not simply a cosmetic covering. They bite deep into you, they affect you. That's why I hate wearing the wrong thing.'

'That dress is hardly the right thing for a take-away curry at home.'

'It doesn't matter if I wear it here. Oh, Sara, isn't it the most perfect dream dress.'

'We already established that. I want to know about your sister. I honestly didn't know you had one.'

'She's been in Australia with my father since Mum died. That's eight years ago. God, so long. I hadn't seen Jane for eight years.'

'Did you invite her to the wedding?'

'I didn't think she'd come. I was gobsmacked when she rang up today. She came and watched me in court and I didn't recognise her at first. She's changed, I've changed, maybe we'll get on now. I used to think she was my evil genius.'

The phone rings again, it's Dave for Sara; she promptly invites him to come over, plus the friends who share his squat with him. He makes a suggestion and she replies:

'Bring them too. I've always wanted to meet the legendary André. Don't forget some booze. We're drinking vodka. I agree, it's midweek and not wise but what the fuck, we're all getting so bloody *sensible* these days. See you soon.'

She puts the phone down and turns to me. I'm sitting on the only kitchen stool, a red plastic affair that's long past its best, while Sara sits at the pine table with four matching chairs she bought in a mad moment in the January sales. One of the chairs is already broken.

'You're right about clothes, Nat. All that black and white you have to wear every day is bad for you, in my humble opinion. I could see you becoming more buttoned-up and conventional by the minute. Sorry, but it's true. This is the first civilised conversation we've had in six months.' We both start to laugh. Sara hiccups and gets herself a glass of water. 'It was getting me down.'

'You should have said something.'

'Why? You know it's not my style to interfere. Comment, yes, but not interfere. If people want to string up nooses for themselves, good luck to them.'

'Nooses seems to be an extreme way of putting it.'

'Don't barristers talk in metaphors?'

'All the time. I sometimes think that the whole legal system is a metaphor for something that can't be defined any better.'

'What a fascinating idea—' Then the doorbell rings and Sara goes to let Jane in telling me to stand against the lighted bedroom door.

So when Jane enters she sees me dramatically silhouetted, but being Jane she doesn't give anything away.

'A Bloody Mary, thanks. Getting into training for the big day, then, Nat?' Her Australian accent hits me afresh.

'Isn't the dress magnificent?'

'You said it was going to be a simple wedding.'

'It is. This dress isn't for the wedding.'

The phone rings – it's Dave again, offering to bring more people. Sara says yes to everything, while slopping tomato juice into Jane's vodka.

'But come off it, Nat. That dress says Wedding Dress in letters a mile high.'

'It is a wedding dress, but not mine.' I couldn't tell her the truth. 'It was made for someone else, her wedding's off so she's just lent it to me to see if I like it. But it's far too grand. Freddie would have a heart attack if I turned up in anything so elaborate . . .'

I can see Sara standing grinning behind Jane. 'I think you should say sod him and wear it. Don't you agree it's the apotheosis of all wedding dresses, Jane? But you ought to have bridesmaids, Nat, the works, Ginny and Lucy parading behind you. You look so wonderful in it.'

'Anyone would look wonderful in it.' Jane gives the skirt a guarded pat as the phone rings again. This time it's Mark, third member of our flat, asking if there were any messages on the answerphone.

'No, but come back because there's a party brewing.'

'You mentioned some curry,' says Jane, looking at the sad remains of the meal. 'I'm really hungry all of a sudden. Shall I go out and get more?'

'We're going to need food for the party. We'll go in a minute.' The evening is slipping out of control but I don't care. It's a couple of years since I spent an evening drinking with Dave Rosenberg and his friends: they are part of the capital's arty fringe, most live in squats on the dole and few need to get up in the morning. Dave writes occasional short plays which his friends perform in rooms at the backs of pubs. Sara and I went to one last year called *Echo Man* in which the action ran backwards. I refused to stay for the party afterwards because I was in court next morning, and Dave put his hands inside my shirt, took me by my shoulders, shook me, and told me I was sacrificing my life to false gods.

'Give in. Let go. Stay.'

'No.'

I waltz round the kitchen, my dress flowing. My feeling of release, of total living for the moment reminds me of only one thing: of my new floating abandonment when Freddie and I are making love in his house. No one will interrupt, no one can hear, we are utterly lost in each other, we go to the edge and beyond.

I waltz; I can hear Jane and Sara are talking but not what they say; I'm half-drunk; I'm invaded by the illusion of Freddie's body, my skin puckers, I shudder as if in orgasm . . .

'Of course the quality of life in Melbourne is high—'

'What do you mean by quality of life – what sort of things—'

Freddie. I'm so lucky. I love him. He will lift me out of this filthy flat, this post-university pre-settling-down existence where a party invents itself in half an hour and can last two days. Everyone except Dave's lot has their feet on the steps of the ladder – from the diplomatic service (Simon and Lucy) to television (Sam) to publishing and journalism (Amy, Charlie, Ginny) to temping (those who aren't on the dole) – but the ladder itself is shadowy and the steps unclear. Amongst Freddie's friends the ladder is clear, ever present, and those who've fallen off it don't tend to meet those who hang on or rise. Ladders. Freddie. Do I want to be whisked up one so fast . . .

'Has she always been like this?'

'Shout in her ear. NAT. Like that. Oops, sorry.'

'Now there's a Bloody Mary down the dress – quick – tomato stains like the devil. Quick, Nat, take the dress off.'

'No. Look, it hasn't marked it at all, well, hardly. Don't worry, Jane.'

'Take the dress off, for God's sake. It's crazy to stand in this dirty kitchen – sorry, but it is – in something that ought to be in a costume museum.'

'No, Jane. It's my party dress for tonight. I'll take it off when I'm good and ready.'

Jane is frowning at me, looking at me from the corner of her eye, head tilted, wearing an expression I've seen all my life. Assessing, aggressive. 'Is your fiancé coming to this party?'

'No. He's gone to see his mother.'

'Why doesn't he come on here later? I want to meet him.'

'He'd hate this sort of party.' Sara says this over her shoulder as she digs out an assortment of glasses from the cupboard. 'Wouldn't he, Nat? Anything could happen. Dave is highly unreliable, he collects all sorts of people on the way. Plus the odd drug.'

'Do you remember that minicab driver he brought over once, the one who said he was a poet—'

'We must be mad to be having a party with Dave.'

'I've got my second wind,' says Jane as she downs her Bloody Mary. 'All I need to keep going is more food. Tell me where the take-away is and I'll get what you need.'

'I'll come with you. Hang on, just let me get my purse.'

'You're not going out like that.' Sara and Jane say this in chorus.

'Why not? I can't take it off, I've just made a vow to the gods that I'll wear it all night. It's my offering on the altar of Hymen.'

'Sober up, Nat. You're going to regret this.'

'What else do we need?'

'Don't ruin that dress.'

'Sara, it's my sacrifice to the gods. Come on, Jane.'

'I think you're mad.'

We set off down the stairs, Jane leading. The dress rasps against the stair rails. Jane turns when she gets to the hallway, a dimly lit area of dismal common space. There's a strong smell of burning food from the flat nearest us

'Nat, what's got into you? Or are you just much drunker than you seem?'

'I'm pretty drunk. I can still walk straight, though.'

'Ruining that dress is just not you. What's happened to you?'

'Nothing's *happened* to me – I've changed, you've changed, time's passed, all that jazz.'

'Let's go back upstairs, you take it off and save it for the wedding.'

'Jane, you and Sara seem unable to accept the fact that I'm not wearing this dress at my wedding. I'm wearing it tonight instead.'

'You're out of your skull.'

'If you're too self-conscious to come with me down the street I'll go on my own. Just tell me what you want to eat—'

'I'm not bloody self-conscious – I just know you'll regret all this in the cold sober light of tomorrow.'

'Let's go then.'

At this moment the front door opens and the tenant of another flat comes in past us. He's a research chemist called Mike. He gives me his usual shy smile and disappears through his door without looking twice at my dress. Cheered by this I lead the way into the street.

As I walk the dress billows round me, its creamy colour turned acid by the street lighting. The soft silk is delightful against my skin; I feel kissed, caressed, by it. Corny but true. Few people passing me give me much more than a low sideways flick of the eyes. A girl giggles, a face in a car swings round in surprise. But in the main, most people behave as if they see wedding dresses going to the Indian take-away every evening of their lives. Even the taciturn Bengali who runs the take-away makes no comment beyond saying: 'Having a party, are you then?' as I give our order. There's no one else at the counter, and we're served in minutes.

'Aren't you cold?' asks Jane as we leave; she has insisted on carrying the food.

'No, not at all. Silk's so warm.' And it's true: my bare arms are smooth, without a single goose pimple. As I hold my arms up a car stops abruptly beside us.

'I see a vision.' Dave Rosenberg leaps out of the crowded back seat and kneels before me. 'A vision. I've never seen anything so unexpected. Divine.' He kisses my skirt, then my hand. 'Particularly framed by this superbly urban setting.' Traffic roars past, debris lies thick on the pavement, an empty Coke can rolls along the gutter. 'Princess, shall we dance?'

He bows and puts his arms round me in a correct ballroom dancing hold; the music coming from the car is a slow blues and Dave circles me dreamily round and round. He is an expert dancer, his feet are neat, his hand in the small of my back is assured. He speeds up the steps and up and down and round the pavement we go, my dress whirling around our feet. It is exhilarating, the most exhilarating dancing I've ever done. I could go on for hours . . .

But the music is interrupted by the gabbling of a DJ, and we slowly stop. My dress seems to sigh as it settles again. The carload of people clap ironically, and Jane stares at me with bruised and calculating eyes.

2

Freddie left his mother's flat in Hampstead earlier than usual and decided to see Natalie after all. There was still time to take her to a tapas bar for a beer and a little snack – something sharp and full-flavoured, like anchovies. He ran his tongue round his teeth again in an effort to dispel the taste of his mother's trifle.

The centre of London was surprisingly clear of traffic – theatres not out yet – and he crossed the river into South London in record time. He hated South London. He'd lived north of the Thames for his twenty years in London, and before he met Natalie had rarely crossed south for choice. North London had better hills, better air, prettier streets—

'You're biased.'

Yes, he was biased. Since Anthea died he could feel a stiffness creeping over him, making him set in his ways and ideas. He was not a naturally open person; he needed someone close to him to lift the tent-flap and let life in. Of course, he remained objective and fair-minded in court; he left personal prejudice behind then—

'You're biased, Freddie.'

In life, but not in work.

'They can't be separated so neatly.'

Yes, they can.

Freddie drove fast to Clapham with an eye constantly open for a police car. Because of this he almost missed a scene progressing on the pavement; he had already turned into Natalie's street when he saw, reflected in his mirror, his wife-to-be dancing in what looked like a wedding dress with a scruffy man wearing his hair in a long plait.

He braked sharply. Natalie twirled, her eyes shut, her huge skirt billowing round her partner's legs as he led the dance. She danced as if to violins in the most beautiful ballroom on earth. Freddie watched for three seconds and then in an involuntary spasm switched his foot back to the accelerator and fled.

That dress. As he raced back through London, his mind was filled with an image of sculpted folds and frills; cream silk pressed into his retina. It was definitely a wedding dress, of the highest quality, made by a top designer. Anthea, who had only bought the best, had trained him to recognise and appreciate a Jean Muir or a Bruce Oldfield at a glance. There was Natalie circling the filthy pavement in the arms of an unsavoury character wearing a dress she could not possibly have afforded to buy. It was inexplicable.

Freddie unlocked the heavy white-painted door of his Victorian house and went with relief into its familiar rooms. He poured himself a brandy, looking at his reflection automatically in the mirror above the mantelpiece – tired, hair needs cutting – before going downstairs to the kitchen. He opened a tin of anchovies and spread a couple on some crispbread, added a few black olives from the jar in the fridge, and sat down on the kitchen sofa. Anthea had had an obsession with sofas – she tucked them in all over the house. She said they were so nice to sink into when you were bored with what you were doing; her favourite one was small, triangular, and placed conveniently near the ironing board.

Anthea. Natalie. Anthea. That dress has brought back Anthea; she's with me, disapproving of its misuse, horrified to see the soft silk trailing in waste paper and dogshit and grimy fallen leaves. Anthea. Her own best clothes are still in the house, hung in the spare-room cupboard; when Meryl cleared her sister's things I made sure those outfits she most treasured were saved.

'Are you sure you want to keep these?'

'Quite sure.'

Brandy in hand, Freddie got up and climbed the pale gold-carpeted stairs again. Meryl had had her eye on those clothes and it annoyed her they hung unused. Freddie had it vaguely in mind to offer them one day to the Victoria and Albert Museum's costume collection. Then at least his childless wife would have left something tangible with a posthumous purpose.

He opened the cupboard and released a waft of camphor. The clothes hung limp and extra silent. He took out a black and white dress he'd always liked and laid the silk organza over his arm. The soft understated garment, constucted in intricate layers, weighed virtually nothing. Zandra Rhodes, said the label. He hung the dress back as Natalie in creamy white flicked through his mind again. He ran his hand along the hangers until he came to a Frank Usher taffeta dress which Anthea had worn a few weeks before she died, at the Middle Temple Ball.

It was green. 'So that the grass stains won't show . . .' Freddie pinched the shiny cloth, Anthea's voice in his mind's ear but his eyes only seeing swirling cream skirts brushing the Clapham pavement, debris flying before them.

He shut the cupboard door and relocked it. Natalie used this room when she stayed over – she had a superstitious dread of storing her things in the bedroom he had shared with Anthea, and he hadn't told her about the existence of Anthea's clothes. A room in Bluebeard's Castle. He drank off his brandy and went downstairs for some more. Then he settled himself on the sitting-room sofa and put his briefcase beside him.

The phone rang, late though it was, and he ignored it. Perhaps it was Natalie – she might have caught sight of his car and seen his swift departure. He wasn't ready to speak to her. On and on went the ringing, but as he gave in and heaved himself out of the sofa, it stopped.

If she hadn't seen him, would he tell her he'd seen her? He sat for some time staring at his glass, uneasy, aware that he ought to give his mind to considering the speech he had to give the jury tomorrow. The whole episode this evening upset him and he couldn't pin down the main reason why. Yes, the first sight had filled him with a quick burst of pain: jealousy? anger? incomprehension? Certainly incomprehension. Confusion. No jealousy or anger. After all, she was free to do as she liked. He'd put off their dinner together at short notice. But that dress: would she wear it again next week? Why else would she possess a wedding dress? The thought of it rustling soiled through Temple Church was disturbing.

With an immense effort of will he opened his briefcase and pulled out its contents. Within minutes he was lost in concentration as he continued to prepare his summing-up of the case against Geoffrey Poole and Roger Betty, accused of wounding a woman police constable with intent. The accused, picked up outside a pub for drunken and abusive behaviour, had been in the back of a police van on its way to the station; the van had swerved violently to avoid a child and mayhem had ensued in the back.

'We will never have a clear picture of what exactly happened in the back of that police van, members of the jury. The truth lies somewhere in the exceptionally diverse accounts given you, but the one person in the van who could have clarified things, WPC Perkins, remembers nothing of the dreadful ordeal because of the blow to her head.'

The five human beings involved told unconvincing stories of the minutes of cramped violence: the police versions tallied too neatly, and the two defendants tallied not at all with them and hardly with each other. Freddie ran through the sequence of events and was still unsure which party was furthest from the truth. The defence had made much of the fact that the policeman driving the van had braked sharply after swerving when he heard the fracas start, thereby precipitating the already aggressive figures of the two defendants forward on to their captors. Freddie thought of a painful incident in his childhood when his father had braked suddenly and the family Labrador had been thrown on to him in the passenger seat. It was quite possible for the WPC to have been knocked out against the side of the van. The police claimed she had been beaten against it.

Civil rights activists were packing the public gallery: whatever verdict the jury came up with there would be publicity. As a QC who had specialised in civil rights and environmental issues, he had had plenty of experience of publicity, particularly in the previous year's Greenpeace case when he defended activists accused of malicious damage to a nuclear outfall pipe; but he'd never judged a civil rights case before. In fact, since he only sat for short periods at a time to make up the statutory four weeks a year he had to put in as a recorder, he tended to get given short meatless cases to judge. This was the first that had attracted a big press presence.

Another week of judging, then his wedding, and then Budapest. He dragged his mind back to the transcripts of the cross-examinations of Poole and Betty.

'Why are you marrying her?'

'Is it really your business, Meryl?'

'No, but can you blame me for asking?'

'If you met her you'd understand.'

'But you know I haven't met her. You've been so secretive about her.'

'I invited you to a party to meet her. I don't call that secretive.'

'You gave me two days' notice – of course I couldn't come—'

'Our diaries rule our lives.'

'Freddie, you're filling the air with smoke and hiding behind it. As usual.'

'Why should I change?'

'But you have changed already. You're getting married to a girl half your age—'

'Not true.'

'You mean, it's off?'

'I mean she's only fourteen years younger than me. Twenty-eight, nearly twenty-nine.'

'When you were twenty-eight she was fourteen, half your age.'

'What are you getting at, Meryl?'

'Oh, I just feel sad and bitchy today. I miss Anthea. At twenty-eight you were married to Anthea, come to think of it. Don't you miss her still?'

'Of course I do. I think of her most days. It didn't stop me falling in love with Natalie, and it won't stop me marrying her.'

'Lucky Natalie. Lucky Natalie.'

'Oh Meryl, not tears.'

'Don't mind me, Freddie. I can't help it – when I'm in this house I think of Anthea with every breath I take. I miss her, I mourn her, I feel the loss of my sister. My only sister. I've got no one left to be absolutely frank with, to tell everything to, moan to without feeling guilty. Oh, God. Yes do fill my glass up.'

'Meryl, please don't cry. Have my handkerchief.'

'Look at it.'

'Look at what?'

'This hanky. It's sparkling clean, it's ironed, it's crisply folded. You're so organised you make me sick. I bet you ironed it yourself.'

'I don't do my shirts—'

'If Natalie's got any sense she'll keep you ironing.'

'I wouldn't mind. I do a lot of thinking when I'm ironing. I've made this one quite strong, by the way. And when we've finished these drinks I'll take you out to supper.'

'Dennis is expecting me back—'

'Give him a ring. I need to talk about Anthea, and you need to, and in three weeks I'll be married to Natalie. So it's now or never, really.'

Meryl's face is red and blotched; she blows her nose energetically on the handkerchief and sits back to take some deep breaths before ringing her husband.

'That's fine. He's got a bridge evening anyway.'

'I'll leave you to your own devices while I change out of this suit.'

Meryl goes to the overmantel mirror and makes up her face. She can hear the boards creaking upstairs as Freddie moves from the bedroom to the bathroom, a lovely luxurious bathroom that she's always envied. The design of the whole suite upstairs left Meryl wordless when she first saw it. You and I, said Anthea once, are both obsessed with our physical surroundings and coverings. I'd rather buy a perfect pair of shoes and store them in a custom-built beautiful cupboard than go to the opera or eat a fine meal. You're the same. But without the means, said Meryl. Without the bloody means.

Freddie appears again, now in a dark blue sweatshirt and jeans.

'I've never seen you in jeans before. They suit you. You are lucky to stay so thin.'

'Nat bought these for me.'

'If you dyed the grey bits in your hair people would think you were her age. Show me a photo of her, I'm curious.'

'I haven't got a photo and we're not going to talk about Nat. This is Anthea's evening. Let's go to the Italian trattoria on the corner, the food's always good there. I eat there so often they practically keep a napkin aside for me.'

'Dennis said how impressed he was at the way you've coped on your own in this big house.'

'No children, Meryl, that's how. If we'd had children, it would have been much harder.'

'Most people would say children are a comfort.'

'I wouldn't know.'

The street is bright with lights in uncurtained windows in the warm autumn evening. There is still a smell of rotting leaves and bonfires in the air, strong enough to drown out car fumes. Shiny horse chestnuts lie thick under one tree, and Freddie bends to pick one up.

'Aren't they wonderful. That brown: it's the best of all browns. This tree has given me such pleasure over the years.'

Freddie puts the horse chestnut on their table where it sits like a buff-faced small animal. Their order is swiftly taken, and Freddie sits back and returns his half-glasses to their case. Meryl notices that his eyes are slightly bloodshot, and there are broken veins in his cheeks.

'Anthea wouldn't approve.'

'Of what?'

'Of Natalie, of my jeans, of the things I now find myself thinking and doing.'

Meryl waits, but he doesn't elaborate. The bread and wine and water arrive, and the waiter stays for a few moments to gossip. Then the starters are served and both Meryl and Freddie are hungry enough to eat them without talking.

'That was delicious, the best seafood salad I've had for ages.'

'Anthea always chose it.'

'Why wouldn't she have approved of Natalie?'

'Too young and brash. And she would have hated these jeans because she used to complain about the fact that ninety per cent of legs were covered by boring blue fabric. She couldn't think why something so unstylish – to her – had become a worldwide phenomenon. But then, no one could match her for style.'

'She was stylish from the age of three. She would stay in bed, go without food and treats, rather than wear something bought for her that she didn't approve of.'

'The trouble is, Meryl, that when I think of her I increasingly recall only her shell: her elegant, tasteful shell. But she was extraordinary in that way – I've never known anyone else who could make things look so attractive. House, garden, clothes. Not a jarring note anywhere, ever. And she wasn't obsessive about unimportant things like cleanliness or tidiness: she got everything right so that a little bit of mess did nothing to detract.'

'Children would have detracted I can tell you. As I discovered. You talk about a "little mess" – Freddie, you don't live in the real world. Your place is always immaculate.'

'I know children make a difference.'

'I had to give up on things when the boys were young.'

'Anthea wasn't *all* surface, was she?'

'Freddie—'

'I get frightened sometimes. I can't remember her ever laughing much. Were we really so serious and solemn?'

'No, no, of course not. No.'

'You sound like a Greek chorus.'

'But Anthea wasn't a giggler, ever. She'd smile rather than laugh. With her eyes too.'

'She had a lovely smile. You've got it too. Dimples. Delightfully old-fashioned.'

He pours more wine and toasts Meryl, whose eyes are looking suspiciously full of tears again. The plates are cleared, more food comes, Freddie finishes the white wine and orders red.

'A bottle each!'

'Easy.'

'You'll be drinking most of it. The Italians say the English are terrible boozers—'

'So what. It's Friday, I can lie in, I've got a clear weekend ahead – in fact, Natalie and I have planned to go off—'

Freddie stops when the red wine arrives, remembering he hasn't told Meryl and Dennis about the cottage he bought last year near Altrincham. He picks up the chestnut, rolling it between his fingers, rolling it hard. There's a big chestnut tree behind the cottage, which will by now have a thick layer of nuts below it—

'Somewhere nice?'

'Haven't decided yet.'

'Does Natalie make you laugh?'

Unbidden comes the memory of a post-coital scene at the cottage, when Natalie told him the story of the couple who stayed in a hotel and indulged in a little gentle bondage – she tied up on the bed, he climbing into a wardrobe the better to spring out with wicked intent. Unfortunately the cupboard closed on him, and in his efforts to get out it fell forward onto the struggling figure on the bed. Eventually they were freed by hotel staff. Freddie and Natalie had laughed until they were weak; outside the window, the chestnut filled the view with leaves.

'Yes.'

'Dennis is very envious of you. I'm sure he'd like to trade me in for a younger model who made him laugh.'

'He'd find Natalie very nerve-racking.'

'What do you mean?'

'She's got no taste, she puts her foot in it, I never quite know what's going to happen next—'

'And Anthea never put a foot wrong.'

'No.'

'We're making her sound dull.'

'Not dull, Meryl. Never dull. Restful, supportive, sensitive—'

'That sounds dull.'

'She was too intelligent to be dull. And she had a secret.'

'What secret?'

'Did you know your sister was a gambler?'

'*What?*'

'I didn't either. No one did. I found out when I was going through her gardening file. There was a packet of betting slips. Horses. The odd flutter on things like the Booker Prize.'

'You've winded me.'

'So she had a secret passion. It was like discovering she had a lover.'

'Anthea a gambler. I can hardly believe it. I feel cheated – I told her everything, but she never gave me the slightest suspicion of this. Do you know, Freddie, I am cross. I thought we had no secrets from each other. I could shake her.'

'I know how you feel.'

'She probably thought you'd find it hard to accept, given your way of life.'

'Nonsense. She just wanted to keep it secret. And you must keep it secret too.'

'She must have paid for lots of things with her winnings – all those lovely clothes perhaps—'

'Not all of them, I can assure you.'

'Perhaps she didn't win much. Where did she go?'

'I honestly don't recall the details on the slips. I destroyed everything because she'd kept it all hidden and I didn't want to blow her secret apart. And I beg you, Meryl, to keep it to yourself – don't even tell Dennis. I wasn't going to tell you, perhaps I shouldn't have anyway—'

'I'm so glad you did.' Meryl's face is pinched and pensive, her skin blotchy from tears and alcohol. 'My sister, my sneaky sister, a gambler. Who'd have thought it.'

No one, and they'd have been right. Freddie sat up late in his quiet house, his work on the speech done, his brandy long finished. What on earth had made him think up that lie on the spur of the moment? As the words came out he'd surprised himself as much as Meryl. Pride? Did he hate to admit he'd been married to a dull wife? Dull. Dull. Anthea had been dull. Yet the surroundings she created were far from dull. The house around him contained subtle surprises, unexpected patches of startling colour, shapes that jarred for a second and then modified and enriched what was around them. That harsh abstract painting placed beside a misty autumnal landscape – the use of the colour orange in each picture constantly teased the glance into comparison.

Anthea put everything she had into the surfaces around her. She seemed squeezed out; even her own pleasure in her stylishness didn't make itself felt. She was dull. How Freddie had longed, as he mourned her, as he sorted numbly through her papers and possessions, to find something as breathtakingly unlikely as a bunch of betting slips.

3

The party is like all parties taken over by Dave. They become vehicles for his current obsession (the latest is the narrative techniques of pornographic films) about which he holds forth loquaciously but with diminishing brilliance until he slides into a corner, too drunk to open his mouth, and sleeps what is left of the night. It was lucky we don't have a video, because he was keen to show us some of his latest acquisitions which he carried round in a Peter Jones bag.

'I wish I could show you *Lift*, Natalie. It is more original than some of the typical triangle set-ups. A man and two women are trapped in a lift – a lift lined with mirrors of course – and the threesome develops with some rather neat social comment – one girl's a secretary and the other's a trapeze artist—'

Dave has imported the usual captive audience but they are neither interesting nor exotic and I can tell that Sara feels as cool about them as I do. Luckily Amy Jenkins drops in at around midnight and she and Sara and I retreat to a corner to catch up on gossip. People start dancing. The neighbours complain about the noise and threaten to call the police. As it's now after three, and the smell of cannabis is unmistakable, Sara and I manage to throw most of the guests out before this happens. Dave is too far gone to be roused and we leave him in his corner; Jane ends up in my bed.

'That man's a pretentious slob, and in ten years' time you'll all be avoiding him. If not before.'

'Shh. He's still asleep next door. You're probably right, but I like Dave.'

'I liked him too. I'm just giving you my objective opinion.'

Jane and I sit in bed drinking tea. The wrecked remains of the wedding dress billow in the corner; I'm relieved though feel guilty that it is now past redemption. I've got ten days to find a replacement.

'I must get going, Jane. I've got to get to Clerkenwell County Court by ten.'

'You look awful.'

'So do you. The only comfort is that vodka gives me less of a hangover than anything else. I could have felt worse.'

I shower – the water's lukewarm – and dress in my usual black suit and white shirt. By the time I've done my hair and made up my face, no one would guess from looking at me that I'd had three hours' sleep. Jane is watching me from the bed as I check myself in the long mirror.

'It never ceases to amaze me that we can live in total and absolute squalor and yet leave home looking as if we live at the Ritz. See you at six, Jane – I've left all the details about how to find Chambers on the pad in the kitchen.'

I rush out of the house towards the tube station, uneasy that I've left my sister alone in my room. Jane is not one to respect privacy. There are two letters from Freddie somewhere which I'd die if she saw; I almost turn back when I remember them. But I'd be late if I did, and as I run on I pray fervently that the confusion of my room will stop her being too inquisitive.

'Miss Harper, I'm a self-employed man. I work from home, but only in the sense that the jobs come in by phone – I'm a gardener, right—'

My client is a tiny man with a birthmark on his forehead like a caste mark. He looks like a gnome.

'Mr Greenfingers.' I'm holding his photocopied flyer.

'Some bastard done me in, reported me to the council that I was running a business at home – could you call this a fucking business? I do three jobs a week if I'm lucky—'

'Unfortunately any breach of the lease puts you at risk—'

'Last week I didn't get no jobs at all, that's what makes me sick—'

'My suggestion, Mr Peagram, is that you should undertake

to stop what you're doing since it isn't very lucrative at the best of times, and I'll do my best to get the council to drop proceedings.'

'You try to drag yourself out of the mud and they push you back in.'

The morning's proceedings start and Peagram's case is not called until eleven. While I'm waiting I eat two tuna sandwiches and drink a pint of water in the canteen and feel a lot better. Luckily, the housing officer is a human being and it is not difficult to get the proceedings dropped. Peagram and his large wife insist on taking me to the pub to celebrate and as Peagram gets the three lagers she pats my knee and starts to cry.

'I told him not to do it. Calling hisself Mr Greenfingers, gardening expert. Putting notices on people's cars and all.'

'To be honest, I'm surprised anyone bothered to report him.'

'He's fond of an argument, is my Ron. Does him no good.' She wipes her eyes. 'Anyways, thanks for all you done, love. That's a lovely ring you're wearing. Dame Edna Everage – can't stand her but Ron likes her – she wears one just like that. Flashes a lot. Cheers then.'

I have a Scotch egg and two black coffees for my lunch on my way back to Chambers; the gentle euphoria of my win has ebbed and I feel rough, very rough. The thought of introducing Jane to Freddie this evening makes me quail. That Scotch egg was a mistake, too. Why do I always think my childhood fondness for them is still with me?

I lie on the floor of the room I share with Colin Stimson and Patricia Saban and have a refreshing half-hour nap.

Jane is early and sits reading Colin's copy of *Private Eye* while I get on with the set of papers I have been working slowly at all afternoon. When I finally finish and focus on my sister, I blink: under the coat she has at some point removed she's wearing a beautiful vivid blue dress which suits her so well it's a pleasure just to look at her. I feel like a magpie in my black and white. She has put her blonde hair up with combs and this too looks stunning. She stares back at me with a faint air of defiance.

'I decided not to let you down.'

'You'll electrify everybody.'

As if on cue, a head comes round the door.

'Sorry to disturb you, Natalie, but do you have Archbold?'

'No, I put it back, but meet my sister Jane. Jane, this is Simon Hardy.' I want to add he's the most lecherous bastard in Chambers but Simon's performance for the next five minutes says it all anyway.

'What a scumbag,' murmurs Jane as the door closes.

'Shh.'

'How much do you earn, Nat? None of this set-up gives me any idea.' She gestures round the overcrowded room. 'The staircase was positively Dickensian.'

When I tell her the gross figure I've earned last year she whistles.

'That's gross though, don't forget. Half will go on tax, rent, clerk's fees, expenses. I have to pay every inch of my way in Chambers, we all do.'

'No perks in being engaged to the boss?'

'Freddie isn't my boss.'

'But it says loud and clear over the bloody door: the Chambers of Mr Frederick Mentieth QC—'

'He's head but not our boss as such – as I told you, we're all self-employed colleagues jointly responsible for the rent and running of our Chambers—'

'Oh, it's so confusing. Boss or head, what does it matter? Who shares this room with you?'

'You're sitting at Colin Stimson's desk and over there is Patricia Saban. Look, Jane, please don't talk about the wedding. We haven't asked anyone in Chambers so we're keeping it secret until the day. It's just a family affair—'

'Someone's coming in.'

Colin Stimson comes in backwards, carrying a pile of files. Jane slides out of his chair as he turns round.

'Hullo.'

'Ah, the famous sister! Word has got about that a celestial being has been gracing my desk.' He puts down his load and shakes her hand, beaming at her. Colin is the nicest man, far too nice to be a success. 'That blue – you must go and see the Wilton Diptych at the National Gallery – same blue.'

Jane grins back. She's a good bit taller than Colin; I notice he's sort of standing on tiptoe.

'What's this Wilton thingy?'

'It's a splendid early painting of the Virgin Mary surrounded by angels and they're all dressed in your blue. Lapis lazuli, pure lapis. The most precious of all pigments.'

'Do you mean to say they crushed up real lapis to make the colour?' Jane sounds faintly indignant.

'Absolutely.'

'I didn't know that either, Colin.'

'Take your sister to see it, Natalie, it's in the new Renaissance wing as I expect you know.'

'I'm such a philistine I've barely seen the outside of the new wing much less gone inside.'

'You appal me, brat.'

'Poor Colin does his best to educate me, Jane. He even got me to an exhibition which consisted of piles of stones.'

'I didn't know you'd finally gone to the Richard Long.'

'I was so disappointed in them I didn't want to tell you I'd been.'

'At least you went.'

As we chatter and tidy our desks Jane looks out of the window at the view of lawn, trees, the Thames beyond. A boat sounds its horn and another answers. Gulls peck the grass before rising in a screaming group as if they've had a telepathic communication of better pickings elsewhere. I join Jane at the window and we watch an old man – a retired judge – throwing a ball for his over-excited Pekingese.

Heads come round the door and I make more introductions. There are twenty-three men and seven women in Chambers, and by the time six o'clock comes a good half of them have passed through the room, many urging us to join them for a drink at the Devereux.

'Not tonight. We're a bit tied up. Is Freddie free yet?'

'I saw McTavish and two other solicitors going down the stairs so they must have finished their consultation.' Colin stands by the door ready to go home, wearing his rather military raincoat which has a button missing. 'McTavish owes me more than all my solicitors put together.'

'Not just you, Colin.'

'I wonder sometimes how he has the gall to put his face through the door. I find it very hard to be civil to him when I think of the size of my overdraft.' Colin has four children and does too much legal aid work to make big money. He's the only member of Chambers who talks openly about his cash flow and earnings; everyone else is secretive and paranoid. Me included. 'Lovely to meet you, Jane. Are you staying in London long?'

'I'm not sure.'

'Bye-bye then, you two beautiful chicks.'

'That man is such a darling – I'm so lucky to be sharing with him. Lean against the door, Jane, the lock's broken and I want to change my shirt and tart up a bit.'

I take the red silk shirt that's been hanging in my cupboard and swop it for the white one. I let my hair down, add a silver choker and huge silver earrings, and freshen my make-up. Jane watches me. It unnerves me and I make a mess of my eyelids and have to start again. Someone tries the door.

'Who is it?'

'Freddie. I've been waiting for you, what on earth are you up to?'

'Two minutes, Freddie.'

'You look fine, come on.' Jane opens the door, but Freddie has already disappeared, back to his room down the corridor and across the landing. We follow. I can't delay the meeting of Jane and Freddie any longer.

Gulls, sand, wet rope, tar . . . When I open my eyes I see Freddie's hand holding a champagne glass against my cheek. It's cold and damp with condensation.

'What's the matter, Natalie? Aren't you feeling well?'

'I overdid the booze last night, and stayed up far too late.'

'Celebrating Jane's unexpected arrival?'

Freddie clinks his glass with Jane's and then with mine.

'Sort of. A party developed, spurred on by Sara. It was very chaotic. You'd have hated it.'

Freddie meets my eyes and smiles, but I can tell he's thinking of something else.

'How was your mother?'

'Fine, considering.'

Jane is prowling round the room looking at the pictures (Freddie collects modern art). She stretches and cranes, showing off her body; we're both acutely aware of her.

'What a terrific office you've got here, Freddie. Perfect. Marvellous panelled room, all these matching books, lots of pictures, great view – the Temple is out of this world.' Jane perches on the edge of the desk, swinging slim black legs ending in black suede ankle boots. Both her dress and footwear look brand new; she probably bought them today.

'Freddie's room is the envy of us all.'

'It's the only perk for the hassle of being Head of Chambers, believe me.'

'Don't moan, Freddie. You don't really mean it.' I kiss his cheek. 'How did the case go today?'

'The jury are still out. So they're in a hotel overnight. It adds to the steam building up – civil rights protesters thick on the ground, press greedy for a story. I'm not looking forward to their verdict.'

'Have you any inkling which way they'll go?'

'If the recent cases of alleged police brutality are any guide, they'll find the defendants innocent. Juries are as anti-police as the rest of the populace. More champagne?'

'Thanks. What is this case about?' Jane has stopped swinging her legs.

'No, no, we mustn't talk shop. This is your evening, Jane – we were supposed to be at a dinner but when I heard you'd arrived I made our apologies.'

'I'd like to hear about the case – it sounded interesting.'

'Tell you later. I want to hear about you – when did you decide to come? It's such a lovely surprise you've appeared.'

'The only member of our family at Nat's wedding.'

'I was afraid Natalie was going to be drowned out by Mentieths. What a pity your father hasn't come over as well.'

'Dad's become so involved with his new life he hasn't time for anybody. He has hundreds of patients, he never stops. I got so fed up I couldn't see him I made an appointment – gave the name Joan Sutherland – he was furious it was me and not her, thought he was into the big time, but at least we had twenty minutes' chat.'

'Did he make you pay for it?'

'Do you know, I thought for a moment he would – when his secretary started to fill out an invoice he was seriously tempted. Dad's always been a bastard, so what's new? Being successful gives him an excuse to behave badly.'

'So Dad's doing well.'

'He works hard for it. Don't get me wrong, he's often very good to me. He bought me my flight over.'

'Let's finish the champagne, and then I'll take you both out for some dinner. Where are you staying, Jane?'

'At a ghastly hotel in the Cromwell Road. It's a rip-off. But I'm moving tomorrow.'

The phone rings and I can tell it's Freddie's mother by the way he answers.

'Where to?'

'Dave's place.'

'*Dave's!* You said you thought he was a slob.'

'I had a long talk to him today in your kitchen when he finally woke up. I've changed my mind.'

'He lives in a squat, Jane.'

'So what? He says there's plenty of room. I'll only be there for a few days until I can sort something else out. But anything's better than paying huge sums of money for a horrible room on a freeway.'

The news that Jane is going to live with Dave is unsettling; I watch Freddie put the receiver down and change his expression from resigned irritation back to pleasure.

'Well, shall we go?'

'Dave said he was hurt he hadn't been invited to the wedding.'

'Who is this Dave?'

'David Rosenberg. You haven't met him, Freddie. He's an old college friend.'

'He's threatening to turn up anyway, Nat.'

'Fine, fine.' I just don't want to discuss Dave Rosenberg or the wedding any more right now in case the subject of the wedding dress comes up. I've told Jane not to mention it ever, but Jane will do as she pleases.

* * *

'What is this place?'

Freddie has taken us to the Garrick Club for dinner; Jane went very silent as I took her up a picture-encrusted staircase to the pretty suite put aside for women. More pictures everywhere, even in the lavatory.

'All these pictures are to do with actors and plays.' Jane is peering closely.

'It's the Garrick – named after David Garrick, the eighteenth-century actor. It's a club for theatre people, television people, the Bar, all sorts. But it's apparently hard to become a member.'

'So it's exclusive.'

'Yes.'

Jane sits at the kidney-shaped dressing table and gets out her make-up. She meets my eye in the mirror, her gaze challenging.

'You sure have done well for yourself, Miss Natalie Harper. Straight in at the top.'

'It's only because of Freddie—'

'How did you get him to notice you?' Jane speaks through spread lips as she colours them. I want to shake her.

'I didn't *get* him to notice me, as you elegantly put it.' At that moment two large formally dressed women come in, laughing noisily together and clearly very familiar with arrangements. Jane and I leave in silence, and find Freddie sitting at a low table surrounded by armchairs, a fire burning nearby.

'I've ordered some more fizz while we look at a menu.'

'Freddie, you're obviously the ultimate host.' Jane smiles radiantly at him. 'This place is amazing.'

'Talking of places, you can't possibly go and stay in a squat. Isn't that what I heard you say you were doing?'

'I'm hardy. I'll cope.'

'Nat, she must come and stay with me. She can have the basement flat. It's an excellent solution, I'm sure you agree, Nat.' He takes my hand but keeps looking at Jane. 'I would feel quite dreadful if you froze in a squat while I live alone in a big house. Alone that is until next week, and then you'd be doing us a favour by living in the place while we're away.'

All this comes out well-prepared. Freddie has obviously been mulling over how to present his suggestion, and I can feel my lack of enthusiasm for it oozing out of me.

'No, no, no, I wouldn't dream of imposing on you, I'm sure you don't want me around. I can see Nat isn't keen—'

'For heaven's sake—'

'Nat wouldn't mind, would you, darling? Jane can be quite separate, she has her own front door, she can come and go as she pleases—'

'Of course it's a good idea. Dave's squat would be dire.' I wish I could hide my feelings better. Freddie probably thinks I'm just jealous because I don't want my sister to live for a week in the same house as my husband-to-be, while I spend my last days in bachelor freedom. I chose to do that – Freddie wanted me to move in weeks ago. I resisted it for reasons which I'm still not clear about, but which are partly to do with the perfection of the Mentieth house. Anthea's taste was unerring. I can't even get two cushions to look good together.

'Such a lovely club—'

'Started by the Duke of Sussex in the 1830s as a place where, I quote the charter, "actors and men of education and refinement might meet on equal terms". I often wonder what the original members got up to.'

'What was the problem about meeting actors?'

'They were definitely off bounds then – dined with the servants and all that.'

'But I seem to remember that Elizabethan actors mixed with the nobility? Shakespeare and the Earl of Southampton, for instance.'

'The Puritans put an end to all that dangerous fraternisation.'

Freddie and Jane chatter on while I sit in a silent turmoil. Huge pictures on the walls press in on me, the fire flickers, my ears buzz. Behind Freddie a group of bald heads nod together over glasses of whisky; Freddie recedes, growing older and older. Jane laughs often, saying really, how wonderful, I don't believe it. A waiter pads over and tells Freddie our table is ready when we are; Freddie thanks him, using his Christian name. Henry. I don't know why this finishes me off, but it does. I can't get out of the soft musty armchair, I feel as if I'm drowning in a world I want no part of. Freddie and Jane are still talking busily and have almost reached the door. I sit there, smothered. The film has stopped.

Then Freddie rushes over, kneels beside me, all solicitude.

'Dear heart, what's the matter? Aren't you well? Come on, I expect what you need is some solid food.'

He pulls me up and we stand close together, our hands interlinked.

'Henry's got holes in his socks.'

'What?'

'Henry. I noticed just now.'

'I don't suppose the staff here get paid all that much.' Freddie's eyes are on mine, puzzled.

'Freddie, do you really want to marry me?'

'Of course I do.'

'I'm hopeless, I'll let you down constantly, I still do mad things—'

'What does it matter, darling—'

'When I'm in a place like this I feel a fraud, I feel all my fine clothes are so much camouflage, I know I'm really still a struggling bigmouth with no class.'

'Silly Nat, what has got into you? Don't be taken in by outward appearances – the Garrick is not as imposing as it looks.'

'I just feel everyone who comes here is grown up and I never will be at this rate.'

'You're being ridiculous now. Come on, Nat, we can't leave Jane out there waiting for us—'

'Freddie, beware of Jane.' The words slipped out.

'Are you drunk, by any chance?'

'No, just exhausted. Take no notice of me. I don't mean beware of Jane, of course I don't. She used to do awful things to me when we were children, but that's all in the past . . .' Lame, lame, and Freddie's stopped listening because Jane has come towards us with her hands up in enthusiasm, bubbling.

'The pictures in this place are just fantastic – I want to know the story behind every face!'

Normally this sort of remark would make Freddie clam up, but instead he beams at Jane and tells her about some of the portraits we pass on the way to the dining room and the pleasures of potted shrimps and pheasant and good wine. There is a well-known actor at the next table dining with his boyfriend, and some self-conscious television personalities in the far corner having dinner with a politician.

'Actors and men of refinement and education having a good time,' murmured Freddie, and winked at Jane.

'Can women join?'

'Afraid not.'

'So we're only allowed in on sufferance?'

'In the evenings. Not at lunchtime.'

'It's worse than outback Australia. I thought England had done away with all that sexist rubbish.' Jane's voice is penetrating, and there is a lull when she says this and more. Freddie fidgets, and our neighbours immediately start talking loudly again. I cheer up considerably. Nothing annoys Freddie more than tub-thumping at meals.

My sister is here. She is here, she is here, and slowly slowly the implications are battering themselves into my brain. She doesn't know anyone. She has lost touch with her old friends or has no desire to chase them up. We have no family backup here. There is me. There is Freddie too now. She made a mark with Dave so there is Dave, for what that's worth. But mainly there is me, Natalie, the successful elder sister. Jane doesn't cling of course, she uses. As the dinner in the Garrick Club passes I can see how pleased she is with Freddie and therefore with me. We are going to be more use than she ever dreamed as she sat in that cramped aircraft and tried to blot out the infant screaming next to her and thought of cold wet England.

'Delayed jet lag has caught up with me. Don't get up, Freddie, and thanks a million for a lovely evening, the best I've had in years. No, no, I mean it, I'll see myself out. You two need some time together.' And off without warning goes Jane in her memorable blue dress, leaving us in a vacuum, surrounded by half-empty coffee cups. Freddie looks quite put out by her sudden departure, but it comes back to me that she has always practised the quick exit. As a child she would disappear in the middle of a game and when tackled would simply say 'I had to go', uncomprehending that I should take it amiss.

'I can't believe she really means it was the best evening she had in years.' Freddie stares at the door as if willing the blue dress to reappear.

'We all say these things.'

'Jane sounded as if she meant it. Has her life down under been difficult?'

'I don't know much about it yet.'

'And she left so suddenly – did I say something to upset her?'

'I'm sure you didn't. My sister Jane—' I stop. There's a pause, and Freddie sips his brandy; I refused it, Jane hardly touched hers.

'I'm going to drink Jane's brandy.'

'Go ahead. Tell me about your mother, you never talk about her. What was she like?'

'Mum was a depressive. I didn't realise this until I was about fifteen. She found all living hard, she never seemed to enjoy what she did. She would tackle a job – gardening, say, or decorating – with clenched teeth, hating it, a fury of energy for a bit, then she'd stop, stand and stare for minutes on end, leave the work half done. I spent my home life skirting round the evidence of her unfinished activity – rotting weeds in heaps on the lawn, partly painted doors, unhemmed curtains. I was so used to it, and to seeing Mum lying on the sofa with slices of cucumber all over her face that I didn't realise other families lived differently.'

'Cucumber?'

'She said it eased her headaches and did her skin good at the same time. When she'd finished with the cucumber she gave it to the rabbits. She often watched the rabbits. They had better care than we did, when I think about it.'

'Do either of you look like her?'

'Jane more than me. Actually, Mum could have been beautiful but that was another thing that went wrong in her life. She got fat. That depressed her too. I'm not surprised my father had enough of it all really. When her cancer started and the weight came off her, there was a stage when she looked wonderful. Dad had already left, so Jane and I thought she was slimming to catch a new man. Then cancer was diagnosed, and soon she didn't look wonderful any more.'

'She sounds a sad woman.'

'Freddie, she was tragic. None of us were sympathetic when she was fat and unhappy, least of all Dad.'

'I was about to ask you about your father. Jane seemed bitter.'

'She was his favourite when we were young.' I sip at Jane's glass. The famous actor has joined the other party in the corner and is doing imitations to much laughter. 'Dad travelled a lot, he was always working. He survived marriage by sitting on the sidelines. When he was made redundant and changed career, Mum cheered up for the only time I remember. He was studying from home, we saw him often. But he was so wound up in his homeopathy he couldn't think of much else. Then he qualified, and was gone. One day he was with us, the next he'd gone to Australia. We didn't suspect a thing.'

'Quick departures seem to run in the family, then. Your mother must have been devastated, Nat.'

'She was.' There's a pause; I'm thinking about Freddie's remark. 'Do you think it's a sign of strength or weakness, the quick departure with no notice given?'

'Cowardice disguised as strength.'

'But I wouldn't be strong enough to do it, cowardice or not.'

'You've got too much goodness in you. Come on, it's late.'

As we walk through the club an acquaintance of Freddie's stops him to chat. Though I'm introduced the man more or less ignores me. When he's gone, Freddie tells me he's just become a Law Lord.

'Not official yet.'

'He was rude. I could see him thinking, ah, Mentieth's bit of brainless fluff.'

'He's not married. He's probably terrified of women.' Freddie takes my arm as we walk up Garrick Street towards the car. 'Does my brainless bit of fluff want to go south or north to bed?'

'I suppose I ought to go home to the flat.' We get into the car and Freddie starts the engine. I think of the dirt and desolation left in the wake of the party. 'What would you like me to do?'

'I'd like you to come home with me.'

'Then go north.' I touch his hand as it changes the gears.

'The house feels empty these days. It didn't use to. I suppose that's because I'm on the point of sharing it again—'

'Is that why you offered Jane a room?'

'Not at all. It's you the house needs. As for Jane, I felt sorry for her – I hate people to visit this country and find themselves in a nasty hotel. When I heard about the squat it decided me. I could see you weren't keen – but apart from possible gossip that I'm sharing the house with my future sister-in-law, what's the problem?'

'Oh, forget the gossip. No, it's because Jane is a manipulator. Freddie, it's an awful thing to say, but I don't really trust her. I never have and I never will. I love her but I don't trust her.'

Heavy rain has started to fall, beating on the windscreen, thudding on the roof. The windscreen wipers swing dizzily, hunched figures dash for cover on the streets. I yawn, my eyes heavy from lack of sleep.

'In my opinion, love and trust go together. Obverse, love. Reverse, trust.' Freddie gazes at a red light; beyond, a tramp slumps in the doorway with his feet in the rain.

'Siblings are different. I disagree with you anyway – I can think of several people I'm fond of but don't trust.' Dave Rosenberg for one.

'I was talking about love, not affection. They're separate things.'

'I'm too tired to think straight.' I lie back and shut my eyes. The rain drums even harder, traffic crawls through swishing lakes of water. Gulls, sand, wet rope, tar. When I open my eyes Freddie is pulling into his concreted carport. He kisses my cheek.

'Wake up.'

4 ∫

Natalie surprised Freddie that night. She asked to sleep in the spare room; she said she wanted to try and keep the last week chaste.

'Would you have preferred to go back to your flat?'

'No, I'd much prefer to be here. It's lovely to be with you in the same house. Do you think I'm being unreasonable?'

'Darling Nat, no, I don't. I think you're probably right. I inflicted a church wedding on you, you've every right to have your own rites of passage.'

'It sounds silly put like that—'

'I didn't mean it to.' They stood in the doorway of the spare room, holding each other closely. Natalie broke away first, slipped off her jacket and wandered towards the wardrobe to hang it up. As she tried the door and found it locked as usual, Freddie said he'd fetch her some hangers. He collected a couple from his own cupboard, seeing her twirling on the grimy pavement in that ravishing wedding dress – the image was so strong that he almost expected to see her standing in the middle of the spare room resplendent in cream silk. But the room was empty (he could hear her in the bathroom off it) and he threw the hangers on the bed before going downstairs.

Natalie, I saw you dancing in the street in your wedding dress. He just could not say it. Perhaps he'd been hallucinating, perhaps it hadn't been her, perhaps there'd been a group of people going to a fancy dress party. Perhaps. But Nat's rapt face as she circled in the arms of the stranger was too clear for perhaps.

Freddie locked up the house, turned off lights, made sure the doors which activated the burglar alarm were shut. By the time he returned to the first floor, Natalie had fetched the overnight things she kept in his bathroom and was already in bed. He stood in the doorway and stared at her; she gazed back from the twin bed nearest the window, her eyes solemn, her hair brushed flat off her forehead. Then they smiled at each other, a smile of warmth and complicity, and Freddie gave a bow, blew a kiss and left her, shutting the door quietly behind him. He heard her call "Night.'

He took off his jacket and remembered the letter from his brother lying in a pocket, still unopened. Thomas Mentieth, globe-trotting economic adviser to the UN, currently working in Delhi. Weeks ago Freddie had telephoned his brother and asked him to be best man and Thomas had promised he would. Freddie turned the letter over knowing precisely what it would contain: profuse apologies: a work crisis has developed and I simply cannot leave . . .

The crisis this time was different. Thomas had broken his ankle. 'A severe Pott's fracture, I'm afraid – my leg is full of steel and I'm on crutches. It's a bloody nuisance all round. Frightfully sorry and all that.'

Freddie took off his shoes and lay on the bed. Thomas had let him down all his life, usually for reasons which seemed good at the time but were in fact the result of his sense of priorities. This time Thomas was failing him for a reason out of his control, and Freddie should have been less upset. Instead his sense of frustration and disappointment were so intense he felt breathless.

HIs wedding to Anthea. Thomas couldn't come, he was stuck in a conference in Washington. But the day Freddie was made a QC Thomas was in London, and Freddie rang him with a real sense of excitement to say there was a seat in the House of Lords for him if he wanted it. But Thomas had an appointment with a cabinet minister he simply could not change or miss; he said he'd come to the party afterwards in Chambers and drink champagne to celebrate. He'd arrived so late the party was over, full of apologies that one meeting had led to another, all essential . . .

Anthea's funeral. Freddie could hardly bear to think of how betrayed he'd felt by Thomas during that ghastly day. His brother was in Milan, but there was no problem about coming over, none at all, he had a working breakfast that day, then he'd take the mid-morning plane and be at the crematorium by three, no problem, no problem whatsoever. But Thomas had reckoned without the fog that frequently cloaks the Po valley, and by the time he arrived the post funeral tea party was long over and Meryl, Dennis and Freddie were clearing up in a numb and muddle-headed way.

'You're here!'

'Bloody fog.'

Freddie burst into tears, so great was his relief at seeing Thomas. He sat weeping on the sofa, still holding a dustpan and brush, while Thomas patted his shoulder and grunted incoherently. He semaphored at Meryl and Dennis to go, and took his younger brother out to dinner to cheer him up. He chose as he always did, the Indian restaurant near his flat. If Thomas ate out that was where he ate. It was cheap, he liked the staff, it was convenient, so why go further? He never did.

Freddie got off the bed and went to a particular photo hanging in a group of family photographs. The two Mentieth boys stood together behind a wire grille, above which was the sign: The Most Dangerous Animal in the World. Both boys were pretending to claw the wire and roar through it. He remembered a zoo, and his father saying, Come on, boys, a funny picture to make your mother laugh. So Freddie bared his teeth and looked wholeheartedly ferocious, while Thomas went through the motions in palpable embarrassment.

Freddie took the photo off the wall and stared at his brother's face. Thomas at thirteen looked little different from Thomas Mentieth in his late forties. Separate, obsessive, clever, eccentric. His clothes always looked rumpled and stale, his hair faintly unkempt. (His hair never changed in length or stye, and Freddie wondered how Thomas kept control of its lack of control, so to speak. Perhaps it never grew.)

After that Indian meal together on the day of the funeral, Thomas took Freddie back to his flat. Thomas had bought the flat before Freddie got married, and lived in it alone on the rare occasions he was in London.

It was the most dismal place imaginable. Thomas bustled

happily around, lighting dusty gas fires and drawing thin dirty curtains all made from the same batch of green brocade, unlined, and barely meeting over the windows. The chairs in the sitting room faced any old way, as if removal men had just dumped them there. Paper was peeling off the walls and the single overhead light bulb had no shade. A broken lampshade rested on one of the chairs; it had probably done so for years. The pictures on the walls – views of Scottish glens and lochs near the old Mentieth family home – had glass so dirty that it was hard to see the scenery behind.

'Make yourself comfortable, Fred. Coffee or tea? I'd recommend the coffee because I only use powdered milk and it marries better with Nescafé than with tea. Sit down, old fellow.'

But Freddie couldn't endure being alone in the cheerless sitting room and followed his brother into the kitchen, immediately running into a string suspended from corner to corner. On it hung teacloths (grey and spotted with stains) and a series of hooks from which dangled a ladle, a wooden spoon, and a rusty metal sieve. One end of the kitchen table was covered with a layer of newspaper, on which stood a permanent collection of jam and sauce bottles, many so empty and old they appeared to contain fossilized remains. The gas cooker, an antique, had come with the flat, and Freddie dimly remembered how pleased Thomas had been when he'd managed to persuade the gas board that it could be converted to natural gas.

'So the old cooker is still going strong.'

'Of course. It'll see me out.' Thomas slid a tin kettle with a whistling spout over a gas ring. 'Now, what about a little snort? I've got some duty-free Glen Morangie.' He poured two large measures of malt whisky into two glasses that had started life containing mustard.

'You've got a bit of a damp problem here, haven't you?'

'Have I? I'm so used to this place I don't notice anything. That's why it suits me so well – every inch is totally familiar, and since I spend my life going to work in new places, I like home to be home. Sugar? Now let's go and sit down next door.'

'I'd forgotten you'd rescued all those old watercolours when the house was sold.'

'Saved me buying anything. I never look at them.'

'That one of Loch Fyne used to be in the hall, didn't it?' Freddie peered through the grime. 'Nice to see it again.'

'Do have it if you'd like it.'

'No, no, I don't want it. You keep it.'

'If you change your mind—' Thomas decided to sit in the chair containing the broken lampshade, which he carefully put on the mantelpiece along with a standing army of Christmas cards going back years. 'Sometimes one needs reminders of one's past.'

'Anthea refused to have anything in the house from her family or mine.'

'Anthea. I'm so sorry, Freddie, I didn't make it in time. I really am. There I was at the airport for hours storming up and down because of the fog. *La nebbia*. It was as thick as a white blanket, and it lifted as suddenly as a blanket can when it finally did lift. I hope there was a good turnout for the funeral.'

'At least a hundred. Perhaps more.'

'Really. How heart-warming.'

'It did help.'

'As I sat waiting to fly it occurred to me that the only people who would come to my funeral would be you, Mother and Elsie. How is Mother?'

'She's still got shingles.'

'Oh dear. And Elsie?'

'She was there today, very disappointed not to see you. Aggrieved. Said you haven't been to see her for nearly a year.'

'What rubbish. I went to see her before I left for Sri Lanka.'

'Which was April – last year.'

'So it was. Ten months. Oh dear. My work is so absorbing I forget everyone and everything. But I mean it, Freddie, only you three would come to my funeral if I died tomorrow. Chilling thought.' But Thomas didn't look very chilled; if anything, he looked proud of his solitary state. 'And since it's more likely my mother and Elsie will die before me, there'll only be you. Elsie's funeral will be fascinating, won't it? All those children she's looked after coming back, some even older than us. She's a terror for keeping in touch. They'll all be there.'

'Elsie approved of Anthea. Said no one had higher standards in the house. Even made a point of telling me today that she could always tell a house where the spring cleaning was properly done.'

Thomas gave a shout of laughter. 'Just as well I've never allowed her through my door. She'd be horrified. Absolutely horrified. By the way, what causes a lavatory to go completely black? I gave the black a poke with the lavatory brush, but it's like a veneer. Doesn't smell at all, though. You must admit, Freddie, that despite the fact I hardly ever give the flat a clean, it doesn't smell.'

'It smells of dust.'

'Who cares about dust? I'm only here a few months any year, and I give it a go with the Hoover at least once a year. I keep the rooms pretty bare so that there's nowhere much for the dust to go except the floor, and what else are floors for? Top-up?'

'Thanks. This is just what I need.'

'Nothing better than Glen Morangie.'

'Anthea never touched whisky, so I tended not to keep it in the house.'

'Are you going to stay on alone in that place?'

'Of course. Why not?'

'It's big.'

'I've got used to it.'

'It's very much Anthea's house. I thought it might be a problem.'

'The opposite. It comforts me.'

'I can understand that.' Thomas pursed his lips and suddenly looked very much like their father, who was thin, craggy, always sucking a pipe. There was a pause, filled by the wailing of police sirens.

'When are you going back to Milan?'

'I'm not, as it happens. I've got four days' leave before I have to be in Geneva. Then after that there's a UN mission looming in China.' Thomas yawned, Freddie caught it.

'I ought to go back. I'm shattered. Grief is bloody exhausting.'

'I'd ask you to stay but my spare room—' They both laughed. 'And come to think of it my bed will be rather unpleasant if I don't go and switch on the electric blanket. Won't be a moment.'

When he returned, he touched Freddie on the shoulder awkwardly and said: 'Why don't you take a couple of days off and we'll go somewhere for a break together? We haven't had a holiday à deux since we hitchhiked to Greece when you left school.'

'Not a bad idea. My clerk's kept me out of court this week.'

'Right. Where shall we go?'

'Scotland?'

'Glasgow. Let's go to Glasgow. I haven't seen it for twenty years. I'm told it's become a cultural Mecca. And we can easily get out of the city and walk in the hills if we want to.'

'We could catch the morning shuttle tomorrow.'

'Nine o'clock? Ten?'

'Ten. It'll give me a chance to talk to the clerks' room before I leave.'

'Excellent, Fred, excellent. I won't even bother to unpack. My last hotel did my laundry.' Thomas yawned again, and as he did so a piece of wallpaper detached itself above the fire and peeled down, hanging over the broken lampshade. 'Funny things happen when I put the heating on.' He was unconcerned, and followed Freddie to the front door.

The brothers stared at each other. A street light down in the square behind Freddie gave him a halo; someone was playing Mozart on a piano. Their gazes held until, for the first time in their adult lives, they hugged each other.

'See you at the stand-by shuttle desk then.'

'I shouldn't really be going off now, there are so many letters to write to people who've written to me—'

'Do some while we're away. Planes are excellent for work. I intend to brush up my Chinese.'

'I didn't know you'd added Chinese to your amazing list of languages.'

'Mandarin.' Thomas rubbed his hands together. 'One day I'll brave Hungarian. And Finnish.'

Thomas alone in Delhi with a broken leg. There was a telephone number on the letter, and Freddie dialled it without working out the time difference. He knew his brother only slept five hours per night, and took the view that sleep was not important.

'Dr Mentieth speaking.' As Thomas answered there was the sound of something metallic – a crutch? – falling.

'It's Freddie. How's the leg?'

'Freddie – isn't this accident the end? Such a bloody nuisance. I'm in despair.'

'How on earth did you do it?'

'Classic Pott's fracture – wasn't looking where I was going and came across a sudden deep step down. Only a couple of feet, but the result was my ankle, tibia and fibula in pieces.'

'Has it been properly pinned together?'

'I certainly hope so, Freddie. They took long enough about it. I was out for hours.'

'Come home and have it checked. And then you'll be here for the wedding.'

'I wish I could.'

'Why can't you? I need you, Tom. There's no one else I want to ask to be best man.'

'My doctor said travelling would be unwise.'

'When did an opinion like that stop you?'

'True. I'd have to travel in a wheelchair, though. I'm not sure I can face it. Pride and – well, pride.'

'I need you, Tom. It won't be the same without you. Please come.'

'I can't cope on my own yet, I couldn't manage living in my flat—'

'You could stay here. Natalie's sister is around to help. We could put a bed in the dining room, and there's a loo and shower all on the ground floor too, don't forget. You'd be very comfortable.'

'You're determined.'

'I am.'

'I'm certainly not enjoying life in Delhi on crutches.'

'So you'll come. I'll make an appointment with someone good at orthopaedics to check you over.'

'Remind me when the wedding is?'

'Saturday week.'

'I'll be with you by Thursday if possible. Perhaps before.'

'Fax me the details in Chambers, and I'll make sure you're met off the plane.'

'Hire an ambulance. I'm serious, I couldn't fold into a car at the moment.'

'Are you being well looked after, Tom?'

'I've set up camp in my office – it's all on ground level so it seemed the best thing to do. A male nurse wallah keeps an eye on me, I've got someone else to cook and bottlewash. It's costing a small fortune even at Indian prices.'

'Shall I get Elsie in to come and nurse you?'

'Don't you dare. She'd drive me insane.'

'Don't forget to fax the flight details. Bon voyage and all that.'

Freddie replaced the receiver and lay back on the bed again, delight flooding him. Thomas was coming. For the first time ever he had managed to changed Thomas's mind. Since Thomas lived life as if doubt in the wisdom of his own arrangements was impossible, this was quite an achievement.

'Are you rich, Tom?'

'I've no idea. I don't think about it; I spend what I need and the rest sits in my deposit account.'

'I've noticed how as people grow richer they travel more – money seems to bring a desire for incessant movement. Look at us now, off to Glasgow when we could spend the weekend together in London—'

'I move incessantly, but it's because of my work.'

'I expect when you retire you'll go on travelling half the year.'

'You couldn't be more wrong. My travelling has nothing to do with luxury or leisure. I like nondescript hotels, I spend most evenings in my room, I always eat at the same restaurant once I've established the nearest and most reasonable. I am in Delhi, in Milan, in Sri Lanka, but in many ways I could be in London. My pattern is much the same. The only variety comes with the language and of course the field trips – those are delightful, but they're also work. I'm not there to admire the scenery but assess it. No luxury, no leisure. I prefer it that way.'

The stewardess reached them with breakfast at this moment, and Thomas tucked energetically into his trayful.

'I always eat every scrap they give me. I can never understand why people complain about airline food.'

Freddie thought of Anthea's dislike of it, and said nothing.

'You're not doing it justice.'

'I ate breakfast earlier.'

'Pass me your croissant, then.'

Anthea. A holiday house booked in Umbria, airline tickets, the summer holiday he'd have to unscramble. Holidays alone. He'd never learned how. He watched the clouds beneath the aircraft, a sea of gigantic grey pillows, and felt afraid.

'I keep meeting people who ask me to tip them off about the unspoiled places I come across, and I never do. Cities can absorb tourism, the countryside is destroyed by it. When discerning travellers seek out the unspoiled place, inevitably they spoil it. Clichés but true. The unending ambivalence of travel. No, I'm not interested in travel for its own sake, Fred. But we're going to have fun in Glasgow – just the kind of place I'd like to work in and never have. I'm greatly looking forward to seeing the Burrell Collection and the Kelvingrove Art Gallery. Could I possibly have some more coffee?'

The buck-toothed fiercely smiling air hostess filled up Thomas's white plastic cup, ridiculously small and inadequate in his large hand. Thomas had curved, oddly convex nails, ridged and clawlike.

'Now for some Chinese.'

But Freddie did not get out his folder of letters to answer. All those dozens of letters. Thank you so much for writing. I still can't accept Anthea's really dead; six days ago she was booking our summer holiday. I can't believe she won't come through the front door with her usual it's me called from the hall. I can't believe she's dead. I've still got all her dry-cleaning stubs in my wallet. Oh, God.

Freddie stared out at the unbroken range of grey pillows. Pits of grief opened, but there was Thomas beside him, self-absorbed, solid, insensitive, his aged Harris tweed jacket smelling faintly of mothballs. Freddie shut his eyes to stem tears, these tears as much for his brother's comforting presence as for Anthea's untimely death.

5

Freddie gives me the news at breakfast that his globe-trotting brother, the economic guru Dr Thomas Mentieth, is coming to the wedding in a wheelchair because he's smashed up his leg. I haven't met Freddie's brother, and I'm apprehensive; he sounds totally intimidating.

'He's staying here since his own flat isn't suitable for a person on crutches.'

'What a good idea. Jane can give him a hand.' I don't meet Freddie's eye; I'm sure he's thinking what I'm thinking, that Jane isn't cut out for nursing anyone. She will be pleased when she learns what's in store.

'Does Thomas live alone?'

'As far as I know he's one of nature's bachelors. Never married, never mentioned there was a woman in his life.'

'A natural bachelor! What a rarity – is he born with no sex drive, is he a latent homosexual, is he celibate by choice and self-control, is he a roué who doesn't need a regular companion? Fascinating.'

'I don't really know. We've never discussed it.'

'Sibling relationships are so strange. One knows a lot and one knows nothing at the same time. This marmalade is delicious – who made it?'

'Meryl. She makes excellent preserves.'

'Meryl – there's another key person I haven't met.'

'She was complaining she hadn't met you either.'

'Then give me her phone number and I'll ring up and suggest we meet for a drink.'

'I'm not sure that's such a good idea.'

'Why not? We're going to meet at the wedding—'

'That's soon enough. Meryl can be difficult – I never quite know which way she's going to jump. Things will be easier when we're married.'

I'm about to disagree with him but I decide it won't achieve anything. After all, Meryl is his dead wife's sister. She's bound to resent me. Do I really want to run the risk of being upset by a woman with an in-built resistance to my arrival on the scene? And anyway, this breakfast is so pleasant – warm kitchen, toasty smells, good coffee, Freddie in an unexpectedly chatty mood for so early in the day.

'You haven't really answered my question about Thomas.'

'It's not easy to answer, except to say no to every category you mentioned except the celibate – and of course I don't know if he's celibate by choice or design or circumstance or what. And of course I couldn't be sure he's not the opposite, a roué as you colourfully put it. My impression is that women don't mean much to him as sexual objects. Nor men. Anthea agreed. He's a workaholic, he loves what he does, he's always travelling, so I imagine it never seems anything but an advantage to him to remain unattached.'

'Do you get on well with him?'

'Yes. We've got closer over the years. But I don't see him often. More coffee? Actually, I ought to get going. I'd like to be at the court early today. There's a queue every morning now for the public gallery. Whatever verdict the jury comes to, there's going to be publicity – if they acquit, there's going to be some tasteless civil rights celebrations, if they find in favour of the police all hell will break lose. I think in this case the police are probably in the right, but they haven't conducted themselves well in court, not well at all. They don't deserve to win.'

'Poor Freddie. I don't envy you. What are you hoping will happen?'

'Not guilty, even though the blighters probably are. Sentencing this kind of case is extremely tricky. Unfortunately the jury is predominantly white and one of the defendants is black. His dreadlocks are spectacular – they go half down his back.'

'They'll be grafted on.'

'You're joking—'

'Not at all. It's the easiest thing. If you'd had sisters you'd have seen them extending their plaits with dressing-gown cords. I wish I could come and watch for a bit, but Douglas is sending me to Maidstone for another repossession. Shall I clear all this away?'

'Mrs Wilks comes today. Leave everything. She likes to feel she's needed – she gets annoyed if I tidy the kitchen. If you want that lift to the tube, I'm off in five minutes.'

I enjoy collecting myself together in this house – my coat and scarf and shoes are warm and dry from the efficient heating, surfaces sparkle as I pass, my feet are silent on the thick carpet. But it's also unreal – I feel as if I'm staying at the Savoy on a bottomless expense account.

'Hang on – I didn't put the answerphone on.' Freddie runs back downstairs.

In the hall there is a pottery bowl full of almost spherical pebbles. They are fascinating, these pebbles; you want to pick them up and roll them in your fingers, crunch them together in the palm of your hand. This time I choose a pure white one, clearly chalk, a grey flinty one with a white belt and an egg-shaped pebble of curdled grey and cream like solidified porridge. They grate and squeak together under the pressure of my fingers.

'Where did these come from?'

'A beach at the foot of the cliffs near Beachy Head.' Freddie's face is sombre as he glances at them. He opens the front door. 'Come on. We must go.'

I turn and as I lower my hand to the bowl the egg-shaped pebble shoots through my fingers and lands with a crack on the rim. The bowl shatters and after a poised moment the collection of pebbles loses form, escapes, rolls slowly in all directions, drumming on the polished chest of drawers before leaping for the carpet.

'Oh, my God! How did that happen! Freddie, I'm sorry—' I'm bright red, I start to retrieve pebbles but they roll straight off the chest again.

'Leave it, leave them. It doesn't matter. Come on, Natalie, we *must* go. Just leave them, Mrs Wilks will clear them up. She'll think we've had a poltergeist in the house.'

I follow him to the car, a pebble still in my hands. Flustered, I put it in my pocket, apologising again as I get into the passenger seat.

'Actually, those stones were collected on a bad day in my life, and this is the time to get rid of them.'

'But it was such a beautiful bowl—'

'Put it out of your mind.'

I can feel the round comfortable shape in my pocket. I take a surreptitious peep at the pebble, but it isn't one of the three I originally picked out. My trophy is flint, but wholly dark.

In the end Patricia Saban goes down to Maidstone to do my case, since our head clerk, Douglas Dean, wants to keep me free for a conference on a new case he's swinging my way. Douglas likes me, and lets me know it; in fact, I sometimes think Freddie noticed me more because of Douglas's enthusiasm than anything else. It's just chemistry between Douglas and me: he likes forthright women who stand up to him and make him laugh, and I did that from the start. He also prefers brunettes to blondes, and told me one heady day that he thought I had the perfect looks for a barrister. 'Tall, dark and composed. The little, shy, eager ones never get anywhere.'

'You mean, they don't get anywhere because you don't push them, you old chauvinist. Do you approve of women at the Bar in your heart of hearts, Douglas?'

'Of course I do, of course I do. But they've got to have the right physique, Miss Harper. It's all in the physique, in my opinion. A small woman in a wig and gown looks a bit ludicrous, if you don't mind my saying so. They'd be better off as solicitors if the law is what they want to do. Luckily, Miss Harper, we don't have any small women in Chambers.'

Patricia Saban isn't exactly tall, and he knows it. Douglas Dean is an enigma in many ways, in other ways a typical successful senior clerk. He wears handmade suits, he drives a Lotus Elan, he has a house in Kent (atypical – most clerks seem to live in Essex). Douglas left school at fourteen and followed his father, a famous clerk known as the Dean, into the lucrative flipside of the Bar, the clerks' room. Douglas is a clerk of the old school, which actually means he's still on a percentage of Chambers' turnover;

not for him a salary and bonus system. He earns a huge amount for a man of his lack of education and lack of accepted official skills, and if he's anything like his father he'll be earning it into his seventies. The Dean died aged seventy-three, while lunching at the Wig and Pen with his favourite solicitor.

So our Douglas is smart, and rich, and aloof. He trades on this aloofness, it's what makes him different from other clerks. I'm sure he developed it early on to cover up initial social unease, but I could be wrong. He has a secret obsession, he collects pewter – I discovered this by sheer chance. I caught him looking at a Sotheby's auction catalogue after work one day, a catalogue he whisked out of sight as if it had been pornography. But it slipped out of his hands on to the floor at my feet, and I picked it up.

'Sotheby's.' There are yellow post-it stickers dotted through the catalogue. 'I've never been to an auction.'

He puts his hand out, staring at me with his pale greeny-blue eyes. His tie is also green, in heavy silk. 'You should try one.'

'You obviously go for a reason.'

He takes the catalogue back and puts it away safely in a drawer. 'I do, as a matter of fact. I collect pewter, and there's some nice eighteenth-century stuff coming up.'

'Pewter – what precisely is pewter, I mean, what metals?'

'It's a mixture of lead and tin. My father had a couple of pewter tankards he left me in his will, and that's how it began. One turned out to be quite valuable, so I got interested.'

'Lead and tin – that can't have done the drinkers much good.'

'Lead pipes, lead paint, pewter tankards in every pub – no, it didn't.'

'Think of all the missed Personal Injury cases—'

Douglas laughs. 'It was the PI aspect that got to me, I suppose, now you mention it. Pewter's more interesting in that way than silver. I like the look of it, too.'

'But you don't drink out of it.'

'No way.'

'What are you going to bid for?'

But Douglas isn't going to tell me, and changes the subject. 'Talking of PI, Miss Harper, there's a chance that the Mackleton ferry disaster is coming our way. I'm hoping to get a leading brief for Mr Stimson, and Mr Stimson will need a junior.'

'Douglas, you're a genius. I thought the Mackleton would go to our friends in Mitre Court. They seem to get all the big PI work.'

'Not this time.' Douglas smiles, a smile which switches off when a head comes round the door behind me. 'Good afternoon, Miss Saban. Anything I can do for you?'

'Never send me to Sittingbourne again. The defendant didn't even turn up.'

'Oh dear, what a pity.'

Douglas is wicked. He doesn't like Patricia, whose name he always mispronounces, putting a stress on the final syllable instead of giving both syllables the same weight. Patricia has stopped trying to correct him. We walk down the corridor together; she is clearly about to explode, and does so when she's in our room. She slams the door.

'Douglas is determined I'm not going to succeed at the Bar.'

'Patricia—'

'I get on fine with Paul. I wish he was senior clerk. I know for a fact that Douglas swings work away from me; that case you did for Kingman and Fletcher was meant for me. They actually asked for me, apparently, but were told Miss Suh*ban* was already booked for that date. Lies.'

'If that's true, I'm really sorry.'

'Of course it's true. I checked out the dates.'

'Sometimes when they're under pressure the clerks miss things in the diary, or put entries on the wrong day—'

'And you think that's excusable?'

'I don't. I think it's disgraceful. But it does happen, and it's not intentional—'

'It doesn't seem to happen to you.'

Patricia is powered by jealous fury. Her mouth is drawn tight, her grey eyes like slate.

'Stand up to Douglas, Patricia. He likes people being tough. Shout at him, not me.'

'I've tried being tough. I can see it has no effect. I once overheard him say at a solicitors' party – he was drunk, but not very – actually overheard him say: "Of course the power gives me a buzz. I can make or break any member of Chambers and they know it." He knew I'd heard. I've never forgotten it.'

'They can be shits.'

'They have too much power. There must be a better system.'

'Think of one.'

'I just might.'

'What we have is flexible, efficient when it's working well, and personal. Freddie always says that with other systems you let in bureaucracy and then the flexibility and speed of reaction would go.'

'But a clerk can abuse his power so easily.' Patricia is still standing in the doorway, tense and angry. 'They can load their favourites and ignore the rest—'

'Patricia, I hate to say this, but you're getting paranoid. You'll go mad if you keep thinking about how everyone else is doing, you really will. Stop worrying about me, about the others you think are getting your work. You're doing better than you think. People rate you highly.'

'Who?'

'Lots of people. Freddie, for one.'

'Oh, Nat, I wish I could trust Douglas, I wish to God I could. I even began to wonder today if he'd sent me to Sittingbourne on a wild-goose chase, knowing that the case had been stood out.'

'Don't be ridiculous. That's what I mean by paranoid.'

'I know, I know.' Patricia sits down heavily on her desk.

'Have faith in yourself.' I sound like an agony aunt.

'Part of the trouble is, I've broken up with my partner and it's been hitting me with a sort of delayed reaction.'

'God, I'm sorry—'

'Don't be sorry, it's a good thing it's over. But I've got used to having someone there to talk to and suddenly there's no one. Even knowing it was the right decision doesn't help when you get in from work and the flat is empty and will stay that way.'

'And you've been together a long time.'

'Five bloody years. The last few months have been hell. I haven't told anyone because I didn't want people to say, "Oh Patricia, she lets her private life affect her too much".'

'Well, I hadn't guessed and I share a room with you. Don't let Douglas know though—'

'Hell, Natalie, you don't think I'd breathe a word of this to him or anyone in the clerks' room. Shit, I'm not that stupid. And don't you tell anyone, please. I didn't mean to let it out.'

'Of course I won't tell anyone.'

'Not even Freddie.'

'Not even Freddie.'

'The real hell about this life is that you're on your own, absolutely on your bloody own.'

Patricia has a reputation for incessant chatter, and for being slow with paperwork. Chatter doesn't matter, but she's a fool to let briefs hang about on her desk for as long as she does. I make it a rule to write an opinion within a week of receiving the papers, and I know my speed has pleased Douglas because it pleases solicitors. But I don't do it to please them – I do it because I know women have to be twice as quick and efficient as men to make their mark. Patricia lets herself be fooled by the fact that someone of her call, like Simon Hardy, takes his time over his paperwork too. She forgets that Simon got a double first at Cambridge, has a father who's a High Court judge, and above all, is male. Things are changing for women at the Bar, have changed, but it's silly to ignore the obvious.

'What a busy little bee we are, Natalie. So industrious. You put us all to shame.' And Simon gives his braying laugh. I don't like Simon – his affected manner and that hideous laugh make him seem like the caricature of every Hooray Henry ever portrayed on stage and screen. He has a huge nose, tombstone teeth, and a high complexion; his black hair is so straight and stiff it looks as if it's been glued on him by a child. I can't understand why Simon is such a success with solicitors and clients; his court manner strikes me as being very off-putting but clearly the punters love it. He gets results too; he's always winning cases. And that can't be due to his background.

Poor Patricia. I can sense her at her desk, oozing desperation. She's turning over the pages of a brief too quickly to be working at it.

'All I need is fair treatment.'

She's right, too. Confidence in her abilities from the clerks, a few successes, a growing reputation, and she'd be transformed.

Perhaps I ought to try and put her position to Douglas next time I get him on his own in an expansive mood —

The phone on my desk rings. It's Jane.

'Nat, did Freddie mean what he said last night, about offering me a room in his house?'

'Of course he did. He doesn't usually make offers he doesn't mean.'

'What a treasure. I thought he was gorgeous, by the way. Lucky you.'

'Lucky me.'

'So what do I do about moving?'

'I'll give you the address now. By the way, Freddie's brother Thomas will also be staying—'

'The more the merrier.'

The more the safer. 'Jane, are you any good at nursing?'

'Am I what?'

'Thomas has broken his leg or something – anyway he's in a wheelchair, it seems. He's flying in from Delhi later this week.'

'You're not seriously suggesting I should nurse him—'

'No, but you'll obviously be someone in the house to help him when necessary.'

How naughty of me to feel pleased at her lack of enthusiasm. We make arrangements about her transfer, about access, keys, the weekend's plans, and I can hear the reserve in her voice. I know she's wondering whether to back out now since it will probably be less hassle staying in a squat. Too late. Jane would never offend Freddie if she could help it: he has too much to offer her. But I know my sister well enough to realise that is the only reason she's taking up his offer.

'What's this brother like?'

'I've never met him.'

'When Jake broke his arm he moaned the whole time. Men are useless about pain.'

Shopping for clothes is a strange business – I can't do it if anyone's with me, and my best buys are always on impulse and unneeded. I need something to wear on my wedding day; a crumpled stained dress lies in the corner of my mind and needs banishing. I use my lunch hour to go to Liberty's – I hate department stores unless they have central wells and as far as I know only Liberty's and Peter Jones are built with this alleviation of claustrophobia.

I run up the creaking wooden panelled staircase to the first floor, conscious of pressures of time and need. I take armfuls of dresses to try on – they are all wrong, too tight, too loose, too long, too boring. My bra is dirty and I look raddled; nothing suits me. In a rage I put my work clothes back on and take all the dresses back. Then I notice a pale grey silk dress on a stand, one of those deceptively simple Japanese outfits of superb cut. I rush over to it and read the price; it leaves me limp with shock. Double the maximum I'd set aside. But the simplicity of the dress gives me an idea and I hurry upstairs to the fabric department. I used to make lots of clothes – why don't I run up something simple in a very expensive silk?

I actually waste half an hour deceiving myself, looking at patterns and feeling fabrics. You have no time, you fool. You're out of practice, your machine needs a service. It won't have lost its ability to knot up and snap the thread. I still persist in my daydream, clearly seeing an elegant straight simple dress in my mind's eye, run up in a couple of hours, no problem . . . I even carry a bolt of silk to a counter before I come to my senses.

When I get back to Chambers, wedding dress-less still, Paul is hovering about looking for me with an agonised expression. He's forgotten to tell me the changed time of a conference which I should have been warned about.

'It's Mr Stimson's client from the Mackleton disaster, Miss Harper. They're up there, they've just started.'

'Mrs Henchard?'

'And her solicitor.'

'This isn't good enough, Paul.'

'Sorry.'

I tear upstairs, feeling the effect of hurry and sweat all over me. Colin introduces me and I sit down quickly at Patricia's desk and use one of her notebooks. My copy of the Mackleton brief is behind the client, and I've no desire to disturb her.

Mrs Henchard is short and heavily pregnant; she's very pale, with deep lines at eyes and mouth ploughing through puffy skin; her pea-green jumpsuit is stretched tight over her huge abdomen. Her voice is monotonous, traumatised.

'I'd have drowned too if I'd gone to that party, but like I said, I was feeling too sick. My mum keeps on about my luck, not going at the last moment, but I'm beginning to wish I was with Brian on that boat and dead now. I've got too many problems, and this baby coming. Everything's getting me down.'

'It's been a very painful few months for you.' Colin has the most sympathetic voice I know, and his face exudes kindness. Mrs Henchard pours out her feelings for another ten minutes, while her solicitor keeps his to himself. She reminds us she's lost the flat she was buying with her husband, she's had to move back with her mother, she's dreading the expense of the baby, plus the fact that no kids are allowed in her mother's block.

'I tell you, it's a nightmare. And if that ship was unsafe, I want to get them men that own it, I want them to feel what it's like to be charged with murder.'

'It couldn't be murder, Mrs Henchard. Manslaughter possibly—'

'Same difference. Can I smoke? That's another bad thing – I've gone back to smoking since all this happened.'

'Feel free.'

'And I want to get some money out of them, lots of money. I've lost everything because of those bastards, everything. My lighter's out of fuel.'

None of us smoke or can produce a match, and I have to run down to the clerks' room to fetch matches. Paul takes a box out of his pocket.

'How's it going? Mrs Henchard was well away down here in the waiting room, shouting at her solicitor like nobody's business.' Paul's manner is always on the edge of cheeky; he gives the impression he's going to drop the usual formality always adhered to between every barrister and clerk and call me Nat. I smile at him frostily without replying; I'm still cross at being put at a disadvantage over this conference.

Mrs Henchard falls on the matches. Colin is going over the current state of the case.

'Of course, no one is admitting liability at this stage. Unfortunately, there was no proper police investigation and the HSE have been very cursory—'

'What's this HSE?' Mrs Henchard starts a coughing fit as she speaks and Colin has to wait several minutes until the paroxysm ends. I give her a glass of water. She sits gasping, tears in her eyes.

'HSE stands for the Health and Safety Executive. They're responsible for enforcing safety, and safe working systems. They are overworked and undermanned like everybody else, but they're also rather unimaginative in their approach. They don't seem to investigate top men, the managers, the decision-makers behind the scenes.'

'The bastards who are really to blame.'

'You could put it that way.'

'But them directors, the ones that were taken to court over the *Herald of Free Enterprise*, they copped it, didn't they? They got it in the neck—'

'Absolutely right, Mrs Henchard. A precedent was established that managers can be charged despite being absent when deaths occur—'

'There you are then. I've got hope.' Another bout of coughing, worse than before. Mrs Henchard stubs out her half-smoked cigarette and puts her grubby ragged-nailed fingers over her face as she gasps for breath. 'I got to stop this smoking, it's doing me no good,' she manages to whisper.

'Hope is definitely what you should have. I have, and I'm sure Mr Farmer has too.' The solicitor doesn't look as if hope is an emotion he's greatly acquainted with. 'But a prosecution has yet to be brought against the company, and unfortunately the investigations into the disaster were rather cursory, as I mentioned before. The case is with the Crown Prosecution Service at the moment, being assessed.'

'What can I do to make them prosecute?'

'Pray, Mrs Henchard. Not much else you can do.'

'Oh, God, don't say that. I never had no luck at praying.'

'I feel so sorry for her, poor thing.' Colin stands staring out of the window after Mrs Henchard has waddled out in the wake of Mr Farmer.

'She's so helpless. What can she do to improve things?'

'Not a lot. She's broke, she will get damages eventually but it's now she needs money, now while her life has fallen apart, her feelings are raw, her equilibrium nonexistent.'

I join Colin at the window; amongst the figures scurrying below is the unmistakable shape of George Warne QC.

'Do you know what that man said to me at lunch yesterday?'

'George?'

'George. Very loudly, so that the whole table heard. He said he thought Chambers was doing too much legally aided work, and certainly too much of it was PI. More or less told me I was a fool to concentrate my practice on both.'

'He's so thick-skinned he has no idea how much he hurts people, Colin.'

'His final remark was that he deeply suspected I'd come to the Bar to Do Good. The disgust he put into those two words was wonderful.'

Colin is chuckling at the memory as he puts the Mackleton papers in order and ties the pink tape round them.

'And did you?'

'Did I what?'

'Come to the Bar to do good?'

Colin's eyes, still full of amusement, meet mine. He shrugs. 'Of course, dearest Nat. But never tell George. Or Freddie. They'd banish me to a Citizens' Advice Bureau in a trice!'

6

'Meryl?'

'Goodness, it's Freddie. How nice.'

'How are you?'

'Surviving.'

'Are you desperately busy this afternoon?'

'Not specially. It's not even my turn to collect the boys.'

'I'm stuck in court all day, and there's a house guest arriving at about four at Elsworth Avenue. Mrs Wilks was supposed to stay on late but some crisis has developed in her life too complicated to explain, and so I need someone to let Jane in. Jane Harper, Natalie's younger sister. She's just arrived from Australia for the wedding. Unfortunately Nat's tied up too. Can you help?'

'Of course. I wanted to drop a wedding present in on you anyway.'

'I could have sworn you'd already given us one.'

'Freddie, you're confusing me with someone else.'

'My mind's not on presents to be honest. I'm in the thick of a complex case. Must go, and thanks a lot for doing this. You're a brick.'

Meryl was pleased. In all ways, she was pleased. She liked oblique approaches to people, and to meet Jane before meeting Natalie was just what she preferred. She'd learn all sorts of sisterly things.

And she wanted a reason for visiting the house, had wanted it ever since Freddie had told her about Anthea's extraordinary secret. She'd been longing to wander through her sister's house, looking for clues. She had a set of keys as a fail-safe for Freddie, and of course she could have used them. She'd picked them up more than once, on the point of making a clandestine visit. But she didn't know Mrs Wilks's hours, and she couldn't bring herself to ask. And she also knew that sometimes Freddie worked at home.

Now she left immediately, lunch forgotten.

'Care in the community! Care in the community! Care! CARE!' A tramp banged on the bonnet of the car as Meryl sat in a traffic jam caused by extensive roadworks. He was railing at the drivers around him in deranged desperation, his hair wild, his skin mottled with long-term dirt.

'Care in the community! Care! Care!' He continued to bang on the cars as they inched slowly along. Intimidated, embarrassed, drivers were handing coins through barely open windows. Meryl had left in such a hurry she hadn't brought any money; the man leaned down and stared at her, still shouting, his bloodshot eyes a foot from hers, his spittle on the window.

'I'm sorry, I haven't got any money on me—'

'Care in the community! Care!'

'Terribly sorry—'

But he hardly seemed to hear her or register she had put nothing in his hand. He moved on again, banging and shouting, even though the cars were speeding up as the blockage eased. He walked straight in front of one car, causing it to brake sharply, and even then his distressing cry of Care! Care! was unvarying in its intonation. Meryl was glad when she could no longer hear it. Then she noticed that a glob of the tramp's spittle was lodged in the corner of the window, thick and glaucous. The sight of it made her feel like retching.

As soon as she arrived at Freddie's house she ran down to the utility room to fetch a bucket of water to wash away the spittle, her hands shaking and her breath short. The main reason the tramp had upset her so profoundly was his physical degradation – in her heart of hearts she couldn't understand how any human being could sink so far. Surely there must have been a moment when they could have halted things – she banged the bucket down in the utility room sink, and knew that Anthea would have felt the same. Self-help – a basic human instinct – Anthea would have agreed with her. But the tramp's raucous cry was hard to forget.

She washed her hands fiercely and then sank onto a small sofa in the corner of the room. The utility room. Sometimes Meryl used to say acidly to Dennis that she couldn't imagine why two adults living on their own needed such a thing, while she had to struggle with a washing machine in the kitchen and two boys whose games kit alone would have given Anthea fifty fits.

Today the utility room gave her nothing but pleasure. She put the tramp out of her mind as she looked at the pale green walls, white cupboards, elaborate hi-tech ironing board, the white-tiled floor. The sofa she sat on was triangular and upholstered in a strong rose colour. There was a watercolour of a vase of dark red peonies beside the small square window.

Calm flooded her as she continued to sit. Anthea. Anthea was everywhere. Anthea, compulsive secret gambler. Meryl smiled at the absurdity of it. Anthea, did you stand pressing Freddie's underpants (I know you ironed them, you ironed everything) as you thought about Red Rum winning or losing in the 2.35 at Kempton? It's so unexpected. Red Rum. The only horse I've heard of. Horses have such stupid names.

'Red Rum. Red Rum.' Meryl said the words out loud. A nearby tap was dripping in the otherwise silent house. Meryl got up to turn it off more firmly, and opened some of the cupboards. Empty except for one big box of soap powder. None of the many products Anthea used to think were essential: different types of fabric softeners, of whiteners, of colour enhancers, of stain removers. Her collection was gone. Instead, on one of the shelves there was a row of round pebbles, each carefully put well apart from one another, looking surreal. Meryl wondered what on earth Freddie used them for, and shut the cupboard on the faintly disturbing sight.

There was a newspaper lying over a chairback in the kitchen, and Meryl opened it at the racing section. List after list of runners at Newmarket, at Stratford, at Fontwell, at Kempton – horses with names like Old Speckled Hen, Smartie Express, Shine on Brightly, For Heaven's Sake, Gladtogetit. The nearest to Red Rum was Red Rainbow. Muddy Lane, Wily Trick, Adjacent. Once upon a time Old Speckled Hen was dragged by a wily trick into an adjacent muddy lane – as Meryl started to laugh, the phone rang twice before switching over to answerphone. A harsh male voice filled the kitchen.

'It's Tom. Just to tell you I'm on Monday's Cathay Pacific flight from Delhi, arriving twelve twenty-five London time. Can't read the flight number. Don't think you need it. Freddie, don't forget about the ambulance. Er – end of message.'

Meryl guessed it was Thomas Mentieth's voice and stood musing, intrigued by the mention of the ambulance. Then she sighed, peeled a banana (lack of lunch was beginning to make itself felt) and made her way to a cupboard near the basement side door. Anthea had kept all her old coats and gardening clobber here, and Meryl wanted to search those pockets for the sort of revealing oddments that get left in them, like betting slips.

But the cupboard had nothing in it except Freddie's things for gardening – an old jacket, Wellingtons, gardening gloves. Nothing else except a pile of plant and seed catalogues, many of them annotated by Anthea.

'Try hostas under cherry tree – Meryl's stripy ones.'

The sight of her name in her sister's hand turned Meryl cold. She stared out of the half-glass door at the wall of the side passage, painted by Anthea with a line of hollyhocks to cheer up the narrow gap. The hollyhocks and their attendant bees and butterflies were roughly done but had great charm. Meryl's gaze fixed on a particular chubby bee as tears coursed down her face. Anthea's life was her surroundings; her spirit was pungently in this house. Meryl shook the catalogues in case anything fell out, her tears still flowing, dripping on to her front. Nothing did.

Meryl dried her eyes on kitchen roll and ate another banana. She wandered all over the house, mourning her sister while searching for something that would show that Anthea had a second secret life. She found nothing personal of Anthea's anywhere, and no locked drawers or cupboards except one. She tugged at the double doors in the spare room but they held. Solid joinery, typical of Anthea.

Meryl looked in vain for a key; she stuck her head in the adjacent bathroom just in case it was hidden there. A minuscule pair of black lace briefs hung from the shower head, and an array of Body Shop bottles and jars sat neatly on a shelf. She shut the door smartly.

Freddie's bedroom was immaculate; Mrs Wilks left everything lined up in rows. Meryl opened the drawers in deep unease, conscious of Anthea's eyes in many a photograph. There was no sign of the cupboard key anywhere. She went into the bathroom to use the lavatory, and as she sat relieving herself she stared glumly at the *tour de force* of design around her. Bath and two handbasins stood on a central plinth; the lavatory had its own niche with sliding door. The walls were lined with phalanxes of custom-built cupboards to hold every different sort of item from underwear to shoes. Subdivisions, racks, all sorts of hooks and cubby holes. All empty. Freddie's possessions took up a small section of one wall; instead of expanding to fill the gaps, his appeared to have shrunk. Or maybe Meryl had never noticed before how lightly his presence lay in the house—

Then she saw it, hanging high up behind the bathroom door. A little brass key on a brass hook. Holding her breath, Meryl reached for it, sure she knew which lock it matched. As she went through to the spare room and unlocked the cupboard doors, she was possessed by childhood fiction, by Alice, by the children who step through the back of a cupboard and out of our time. She had read *Alice Through the Looking Glass* and *The Lion, the Witch and the Wardrobe* to Piers and Harry so many times. The doors swung open.

The scent of Anthea's skin flowed into the room. None of the dresses had been dry-cleaned; they retained Anthea's aroma uncannily. She had never used commercial perfumes, only a mixture of natural oils which she put together herself. Musk, rose oil. The aroma was faint now, but to Meryl it was as if her sister was hiding behind those soft expensive folds.

She stood frozen for some time, and then ran her hands through the row of garments, only half of which were at all familiar. The labels in them made her lips tighten. Anthea must have spent thousands. Thousands and thousands.

'Dennis, look what Anthea's given me for my birthday.'

'How nice.'

'*How nice!* It's not at all nice. I saw them on the special offer rail at Marks and Spencer not long ago. Things only go on the special offer rail if they're not selling well. I had a look at these shirts myself and decided that even on my budget I could do better.'

'She probably bought it when they were full price.'

'Either way, I feel hurt. It's horrid.'

Meryl shut the cupboard doors as she remembered the meanness of her sister's presents. She lay down on the bed Natalie had slept in the night before and shut her eyes as the hurt built in volume. A fresh lot of tears collected and flowed. Anthea never gave the boys splendid presents either: they were always halfway good, subtly wrong. Roller skates that fell apart because they were too lightweight or too small, guns with no caps, T-shirts that shrank and ran in the wash.

Once Meryl had overheard her sister say it was important to match presents to the pockets of the receiver. That hurt too.

Anthea, Anthea, were the dresses the rewards of your gambling? Does Freddie keep the cupboard shut because he knows this and finds it hard to face? Did you go constantly to gamble, under cover of that sculpture course at the Tate, those Renaissance lectures at the V&A? I hate you, Anthea, I feel cheated of all my good memories of you, I can only think of the bad, of your meanness, your indifference to my boys. Bugger you.

Meryl lay utterly still, her body stiff, her mind slowing into a state of frozen quietude. The phone followed by the distant burble of the answerphone roused her eventually and she sat up. The cupboard doors had swung open of their own accord.

Suddenly she leapt up and started to undress until she stood in her white slip and black bra (her two white ones were dirty). She ran her hand through the luxurious row, and chose a black and white Bruce Oldfield. It was ingeniously constructed in asymmetrical panels, and though a delight to feel against her skin and elegantly becoming, it was too long. She dropped it on the floor and looked for something where Anthea's extra height wouldn't matter. An Issey Miyake outfit of black silk consisting of short trousers (ankle length on Meryl) and a pleated loose jacket was perfect: she gazed at herself. She was transformed. And in that moment, she knew that she would steal it.

It's fair, Anthea, it's fair at last. You had all the lovely things, I've never had a single piece of clothing that wasn't ordinary. Never. Clothes, clothes; you were obsessed by appearances so clothes were your own apex of achievement. The house, you in it, you out of it – all perfect. Superb. You tried not to look at my homemade skirts, the chipped paintwork, the tricycles in the hall, the dried baby food on the kitchen walls flung by the boys as they learned to eat. I used to tell Dennis I was sorry for you. But I wasn't, I wasn't. I was green with envy.

As Meryl stood there admiring what the black silk outfit did for her, the doorbell rang. Christ. Four o'clock, it was four o'clock already. She fumbled her way out of the suit into her own clothes and rushed tousled downstairs as the bell went for the third time, a short despairing ring.

'Jane Harper? Hello, hello, I'm Meryl, Freddie's sister-in-law – so sorry I kept you waiting but I was at the top of the house – *do* come in!'

By the time this effusion ended Jane had dumped her large case and a canvas holdall on the hall floor.

'I was expecting to be let in by a Mrs Wilks, the cleaner. I thought she must have forgotten and gone.'

'Oh, no, some problem cropped up, so Freddie rang me and I rushed over.'

'It's very kind of you.'

'And of course I know this house backwards, home from home so to speak—' Jane had a cool composed manner that intimidated Meryl, so she gushed away to cover her unease even while she tried in vain to check herself.

'I tried the door in the basement—'

'Very sensible, since that's where you're going to be staying. We can get to the flat from inside though, downstairs and through the kitchen. And I'm sure you'd like a cup of tea or something, long air journeys are so exhausting what with jet lag—'

'I'm all right, thanks. I've been here several days, in fact. If you take this, I'll manage that heavy one.'

Meryl took the holdall and was surprised at its weight. She led the way, unable to get the image of designer clothes strewn all over the spare room out of her mind. She pined to get back there to restore order and hide the Miyake. She had a vision of Freddie making a special effort to get home early to welcome his future sister-in-law and sweat broke out all over her body.

'So here's the bathroom – very sweet and neat, isn't it – and there's lots of cupboard space – Anthea was so clever at creating space out of nothing – Mrs Wilks has put out some towels I see – so I'll leave you to settle in while I put a kettle on and – well, put a kettle on—'

Meryl crashed about filling the electric kettle, then ran upstairs, then down again to find a large carrier bag in the utility room cupboard where Anthea had always kept them. Heal's. She had loved Heal's. Even the bag smelt of Anthea.

Meryl folded the Miyake suit with care and hid it under some loose tissue paper. She hung up the Bruce Oldfield, which she'd torn slightly while getting it off, and locked the cupboard after arranging all the clothes as they had been. She pushed the thought that Freddie would notice the absence of the black silk out of her mind – Dennis never noticed anything she wore, he always looked completely blank when she referred to some familiar old garment he must have seen a thousand times. Besides, there were several black outfits in the cupboard, lots in fact, and one more or less wouldn't show. Freddie probably never looked at them; after all, he hadn't even had them cleaned.

'Hullo – o.' Jane's voice carried up the stairwell. 'Sorry, I didn't catch your name.'

'Meryl. Meryl Peak.'

'I've run out of hangers, Mrs Peak.'

'Call me Meryl, please call me Meryl. After all we're going to be relatives in no time at all. Hangers. Let me find you some, there should be some in this cupboard, oh dear, they're all in use. Plenty upstairs, I'll go and fetch you some in a minute. Clothes are such a bore, aren't they, they need washing, they need ironing, they need hangers, they're almost worse than children.' Oh why, oh why did she witter on at this deadpan Australian?

'Since I don't have any children, I rather like looking after my clothes.'

'Oh, well, yes, I could quite see that—'

To Meryl's relief, the phone rang. On to the answerphone came Freddie's voice. 'Pick it up, Meryl, it's Freddie here. Hullo, has Jane arrived? Good, good. Pass her to me a moment, would you?'

Meryl watched the softness, warmth and pleasure spread across Jane's face as she took the phone and listened to Freddie. Her tones in reply were no longer cool. When she put the receiver down her expression was decidedly smug. She went back to her new quarters ignoring Meryl completely.

Meryl found some tin hangers and made tea out of Mrs Wilks's supply of PG Tips rather than Freddie's finest Darjeeling. She called Jane to say it was ready and was surprised when Jane came at once looking more friendly.

'So what do you think of my sister Natalie?'

'I haven't met her yet.'

'Haven't *met* her!'

'Freddie kept her very quiet. Until they were actually engaged, the family didn't know she even existed. Since then, they've been too busy to arrange a meeting. You know how it is.'

Meryl could see from Jane's expression she knew exactly how it was. Freddie did not particularly want his future wife to meet his ex-wife's gushing sister until it was unavoidable.

'Natalie kept me in the dark too, until the wedding invitation came.'

'What did you feel?'

'Bloody gobsmacked. I didn't even know she was a barrister, let alone she was going out with one. But there you go, Sydney is a long way from London. And we were never close as sisters. We never rang each other, we just wrote occasionally. I told her about my life, she kept quiet about hers. Yes, I was gobsmacked.'

'And what do you think of Freddie?'

'Too old for her, but he's a dear. She's certainly done well for herself.' Jane kept her eyes on the kitchen table, tapping nervously with a finger.

'I worry about the age gap too.'

'It's Nat's problem. Nothing to do with us. But she's skipped from being an impoverished student to an affluent middle-class wife with a middle-aged husband, and she'll pay for it.'

'More tea?'

'No thanks.'

'A drink? It's after half five—'

'A beer would be great.'

'A beer. Now where would Freddie keep beer, I wonder—'

'There's a crate of Foster's in that corner.'

'Foster's?'

'Aussie beer. He's obviously got it in specially for me. That man is too wonderful.'

'Actually, Freddie's very fond of beer. He often drinks it.'

Meryl got herself a glass of white wine from a half-finished bottle in the fridge, and watched Jane swallow half a pint of beer in seconds.

'What do you mean by Natalie paying for marrying Freddie?'

'Oh, forget it. She'll cope. She's tough. She won't notice the price, she'll enjoy the perks too much. She's got a strong materialistic streak, has my big sister.'

'You're not implying anything unpleasant, are you?'

'What's unpleasant about being materialistic?'

'I meant, that she's marrying Freddie just for his money.'

'Why not? He's obviously loaded. And he's a top dog, belongs to all the right clubs, all that jazz. Very tempting for a rootless young girl who's struggling to make her way in the world. It would tempt me.'

Jane fetched another can of Foster's. Meryl sipped her rather acid wine in silence, unable to find anything to say.

'Of course, Nat's in love with him. Don't get me wrong. And she's no fool, she's good at her work, she'd have probably done well anyway, but not with the speed being married to the Head of Chambers is going to give her. I'll be honest with you, I was mistaken about Nat.'

'Mistaken?'

'Yes, I always thought that without me around to spur her on she'd choose the slow lane. All our lives as kids I was the pushy little sister giving her hell, putting a tiger in her tank.' Jane laughed as she stretched out in her chair, running her right hand down her left side as if testing the firmness of her flesh. She has a beautiful body despite this fondness for beer, thought Meryl, and hoped that one day the beer would win. She did not like Jane.

'So you were wrong about her. It's easy to assume one knows one's sister well, only to find one doesn't.'

'Too right.'

'Why did you describe Natalie as rootless?'

'I include myself in that. We're both rootless. No family ties, no breeding as defined by people like you, just brains and pzazz.'

'You make us sound very judgmental, we're not really like that.'

But even as she spoke she thought of those armies of relatives on all sides – the Gittingses, the Belling-Johnsons, the Mentieths – and felt deadened by the prospect of them all congregating at the wedding. And of course being judgmental however hard they tried to hide it.

'I have another question for you.'

Jane gazed at her, her eyes bright despite brown shadows of exhaustion beneath them.

'Fire ahead.' Meryl downed the last of her wine.

'This house is terrific, it's wonderful, but whose taste does it reflect? Did Freddie have a top interior decorator in, or what?'

'No, no, it's nothing to do with him. He hasn't touched anything since Anthea died. This house is my sister through and through.'

'And through. Well, she certainly had style. And my last question is, how do you lock this place up? I want to go out briefly, and Freddie said you would give me your set of keys before you left and take me through the security routine.'

'Goodness, of course, yes—' Meryl was so thrown by the firm way Jane showed her out that she forgot the all-important carrier bag and had to ring the bell, leaving the car running outside.

'My shopping. Frightfully sorry, left it somewhere.' Though Jane paid no attention whatsoever to the Heal's bag, Meryl could feel she had gone bright red from her collar up. Her hands were damp on the steering wheel and she stalled the car twice before driving away, the taste of flat wine acrid on her tongue.

7

'*Ma che fai qui, Signorina?*'

'Dave, you mustn't do that to me. I nearly died of shock.'

'Couldn't resist it. Why are you here in Lavender Hill and what bus are you waiting for so distractedly?' Dave moves his hands from my shoulders to my waist. I pick them off.

'I've been earning my crust in South Western Magistrates' Court. Some of us have to. And now I'm trying to get back to the Temple. I'm fed up with waiting for a bus, and no taxi has gone past.'

'So you're stuck. Good. Come and have lunch with me, darling Nat.' Dave is looking a little less seedy than usual: he has trimmed his beard, and his hair is clean. His clothes smell but not unpleasantly: it's that sweetish musty smell of outer garments that need a visit to the dry-cleaners.

'I can't. I must get back.'

'Oh, come on. I so enjoyed our dance the other night, by the way. Surreal. Did you know that someone photographed us and it's going to come out in some article on social contrasts?'

'Oh, God, no.'

'Relax, you're unrecognisable, eclipsed by that dress, that totally *meraviglioso* dress.'

'Where is it coming out?'

'One of those society rags, *Tatler*, something like that.'

'Did *you* send them the photograph?'

'Would I do a thing like that?'

'Absolutely, while you were selling your sister, your mother—'

'I love you when you're angry. Come and have lunch, Nat. Please.'

'Oh, all right then. A very quick bite.'

'I'm good at bites. Try me.'

'Dave, if you've got anything other than lunch in mind, forget it.'

'This way. There's a deli-cum-snack bar which isn't bad for a cheap quick bite.' He takes my arm. 'And of course I've got other things in mind. I always have. I think I must be developing whatever syndrome it is that afflicted Don Juan. I suffer from rapacious sexual curiosity, and it gets worse all the time. But one fuck's enough, then I move on to the next girl. Just like the Don, always adding to the list.' He chats as if discussing the weather. 'In here. Now what would you like? Lunch is on me.'

I choose quiche and salad, this time avoiding some evil-looking Scotch eggs. Dave chooses four long sausage rolls which he jokes about before eating at great speed. He then has a bowl of baked beans.

'How come you're here in Wandsworth yourself, Mr Big Spender?'

'I've been flat-sitting, just till tomorrow. Mick Mackintosh – you remember him, third year in our first?'

'No.'

'He landed a very flash job in the City. He's got a flat just down the road with more plants in it than Kew Gardens. I keep them watered and live free in luxury while he's busy abroad. I can see by your expression you find this domestic responsibility hard to believe.'

'I thought you were fixed on the idea of squats and freedom.'

'Squats are a necessity, not a choice. Having said that, I'm in a very good squat. You ought to come and see it, it's not far from your future hubby's elegant abode, the grotty end of Camden Town but we can't all live in Primrose Hill.'

'Hubby. What an appalling word. How's the novel getting on, Dave?'

'Slowly. But contrary to what you all think, it exists. It's real. I have a hundred thousand words to prove it.'

'Sounds as if you've nearly finished it, if it's that length. Unless you're aiming at a blockbuster—'

'I'm not aiming at any length. I'll probably ditch half of it when I start revising.'

'What's it about?'

'This and that. That and this. It's highly experimental and boring. *Really* boring.'

'Why go on with it if it's boring?'

'But I'm aiming at boredom, dear Nat. Life is boring ninety per cent of the time, with ten per cent of good flashes. I'm after the same effect. I don't want the interesting bits to take over.'

I never know whether to believe Dave. He changes his ground constantly. The next time he talks about this novel he'll probably say it's all a homage to Dickens.

A pretty fair-haired girl comes and sits nearby, laying out her lunch with demure self-consciousness as Dave watches her avidly. Still keeping an eye on her, he takes out a little notebook full of columns like a cash book, and scribbles along a line.

'You need a Leporello.'

'A what?'

'Don Giovanni's manservant in the Mozart opera.'

'Never been to an opera. Not interested. But what does this manservant do?'

'Keeps a list of his master's amours.'

'After or before he's had them?'

'After.'

'I only list descriptions of the ones I lust after. When I have them they get crossed out. You're down. I listed you months ago, after you started going out with your hubby-to-be.'

'You're mad. And stop using that phrase.'

'Here you are. Look – Natalie Harper. The rest is in code. No, you can't see any more of it. Hands off.'

'Is Jane down?'

'*Ma certo. Eccola qui.*'

'You are mad, David Rosenberg. You really are.'

'Mad, bad, and dangerous to know. But that's so attractive.' He's holding my gaze with his mocking one. 'Come back to Mick's flat and have some coffee.'

'No.'

'You want your name to come off this list, don't you? Of course you do. So come back to Mick's flat and cross yourself off. There's only one way you can do that.' He picks up my hand and kisses it, his eyes still on mine.

'Oh, what the hell. OK.' I stand up. Fifty per cent of me is calling his bluff. I haven't slept around since Freddie came into my life, and I don't plan to do so when I'm married. Somehow this demand of Dave's doesn't seem to have anything to do with my new life, just as he himself is now outside it. He and I have flirted since we met in my first year at university, we've occasionally kissed and stopped and stared at each other, knowing it would be easy to go further. Sexual possibilities are a staple of student life, after all. Some you take up, some you don't. I've been years out of the ambiance, but today I suddenly want to act like a student again, before it is too late.

'Well, well.' Dave stands up too. Do I see just a spark of dismay in the back of his eye? I smile, he smiles back, the spark gone (if it ever existed), supplanted by an intent businesslike look. He takes my arm again and walks me with great speed down through a maze of little streets into a house that has been converted into two halves with an outdoor staircase of metal. We clatter up this.

'Very hi-tech, Mick's place.' I watch Dave flick complicated switches with a practised hand.

'Coffee? He has a Gaggia machine.'

'Just to watch you use it. For someone who believes in the simple life, no unnecessary refinements or possessions, you seem remarkably at ease with all this.'

Dave takes no notice, except to tell me to take my shoes off. Mick has thick cream-coloured carpet everywhere, and shoes, says Dave, are not allowed. He takes his off. He has no socks on, and his long white feet have extra-long toes, each with a tuft of black hair like decorations on a child's slipper. I then notice how much hair is creeping down the back of his hand, and realise for the first time what a hairy man Dave is. How could I have never noticed before? Perhaps because I never looked past the long hair on his head and face. I follow Dave into the kitchen; the white-tiled floor is warm underfoot. Dave starts up the Gaggia.

'Your sister Jane is a real ball-crusher.'

'What makes you say that?'

'Long experience. I used to avoid her kind, but these days curiosity has got the better of caution.'

'Caution has a role to play in this game.'

'If you're talking about protection, then don't worry. I get no kicks out of taking risks, and I don't suppose Don Juan did either. We get our kicks from other things. Sugar?'

'Half a spoon. Umm. Smells divine.'

I sip my coffee from a white porcelain cup, and wander about the kitchen. I am fascinated to see how Dave will get me into the bedroom, and I'm giving him no help. We admire the roof garden, we look at the pictures in the living room. Then Dave takes my cup and disappears into the kitchen, returning a few moments later completely naked. Sleek black hair covers his body all over, in sharp contrast to the brownish-red of his mouth, nipples and erect penis. I've never seen a man so hairy. Freddie is white and almost hairless by contrast.

'You undressed at the speed of light.'

'I only have two garments to take off. I never wear underwear, haven't for years.'

'This is a crazy idea, Dave. I don't feel like making love—'

'Who says you won't in a minute? Come on.' Dave disappears again, into Mick's bedroom (even his bottom has hair on it). 'Come on, Nat. Think of that list. Lie back and think of that list.' I can hear the smile in his voice. 'I'm waiting.'

It is a strange experience. Dave is oddly neat and gentle in the way he touches me, precise and not tentative, and all the time his intent businesslike expression does not change and all the time he keeps up a soft monologue in my ear. It is his voice that gets me going and carries me until I'm lost in a protracted climax.

'Red-haired girls with gorgeous red bushes, thin girls with super-reactive nerve ends, fat girls, oh pneumatic bliss of fat thighs, come on, Nat, come on, blondes with their nipples tight in their T-shirts, black girls with lush pink pussies in that wonderful skin, come on Nat, girls with freckles everywhere, girls with moles in secret places, go, Nat, go, go, told you feelings didn't matter, told you, told you, TOLD YOU.'

We don't lie for long on Mick's futon – there's a huge silent clock implanted into one wall and it tells me it's two o'clock already. I roll away to go and clean up and dress; Dave wanders off to the kitchen to find his jeans and jersey. He returns fully dressed before I've even done up my white shirt and waves his notebook at me.

'Will you sign it?'

'Sign what?'

'Sign your name beside your name.'

'No bloody fear.'

'Lots of girls have.'

'More fool them. I'm just waiting to see you scrub my name out.'

'It looks so nice to have the signature there, beside the date.'

'Dave Rosenberg, I'm sure you're mad, I don't trust you, and I'm not signing your fucking fucking notebook.' As Dave starts to laugh, a nasty thought crosses my mind. 'Do you show that thing to every girl you get to bed?'

'It depends. Not usually. Some I never tell at all about the notebook. It depends. I've known you for so long—'

'If you dare show it to my sister ever, *ever*, Dave, I'll never speak to you again. I mean it.'

'Oh, what a fate. Look, I'm putting a line through your name.'

'Since Jane's on the list, I suppose you will pursue her—'

'Of course. I'll probably get nowhere. Ball-crushers always play hard to get before they get to work. But if I arrive at cross-off point, I won't tell.'

'I don't trust you, Dave. I don't trust you. I should never have come here.'

'Palilogist.'

'What? What do you mean?'

Dave laughs and puts his notebook into his hip pocket.

'What was that word?'

'Palilogist? It's a rhetorical term.'

'I don't trust you. I don't trust you one inch—'

Dave is laughing so much he can't even say goodbye and I storm off alone towards Lavender Hill.

By the time the bus comes the warmth of exercise and the feel of Dave inside me have faded; I am chilled in body and mind. I am a fool to fall for that ploy – cross yourself off my list by having a fuck with me – I am a fool. How ridiculous to think it will end there. He'll use what I've done, I know he will. He loves making trouble.

The bus is old and noisy and shudders its slow way towards the West End. I sit blind to my surroundings, my brain full of the gratuitous act of sex with Dave. I feel his hairy body, so different from Freddie's, so utterly different. Dave is circumcised, Freddie not, and this nudges insistently but meaninglessly at me as if the engorged organ is pressing on my conscious mind.

I used to have plenty of casual affairs as a student and think no more about them; life as a working girl has made me more circumspect and also limited the possibilities. I suppose I've grown out of casual sex, too – Sara says she has – she used to be totally promiscuous.

'I don't get a kick out of it any more. I'm much more likely to notice their smell or their pimples and vow never again.' Sara's giggle makes me take a deep breath now, as the bus groans its way over Lambeth Bridge. I think I'll talk to Sara tonight about Dave. I wonder if she – I have no idea if they've ever slept together, as students or since.

Dave. I see myself as Dave must have seen me earlier, hurrying out of the court along the street to the bus stop. He's on the opposite side of the street, possibly checking out some luscious shop assistant and writing her up in his book when he catches sight of me. It's Nat. Well, well. Natalie who's about to change her life rather dramatically, go middle-class and marry a stereotype older man, boring and rich. Natalie, on my list. Right, let's get her.

I was stalked, I was pinned down and caught. He could have been watching me for some time before he pounced. Sleek black body hair. Damn you, damn you. I don't trust you. But I don't trust myself either. How could I have been so stupid as to give in to him now? I've resisted him for all those years when it would have been no big deal to make love. What was I after? Why now? Why at all? Is it because Dave still has the power to make us all regress into bohemian amorality – except that he would be angry I used the word regress. You're getting so proper, Natalie. Damn you, Dave, damn you.

Remorse. It's not a feeling I'm familiar with. Regret, yes. I've felt regret often enough, who hasn't? But remorse – it's a harsh emotion. Remorse. I have done what I ought not to have done.

In this old London bus smelling of aged plush seats, diesel fumes, human sweat and dirt, remorse fills me as the smell fills my nostrils. Pain floods me, even some anger. This remorse is undesired, unexpected. I don't even believe that the act of making love to Dave is wrong, yet remorse beats round my head and I can do nothing to stop it.

The smell of this bus will be with me for the rest of my life, encapsulating remorse. Damn you, Dave, damn you.

8 ∫

'I've got to go back to the flat first. Things to clear up with Sara.'

'But you'll come in time to eat? I don't feel I can entertain Jane on my own for long—'

'Of course, Freddie.'

Natalie looked white and tired, and was clearly not in a very good mood. Freddie sighed as she banged the door. He'd just been through a very difficult day, the nastiest he could remember, and was hoping for sympathy and interest from Natalie. Instead, she'd given him no chance to say anything and would probably arrive late for dinner, leaving him in the clutches of a feminist Australian. He was holding his head in his hands when the door opened again and Natalie ran back in.

'Sorry for being such a bore. I'll be in a better mood when I've got my act together.' She kissed his cheek and hugged him fiercely.

'Promise you won't be late.'

'I promise.'

'And watch the early evening news. I think they'll be reporting my case.'

'Oh? OK. Love you.'

She went out and immediately put her head back round the door.

'I meant to ask you – what does palilogist mean, Freddie? I can't find it in my dictionary.'

'Palilalia is a medical term for the mental instability which produces endless repetition of words and phrases. Palilogist must be a related word—'

'Thanks.'

*   *   *

When he drove past the court that morning on his way round to the private car park, Freddie scented trouble. There were journalists everywhere, mostly clustered round a tanned blonde woman who behaved as if she was used to and liked publicity.

'That Kerry Poole's in court again, Your Honour. I brought you your coffee. Black, one sugar.'

'Thanks, Mrs Frobisher, wonderful. But who are you talking about? I'm not quite with you.'

'Kerry Poole – she's the star of *Pack Up or Shut Up* – and she does that vodka advertisement, Your Honour, the one where they're drinking vodka in a hot-air balloon.'

'I'm afraid I've never seen *Pack Up or Shut Up* but I did see the hot-air balloon ad between two halves of the news the other night.'

'Kerry Poole's the defendant Geoffrey Poole's sister. The paper said she'd come back from America where she's making a film specially to be here for the end of his trial.'

'I see.'

'I'll just go and check the court, Your Honour.'

Mrs Frobisher was the most talkative of any usher he had come across; she mothered all the judiciary and clearly loved her role.

'The court's ready when you are, Your Honour, and you'll be pleased to hear the jury has reached a verdict.'

Freddie followed her down the corridor, noticing that she had smart new black suede shoes on. As the court rose when he entered, his eyes went immediately to the public gallery. The blonde woman was in the front row, smiling at Geoffrey Poole.

Poole himself was staring fixedly ahead. He looked like a brutish version of his sister: her blonde hair became a stiff yellow stubble on his head, her pink-and-white complexion on him was a rough red skin mined by acne and alcohol, her thin neck a thick column the same diameter as his head. Both had the same glassy bulbous blue eyes.

His co-accused, Roger Betty, was short, black and myopic; he constantly adjusted his glasses, a nervous tic that had become more marked as the case progressed. Poole and Betty were no more than pub acquaintances, and the strain of the case had caused an intense dislike to grow between them – their antagonism was palpable.

The predominantly male jury filed in, and there was complete silence in the tense courtroom when the foreman, a plump bald man with a slight stammer, announced that the jury found both Betty and Poole guilty. Immediate uproar followed, eventually quelled by Mrs Frobisher's shouts of silence. When Freddie opened his mouth to resume proceedings a female voice shouted 'bastard' and more noise developed in the gallery as the duty policeman made the most disruptive members of the public leave. It was the first time in Freddie's short judging experience that a jury had found in favour of the police, and he found the atmosphere in court nerve-racking. By the time he adjourned sentence pending Social Enquiry and Community Service reports, and then granted bail to both defendants, he was more than ready for the court to rise.

'Oh dear, Your Honour, that was a bit of a party. Can I get you a cup of tea?'

'You certainly can, Mrs Frobisher. You handled that very well, if I may so. Good thing you've got a strong voice.'

'Thank you. If I were you, Your Honour, I'd stay put here for a bit until the crowd outside clears.'

'Precisely what I intend to do.'

He drank his tea and read the newspaper, then went out the back way to his car. Beside it were two men; one was tapping on the Saab's bonnet with a roll of documents while he laughed at something the other man was saying. They saw Freddie before he saw them, and fell silent. The rest of the car park was empty. Freddie recognised the men as two civil rights protesters who had followed the whole trial, and felt a pang of real fear. They were both large men.

'Ah, at last His Honour the judge, Mr Mentieth QC. Good afternoon to your Honour.'

'What do you want?'

'We didn't like your speech to the jury at all.'

'I said what I needed to say to sum up the case.'

'You said what you wanted to say. You slanted it towards the police, you tipped the jury towards the verdict of guilty.'

'That's nonsense and you know it. A judge is obliged to be objective.'

'Of course he is.' The man with the roll of documents spoke now. 'Of course he is. That is exactly my friend here's point. A judge should be objective. But you weren't, Mr Mentieth; you were biased, if you'll pardon my being so blunt. You favoured the police throughout and none of us liked it. The police beat those men up in the back of the van and everybody knew it. The WPC just got hurt in the fray.'

'Who are you?'

'Hugh Jones. This is Stan Whicker.'

'I mean, what organisation are you from?'

'That's your trouble, Mr Mentieth. Tunnel vision. We have to belong to an organisation to exist in your eyes.'

'That's simply not true.' Freddie gazed achingly at his car, trying to control his irritation at this pointless yet faintly sinister conversation. 'But I'm afraid that whatever views you two gentlemen hold about the verdict, it was reached by twelve ordinary men and women picked at random, and under no pressure from anyone, me included.'

'Under no pressure! Do you hear that, Stan? He doesn't know what we know, then. He doesn't know that one of the jury was nobbled by a certain policeman who shall remain nameless for the moment.'

'It's a bit late to make an allegation like that.'

'We only just learned about it.'

'The case is over, the jury's given its verdict. There's nothing to be done. Now if you'll excuse me, gentlemen—'

'You were on the side of the police—'

'This conversation has gone on quite long enough.' Freddie was on the point of pushing past to open his car door when he saw to his horror a TV cameraman and a reporter come into the car park. Jones and Whicker brightened at the prospect of media attention and stepped closer, forming a nice filmic group.

'You said in your speech that Mr Poole was lying—'

'I said *if* Mr Poole was lying—'

'It was difficult to hear the if, wasn't it, Hugh? Did you hear the if?'

'I certainly didn't. And if we couldn't, perhaps the jury couldn't either.'

'Please let me pass.'

The reporter was now close, and the camera was running. Freddie felt he was in a nightmare; he normally enjoyed dealing with the media, but not in this company in a deserted car park.

'Good evening, Mr Mentieth. Could I ask you a few questions—'

'Not now, I'm sorry, I have to hurry—'

'What is your reaction to the rumours flying around that a female member of the jury was pressurised by police in the course of the trial?'

'No comment. The case is over. Now, if you'll excuse me—'

'But surely you can't sentence these men if there's been a miscarriage of justice, Mr Mentieth—'

'I can't comment any further. Goodbye.'

Freddie had to shoulder his way past Whicker and Jones, who were now talking loudly to the reporter. He sank into his car feeling more shaken than he had since Anthea died. He needed to sit and recover but was afraid he would be approached again so he started the Saab at once and left, bumping the kerb badly as he turned out. He pulled into a garage within minutes because his hands were still shaking, and topped up his tank to give himself breathing space.

Stan Whicker and Hugh Jones had exuded the curious low-key menace of the fanatical activist. And he hadn't handled them well. Not well at all. They'd got under his skin and they knew it.

The house smelt different. Freddie turned to put his keys on top of the bowl of pebbles as he always did, but the bowl had gone. His head swam. Too many invasions of the norm – then he remembered the accident that morning.

But the house smelt different. Mrs Wilks left behind a whiff of powder and body odour; overlaying it was a new scent, heady and strong. He peered into the drawing room. Empty but scented. There was no sound in the house, just the smell of the souk.

Jane. Of course. He'd forgotten about Jane in his turmoil. In his relief he clattered down the stairs into the kitchen calling her name. The kitchen table seemed full of empty glasses and beer cans. Jane appeared wearing a green towelling robe and a white mask of creamy substance through which her eyes peered blinking.

'Hi, Freddie. Sorry about this. I wasn't expecting you so early.' The whites of her eyes looked yellow against the mask. She spoke hardly moving her lips so her mouth remained a slit. 'I was flat on my back. Give me twenty minutes.' She flapped a hand and disappeared again.

Freddie dealt with his answerphone, listening to Thomas's message twice. He went up to his bedroom and was again assailed by the subtle sense of displacement caused by a strange odour. He put this down to his tense state and decided a long hard shower would do the most to help. Just the week before she was killed Anthea had had a superb new shower installed with pressurised jets playing from all directions. Freddie dropped his clothes where he stood and went into the shower cabinet. Needles of water beat onto his skin as he stood with head bent, inhaling the steam deep into his lungs. He tried to lose awareness of self as the rush of water encased him, but his mind teased at the scene in the car park. He should never have allowed the two men to get into conversation. He had made no error of judgment in his speech to the jury, he had summed up a confused and murky set of circumstances with dispassionate clarity. He was in the right, but he could not dispel his unease.

He stayed in the shower so long his skin throbbed for some while after he'd got dressed again. He sat at his desk, read his post, checked on his diary for the next day, and then went down to the kitchen to find Jane clearing up, still wearing the gown but with her face bare now.

'Your sister-in-law and I had a drink together.'

'Quite right too.'

'It was kind of you to lay in Foster's.'

'Time for another, I'd say. Unless you'd like something different?'

'I'd rather drink beer, to be honest. You look whacked, Freddie.'

'It's been a tough day.'

Jane pulled out a chair and sat at the kitchen table. Freddie, who normally objected to drinking in the kitchen, sat down opposite her. The fridge hummed, the clock ticked, Jane smiled.

'Are you comfortable in the flat?'

'It's perfect. But tell me about your day, Freddie. What happened in your civil rights case?'

'We must switch on the news at seven. The media was there, and no one liked the verdict. The jury found the two men guilty.'

'Was that a surprise?'

'It was. That particular police station is notorious for using their truncheons a little too energetically. Obviously the jury wasn't to know that but word gets about. In this case the evidence was so conflicting nobody could be sure who'd beaten whom, to be honest. In a situation like that you'd expect the case to go against the police.'

'Tell me the details again.'

Freddie found Jane very quick to see points, and their discussion went deeper than he'd foreseen.

'I've always been fascinated by the law, by courts, by crime.'

'Most people are, I've found.'

'But it's the legal points that really interest me.' Jane put her chin on her hands and looked at Freddie warily. 'I got a first in history, and I haven't used my brain properly since. I miss it. Freddie, this is a mad idea maybe, but how would I go about becoming a barrister?'

'By going to law school and sitting your Bar exams. Then you would try to arrange a pupillage for yourself in whatever set of Chambers will take you, and when that six-month period is over you'd probably do the next six months of pupillage somewhere else before you seriously started applying for a place in a set of Chambers. I imagine it's much the same in Australia.'

'I wouldn't do it in Australia. I'm talking about here. I've come to a dead end in Sydney, emotionally and professionally. A dead end. When Nat's letter arrived about your wedding, I suddenly realised how much I missed England. The dead end had an exit after all.'

Freddie smiled and waited. He suspected Jane of editing her past to suit her present, but she did it with great charm.

'Will you keep a secret from Natalie for the moment?'

'It depends what it is.'

'I'll tell her myself soon. I came over on a one-way ticket, Freddie. She thinks I'm going back after two weeks. I haven't got much luggage because I got rid of everything except the essentials. I've finished with Australia. But I'd rather Nat didn't know until after the big day. I don't want to destabilise her.'

Freddie knew that if most people talked to him like this he would dislike it intensely, but Jane simply defused the possibility by her smile, the way she held back her fair hair, the way she candidly met his gaze. He smiled, he began to feel more relaxed, he was pleased she was now going to be a permanent part of his life. She was so pretty.

'And actually, Freddie, I'd rather you didn't say anything about this new idea of mine, coming to the Bar – it's only an idea, and I need to think more about it, to let it grow or die in secret. I'll tell Nat all about it when I'm clear myself.'

'I understand perfectly.'

'I knew you would.'

The phone rang at that moment; it was Meryl, checking that all was well. She sounded flustered, but he could hear Piers and Harry shouting at each other loudly enough to fluster anyone.

'I forgot to bring the wedding present after all, would you believe it? I can't think how I left it behind, it was there in the hall staring me in the face all wrapped up in silver and I still walked out without it. Do be quiet, boys, I can't hear myself think.'

'Never mind, Meryl, you can give it to us any time.'

'It just annoys me to be so scatty.'

'You have plenty on your plate. The boys sound as if they are about to murder each other.'

'It's all about some stupid video. I give up. Now if you need any help next week when your brother's with you as well, let me know.'

'You're very kind. How did you know he was coming to stay?'

'Oh dear, it does sound nosy, but I overheard him leaving his message. Couldn't help hearing—'

Freddie at last managed to end the conversation, but when he turned round Jane's chair was empty. He heard rustling sounds from the flat, but Jane said nothing and did not reappear. He noticed the time and hurried upstairs in time to catch the news. There was no mention of the case until the local news, when it was the main item.

'A surprise verdict against Kerry Poole's brother Geoffrey at Snaresbrook Crown Court this afternoon found him guilty of grievous bodily harm against the policewoman who was injured. Civil rights activists demonstrated outside the court, supported by Miss Poole. Judge Mentieth has reserved judgment.' There were shots of shouting people, and then the screen cut to a familiar face. 'Civil rights expert Stanley Whicker told us that he had been informed this afternoon that one of the jury had been pressurised by police.'

Freddie stared at Whicker as he talked smoothly about police harassment. Then the film cut to the car park.

'Mr Whicker told the judge about this as he left the car park this evening.' This was followed by Freddie's brief conversation with the interviewer which ended with him driving hurriedly out of the car park. It looked what it was, a panicky retreat. Freddie sat stunned. The phone rang beside him at once; it was Natalie.

'Freddie, you poor thing, you must be furious—'

'I am.'

'You didn't tell me there'd been so much trouble—'

'You didn't give me much chance.'

'Sorry. I'm really sorry. I'm coming over now. I'll take a cab.'

'I thought you were seeing Sara—'

'She hasn't turned up and there's no knowing when she'll be back. Anyway, this is more important. So was that juror really leaned on?'

'Natalie, it's probably all rumours cooked up by those lunatics because the police were exonerated.'

'They looked a real pair of thugs.'

'They were. They got me on my own in the car park.'

'How terrifying.'

'It was.'

'I'll be half an hour.'

The pebbles. What had Mrs Wilks done with the pebbles? He searched the house in vain while he waited for Natalie. He missed them, even though they brought back bad memories. He liked to hold them in his hand while he used the telephone; there was an edgy pleasure in the scratchy crunching noise they made as they rubbed together. They still smelt faintly of the sea.

> *The murmuring surge,*
> *That on th' unnumbered idle pebble chafes,*
> *Cannot be heard so high. I'll look no more,*
> *Lest my brain turn ...*

Freddie had been haunted by *King Lear* all that day, as he and Anthea walked the grassy cliffs beyond Beachy Head at a safe distance from the chalk-face edge. He remembered quoting the same passage at her because it was so exact. They couldn't hear the curdled crunch of the pebbles as they were tugged by the waves – the detailed sounds were thinned out to a marine hissing and shushing. It was cold that day; a sharp autumn wind pressed their clothes against their bodies. Anthea's nose was a bright red, her hands when they emerged from their gloves a deadened cream. Tears of cold ran from her eyes.

'Let's go down there, Freddie. It's so exposed up here.'

Birling Gap; that's where they'd gone that day, because Anthea wanted lots of smooth pebbles to make a path. Birling Gap – just there the cliffs diminished into a green-lined cleft through which a stream flowed to the sea. The car park was empty; a couple of summer buildings were shut and forlorn. The majestic cliffs towered above them as they walked along the beech, the chalk face streaked with pale pink in the fading sun. The tide was receding, leaving weed-rimmed pools full of rounded pebbles.

'The unnumber'd idle pebble,' murmured Anthea. 'You left out the bit about the fishermen down on the beach like mice. I played Edgar once at school, you know. Unlikely, but true. My English teacher gave me the part because she knew I'd hate getting into rags and grime to be Poor Tom. I wanted to be Cordelia, naturally.'

'You never told me you'd done any acting.'

'I haven't thought of it for years. It was my only stage part. Miss Rance, that's what she was called, Miss Rance. What a cow she was, and a hopeless teacher. Just to spite her, I played a very convincing Tom.'

'I can't imagine you.'

Anthea picked up two round pebbles, weighed them in her hand, turned and suddenly blocked Freddie's path. Behind her in the growing dark the huge cliffs undulated towards Beachy Head, a frill of seagulls wheeling and screaming in the wind.

'That's what's wrong.'

'What do you mean?'

'You can't imagine me playing Poor Tom. You pigeonhole me, you've always pigeonholed me.'

'Anthea—'

'You have. You see me as excessively neat and stylish and concerned with appearances – admit it—'

'If I do it's only on one level—'

'What other level is there between us?'

'Anthea, what on earth has got into you?'

'Cliffs. Elemental nature. "How fearful and dizzy 'tis." I've never been here before but when I imagined these cliffs all those years ago at school this is exactly how I saw them. Exactly, even to the smell and the scale compared to me.'

'But what did you mean about no other level?'

'We exist on one plane, Freddie. One plane. Our lives are so ordered, so well supported with physical things.' She stared at the pebbles in her hands. 'We really are like these, touching each other but never connecting.' She banged two stones together making a strange clacking like a seabird's repeated call. Clack, clack, clack. The sound reverberated against the wall of chalk behind her.

Then she stumbled away over the treacherously slippery bright green seaweed. Freddie followed, slipping and sliding, his eyes fixed on the viscous weed in an effort to keep his balance.

'Anthea, stop being so melodramatic.'

Clack, clack, clack. 'I can just see how ancient man discovered fire. I can just imagine them sitting at the base of cliffs making fire to cook fish. "Poor Tom's a-cold".'

'Anthea! Wait a minute!'

'*The crows and choughs that wing the midway air Show scarce so gross as beetles.*'

Clack, clack, clack. One behind the other, they stumble on. Then with a final clack Anthea flings the stones towards the sea. 'I give up. We'll never make that fire between us. The chemistry's wrong. I GIVE UP!' Up, up, up goes the echo.

Freddie squelches after her, his whole being as bruised and leaden as the fading light. Seawater has got into one of his boots.

Birling Gap. Afterwards, Anthea said she'd had a brainstorm there, she'd been possessed by the strangeness of the place, she'd said things she didn't mean and couldn't remember.

'I was as mad as Poor Tom.'

'Except he was only pretending to be mad.'

'Didn't you find the place disconcertingly strange? I felt I was back in prehistory. I never want to go back there.'

They never did. And until Natalie had broken the bowl this morning and scattered the pebbles, he'd buried the memory of Anthea's words.

'Mrs Wilks? Yes, it's me – I'm fine thanks. And you? Oh, how awful, ah yes indeed, oh dear. How distressing for you. Well, thanks for keeping me abreast of Mr Wilks's problems – no – I rang up to ask about them, and also to apologise for the broken bowl. Yes, of course – but where are the pebbles that were inside? Oh, in the utility room. No, I didn't think of looking there.'

At last he was able to stem the flow of comment and put the phone down just as Jane came into the room. She looked completely different: she had sleeked her hair into a tight knot and was wearing a black jersey dress with a wide red belt. Her lips and nails were the same bright red, polished, luscious. She disturbed him.

'Nat should be here any minute.'

'Don't mention what I said.'

'Of course not. You asked me not to.'

'Sorry – I've been surrounded for years by people who simply can't keep a secret. Chatter, chatter, chatter, stirring everything up. Is that a photo of Anthea?'

'Yes. I took it myself.'

'She's not a bit like her sister Meryl.'

'Yet they could look very alike sometimes. I admit you don't see it there.'

'She's good-looking. Do you think Nat and I resemble one another?'

'Not really.'

'You wouldn't have picked me out as Nat's sister in a crowd.'

'No.'

'You might have if I'd been wearing a bikini. We've both got precisely the same birthmark.' Jane touched her hip and laughed. 'Odd, isn't it?'

'Unusual. There's today's paper if you want it. I won't be a minute.'

Freddie found the row of pebbles where Mrs Wilks had left them; each sat in separate state, asserting its roundness achieved over millennia. Freddie searched for a suitable bowl and settled in the end on a rather clumsy but charming dish made by either Piers or Harry, he couldn't remember which, and given to him last Christmas. The pebbles looked good in it, and he carried the bowl up to the hall conscious of the fact it would never have been used by Anthea. As he put the bowl down where the old one had been, an appalling crash came from the drawing room.

Jane was sitting in the chair in front of the window, covered in splinters of glass. The red nails of her hands pressed against her face glowed like blood. Her eyes were blank with shock. A brick lay on the carpet not far from her feet; it had shattered a huge pane in the central sash window.

'Somebody doesn't like us,' she said.

9

Your Honour, I realise the defendant bases her fears on very little evidence. Your Honour knows as well as I do that most human actions can be interpreted in conflicting ways. A grin can look like a snarl. A gesture of greeting can look menacing. It all depends on how it is received, Your Honour. And there's the rub. The defendant cannot see her sister without a lifetime's resentment clinging to her, modifying in her eyes everything her sister does. A lifetime's resentment imbedded in her psyche. There has been a long period of remission, so to speak, so long it felt like cure, caused by the absence of the sister in Australia. In fact, Your Honour, the defendant believed she was cured of her burden of resentment against her sister.

She was wrong.

How could a young, attractive, intelligent child so plague her elder sister? Surely, I hear you asking, Your Honour, ordinary family life has its ups and downs which end in reconciliation and bridge-building – why not in your case? People grow up, their priorities change, what a child finds painful will pass the adult by. All this is true, Your Honour, and it should be so for the defendant. Perhaps she has never grown up, but with the return of her sister her sense of resentment has ballooned to its old size, to her infinite depression. Yes, Your Honour, I can give you examples of the kind of family terrorism the younger sister practised. It's a mild form of terrorism, but I have chosen that word deliberately. I have already mentioned the episode of the net – it is not much in itself, but it brought the impression of being ensnared in toils into the defendant's life, an image which has never left her.

I take at random another incident, less trivial in nature. As a child, the defendant was very good at ballet, as was her sister: they had the right sort of trim wiry bodies, and good long necks. The defendant was put forward by her ballet teacher for an audition with the Royal Ballet for a possible place in their ballet school. The audition date was suddenly brought forward and this fact was phoned through immediately by the teacher. Unfortunately the younger sister took the message; she wrote it all carefully down and even rang the teacher back to make sure every detail was correct, thus allaying any fears the teacher might have had that the urgent message could go astray. The younger sister then forgot all about it, having put the message out of sight in what she called a safe place so it wouldn't get lost. As a result the defendant learned about the audition too late to attend it, and all her hard work and hope were wasted. Her sister was filled with compunction about her bad memory, and even gave her a present to cheer her up.

But that slip of the memory was not accidental, Your Honour. And its result was that the defendant lost heart over ballet thereafter, which left the field clear for her sister who successfully auditioned for the Royal Ballet a year or so later and then turned down the place. From this point on the defendant was always searching for activities and skills that her sister would find unattractive or would be bad at. But the range of things available for schoolgirls to do isn't that wide, and in almost everything she undertook she was nudged, pushed, crowded out by her sister. You can say, as I'm sure you will, Your Honour, that it shows a weakness in the defendant that she should mind, and that surely there was room for both of them to indulge in their pursuits, trivial or otherwise. Of course there was room, but her sister's attitude made it irrelevant; she did not only want to excel, she wanted to destroy.

You may wonder, Your Honour, why the defendant's sister didn't continue with her ballet dancing? She was, if anything, the better dancer of the two. I suspect the flavour had gone out of it. I agree, this attitude could be viewed as a great disadvantage to the sister: the fact she was motivated by sibling rivalry only, and not by any deeper appreciation of her skills. And it is also true that she may have seen this for herself, and it caused her to cut herself off from the defendant's influence by emigrating to Australia . . .

I address the back of my taxi driver's head though his lumpy ears hear nothing. I constantly practise my speeches like this, in taxis, buses, trains – my tongue seems to roll the words audibly, and sometimes I have heard everything so clearly I can't believe I'm inaudible to other people.

Your Honour, the problem seemed solved—

'Which end of Elsworth Avenue, love?'

'North end, thanks. Swiss Cottage end.'

'Looks like you got a reception committee. Two police cars and all. No, I tell a lie – they're off.'

Blue lights accelerate past us. Freddie's standing outside his front door, staring up at a smashed window.

'Trouble,' he says as I run across the road after paying off the taxi. 'It's a mercy Jane wasn't hurt.'

By the time I've heard the full story and vacuumed the floor and Jane for splinters, a glazier has arrived and we leave him to it.

'So everyone thinks this attack is a follow-on after the verdict today.'

'The police say this kind of thing is committed in anger soon after the event, and then common sense or caution prevail and nothing more happens.'

'They could come and attack you in your office,' says Jane; she looks shocked, strained round the eyes. I've made them both sweet tea, but neither is drinking it.

'It's a risk I'll have to take. It would be quite difficult to achieve—'

'Oh, go on, Freddie, it would be the easiest thing. They could just wander into Chambers looking legal and no one would question them.'

'Well, there's nothing I can do. Poole and Betty are out on bail consorting with their mates, and no doubt with the charming Mr Whicker and Mr Jones. The police say they're going to keep an eye on them all, and we have to hope they will.'

A sliver of glass slides out of Jane's hair and falls with a faint tinkle on the table. She suddenly puts her hands over her eyes and starts crying.

'Jane—'

'Bang, crash, glass all over me. I thought I'd been bombed.'

Another piece of glass lands on the table, and I pick both up gingerly and put them in the bin before putting my arms round Jane's stiff shoulders. Her tears stop as quickly as they started, but she keeps her eyes covered.

'I'm just shocked.'

'I can see you are. Drink this tea.' I look up and see Freddie staring at us; to him we must look like the model of devoted sisters at this moment. He's smiling and the love in his eyes is for both of us.

'I'm just going up to see how the glazier is getting on before I ring for a take-away dinner for us, and then we'll go off.'

'Off?' There's blood oozing from my thumb – I've cut myself without even noticing it. I take my arm away from Jane's still unresponsive shoulders and go to the sink. Jane takes her hands away from her face and looks up at Freddie.

'Off?' she repeats.

'Natalie and I are going to my little place in the country and you're coming too. I'm not leaving you here on your own after that little episode.'

'I'll be fine.'

'You're coming with us.'

'Don't be so bossy, Freddie. Jane's got her own plans, I'm sure.' As I run my cut thumb under the tap a numbing cold is seeping through me and it isn't coming from the icy water. I can't look at Jane. I don't want her to come with us.

'I'm worried about those lunatics doing something else. Either we all stay here or we all go and leave the police to keep a sharp eye on the house. I mean it, Jane, I'm not leaving you here on your own. Personally I need a break from London. Today has been a strain.'

'You are so kind to me, Freddie. I can't think of anything nicer than a couple of days in the countryside.' Jane uses her wan, please-protect-me little voice which I have heard her turn on all my life. But she uses it very rarely, and everyone immediately responds to it because a chink in her self-sufficiency is such a surprise. Freddie is no exception.

'Then you shall have them. We'll have some good long walks and I'll introduce you to one of England's most underrated bits of countryside.'

The glazier calls down the basement stairs and Freddie goes up to see what he needs. I put a plaster on my thumb to stem the flow of blood, aware that Jane is watching me. I pin a cheerful face on. Luckily she's not one to look below the surface.

'I got glass all over me, and not a single cut. Poor Nat.'

'Life's full of irony.'

'Do you think these people will be back, now they know where Freddie lives?'

'Probably.'

'You don't sound too worried.'

'There's nothing we can do.'

'There was a man with long hair hanging about in the street earlier – perhaps it was him.'

I see a sharp image of Dave, naked, his hair resplendent.

'More likely to be a man in a suit with a brick in his briefcase.'

Dave. I must have been mad to have given in to Dave today. He'll tell whom he pleases, when it pleases him. He'll wander in uninvited to the wedding and start showing Jane his notebook. He loves trouble, he orchestrates trouble.

'I'm feeling more shocked now than I was straight after the crash.'

'Drink your tea, it'll help counteract it.'

'It's cold. I can't stand cold tea.'

'I'll make you some more.'

I could scream.

At last I get Freddie on his own, when we go upstairs after eating to pack a few things. I corner him in the bedroom. What I want to say is: 'Don't take Jane to the cottage. Don't let her into all our special places,' but of course I can't because it sounds so utterly mean and miserable.

'I don't think we should go away.'

'I refuse to give in to those people.'

'There's still so much to do.'

'Nonsense, Nat. What, for example?'

'I still haven't got myself a dress to get married in.' I go to the window and peep through the curtains. Peace outside.

'I thought you had.'

'Nothing that's suitable.'

'Take time off next week then, tell Douglas to keep you out of court.'

'I suppose I could. I hate buying clothes.'

'Come here. You look miserable. What's the matter?'

'Oh, this and that. Niggles.'

'I said come here.'

'Oh, Freddie, I wish we had this weekend to ourselves. It seemed important to be just you and me at the cottage.'

'We've got the rest of our lives to ourselves. What a lovely prospect—'

'I know.'

'Take them off.'

'Not now, Freddie—'

'Yes, now. Come on, I need a quickie, come on—'

'Jane's downstairs—'

'So what? The door's shut. Come on, Nat, I need to fuck you, you need it too, let's blot out the nasty day, come on—'

We take off the minimum. We are rough with each other; the constrictions of clothes seem to intensify the union between our two fleshes, our orgasms are violent and together.

Anthea smiles tidily at us from her oval silver frame.

10

Freddie liked his country life basic – minimum physical comforts, a big wood fire the only form of heating, plenty to eat and drink. Layers of old clothes lived in the cottage on hooks and could be borrowed by those who had underestimated the temperature. (Nat always used an old Aran jersey he had had as long as he could remember; it hung loosely like a tunic over her thick cords, and she often wore grey mittens out of which her fingers peeped like pink mice.)

He hated seeing overdressed women sitting in the shabby arm-chairs he'd picked up at local auctions, he hated inappropriate shoes on the fibre matting. He knew that the cottage represented everything Anthea had denied him while she was alive, and he put the thought away.

'It's stupid in my view to live in the country as one does in London.' Freddie would glare at a house on the corner of the lane leading to his cottage. A stockbroker called Batley had done it up until it looked like a stage set; he and his wife would arrive with the back of their estate car jammed with all the food and drink they would need for the weekend. Freddie went and queued at the local butcher's, and queued again at the greengrocer's; Nat thought he got poor value from the latter, but did not interfere.

'I refuse to use the Duomo di Tesco.' As they drove past the new shopping precinct with its floodlit clock tower and large sign about Sunday openings, Freddie pointed at it. 'Do you think the architect consciously tried to awake in the shopper the idea he was about to perform an act of worship? Spend as long as you can buying a little more than you need for the good of your soul?'

'I think it looks rather nice,' said Jane. She was sitting in
the front seat; Natalie was silent in the back of the Saab.
'Welcoming.'

'Those were green fields when I bought the cottage. It looked
nicer.' If Jane heard the edge to his voice she gave no sign.
Her hands were lying in her lap: soft pampered skin, long
unbroken red nails. Nat's hands were quite different – short
nails, double-jointed thumbs which bent when she held a pen
or a kitchen knife. Workaday hands compared with her sister's.
At least Jane had changed into jeans.

Freddie caught a glimpse of Nat in his mirror. She was staring
out of the window into the darkened countryside looking
depressed and tired. Despite his fear that Jane was not a
country lover, he was glad she had come with them for the
weekend – she and Nat could go off together for good sisterly
chats and leave him in peace to cut down those roses at the end
of the garden.

The enormous arching thicket came from three overgrown
rambler roses which had been neglected for so long it looked
as if, given a little more time, they could spread thorned arms
all over Bedfordshire. Freddie assessed them with pleasure. He
was dressed in what Natalie called his garden combat gear – a
canvas jacket that had belonged to his father and boilerman's
gloves.

'Right, you bastards. You're not going to know what's hit
you.' Freddie always talked sternly to erring plants, uncaring
of who overheard him. 'Your hour has come.' This simple
aggressive work was just what he needed. He cut, he pulled,
he fought with ivy and bramble bound round thorned tentacles,
he sweated. Occasionally the faces of his persecutors, Whicker
and Jones, floated through his mind and he wielded saw and
secateurs with increased fury. The huge awkward pile of cut
growth grew behind him, the growth in front of him receded,
tamed, leaving trampled dying bracken, mulched leaves and
nude earth. Squashy overripe blackberries left purple stains all
over his clothes. At last he reduced the roses to a neat meek
hedge, and stood in triumph before it. Nature tamed until next
year. His hand throbbed. He took off a glove.

'Bloody thing.' A large thorn had gone through a hole straight into the first joint of his right index finger. He bent his finger and pain shot up his arm. 'Sheer spite.'

He couldn't find Nat, but Jane was sitting in the cottage looking bored.

'Dig a thorn out for me, would you?'

'Where would I find a needle?'

'Use this safety pin.'

Jane probed for a minute without success. 'It's not moving. Tweezers would be better.'

'Rose thorns in the joints give you arthritis – it's got to come out. Keep trying.'

'I don't want to hurt you.'

'I don't want arthritis. Have a bash, don't worry about hurting me.' He watched her red nails pushing and pinching at his finger while she probed. Her hands were cold.

'Where's Nat?'

'I've no idea. I think she went for a walk.'

'Didn't you want to go?'

'She didn't give me the choice. It doesn't matter. I'm not a great walker. Got it.'

Jane held up a sizable chunk of thorn before taking his hand again to check if she'd left any of the thorn behind; Freddie looked too, his head practically touching hers. She still smelt faintly eastern – musk or something. Nat walked through the back door into the kitchen at that moment.

'I need a plaster, Nat. Do you know if there are any here?'

'I brought spares because of my thumb.'

'You are in the wars, you two.' Jane, more sardonic than sympathetic, watched her sister bandage Freddie's finger.

'I met the Batleys in the lane, Freddie. They want us to go for a drink tomorrow.'

'No. Absolutely not.'

'They were very insistent.' Nat followed him out to the garden.

'I don't come here to go to drinks parties.'

'Anne Batley kept saying we were her nearest neighbours and she never saw us.'

'Deliberate – she must be thick-skinned not to have guessed

by now. Bloody brambles.' Freddie started cutting into another clogged area.

Nat went up close and put a hand on his arm. 'It would be something for Jane to do,' she muttered.

'You two go then. I want to get the ivy off the kitchen wall when I've finished this.'

'Freddie, why don't you stop and relax? You're always so busy attacking the garden here—'

'This is how I relax. I don't like doing nothing.'

A gust of wind blew dead leaves about their feet. Smoke from Freddie's nearby bonfire changed direction and enveloped them for a moment, making their eyes sting.

'But you did like sitting on the beach doing nothing last summer, didn't you?'

'We were getting to know each other, Nat. It was fun. I wouldn't like that sort of holiday too often.' Freddie picked up an armful of brambles and took them over to the bonfire. Natalie watched him battering the barbed wire-like tangle into submission for a moment, and then started to go back into the cottage.

'Nat! Come back. That sounded very ungracious – I didn't mean to be – I loved our holiday. Come here, darling. What's the matter?'

'I'm feeling a bit vulnerable. It's the effect my sister has on me.'

'Come and help me here. You enjoyed it last time.'

'Freddie, I can't really leave her moping inside on her own. I'd much rather be with you, it's lovely doing things together, making order out of chaos.'

'That's why I like gardening. You make order, but only temporarily, for this month, this year. Nature is always ready to get her own back.'

'Doing the everyday things together at weekends makes – makes me want to cry sometimes I'm so happy.' Natalie's voice had dropped to a whisper.

'*I love thee to the level of everyday's*
Most quiet need, by sun and candlelight.'
Freddie held her tightly in his arms.

'Oh, Freddie. I do love you. Who wrote that?'

'Elizabeth Barrett Browning. It's from a sonnet beginning "How do I love thee? Let me count the ways".'

Jane's voice called from the cottage, and Nat pulled herself away. Freddie watched her go through the kitchen door and then turned to get on with his bonfire. But those words from the sonnet suddenly opened memories, brought back Anthea, brought back a sheet of paper with the whole sonnet written out in her careful italic handwriting which she'd sent to him just before they got married. He stood frozen, blind to the garden around him.

I love thee to the depth and breadth and height
My soul can reach . . .
And the last line. Oh, Anthea, Anthea.
I shall but love thee better after death.

11

Jane is sitting on the sofa (stuffing leaks out of the arms) wrapped in a blanket, flipping through the copy of *Vogue* she's brought with her.

'I'm bored. I thought this was going to be fun.'

'Sorry?'

'The trip to the country. Fun. Forgive me for saying it, but this place is a dump.'

'We don't happen to think so.'

'Come off it, Nat. Welly boots and mud everywhere and arctic temperatures were never your style.'

'How do you know? How do you bloody know? You've no idea what I'm really like.'

'Ditto.' The word comes back across the room like a poisoned dart.

We stare at each other aghast. All friendliness, all efforts at social coexistence have dropped away. The veneer is porcelain thin, thinner than either of us realised. Our lifetime of sibling rivalry lies between us like a sudden miasma, a patch of fog arising from nowhere and making driving lethal. A net.

I break the silence. 'We've been apart for eight years so it's not altogether surprising—'

'Even if we'd been near each other we still wouldn't know each other. You hate me, Nat. Admit it.'

'Don't be ridiculous.'

'I can feel it. Nothing's changed. You always did hate me, ever since I can remember.' Jane's white, pinched face sticks out of the folds of red and black checked blanket; her feet and hands are invisible.

'Jane, Jane, I don't hate you, and I never *hated* you. For God's sake, I was jealous of you, almost scared of you because you kept beating me at my own game. That doesn't mean I hated you. It's much easier now – you've got your life in Australia and I've got mine here. Things have changed.'

'I don't feel much has changed. You're still very cold towards me most of the time. On top of feeling absolutely frozen anyway at the moment, it's more than I can stand.'

'Oh, God, what a stupid mess this is. If I've been cold to you I'm sorry – I suppose I'm still nervous that you're going to muscle in and spoil what I've got—'

'*Spoil* – what on earth are you talking about? Why should I want to spoil your life? You're paranoid, Nat. Paranoid.'

'Maybe I am.'

'At least we're actually talking to each other. You've been really distant to me—'

'I'm stressed.'

'Aren't we all? Shit, can't you light a fire here or something? I'm so cold I could be sitting in a fridge.'

'I'll lay the fire.'

'I left England because of you, to escape you.'

I kneel in front of the messy ash-strewn hearth. My hands are shaking; I can hardly focus on the fireplace. As I try to rake the ashes the fire irons fall over with a great clatter.

'Do you really mean that?'

'Why else would I leave?'

'To make a new life, to do something different, but mainly to join Dad. That's what you really wanted, to join Dad. You were full of excitement about it all. I don't remember you being bitter. You were thrilled.'

'The original reason was you.'

I roll up pieces of newspaper in silence, lay kindling on the top, and logs on top of the heap. It is not a well-built fire. It probably won't even light, but I don't care. I'm about to strike a match when Freddie comes in.

'Right, girls. Time for the pub. What on earth are you doing, Nat? No need for a fire until this evening.'

'The pub. What a lovely idea.' Jane speedily unwraps herself from her cocoon of blanket, and stretches. 'I need to be in an English country pub again. Inglenooks and all that.'

'Don't raise your hopes. The inglenooks in the Bellweather have long ago been tarted up to look like seats in a French brothel. But the beer's not bad. We'll walk – it's only ten minutes across the fields.'

I straighten up, the spent match dying between my fingers. Jane is smiling at Freddie, and has stopped looking so obviously pinched with cold.

'Those nice boots might get a bit muddy, Jane. Borrow these old wellies—'

'Don't worry, Freddie, these boots will be fine.'

'There's been plenty of rain, which means plenty of mud.'

'I'll cope.'

I know that nothing will induce Jane to put on a pair of ancient wellington boots covered with rubber patches and too big for her. I also know she has no idea how bad the mud is.

'We could take the car, Freddie—'

'What is the matter with you today, Nat? First you want a fire, and then you don't want to walk! Come on, love, beer and a pub lunch is what we all need, and a bit of exercise getting there and back.'

So we set off. The mud is bad from the moment we cross into the fields, but Jane hops from tussock to tussock with many a jolly giggle until we reach a gateway where cattle have stirred the earth into liquid chocolate a foot deep. At this point Freddie has to give Jane a piggy-back.

'Whoops! This is serious mud!'

'Don't make me overbalance—'

I struggle to shut the gate behind us as they stumble along laughing; Jane has her arms round Freddie's neck, her head is pressed to his as if she's about to nuzzle his ear. I close the gate behind them, my whole being filled with bile. Perhaps Jane is right, perhaps it is hatred I feel, pure unadulterated hatred. I grip the gate bars and shut my eyes. I have to hang on to the fact Jane is going back to Australia, she will be gone soon. A week to the wedding, exactly a week, then we'll be away and so, soon after, will she. Gone back to the opposite end of the earth.

*   *   *

At breakfast on Sunday Freddie said he'd come to the Batleys', but I knew he wouldn't once he started ripping ivy off the walls. He can't stop – it's as addictive as picking scabs. He keeps exclaiming at the horrors he's uncovering.

Jane doesn't get up until just before we're due at the Batleys'. She's had some coffee and a large plateful of toast in bed.

'This is the only warm place and I'm staying put until it's time for the party.'

'It isn't exactly a party—'

'Whatever.' Jane's little nose is sharply white.

'We were asked for half past twelve. Do you need anything else?'

'Central heating.'

'Australia's weakened you. Remember how cold our house used to be?'

'And remember how we moaned? You evolved that system of wrapping yourself round and round with that old knitted blanket – you looked like a striped mummy when you hopped across the room to get into bed.'

'And I had green bedsocks also, knitted by Granny.'

'And those hot water bottles in knitted coats. And chilblains every winter. God, Nat, it was medieval. If I get a chilblain this weekend I'll sue Freddie.'

'It's not as cold today as yesterday.'

'I'm not feeling a hundred per cent anyway. Staying in bed is probably sensible.'

Jane takes a quick swig of coffee, and retreats under the bedclothes. I go to the kitchen to prepare some lunch – a chilli con carne – mince and tinned kidney beans were about all we could find in the village shop yesterday.

Freddie comes in while I'm messing about at the sink and puts his arms around me from behind. I turn my head and he kisses my cheek. His face is cold and bristly – he never bothers to shave when he's at the cottage. He smells of bonfire.

'I'm sorry I was such a bear yesterday.'

'It's all right. Everybody was a bit edgy yesterday.'

'Where's Jane?'

'Still in bed, says it's the only warm place to be.'

'She's going to have to get used to the cold again or she won't enjoy life in England.'

'Well, she's not here for long.'

'Is that what she's told you?'

'Not in so many words. She implied it – why?'

'She's come home for good. She didn't want you to be told yet, but I can't see any reason why you shouldn't know – I'm sure you'll be pleased to have a sister around again.'

There are tea leaves sticking to the sides of the sink. I run water on them and watch them swirl away, taking with them the one thing I was hanging on to – Jane's departure. Peace of mind – gurgle, gone.

'When did she tell you this?'

'Darling, I don't know – sometime recently. Friday? Life has been so pressurised I can't remember. Let's have a coffee.'

'Did she specifically ask you not to tell me?'

'Well, yes, but not very seriously.' Freddie's face is a little flushed, but it might be from his exertions in the garden.

'What else did she tell you? Since I don't seem to be in my sister's confidence.'

'Oh, Natalie, I'm sure she doesn't mean to hurt you or exclude you. She happened to be asking my advice about something, again not very seriously.'

'What was that?'

'I really do need some coffee. What about you?'

'She's decided she might read for the Bar, hasn't she?'

'There, she's mentioned it to you too.'

I can't bring myself to say anything. I watch Freddie put instant coffee into two mugs, stir in boiling water, stir in milk; the spoon scratches against the rough pottery sides of the mugs and sets my teeth on edge.

'Anyway, she didn't sound particularly keen – she was simply making inquiries. Now, come outside and hear my latest plans about the garden.'

I know there is one way to get close to Freddie, and that is to listen to him on his beloved gardening. I don't know a begonia from a berberis, but we wander arm in arm round the property, admiring the devastation he's created already this weekend.

'So I plan a bed of shrubs here, all early flowerers like mahonia, that look after themselves. Then a tree here, perhaps a walnut. There's a gap that needs filling and a walnut is such a nicely shaped tree. One day we can pickle the nuts. And lots of roses against that wall, haven't decided which yet, but definitely an Albertine over that shed.'

'How did you learn so much about gardening?'

'Anthea taught me.'

'Will you teach me sometime?'

'Of course.'

As we turn towards the house I catch a sight of Jane's face in the window. A distant church bell starts ringing. It's twelve o'clock.

Anne Batley tries to hide a lumpy body by dressing in the brightest, prettiest clothes. Her dark hair is beautifully cut, her jewellery is attractive and unusual, her shoes are expensive and covetable, but she can't do anything about that large bottom and those bulging thighs. Her husband Jeremy is small and thin, with exceptionally narrow hips. Thoughts of nursery rhymes and love-making positions chase through my mind as we're welcomed.

'Is Freddie not coming too?'

'He might later. He's wrestling with the garden.'

'Jeremy is adamant about not doing any hard work at weekends. We use that nice man who used to run the newsagent's. He's very good – I'm sure he'd help you out as well if you asked.'

'Freddie likes doing it all himself.'

'I saw Freddie on the news on Friday night—'

'Champagne, girls?'

Jeremy draws us into a long room with a fire at each end; we are introduced to people whose names do not stick, we chatter about the weather, the dogs (several are hogging the fires) and the new supermarket – all the usual things. A good-looking man arrives, and somehow Jane's at his side in minutes. I can hear them talking about Sydney. I wish I hadn't come.

I haven't told Jane that I know anything about her future plans. I want her to lie to me, so that I can use the lie when it suits me. Ignoble, but I don't care. I want to see her squirm. I wander to the window and stare out at the Batley garden, full of tidy weeded beds and severely controlled plants.

Jane has always brought out the worst in me, always. When I freed myself from that net, I attacked her with teeth and nails and no fair play. I tore at her flesh, her hair, screaming at her.

'It's so lovely being back and seeing really old buildings everywhere, nothing's old in Australia, I never get used to it—'

Jane's using her intense husky voice, the voice she puts on to attract men – there I go again. Ignoble. I must stop it.

'Let me give you a top-up, Natalie.'

'Thanks, Jeremy.'

'You're not at all like your sister.'

'No, I'm not.'

'I gathered she's come over for your wedding – which she tells me is very soon.'

'Next Saturday.' As I say it, panic rushes through me cold and sudden. My wedding is less than a week away. Jeremy tries to clink his glass against mine as he says:

'Let's drink to the day.'

'I'm terrified.'

'Weddings are pretty nerve-racking things. I dreaded mine. I always think that's why stag parties came about: get the groom so drunk that all he's conscious of next day is his hangover.'

'Rather barbaric.' What is Freddie doing the night before we get married? I've no idea.

'Useful though. Rites grow up to serve a purpose. You ought to have a hen party with your sister – or perhaps you already are.'

'Hen parties aren't really my scene. Or hers.'

'What is your scene, Natalie?' Jeremy tops up our glasses again and puts the bottle down on the windowsill beside us. 'If you don't mind my asking. I don't even know what you do.'

'I'm a barrister.'

'I had no idea.'

'That's how I met Freddie. He's my Head of Chambers.'

Jeremy has green eyes, shrewd but oddly shy. 'He's quite a bit older than you then.'

'Fourteen years.'

'Not that it matters. People fuss too much about age. Anne is six years older than me and it's made no difference at all.'

'You asked about my scene. Well, in some ways I'm still part of that post-student feverish life – everyone still job hunting, living in chaos, parties developing at the drop of a hat, clubbing till dawn – as my friends do.'

'How do you reconcile that with reading briefs and getting into court with a clear brain?'

'It can be tricky. I don't go out with my friends very often.'

'If you were defending me and you arrived the worse for wear, I might not like it.'

'Quite.'

'I can't quite see a man like Freddie enjoying the club scene.'

'He wouldn't dream of coming. I suppose when I'm married I'll give it all up.'

'Are you ready to?'

I drink a sip of my champagne and gaze at the stiff little bubbles. Dave's hairy body comes into my mind and I push it out again.

'Whether I am or not is irrelevant. I've made my choice and I wanted to make it.'

'If I were Freddie I'd give you a long rein one night a week. Nat's Night Out.'

I want to tell him he's a patronising bastard, but I don't. Besides, I quite like him.

'Sometimes it's a real relief not to eat pasta on my knees yet again and stay up until three drinking plonk and inhaling other people's fags.'

'Instead you will stay up until midnight drinking malt whisky and inhaling other people's cigars. Big formal dinners in livery halls. Black tie, speeches, loyal toasts, all that mind-numbing stuff. Lousy food, too, half the time. Boring conversations. The only good thing at those events is the wine. Which reminds me, have some more champagne.'

'Why not.'

'You will inevitably have to endure some of those evenings.'

'I have already.'

'That's a very beautiful ring, you know. It sparkles so much you'd think you had a battery inside it.'

'It belonged to Freddie's first wife.'

'I didn't know he'd been married before.'

'She died in a traffic accident. Knocked down by a lorry near her home.'

'How dreadful.' Jeremy is staring at my ring as if expecting bloodstains to appear.

'She never wore this ring. She had a thing against diamonds.'

'Jeremy, everyone's dying of thirst. And you're monopolising Natalie.'

The party swirls round me; I drink more champagne and talk to people whose names I still don't really catch. I can't take my eyes off my ring. I have only Freddie's word for it that Anthea hated it and didn't like wearing it. She may have worn it all the time. She may even have been wearing it the day she died. In the bluish shards of light my diamond gives off, I hear the roar of that lorry, the brutal, inexorable horror of its vast wheels and chassis, the screech of its brakes.

I'm fairly drunk by the time we walk back for lunch. Jane is flushed too but she says it's not alcohol, just the effect of being in a well-heated room after the arctic cold of the cottage. (I think she's probably telling the truth – her voice goes all careful when she's had too much. Mine slurs, is slurred now.)

Large pockets of wind build up inside me as I walk from the shaking up of the champagne: when I burp, it's thunderous.

'There was a woman there whose sister breeds cocker spaniels in the next street to mine in Sydney. Weird.'

'Weird.' More gas escapes.

'The world's so small.'

'I think it's wonderfully big.'

'You haven't travelled much.'

'Lovely big world.'

'Where are you going on your honeymoon?'

'Secret.'

'I think I heard Freddie mention Budapest.'

'Bang goes the secret.'

'You're not walking very straight, Nat.'

'I'm pissed. Fresh air on top of champagne on top of an empty stomach. Lethal.'

'You need some lunch.'

'Chilli con carne. Archetypal student grub. Dave Rosenberg used to call it Spicy Fart Stew.'

'He told me he's writing a novel.'

'He's been doing that for years.'

'I'm seeing him tomorrow. He's asked me to go to some play or other with him – he's been given two complimentary tickets.'

The week ahead is not a pleasant prospect, but I'm too drunk to deal with this latest aspect of it. Dave pursuing Jane. I try to push Dave out of my mind again, but it's difficult, like trying to close an overfilled suitcase. We walk in silence for the last fifty yards, and when we turn into the cottage yard we find a stern-faced Freddie loading up the car. I steady myself against the bonnet and try unsuccessfully to hide another burp.

'What's the matter, Freddie?'

'The police have rung. Another brick, this time through an upstairs window. I can't risk a full-scale break-in. So we're off as soon as we can get going.'

'After some food.'

'I'm not hungry. I'll go and pack my stuff.' Jane goes briskly into the cottage, very much the cool sober sister.

'I've already eaten. You've been so long, Nat – I thought it was just a brief drink.'

'You could have come and got us.'

'It was easier to get on with things here.' He's looking at me accusingly.

'I know, I know, I'm drunk. I'll just go and eat a plateful of beans to mop up the champagne.'

I do my best to walk steadily into the kitchen. The chilli's lukewarm but I don't care. I pile the glistening beans onto a soup plate and stand gobbling them by the cooker. There's a crash outside as Freddie drops something, and he comes in holding up his bandaged hand.

'That thorn's really making itself felt – I think it must be going septic or something. My arm's beginning to throb. And now because of it I've dropped the Jameson's I was going to take back to London, damn it. The bottle just slipped out of my hand. Glass everywhere.'

'I'll clear it up. Just let me finish this.' I wish I could banish at one magic stroke the alcohol in my bloodstream. I stagger as I carry a brush and dustpan out to the yard; it's as if my legs have had the wires loosened. The beans are doing me no good. I bend over to sweep up the shards of glass and the smell of Irish whiskey is too much. I just make it to the flowerbed before I part company with the beans and a great deal more. I've never been so violently sick in my life; I kneel there for some time, unable to move. I can hear Jane sweeping up the glass with brisk thoroughness. Freddie is somewhere inside the cottage – but it's too much to hope that he hasn't seen me vomiting. All the same, I cover the evidence with fresh earth.

'You must have had a skinful.' He's right behind me.

'I'm sorry, Freddie. Jeremy Batley never leaves your glass alone. I wish I hadn't gone.'

'I told you not to.'

I wish I hadn't gone. I went in order to keep Jane amused. I wish she hadn't come here. I wish we'd stayed in London. I wish I hadn't gone to bed with Dave. I wish—

'Nat, what shall I do with the chilli?' Jane is standing in the kitchen door holding the saucepan.

'Chuck it out when you've had some.'

'I told you I wasn't hungry. Unlike you, I had a good breakfast. And not much champagne.'

'Don't be so bloody smug.'

'Sor-*ry*.'

Within half an hour we're ready to leave. I've drunk a pint of water and taken a couple of Alka-Seltzer. I should be feeling better. I try to give the impression I am. As I bring my weekend bag to the car, Freddie and Jane are having a discussion about who should drive.

'If your hand is inflamed, Freddie, it's a bad idea to drive. It might make it worse.'

'I can cope—'

'I've got an up-to-date international driving licence, so if your car's insured for any driver, off we go. I had almost nothing to drink, by the way.'

'I can see that. It's just that I don't like being driven, Jane.'

'Tell me something new. I haven't yet met a man who does.'

'Freddie, let me look at your finger.' I sound convincingly in control of my tongue, but Freddie waves me away.

'Nat, it'll need more than someone with a needle to get at the problem.'

'So I'll drive?'

'Let me have a try, and if it hurts too much we'll switch over.'

'Right on.'

'Nat, did you shut the bathroom window? It doesn't look like it.'

'I'm sorry, I forgot. Give me the keys, I'll go and do it.' I manage to unlock the cottage door without too much fumbling, and go upstairs. As I struggle to do up the safety locks, I can see Freddie showing Jane the car controls.

I have well and truly fucked this weekend up. I stare at my reflection in the fly-blown mirror – white face, messy hair, puffy bruised eyes. The bruising goes a lot further than my eyes.

Freddie's only driven for about ten minutes before he pulls into a Happy Eater and stops in the forecourt.

'It's all yours, Jane. I've had it.' He gets out but Jane slides across, lifting her legs over the gear levers. Her eye catches mine as she swivels her body, a quick expressionless glance. Neither of us speaks. I'm lying with my head on my weekend bag, past caring. This round is so completely Jane's I know the best thing is to opt out. I've never been driven by Jane before. I've never driven the Saab either.

'It's a great car – it handles beautifully. My last car was a clapped-out old four-wheel Subaru – heavy but useful for the outback.'

'How much long-distance driving did you do there?'

I stay silent, hoping that sleep will overtake me, while Jane tells interminable stories about the bush. She drives fast and smoothly; after a while, in the middle of a saga about a trek through a hundred kilometres of deep mud in New South Wales, I hear Freddie give a gentle snore. I know that snore, I've heard it close to my ear from the next pillow. It cheers me up.

Freddie lay awake most of the night, aware that the throbbing of his right hand was going to need medical attention. Monday morning was already a logistical nightmare without having to fit in a visit to a casualty unit at dawn. Natalie had tried to make him go on Sunday night, but he'd refused. She'd muttered about tetanus before disappearing to her flat. Not helpful. She hadn't been helpful all day.

Thomas's arrival was the main worry ahead, just beating the concern about possible future actions of the civil rights group. There was no one free to meet him at the airport except Meryl; the ambulance had been arranged by Natalie, but Freddie hated the thought of things going wrong. He had little faith in his sister-in-law. To add to the difficulties, Mrs Wilks didn't work on a Monday (she kept to a mysterious timetable as rigid as armour) so he'd asked Elsie to come and settle Thomas into the house. The only light note of his wakeful night was the thought of Thomas's reaction when he found he was in the hands not only of Meryl (whom he'd dismissed long ago as a witterer) but his old nannie as well.

Freddie got up at five and stubbed his toe in the dark against a rough hard object. Of course, the brick. He'd left the brick in the room on purpose, in case the police wanted to see it. They hadn't. He picked it up and put it in a corner of the bathroom out of the way, and had a shower. His finger was red and swollen; he held it under the needles of hot water, half-enjoying the agony.

The only advantage in arriving at the hospital by six was the space still available in the visitors' car park. He'd expected the casualty department to be empty at this hour, but early morning accidents filled the seats. A child with a burned arm, an office cleaner who'd fallen downstairs, a milkman who'd been bitten by a dog. Freddie waited in growing impatience, aware how conspicuous he was in his well-tailored dark blue suit, stiff collar, Garrick Club tie, and large black briefcase. (He never, ever left his briefcase in his car.) He was the only person in a suit, but at least his bandage united him to the other injured.

'Wassor nime?' The little boy with a burn stood big-eyed in front of him, gluey runnels hanging from each nostril.

'Fred.'

'Did the kettle burn you too?'

'I was bitten by a rose bush.'

'Roses don't bite.'

'This one did.'

'Roses can't bite.' The boy was accusing: truth mattered.

'You're right. I got a thorn in my finger. It felt like a bite.'

'Show me then.'

'Darren!'

'Tike off yer bandage.'

'Leave 'im alone, Darren.' Darren's mother clearly didn't expect obedience, nor got it.

'I'll show you my burn an' all if you show me.'

Freddie unwound the loose bandage and Darren put his snotty nose perilously near the swollen finger.

'The thorn's in there.'

'P'raps they'll cut yer finger off.'

'I sincerely hope not.'

'*Darren!* Give over.' Darren's mother wore a threadbare coat; her skin was whitish-blue, her hair a frizzy blonde halo. 'Hurry up, they've called us.' She avoided looking at Freddie while she roughly wiped her son's nose.

'You gotter big car then, Mr Fred?'

'Darren, you'll be the death of me.' The boy was dragged away before he could get an answer from Freddie; he watched Darren's retreating backview, touched by his liveliness and sense of curiosity. Nature, nurture. There was nothing wrong with that boy's nature. The pressures of poverty and a poor education would probably turn him into a typical small-time villain by the time he was eighteen. Like the many who appeared before him in court—

'Mr Mentieth.'

'At last. You're very busy this morning.'

'Take a seat please. Doctor will see you shortly.' The nurse hadn't the time or inclination for conversation; she left Freddie sitting alone in a cubicle. He could hear Darren screaming. He stared at charts on the wall. Time passed. Darren's screams turned to sobbing as he was led away by his mother.

By the time the junior doctor, an exhausted six-foot redhead with long bony arms sticking out of his off-white coat, had lanced Freddie's finger and retrieved the rest of the thorn, Freddie was ready to scream too. The antitetanus injection made him feel faint and he had to sit for some time recovering.

'What you need is a nice cup of sweet tea. Next – Mrs Odinga. Hurry along please.' The nurse waved a new set of notes at the dispirited queue. Freddie walked unsteadily to his car and sat for a while with his eyes shut. Quarter past eight. He longed for the comfort of his room in Chambers, but knew he didn't have time to go there first as well as have breakfast, and what he needed was a calm, civilised breakfast.

What he got, after a long, clogged drive through the East End to Snaresbrook Crown Court to continue his week of judging, was a polystyrene cup of weak coffee and a Danish pastry that was neither fresh nor good, both provided from the canteen by Mrs Frobisher. He spat out the glacé cherries and chewed his way through the pastry while he checked through the list for that day.

'Sorry to disturb you, Your Honour. I thought you might like to look at this. That is, if you haven't already seen it.'

She handed Freddie a copy of the *Sun*. On the front page was a colour photo of Kerry Poole wearing a jungle costume consisting of some strategically placed leaves, and showing a great deal of breast. The headlines claimed:

THIS TIME SHE'S REALLY SAVAGE

'It was a stitch-up,' claimed Kerry Poole. 'My brother was framed by the police.'

Freddie read the garbled summary of the case against Geoffrey Poole with a cold heart. Then he put his polystyrene cup down on Kerry Poole's face, blotting out her manic blue eyes. Her hands hung suggestively over her hairless crotch, barely covered by the G-string.

'I don't for a moment think this woman is really after justice for her brother. She's after publicity. The concepts of truth, justice, discretion, restraint are not anathema to her, they're incomprehensible.' He sighed and threw the remains of the Danish pastry at the wastepaper bin. It hit the metal sides with a clang.

'I'm sure you're right, Your Honour. That Danish could have been fresher, I told them it didn't look like today's. Never mind.' She took back the newspaper. 'She looks like she means trouble.'

'The press will lose interest, and then so will she. The whole affair will calm down of its own accord.'

'Let's hope so, Your Honour. Disgusting, that photo.'

'I'd rather there was no gossip about this article, however—'

'You know me, silent as the tomb.'

The phone rang as Mrs Frobisher left the room; it was Douglas Dean, who had also seen the front page of the *Sun*.

'And I'm sorry about all your weekend troubles, sir. Bricks through the window. Not good at all.'

'Who told you about that?'

'Miss Harper, sir.'

'There's too much talk going round the clerks' room—'

'Not when I'm around, sir.'

'How did the attackers know my home address? I don't trust Paul to be totally discreet on personal matters. How did they find out? It's not even listed in *Who's Who*.'

'I'm sure Paul has been discreet, sir. I'll make sure Sharon is extra careful with Chambers' lists. I doubt if the information came from here. There's no weak link in the clerks' room, you can rely on me for that, sir.'

Freddie didn't believe Douglas for a moment. The staff were incorrigible gossips. 'Douglas, may I also remind you that no one except you in Chambers knows I'm getting married next Saturday. I'd be very upset if any whisper of this got out to the press. The last thing I need is a demonstation of Kerry Poole's disruptive abilities outside Temple Church.'

'I have honestly told no one, sir.'

'Good. Is that consultation still on at five today? I saw it pencilled in.'

'Confirmed, sir. The solicitors have just rung. Mr Bates is also apprised.'

'Anything else come in?'

'A stronger nibble from that gentleman who shall be nameless, sir. I'm having lunch with his solicitor today.'

'Excellent. I must go, Douglas, I'm being summoned to the court. I'll be back in Chambers well before five.'

Freddie was smiling as he followed Mrs Frobisher down the corridor. The certain gentleman was a well-known financier accused of massaging pension funds, Maxwell-style. Just the sort of high-profile case Freddie enjoyed. As a bankrupt, Francis de Witz would be on legal aid, but Freddie never scorned legal aid work, unlike some. George Warne, for one.

'You are mad, Freddie. The combination of the Legal Aid Board's inefficiency and inflation make it a financial no-no.'

'That's not a reason for refusing legally aided cases.'

'It's a clincher as far as I am concerned.'

'Somebody's got to do them.'

'Leave it to the likes of Colin Stimson.'

'Perhaps I am his like.'

'Oh, come off it, Freddie! I mean people with low incomes and the gleam of altruism in their eyes.'

'George, you have an acid tongue.'

'It's earned me a fortune, so I'm not complaining.'

'Do you like my new picture, by the way?'

'Which one's new?'

'The Gillian Ayres, over there.'

'Not much, to be frank. Bit of a mess. Have you got this lot properly insured?'

When Freddie took his place on the Bench, his eye immediately flew to the visitors' gallery. Besides the policeman on duty, there were two black women sitting together in the front and no one else there at all. He felt a disproportionate sense of relief as he looked down at the papers dealing with the first case of the day. He noticed spots of blood on his white cuffs, and a small red patch working its way through the bandage on his hand. At least the actual finger joint felt easier.

The day was beginning to improve.

There was an accident on the M4 and Meryl found herself diverted to the A4, which flustered her. She hadn't driven to Heathrow via that route before and arrived at the terminal well after Thomas's flight from Delhi landed. Praying it hadn't come in early, she rushed about looking for a driver called Ron holding a sign saying Mentieth; there were flocks of drivers holding signs – Patel, Singh, Ranjit, Macdonald – but no Mentieth. Streams of numbed people were pushing trolleys out of the arrival doors, gazing about in passive dazed confusion, blocking each other's paths. There was no knowing whether this was Thomas's plane-load; two planes had come in close together from India.

Meryl was distracted by the sight of two English girls wearing saris and carrying colourful rolls of baggage, and then realised that a wheelchair pushed by an airline steward had somehow got past her.

'Oh, my goodness, it's Thomas, isn't it? Yes, it is – how lovely to see you – what a bear garden this place is today!'

'It always is. Hullo, Meryl. Are you my ambulance? Or are you meeting someone else?'

'No, no, I've come to meet you – Freddie asked me to. An ambulance should be here – there's a man called Ron . . .' She tailed off and started to scrabble in her bag. The steward kept his wide smile in place as he suggested:

'If you give me his full name and the firm I can have him paged.'

'Hang on a minute, it should be here—' But she couldn't find the envelope where she'd written all the details nor could she remember anything of Natalie's message except the name Ron. 'Oh dear, this is a bore, I'll have to look around again for this wretched Ron person—' Pink-faced, Meryl pushed herself fruitlessly through the crowds.

I hate airports, I can't think why I said I'd do this, Thomas is looking at me as if I'm a complete twit and I am, the whole thing's turning into a farce, I could get the wheelchair into the Fiat but how on earth would I manage to get it and Thomas up the steps at Freddie's, oh God, I can't even ring him, he's in court – Meryl rushed up and down outside the terminal looking in vain for a parked ambulance. Sweating, distraught, she went back to admit defeat. Thomas was talking to a tall black man wearing a jersey and jeans and a Rastafarian woollen hat swollen with his hair.

'This is Ron, Meryl. While you were trying to find him he found us.'

'I was looking for a sign, or an ambulance.'

'I figured I'd be able to pick out the wheelchair easier than you picking out me.' Ron's slow voice gave the impression it could never change speed. 'Wait here in the warm, sir. I'll bring the vehicle up just outside.' He strolled off.

'I can't believe he's going to produce an ambulance,' Meryl muttered, gazing after him; the steward tried to pretend this problem wasn't his.

'How kind of you to come and meet me, Meryl. There was no need.'

'Of course I had to. And I'm coming on to let you into Freddie's house.'

'Very kind.'

Meryl could have hit him. Her head was still buzzing after her drive in heavy traffic, and she had the return drive ahead. Thomas's thin craggy face was deeply lined, his hair was greyer than she remembered – hunched in the wheelchair, he looked like an old man. On his lap was a newish-looking briefcase, but at his feet was his only other piece of luggage: a very old brown case tied round with rope and covered with worn illegible labels dating from another era.

'Your ambulance, sir.' The steward's smile still gave nothing away. Outside, visible through the glass, was a small white ambulance with ZAP PARAMEDICAL SERVICES painted on its side. Ron and another West Indian jumped out.

'This is a new experience.' Thomas looked cheerful, however, and Meryl watched as he was neatly transferred up a ramp into the converted van. She then had her first and only useful moment: Thomas asked her to bring his suitcase, as there didn't seem to be room for it. She loaded it into a veering trolley and hurried to the short-stay car park; it took her some time to find her car because in all the rush she'd forgotten to note which level it was on.

At last she was on the M4 (the westbound carriageway was open luckily) and driving as fast as she dared in an effort to catch up with Zap Paramedical Services.

'You'll catch us easily,' Ron had said. 'We don't go above fifty.'

But she didn't, and as she took her usual route through Bayswater and Paddington she visualised the ambulance waiting outside Freddie's house. The suitcase sat on her small rear seat like a frowning presence. However, all she found when she arrived was a policeman pacing casually past the house.

'Excuse me, officer, but have you seen a private ambulance with ZAP on the outside and a man with a broken leg—' Meryl stopped and started again. 'Has anyone arrived here while you've been on duty?'

'Very peaceful.' He walked on, clearly not doing any more than checking up on a beat duty. Meryl dragged Thomas's case up the steps – it felt as if it was full of books – and started to unlock the front door. It swung open before she could put a key in.

'Elsie!'

'Didn't he tell you I was coming then?'

'Well, no—'

'It's an emergency, Elsie, he said, the key's under the dustbin, second from the right, and get there by twelve o'clock. He said take a taxi but I didn't like to. Mr Thomas has broken his leg, he said.'

'I know.'

Elsie watched Meryl drag the case through the door. She'd met Mrs Peak on several occasions and formed the opinion she wasn't a patch on her sister. She definitely seemed the sort of person who didn't iron anything except shirts, and then only the front, the collar and the cuffs.

'How's the back, Elsie?'

'It's me knees that kill me.'

'That's a very splendid cardigan.'

Elsie ignored this comment; the shapeless purple garment with cheap gold buttons at irregular intervals hung unevenly, partly because she had skewered a diamanté poodle brooch above one bosom.

'If Mr Freddie or Mr Thomas need me, I drop everything to come.'

'How good of you. Well, this is Mr Thomas's suitcase. Where shall I put it?'

'Mr Freddie said the housekeeper had prepared the dining room,' said Elsie grimly. Meryl could hear her corset creaking as she walked. She pointed to the divan made up in the corner of the room. 'There's not nearly enough on that bed. Mr Thomas will be cold for sure. And get nightmares – you should never sleep in a red room. Never.'

'Oh, nonsense, Elsie.'

'Green is best for a bedroom. Or blue.'

'Our bedroom's yellow and we've survived.'

'I read a book once about colours.'

The doorbell pealed and Elsie hurried off, sore knees temporarily forgotten. She held the door open a mere crack when she saw Ron, even at his announcement of the ambulance. Meryl had to elbow her aside to pull it open.

'Wonderful, Ron, bring him up here, I've only just arrived myself, perfect timing, through here.' Ron and his companion carried the wheelchair with ease up the steps. Aloft, Thomas was staring down in horror at Elsie.

'Don't be worried, Mr Thomas, I'm not going to be cross with you. Though by rights I should, breaking your leg like this. What carelessness. Mind that, young man.'

'This, Ron, is Elsie. She's always found it hard to accept I've grown up. How much do I owe you for all your kind services?'

'Paid in advance, guv. Cheers.' Ron refused a tip and went off whistling.

'I never can trust those darkies—'

'Elsie, what I need more than anything is one of your excellent cups of tea.'

'I can't help feeling they're better off where they came from—'

'Shut up, Elsie, and go and make some *tea*.' When Elsie was out of earshot Thomas raised his fists in a gesture of despair. 'That woman makes the National Front look quite restrained.

How could Freddie have inflicted her on me! I told him expressly not to.'

'To help you.'

'To torment me. He's done it on purpose. You're here to help me. I don't need Elsie.'

'I'm sure he meant it for the best.'

'Take her away, Meryl! Drive her home, anything. I'd rather sit in extreme discomfort than have Elsie around helping me. Pass me those bloody crutches, would you; how I hate the things.'

'Do be careful, Thomas—'

'I need to pee. Urgently.'

'The best thing to do is stay put while I fetch you some empty milk bottles. Much easier to pee in a milk bottle. When Dennis broke his ankle, that's what he did.'

'Excellent idea, but keep Elsie out of here whatever you do.' Thomas lay back in the wheelchair, his face grey.

Meryl found three bottles outside the front door and gave one to Thomas. 'I'll put the other two here, within reach.'

'Bless you.'

Meryl could hear the banging of cupboard doors as she went down the basement stairs.

'Everything's changed. I can't find the traycloths. They used to be in that drawer.'

'I don't think Freddie bothers with traycloths.'

'And this? Does he wear things like this now? By the sink it was.' Elsie held up a bracelet.

'I expect someone washed up for him and left it there. You don't need to lay an elaborate tray, Elsie.'

'Things should be properly done.'

'All Thomas needs – all I need – is a mug of tea. I'll pour it down here and save your legs by taking it up myself.'

'It's no trouble—'

'Off I go.'

'I brought these chicken winglets to make Mr Thomas some soup. I think I'll get on with that then.'

'Good idea.'

'They need a good long boil.'

'So they do.' Meryl spilt some tea on the stair carpet but

ignored it. She hoped Elsie wouldn't notice. She tapped softly on the dining-room door.

'Come in, come in. I'm decent.'

'Elsie's busy making you some chicken soup. Let me empty those.'

'I filled two. I am amazed.'

As Meryl bore the two bottles away to the ground-floor lavatory the phone rang. She put them on the cloakroom windowsill and hurried to answer it before Elsie tried.

'Meryl? Freddie. All well?'

'Fine. Except for Elsie.'

'What do you mean?'

'Your brother's a bit annoyed to find her here.'

'I had to lay her on as a backup.'

'He wants me to take her away.'

'What on earth has she done?'

'Nothing, poor old thing. She's making him soup out of chicken winglets.'

'Chicken what?'

'Winglets.'

'I should never have asked her.'

'That's precisely what Thomas thinks.'

'I didn't want him stuck with no one in case of emergencies. I've got a consultation after court so I won't be back before six thirty at the earliest. Natalie's busy, Jane's out of town all day – that's why I asked Elsie to hold the fort. Tell him all that, will you. Cheer him up.'

'I'll try.'

'No more bricks?'

'What?'

'Never mind. Give the old bugger my love.'

'Freddie, I must go – someone's at the front door.'

A policeman, a different one, smiled at her from the doorstep. 'Sorry, madam, but is Mr Mentieth in?'

'Mr Thomas Mentieth or Mr Frederick Mentieth?'

'The owner of the house. The judge.'

'Ah. No, he's in court actually.'

'I'll call back. Tell him it's about the bricks.'

Meryl shut the door at the sound of a crash from the dining

room. Thomas had been trying to open his briefcase, and it had slipped and knocked over a small table. He was leaning perilously out of his chair.

'Let me, let me. Everyone keeps mentioning bricks. Freddie didn't tell you anything about bricks, did he?'

'Bricks?'

'It doesn't matter. He sends his love and he'll be back as soon as he can, but not before six thirty.'

'What I'd really like to do now is sleep. So if you help me on to the bed that's what I will do. I'm very comfortable, and you've organised things excellently. Just don't leave me here alone with Elsie, I beg you. Drive her home, put her in a taxi, anything.'

'She's in the middle of making that soup.'

So Meryl had to help Elsie with the laboured preparations, and insisted on pressure-cooking the soup for speed, much to Elsie's disgust.

'It won't taste the same. Those things never bring out the full flavour. I don't hold with them at all.'

Meryl then took Elsie off and drove her miles to her flat in Hanwell. As a result she was late collecting Piers and Harry from school; they were standing alone outside the closed gates of the playground looking furious.

'Typical. If any mother's going to be late, it's you, Mum.' Both boys continued in this vein for some minutes, until Meryl suddenly stopped the car.

'If you say *one* more thing to me, boys, you can both get out.'

'You always say that, and you never mean it.'

'Out.'

'Come off it, Mum, you are being ratty today—'

'OUT.'

'That car behind's getting annoyed.'

'Out, both of you.'

'I don't believe this—'

'You're both old enough to take the bus anyway. Here's the money. OUT.'

For the first time in her life she left her sons standing by the side of the road. The only thing to spoil her sense of triumph was the fact she dented the rear bumper when she parked the car.

13

'Why are there two pictures of the same theme so alike?'

'No one knows.'

'I like the one by Mantegna best.'

'I can never decide. Mantegna and Bellini were brothers-in-law, and were both taught by Bellini's father, Jacopo. Perhaps he set the two of them a competition.'

'You know so much, Colin. You must despair of all us philistines.'

'I don't know a lot. I've just got an excellent memory. If you don't forget things, you maximise on the little you know. Come and have a quick bite somewhere near, before we go back to Chambers.'

'I'm so glad you were around today.'

'What's the matter, Natalie? Or can you not tell me?'

I shrug as we go down the wide dark grey stone steps of the staircase in the new wing of the National Gallery. As we collect our coats, I watch the mechanical carousel turn until it eventually, with a clack and a rattle, stops and yields my black overcoat.

'I feel as if I'm one of those. Other people press switches and round I go.' Colin sees me through the huge revolving doors and takes my arm. 'I'm going to tell you something which you must absolutely keep to yourself. I'm getting married to Freddie on Saturday.'

'So soon!'

'We wanted a small family affair and that's why no one in Chambers has been invited or knows about it.'

'Understandable. And you're feeling nervous?'

'I'm terrified. Everything is suddenly out of my control – Freddie is going to lift me out of my chaotic post-student life and it's as if I'm going to be his property.'

'Freddie isn't a man to regard his wife as his *property*.'

'No, of course not—'

'He's much less conservative – with a small c – than he seems.'

'He votes Labour.'

'It doesn't surprise me.'

'It surprised me. I would expect you to, but not him.'

Colin laughs and steers me into a tiny restaurant serving Middle Eastern dishes. We squash into a table built for two very small people and eat a mound of comforting spicy food.

'I had a horrid weekend and you've really cheered me up. Freddie took me and Jane to the cottage he's got and it all went wrong.'

'Jane your beautiful sister – whom I met the other day?'

'Yes.'

'Prettiest nose I've ever seen.'

'I wish she hadn't come to England, Colin. It sounds a terrible thing to say about my only sister but it's true.'

A waitress comes up and Colin orders coffee and baklava. It gives me time to realise I shouldn't talk too freely about my troubles, but I don't care. It's tempting to confide in someone like Colin.

'Well, she's only here for a couple of weeks, isn't she?'

'She's come home for good. I only learned that yesterday. I could cope with the idea of a couple of weeks; to have her permanently on the scene is a different kettle of fish. But I'll get used to the idea. Enough about Jane. I don't think I can manage all this baklava.'

'Cut off what you don't want. I dote on the stuff. Fatal but delicious.'

'I'd noticed you had a sweet tooth.' Colin has a trickle of syrup on his red and white spotted tie. His double-breasted suit is shiny and worn, and one of the buttons doesn't quite match the others.

'I'm just suffering from pre-wedding nerves, and the fact that I still haven't got myself a wedding dress to wear. I'm worried that I can't get worried about it and solve the problem. I keep putting it off. Which is odd, considering what a neurotic I can be about being correctly dressed.'

'Sally says one's attitude to clothing is of profound importance. It is after all the cover, in both senses, you put on to face the world. Sally always asks me what my clients are wearing in court, for instance. She'd probably have something clever to say about the fact you're procrastinating.'

'How's her sabbatical going?'

'It's over. She didn't finish the book, and she's back at the LSE with a full teaching load.'

'I don't know how she manages to do all she does and cope with you all as well.'

'She often doesn't cope. We get by somehow.'

'What did Sally wear to get married in?'

'Guess.'

'Church or registry office wedding?'

'Church. Rather against her will.'

'Then she probably wore white but in a rather original way – satin trouser suit or something.'

'Wrong. She wore red velvet.'

'Did it look good?'

'Wonderful.'

'Colin, I must go and do something about it this afternoon. Otherwise I'll end up in something I've had for ages.'

'What's wrong with that?'

'I *must* wear something new. I don't know why, but I absolutely must. Sally would no doubt have theories about that too, but now I've said it I realise how true it is. I can't possibly wear something I've worn before.'

And that real wedding dress, that confection of cream silk lying in a heap in the corner of my bedroom, crushed, soiled, torn? I can't bear to think about it. I can't bear to touch it. I've pushed it out of sight.

There is an old bag lady sitting outside Liberty's, on the pavement with her back against a window of clothes. Winter clothes: coats trimmed with dutiful fake fur, suits of rich tweeds with silk shirts closing softly round the hard necks of the arrogant mannequins.

The old woman is wearing all the clothes she possesses, by the number of layers cocooning her body. Not much chance of choice for her each morning – her cover is necessity. Then I look closer.

She's wearing a brocade waistcoat, torn and filthy, over her final layer of coat. She could have worn it underneath, but she hasn't; on top like that it looks raffish. She's also picked up a battered rose head from a gutter somewhere and shoved it through a buttonhole. She's halfway through drinking a bottle of wine; her eyes above her red-veined nose are shut, but I can see she's alert to something – her dirty thumb is working back and forth, back and forth, across the top of the bottle. It's impossible to guess her age; her whole existence is unimaginable.

Her free hand suddenly fingers the rose.

The grey Japanese dress I liked and had steeled myself to buy has gone, sold. I stand in dismay, almost in tears as the salesgirl confirms they have none left. She tries to interest me in other dresses, but they are none of them beautiful – I remember the Japanese dress and probably exaggerate its beauty. These colours are ugly, the prices make me reel, the fabrics slide and slip and give off the sweetish smell of luxury, of money.

'Red velvet – do you have anything in red velvet?'

'Red isn't in this winter – we don't have much in red. Green velvet?'

I leave Liberty's and trudge through two more department stores, staring bleakly at more ugly dresses, stiff with buttons and shoulder pads, or long and slithery and décolleté. A harsh fuchsia colour is everywhere; I long for a rich quiet red, I think of Sally Stimson watching my despair and indecision and drawing complex and demoralising conclusions. I feel light-headed, a little mad. I go into a café and sit quietly, trying to collect myself. I know I have to find a dress today – the rest of the week is too busy.

Sally would say that all this indecision and procrastination must hide a deep-seated reluctance to marry Freddie. Is she right? The chocolate scattered on top of my cappuccino swirls and melts away as I stir. Is she right?

My equilibrium has gone since Jane arrived. I didn't have any doubts before; I even bought that dress after all. But don't fool yourself, Natalie, that dress made you nervous. Look what you did to it.

Dave Rosenberg. Another spoiler. And he and Jane are going out together tonight – don't be silly, I'm getting paranoid. It's ridiculous. The important person is Freddie, the important thing is my wedding.

When I marry Freddie I'm changing my life. It's not like living with a boyfriend until you imperceptibly slip towards marriage or a permanent commitment. I'm leaping into his highly constructed life, I'll leave out the in-between stages for ever. And Sara's right, lots of his friends won't be my friends.

But I love Freddie. He says he loves me. He behaves as if he does, too. He'd have to love me to face taking me on permanently. He could have just had the sex whenever he felt like it and I think he realised that.

'You're flattered he's chosen you.' Sara said this while chopping onions; her acid voice comes out below her streaming tears.

'What's wrong with that?'

'It's not a good basis for a permanent relationship.' Chop, chop, sniff. 'Pass me some kitchen roll to blow my nose on.'

'Give me a break, Sara. I know the difference between feeling flattered and loving someone. And we share such a lot – that's a good basis, surely.'

'You're in the same job, that's all. But if you weren't, how much would you share? That's where you should take a good clear look.'

'You're just jealous.'

'I am not jealous. Fuck off, Nat. This conversation is poisoning my cooking.'

Jane. Her thick blonde hair, her figure, her air of confidence, her nose. That small, straight, maddening little nose. Perfection in a nose. The nostrils curve to the tip and resolve with a neatness that is continually drawing the eye.

I don't look at my nose any more – I've accepted its size, its rounded blobby tip, the ample nostrils. 'Grandpa's nose. Full of character.' My mother said this in the jolly tone that never fools a child.

'Whose nose have I got, Mum?'

'Must be from the other side of the family. There are no beautiful noses in mine, Jane – just noses full of character.'

Thank you for that one, Mum. Thank you very much. It made me dread our visits to my grandfather because in front of me was what my nose would become. Nobbly, red, bulbous, narrowing to a bump that shone as if the bone were trying to poke through. Hairs trailing out of his nostrils. I spent hours of my childhood looking into a hand mirror to see if any black hairs were lurking deep in mine.

I buy another coffee and stare out into the street, unable to move on. The bag lady from outside Liberty's walks past outside, shouting. The pavement empties around her. She's still got the rose stuck into her old waistcoat. Her nose is so distended and red it makes mine look positively dainty. She meets my eye through the plate-glass window and waves her bottle at me in a mad salute.

I look down at my coffee, unable to keep my eye on hers. I'm suddenly suffused with self-disgust at my petty worries, my life-long obsession with my sister, my inability even to equip myself with a suitable wedding dress. I march out leaving my coffee and go straight into Dickins and Jones where I buy myself a red silk dress in five minutes. It's not very nice, but at least it's red.

14

The painkiller wore off by mid-morning. Freddie began to feel invaded; his damaged finger drew all his fingers, his hand, his arm, the left side of his body, into the assault. The pain was extraordinary. He knew the thorn was gone, he'd seen it in the infernal tweezers the doctor had waved under his nose. Yet its effect continued to gouge its way into his joint, to spread its poison, to make sure he had a problem for the rest of his life.

His concentration was undermined by the pain. He always saw his mind as a torch or spotlight which he could direct at will. Not a laser – right from boyhood, the image was a spotlight, and early on he realised it was a better one than most – he could work at a speed far greater than his friends. (Only Thomas always outdid him. Solutions came so fast to Thomas that they lost value; Freddie knew the importance of being seen to try.) But today, by the end of a morning dealing with the usual Monday start of bail applications, broken fixtures and pleas of guilty, his spotlight would hardly switch on, and when the chief witness in the afternoon's case did not turn up he was more than relieved.

'Mr Hollowood, have you any idea why the witness has defaulted?'

'No, Your Honour. I saw him on Friday and he was all set to be here at two o'clock. I can't understand it. He might have had an accident of some sort.'

'We will adjourn the case until tomorrow in the hope he can be speedily located.'

The court rose, and as Freddie turned out of his judicial chair he caught his sore hand on the carved arm.

'Are you all right, Your Honour? You're looking very pale.'

'This finger is ridiculously painful.'

'A good thing we have adjourned, Your Honour. Now you must go straight home and give yourself a proper half-day off.'

'Would that I could, Mrs Frobisher. I must ring my clerk and tell him I'll be back early.'

'Let me do that, Your Honour. Have this cup of tea in peace and quiet. Shall I get you a couple of tablets for the pain?' Mrs Frobisher flapped about him, a motherly crow in her gown. She had lost the only two children she'd had in cot deaths, and used her otherwise unexercised maternal instincts at work. She told Freddie about her children when she learned of Anthea's death, confessing it as if it was a shameful secret. Apparently no one else at the court knew, only Freddie. He'd been touched by her need to tell him of the central sadness in her life.

'It's all right, I took something not long ago. Many thanks for everything, Mrs Frobisher. You're definitely the usher with the mostest.'

Mrs Frobisher blushed so hard even her ears went pink.

The car park was empty of suspicious people; the attendant was in his kiosk doing the pools as Freddie passed. But the Saab looked odd: it had shrunk. All four tyres were flat; each tyre had a neat slash in an almost identical spot.

Anger wiped out pain as Freddie ran to the car attendant and raged at him. 'How can you possibly not notice someone slashing my tyres—'

'There's no call to shout, sir, I've only just come on duty.'

'Sorry. But it's too much. This is supposed to be a secure car park. First I'm cornered by thugs and cameramen, then my tyres are slashed.'

'Thugs and cameramen, sir? I haven't seen a soul—' The attendant was new, with an edge to his tone Freddie didn't much like.

'Never mind. What the hell is the best thing to do? My garage is in North London, they can't help. Shall I ring the AA? It really is too much.'

'You need to get it to one of them tyre places.' But he clearly was going to be no help, and Freddie felt so deadened by this latest problem he couldn't think straight. He took a taxi back to Chambers, and to his relief found Paul in the clerks' room.

Paul had a tattoo of a snake's head on one wrist, and its tail on the other; at the back of his neck, just visible over the collar, was a section of snake body. The fact he was a third-generation barrister's clerk cancelled out the effect of this tattoo on a conservative profession. He was also willing and efficient, and promptly took over Freddie's problem.

'Best thing is to get the AA to deliver the car to a tyre dealer, sir. Give us your membership card and leave it to me. Who do you think slashed them, sir?'

'The same charming man that keeps throwing bricks through my windows, I should imagine.'

'Could be a woman.'

'No, Paul. You need real brute strength to get through a tyre.'

'Depends what you use, sir. There's some nifty gadgets available to villains.'

Freddie collected a coffee from the dispenser and poured a large tot of whisky into it before slumping into an armchair in his room. He drank it at a draught and shut his eyes. Paul's knock woke him twenty minutes later, and he knew Paul wasn't fooled by his attempt at wide-awake attention.

'Your car's being delivered to Vulcan Tyres, sir, within the hour. They'll do the job at once so you can collect it about six.'

'I'm not sure I should drive, Paul. This hand is extremely painful. Is Miss Harper around?'

'Been gone since before lunch, sir. Went off with Mr Stimson.'

'I suppose she could fetch the car for me. Ask her to come straight here when she comes in, would you?'

'I could fetch it for you, sir. After I've done the court lists with Douglas.'

Freddie looked at the snake's head on Paul's wrist. 'That's very kind, Paul.' He felt misgivings, but the thought of Natalie behind the wheel of the Saab was worse.

'No problem.'

'Here's a tenner for the taxi. Thanks very much, Paul.'

'You'll need to give me the car keys as well, sir.'

'I'm not myself today. Here you are.' Paul put out his left hand

and the snake's tail made a sinuous movement. 'Does that thing really go all over you?'

'Pardon?'

'The snake.'

'Oh, my tattoo. Up the arm, round the neck, round the body, up again, down the other arm. The girlfriend gave it to me for my twenty-first.'

'She's a tattooist?'

'No, she paid for it, sir. She'd laugh at the idea of her tattooing, she couldn't prick a fly she's that squeamish. Do you want to see how the snake goes?'

'It's all right, Paul, I'll believe you.'

'I'm looking forward to driving your car, sir. Good bit of engine under that bonnet. Vroom, vroom.'

'She's organised me beautifully.'

'So it was a good idea to ask Elsie to come after all—'

'Not Elsie, dammit. Your sister-in-law. Ex. Can't remember her name for the moment, wittery woman but turns out to have a head on her shoulders.'

'Meryl.'

'Of course. Meryl. Elsie was lethal, absolutely lethal. You did that out of pure sadism, Fred.'

'So you're comfortable.'

'Excellent. Books, water, phone, milk bottles. When are you coming home?'

'I've had the car sabotaged this morning. I'm not sure.'

'Oh dear. How badly?'

'Slashed tyres. All four. And I've got an agonising finger, got a thorn in it gardening, hurts like hell.'

'We are a pair.'

'Help yourself to whisky, Tom.'

'I certainly will. Meryl put it handy too. She remembered everything.'

'How surprising – she's not known for her efficiency. Kind but chaotic normally. Did I hear you say milk bottles just now?'

'You did. Meryl's idea. I pee into them. Who's coming to the wedding, by the way?'

'I'll tell you this evening.'

*   *   *

Freddie looked at the guest list for his wedding and suddenly lost hope in it. Why had he ever thought even this weeded group of family would stay charitable and sociable for any length of time – he should have listened to Natalie and had a civil wedding with a few witnesses and a small dinner afterwards.

Not that she'd been insistent; she'd actually seemed perfectly happy to be married in Temple Church and to have the reception and lunch in the Garrick afterwards. She'd said there was nothing she liked better than handing over all the arrangements and just going along with whatever he'd planned. She hadn't interfered at all. In fact, if anything she'd gone to the opposite extreme – not quite uninterested, not quite, but nearly.

Why the hell had he invited Ralph? Because he wanted to impress him, to take that look of mocking amusement off his face? Look, I'm a successful silk, Head of Chambers, I'm marrying a gorgeous young woman, I'm so lucky. Pathetic. Ralph couldn't care less.

His cousin Ralph Mentieth was a singularly unsuccessful painter, he'd married three times, he'd lived through bankruptcy and repossession of the only house he'd ever tried to buy, he currently lived in a council flat with a black policewoman who'd been one of his models, he never had enough money, yet he always succeeded in giving Freddie an inferiority complex.

Freddie stared round his elegant room and said aloud: 'God, I'm a fool. He'll get drunk and disrupt everything.' (His habit of speaking aloud was increasing; he'd found himself saying 'Love is a lottery' on the staircase in George Warne's hearing, and got a strange look.)

But he knew why he'd invited Ralph, if he was honest. He wanted to earn his respect, because Ralph was the only person he truly respected.

Respect. What a dusty, crisp word. Respect. Freddie got up and stared out of his window at the immaculate green lawns, the huge bare planes, the Thames beyond the Embankment. There must be other people he respected. He loved Natalie but he didn't exactly respect her, nor had he Anthea. Nor any member of Chambers; he did respect some of the judiciary for their minds, but not as people. His old headmaster, recently dead, he'd respected him, but that was a respect that had never been tested outside the confines of the education system.

Of his family, he only felt respect for Ralph. Thomas was too selfish to win respect for anything except his exceptional brain and abilities. He was an emotional child. Not Ralph; Ralph lived life to the full, he never compromised, he survived appalling bad luck, traumas, mess, he made mistakes and dragged others into them, he was impossible, he was beyond the pale. And Freddie respected him and had done since they were children. Ralph was the most 'unrespectable' person he knew, which proved that respect had nothing to do with proper behaviour.

The door opened and George Warne put his head in. 'I say, Freddie, I've got a problem. Wonder if I could run it past you?'

You couldn't respect George. You couldn't respect his fees (too big), his lifestyle (too flashy), his performance in court (ditto), his—

'Are you feeling all right, Freddie?'

'I've got an inflamed finger.'

'Thought it was something worse. Flu. Everyone seems to be going down with it. Anyway, my problem is this: two tickets for Covent Garden clash with Grand Night in Hall next week, can't think how it's happened, wonder if you'd like the tickets?'

'What's on?'

'*Tosca* – that new tenor everyone's raving about, saying he's the new Domingo. Got terrific reviews. It's amazing but I'm beginning to like that picture over there.'

'Next week – no of course I can't, what am I thinking about. I'm away.'

'Never mind. Tried you first because the tickets are rather expensive. Who did you say painted it?'

'Gillian Ayres.'

'Well, it's growing on me. How much did you say you paid for it?'

'I didn't.'

'You mean it was a gift?'

'I didn't say.'

Freddie watched George staring at the painting, nose close, assessing, touching.

'I wish she hadn't added this red thing here. Spoils the picture.'

'A matter of opinion.'

'Looks like a horse's penis.'

Freddie leaned back and stared at the picture as George closed the door. He wondered what Ralph would think of it. Perhaps Ralph would have time to pop up here after the wedding and look at his new acquisitions on Saturday. Of course he wouldn't. They would all be hurrying to the Garrick straight after church.

Freddie picked up the list and the seating plan and looked dispiritedly through them. He wondered if Ralph was going to bring his black policewoman. She wasn't invited mainly because Freddie had no idea of her name or her part in Ralph's life. He decided to play safe and allow for her on the plan. As he wrote BP into a gap, Natalie came in.

'Freddie darling, are you all right? Paul told me there's been another attack.'

'They slashed the tyres of the Saab this time.'

'Oh, Freddie. I am sorry. All this is beginning to scare me. Next you're going to get hurt.'

'They won't go further than this sort of thing. They are just petty mindless villains making a point. Vandalism is the only method they can think of. I really think it will tail off now. So do the police – three incidents and that's it.'

'I wouldn't be too sure. If they find out about the wedding, they might try something to mess it up.'

'The wedding has been an exceptionally well-kept secret. Outside the family, only Douglas knows it's on Saturday, and he hasn't told a soul.'

'I told Colin.'

'Well, make sure he keeps quiet about it. You shouldn't have told him, Nat, what came over you?'

'He's been so sweet to me today. He promised not to say a word. But are you all right, Freddie? You look a bit under the weather.'

'This stupid finger.'

'Did you get to the hospital?'

'Yes, but it's hurt like hell ever since.'

Natalie put her arms round him, but he remained stiff; her gesture became perfunctory, and she moved away again. She looked tired and jaded, and her clothes smelt of cigarette smoke. Freddie reached out and took her hand.

'Well, at least Thomas got here safe and sound – your ambulance did him proud apparently, as did Meryl. Come home with me now and meet him. I'll order a taxi. My meeting is cancelled, and Paul is collecting the car and driving it up to the house, bless him.'

'I can't, Freddie. I really must finish a set of papers by half five. Douglas says the solicitors are agitating.'

'Which solicitors?'

'Berry and Harman.'

'How long will you be?'

'A good hour. I've been out all afternoon, I really must put my head down. Life is so out of control at the moment.'

Freddie gazed at her thick hair, her neat ankles below her mid-calf-length black skirt, and her waist defined by a black leather belt. She had such a tiny waist, looking at it made him dizzy. He got up to put his hands round it as he often did, but his finger gave a spurt of pure agony as he touched the warm leather so instead of a gesture of affection he gave a hiss of pain and moved away.

'Perhaps it's infected. Take the bandage off, Freddie.'

'Not now. I'll do it at home. So when do you expect to arrive?' He sounded sharp, domineering.

'I'll give you a ring when I've finished.' Nat's kiss on his cheek was cool.

'I don't know what we're going to eat tonight.'

'Get the taxi to stop at that Italian delicatessen – they do such fab fresh sauces for pasta.'

Natalie hurried off. Freddie suddenly felt old; he looked in the mirror inside his robe cupboard and saw a sallow, lined face and too much grey hair.

Thomas looked old too. He was propped up in bed with half-moon glasses on the very end of his nose; his grey stubbly hair was matted and untidy; the dining room smelt of unwashed body and stale clothing.

'Freddie, I'm really enjoying this – found the book in that corner shelf. I had no idea Aretino was so amusing – I thought he was simply a scurrilous pornographer. My heart warms to him. Listen to this:

It's true that I refused the knighthood with which the Emperor wished to honour me. The reason is that it's more to my credit to have people going round trying to discover why I was *not* given such a rank than it would be to have them clamouring to find out *why* I was given it.

Did you know I'd turned down a CBE?'

'Hullo, Tom. Nice to see you've settled in so well. No, I didn't. Same reason as Aretino?'

'I don't believe in honours, you know that. Ridiculous out-dated system.'

'How's the leg?'

'Not too bad. It got very swollen on the plane but it seems to have gone down. Here's another very amusing bit, listen—'

'Not now, for goodness' sake. I've only just walked in the door. Give me time to take my coat off. Is Jane here?'

'Who's Jane?'

'So there's no one in the house, no sounds from the flat?'

'Not to my knowledge. Meryl removed Elsie not a moment too soon. She'd already managed to make that disgusting chicken soup with barley which plagued our childhood. The smell has filled the house. Ugh.'

'I'll go and deal with it.'

Thomas pointed to his milk bottles. 'If you bring a bucket I could empty them myself.'

'I'll deal with them later. Chicken soup first.'

Freddie went downstairs and opened the lukewarm pressure cooker. A concentrated blast of over-boiled chicken wings and vegetables filled his nostrils. Slimy-looking winglets floated amongst chunks of carrots and potatoes, each winglet coated in withered-looking white skin. Barley floated in the thin broth like frog spawn. Almost gagging, Freddie put the whole lot outside the back door and switched on the extractor fan. Elsie had left a laid-up tray for their tea; she'd managed to find an embroidered napkin to use as a traycloth, she'd put out the bone china cups with finicky handles which he'd always pushed to the back of the shelf because he didn't like them, she'd even found the little matching cream jug which hadn't been used in years. Freddie put all the china back in its cupboard and put tea bags, mugs and a bottle of milk on the tray instead. (He usually decanted milk into a jug, but needed to make a stand against the all-pervading sense of Elsie's gentility.)

Before going upstairs, he had a quick look into the flat. It was wildly untidy and in darkness. He shut the door again.

Thomas was shouting his name as he carried the tray upstairs. He'd switched the television on and was pointing at the screen.

'You've just missed it. They were saying you had trouble as a result of a case – "Frederick Mentieth, the well-known civil rights QC, has experienced days of minor intimidation as a result of the verdict in the Poole case" – tyres slashed, bricks through windows, they said. What is all this?'

'Are you sure they mentioned the tyres?'

'Absolutely. Why should I invent that?'

'It only happened today – I found them slashed this afternoon. Whoever did it must have contacted the media.'

'Put some whisky in that tea. Best anaesthetic there is.'

'I was going to.'

'Well, go on, tell me about the Poole case. What did you do to excite all this violence?'

'I was judging it, and judging it absolutely fairly.' Freddie summarised the case. 'To my surprise the jury found the defendants guilty and the police came out of it unscathed. The public gallery didn't like that at all.'

'Was it a fair verdict?'

'Impossible to say. The stories were so conflicting; the police gave a very different version of events from the defendants. Both defendants contradicted each other and neither was good in the witness box. The jury took against them. There's now an allegation that one of the jurors was nobbled by the police.'

'True?'

'God knows. Probably not. But the real cause of the trouble has been the fact that one of the defendants has a sister with a high profile in the popular press because she's a TV celebrity. The police tell me she's married to a very shady character, keen on the rough stuff. Could be behind these attacks. I should doubt it – I think they are more likely to be the bright ideas of the civil rights mob element.'

'What a colourful life you lead, Freddie.'

'It doesn't seem colourful to me. Just very hard work and full of unpleasant surprises at the moment. The last few days have been altogether too much.'

'Could you possibly do the honours with these milk bottles before I knock one over? And bring them back, they're an essential part of my independence.'

Seething, Freddie took the unpleasant bottles to his upstairs bathroom and dealt with them before changing into jeans and his most holey jersey. When he got back to the dining room he found Thomas half off the bed – he'd been trying to reach his duty-free bottle of whisky.

'Do be careful, Tom. We can't have you back in hospital.'

'Sorry. I wanted to give you that bottle since I seem to have made such a dent in yours.'

'Don't you think you're going to need a special nurse?'

'Whatever gave you that idea?'

'How are you going to have things like baths? I'm no nurse, and I can't ask the girls to help.'

'Ron the Rastafarian, alias Zap Paramedics, might be of use – he gave me his card and said he covered all sorts of medical care. Let's ring him tomorrow.'

'I'll ask Natalie if she can do it for us – she found him initially.' Freddie was cheered by his brother's lack of resistance, and put the bottles under Thomas's bed with a better grace than he had taken them. 'She'll be here soon.'

'That's what I mean by a colourful life – there you are, marrying a young thing, moving into a world I can't begin to enter. And you're wearing jeans, dear boy. An outward and visible sign. I've never worn them in my life.'

'Anthea would have hated them.'

'Does that bother you?'

'Not any more.'

'Good.'

'Do you dislike them?'

'Dislike what?'

'These jeans.'

'Freddie, I have no views about clothes. You know that. You could wear pink pantaloons and it wouldn't offend me. Tell me who's coming to the great wedding.'

'You're not going to like the list.'

'I wasn't expecting to. As long as Elsie isn't on it I can bear anything. Ralph must be coming.'

'Why do you say that?'

'Because you've got some obsession about him. I've noticed. You always have had.'

'Rubbish.'

'Did you know he's living with a black policewoman six foot tall?'

'I didn't know she was six foot.'

'Mother was probably exaggerating. Mind you, most people look tall beside Ralph.'

'Here's the list.'

'Meryl and Dennis, Henry and Isabel, Crawford and Zoe and their girls – how old are they now?'

'Lalage is sixteen. Esther's about eighteen.'

'She can't be eighteen already. What a hopeless godfather I've been to her.'

'Precisely what Crawford was saying last time I saw him. He came to a guest night in hall.'

'I'll make sure I name her in my will. Have you made your will yet, Freddie?'

'Well, no, I haven't. But since I would have had to have changed it, perhaps it's just as well.'

'People without children don't think about wills. When you have a family – as I suppose you hope to – you'll be drawing one up at once.'

'Natalie doesn't want children yet. She needs to establish herself first.'

'Don't you want them?'

'Of course I do one day. But I've got used to life without them. So have you made a will, Tom?'

'Of course not. This accident brought it home to me. In fact, perhaps you'd help me draw one up while I'm here. Back to the wedding list. I'm surprised you've only asked the inner family. No Bar.'

'We've kept the fact we're getting married on Saturday a secret from Chambers. I can't ask them all, so I decided to ask none.'

'But they know you're engaged?'

'Oh, yes.'

'Did that go down well?'

'Why shouldn't it?'

'You might be accused of cradle-snatching, marrying someone doing their pupillage.'

'She's not a pupil any more, she's a full junior member of Chambers and she's doing extremely well in her own right. Douglas reckons she'll go far.'

'I remember you saying he was bad at promoting women at the Bar.'

'Even a clerk can change. He likes Natalie – she possesses his three requirements for women to succeed as barristers – she's tall, she's dark, and she's got a good strong voice. It's the small blonde ones with high-pitched voices he can't be doing with.'

'Pity Douglas isn't coming to the wedding. I had a very good conversation with him once when I was waiting for you. About hop-picking in Kent. I've never forgotten it.'

'You never forget anything.'

'I'm beginning to. It's got worse since this accident. But tell me about Henry's operation. Mother said he nearly died.'

Freddie found it very comfortable and comforting to sit and talk about the family with his brother. The family, the unexciting, unexceptional (except for Ralph) family, the given web of blood relations and their partners, the shared genes that caused the crinkly hair, the tipped-up nose, the large ears, the long bones. He smiled at his brother, who smiled back, sharing his content.

Within minutes the doorbell went. Paul stood whistling on the doorstep, twirling the Saab's keys.

'All serene, Paul? No problems?'

'Your spare was flat and all, they said, sir.'

'Oh dear.'

'Yeah, slow puncture. Astronomical price, those tyres, sir. Astronomical. They're sending the bill to Chambers. I fixed that.'

'I'm so grateful to you, Paul. Have a drink before you go.'

'Don't mind if I do, sir.'

'You deserve one. What's it to be?'

'Beer, sir, if you've got it.'

'A Foster's is on the way. Come in here and sit down while I do the honours.' Freddie decided not to inflict Thomas and Paul on each other, and led Paul into the sitting room. He popped his head in on Thomas and saw him deep in Aretino. As Freddie came upstairs with some cans of beer and two glasses, the bell went again. Expecting Natalie, he opened the door.

'Good evening, sir.' Two policemen stood there, one familiar.

'Good evening, officers. PC Partridge, isn't it?'

'We heard on the news about your tyres being slashed, sir. Sorry to hear you've had more trouble.'

'Not in your manor, Constable.'

'Have you reported the incident, sir?'

'Yes.' He hadn't got round to it.

'Been in the wars yourself, sir?'

'No, this was just from being careless while gardening.' There was a pause; Freddie could hear Paul's footsteps creaking in the sitting room, and knew he was all ears.

'Well, we'll be off now, sir. Just keep us informed of every little thing – you never know if it could lead us to the villains.'

'Naturally. Thanks for dropping in.'

As the door shut Paul's face came into view. 'You get a good service from the fuzz in these parts.'

'This level of attention is highly unusual.'

'Cheers, then, sir. Down the hatch.' Half the glass disappeared. 'Got a lot of pictures here too, sir.'

'It's always been an interest of mine.'

'That black and red one there, it's just done with a spray gun. I could do something like that in five minutes. Don't mean to be rude, sir, but it's the truth.'

'Yes, theoretically you could.'

'So what's the difference then, apart from ten thousand pounds?' Paul laughed as he finished his glass of beer.

'It's difficult to put into words. But if you or I produced something like that it would be a happy accident. The artist knew precisely what he was doing and there is no element of accident at all about it. The whole picture has a most satisfactory balance; I never get bored looking at it. Have another beer, I brought one up for you.'

'Don't mind if I do, thanks. So making a mess on purpose is better than making it by accident, even if the end result is exactly the same?'

'You could put it like that.'

'You're not offended, sir?'

'Not at all. I don't expect people to have the same tastes as me.'

'That woman ought to be locked up, the one who filled a house with concrete and then took the house away, she must be off her trolley.'

'Installations aren't really my thing either.'

'Then some fellow put mounds of rice all over the floor, I mean I ask you—'

Three little rings on the front door announced Natalie's arrival, and as Freddie let her in he immediately warned her of Paul's presence in the sitting room.

'And Thomas is in the dining room, reading. I'll introduce you later.'

'I must disappear first. Give me five minutes.' Natalie went into the downstairs cloakroom and Freddie returned to Paul, praying that he'd drunk his second beer at the speed of his first. But Paul was sipping it.

'That was Miss Harper.'

'In that case I'll get a move on, then—'

'Do finish your beer—'

'No, no, sir, I must go and leave you in peace. Now that picture I do like.' He pointed to a small oil of a field of hay under bulging grey clouds.

'I like it too. It came from my grandfather's house.'

'The only picture we've got indoors is of a bunch of roses. My mum had it framed, it was just a card but she liked it. Good night, sir, and thanks for that beer. Didn't expect you to stock Foster's and all.'

'Thank you for bringing my car back.'

'Any time.'

'I'm rather hoping there won't be another.'

'Fingers crossed, sir. Those villains seem to be full of ideas as far as your property is concerned.'

'Goodbye, Paul, and thanks again.'

'No sweat. All the best to Miss Harper, sir. Ta-ta.'

15 ∫

I can't help being surprised – well, shocked would be better
– by Thomas Mentieth. When Freddie described his brother's
jet-setting life I assumed he'd be the sauve, worldly, neat-suited
type, greying hair immaculate.

I know he saw my expression as I followed Freddie into the
dining room. It's a split second of reaction that I cover by smiling
a lot, being charming, doing my best to erase the fact that my face
must have said as clearly as words: What a smelly old tramp.

He looks so much older than Freddie, though there's only
supposed to be a few years between them. The odd thing is,
when Freddie sits beside his brother he suddenly looks old too.
It's catching. Thomas wrinkles his nose, then Freddie does it too
and adds another five years. It's alarming. They both purse their
lips in the same way; deep lines form around their mouths when
they do this, and if I just look at their mouths—

'I'll go and get supper organised. Did you get to the deli?'

'Everything's in the fridge, darling.'

I try and walk out of the room slowly but it still feels like a
rushed escape. The smell of old man seems to have permeated
the kitchen, or perhaps it's something else. The whole house
smells odd.

I stick my head into the flat to see if Jane's been back, but all
the evidence points to an early morning departure. She hadn't
been feeling too well by the time we got back to London last
night, and went straight off to bed. Said it was prolonged jet lag.
She must have already gone to meet Dave by now; she won't be
back till the small hours. If then.

Frying garlic in olive oil makes the kitchen smell better at once. I fry small cubes of bread, and make a big salad ready for the warm croutons to be added at the last moment. I warm the water for the pasta, and get the sauce out – pesto. All this takes me ages; normally I would have done it in five minutes. I'm consciously putting off the return to two old men.

Freddie's feet bang down the stairs and he positively bounces into the kitchen.

'I'm feeling so much better, Nat. The whisky seems to have dealt with the pain.'

'Perhaps it was going to stop anyway.'

'Are you all right, my love?'

'Tired. And all the aggro, the attacks on you, the tensions – they're all getting to me.'

He puts his arms round me, kisses me. He's looking his proper age again. I put my hands round the two cheeks of his bottom in the way he likes.

'Having Tom here is going to cramp our style—'

'I was going to have a chaste week, remember. And Jane is here too.'

'Where *is* Jane?'

'I think she's gone to the theatre.'

'It seems odd she's left me no message.'

'Jane's like that.'

'I thought she was here for supper so I catered for her.'

'She's finding her feet. With luck she'll find somewhere to live too.'

'Not too soon – I'd prefer she was here when we're on honeymoon.'

We stand together very still and comfortable with each other. The boiling water bubbles gently on the cooker.

'Nat, I'm afraid she's going to find the wedding very boring. I'm afraid you are too.'

'Freddie, I don't mind. I always said I wanted a small wedding and it's a small wedding. I didn't want to invite dozens of my friends, or have the Bar en masse; I'm perfectly happy with a bunch of your relations and a few friends. I haven't got a family, you have. Great. End of story. Does your brother like Italian food?'

'He'd better. He's got no choice.' Freddie smiles. 'But he's easy – he doesn't really notice what he eats. He's got his whisky and he's chuckling over Aretino. If we just took up bread and cheese he'd be perfectly happy.'

'Who's Aretino? What dish shall I put the pasta into?'

'A sixteenth-century Venetian roué, writer, wit, and pornographer. Use this one. Anthea's favourite. We bought it in Italy.'

'Mine too. Colin took me to the National Gallery today, talking of Italy. He took me round the new wing with all the Renaissance pictures – it was lovely. He knows such a lot. Then he took me out to lunch, to a tiny little place, very cheap and cheerful.'

'I'm glad he didn't spend a fortune on you. He's behind with his Chambers' rent at the moment.'

'Poor Colin. Life's a struggle for them.'

'He oughtn't to do so much legal aid work.'

'Patricia Saban's having a hard time too at the moment. She says Douglas discriminates against her.'

'Douglas's view is that she doesn't work hard enough. You do. But don't let's discuss Chambers now. Everyone will have a chance to have their say next month when we have our review of working practices in the clerks' room. Patricia can air her grievances then. Let's get dinner going.'

'Are we eating in the dining room?'

'Thomas has got back into his wheelchair so that he can sit at the table.'

'I'm a bit nervous of him.'

'He's terrified of you.'

'Don't be silly.'

'Says he never meets people under thirty. Says he's forgotten how to talk to them, what they're like.'

As we sit at the candle-lit table I think to myself I might forget too, if this is to be the pattern of my future.

Then the phone rings.

'Nat? There's some crackpot at the door saying he's from Zap Paramedical Services – that's on his card – he says you owe him a lot of money.'

'I sent him a cheque!'

'You forgot to sign it. He's brought it round.'

'Hell. Sara, can you be a love and pay him?'

'I've left my cheque book at the office.'

'Tell him we need him for more nursing work, that'll cheer him up. Let me speak to him.'

'Look, Nat, I'm here on my own and I've no desire to let a strange Rasta or any other kind of stranger into the flat. He's outside and he said he'd hang on and wait for you.'

'Tell him I'll be half an hour, I'll get a cab now.'

'Great. I need to talk to someone.'

'Are you OK? You sound depressed.'

'I'll tell you all when you come.'

Freddie is making coffee downstairs when I tell him I'm off. He looks startled.

'Sara is in trouble.'

'Oh.'

'I needed to go home early anyway. I feel shattered. When does your brother need the male nurse to come?'

'Go and ask him while I just finish doing the coffee.'

Thomas has now been pushed into the sitting room, where he's reading the newspaper. As I come in he looks past me for Freddie. When he realises I am alone he starts fussing with the paper, trying to fold it up. Most of it cascades onto the floor.

'Don't stop reading – I've only come to say goodbye and ask you when you'd like the nurse to come.' I hand him the loose sheets. He stares at me over glasses blankly.

'The nurse?'

'Ron.'

'Oh, yes. Any time. Say ten if it suits him.'

'Fine. I hope you sleep well despite your leg.'

'Oh, yes. I will. Valium helps. Where are you off to?'

'My flat.'

'I thought you lived downstairs.'

'That's my sister.'

'I'm confused. It's been a long day.'

'It's very good of you to come over specially for the wedding.'

'Well, I – yes. I have a feeling I'm going to be more of a liability than an asset.'

Freddie comes in at that moment. 'You're going to make a brilliant, short, best man's speech. You can take the whole of the rest of this week to compose it.'

'Full of quotations from Aretino.'

'No doubt. Nat, I think your taxi's here. I'll see you out.'

It isn't wise to make a small detour past Dave's squat, but I can't resist it. There is light in some of the windows, behind makeshift curtains. Visible through one uncovered window is a man who because of his mane of black hair for a moment looks like Dave. He's wearing a dirty red singlet and taking a motor bike to bits in an otherwise bare room. There's a girl sitting on the floor smoking.

As the taxi turns out of the street, I see Dave and Jane getting off a bus on the opposite side. Dave's laughing and holding Jane up, as if she's tripped getting off. She's got her hair in a ponytail, her face is devoid of make-up, she's wearing a denim jacket and jeans. She looks pale, tired, interesting and about fifteen. She does a little dance for Dave to show she's all right, a little rhythmic movement of the feet and hips that's so familiar. She used to do it in the kitchen at home when she'd won a point or escaped doing a chore.

I suppose they're in my line of vision for ten seconds at most, yet the image stays with me all the way home. Dave is clearly going to cross her off the list in his little book. And probably show her the list as well.

My encounter with Dave was only a few days ago, but it feels like a another life.

Ron leaps out of the Zap Paramedical van when he sees me put my key into the door.

'Sorry to hassle you, lady, but you never signed this. Your friend said wait.'

'I'm so sorry. You did a great job, I hear. Mr Mentieth wants you to go back regularly and give him some help while he's here.'

'No problem.'

'He suggested tomorrow morning, about ten.'

'Sure thing. Same address, I take it?'

'Here's the phone number on the back of the cheque. I'm really sorry you had to chase me for this – I'm a bit stressed at the moment. Not thinking straight.'

'All sorted. Just you go and relax now.' Ron pockets the cheque and grins at me. 'There was I, thinking I'd been two-timed.'

I am so tired I can hardly drag myself up the stairs. I can hear Sara playing Edith Piaf. She only does that when she's been let down by someone. I can see a long evening ahead.

Sara's in the bath. I sit on the loo, having brought the end of a bottle of wine from the kitchen. Sara's body is startlingly white, and even more startling, given her auburn hair, is her blonde bush. Her eyebrows and lashes are fair, and that should warn one, but somehow it doesn't. (Freddie says he's never seen a blonde bush.)

'Well, I got my wedding dress number two. Want to see it?'

'Of course. *Red*. Nat, you're mad.' She stares at the dress and then lies back again in the bath, shutting her eyes. 'It looks very eveningy. I liked the other one better.'

'I'll be happier in this one.'

'Suit yourself. It's your wedding.'

'So what's your problem, Sara?'

'What do you mean, my problem?'

'You said you wanted to talk.'

'That doesn't necessarily mean I've got a problem.'

'In that case, I'm off to bed. I'm knackered, I need an early night.'

'Don't be a pig. We hardly ever talk now.' Sara stands up and reaches for a towel, scattering water everywhere but luckily not on the new red silk dress. I go and hang it on the back of my door. Behind me I hear Sara say:

'Gus is going to Washington.'

'Since when?'

'Apparently he applied for a transfer there ages ago. It's come through.'

'So he told you today.'

'Not him. The rat. The bastard. The utter bastard. I knew nothing about it at all. He made sure I learned through the office grapevine because he didn't have the guts to tell me himself. The bastard! I've never felt such an idiot. God, I'm furious.'

I follow her to the kitchen where she paces up and down in

her clogs, a towel wound under her arms, her hair turbaned in another.

'Why do men always do this to me, Nat? They escape in the most shitty way. I don't even get the pleasure of a stand-up row. They just ooze away suddenly. They don't return my calls. It's getting to me. What's the matter with me?'

'Sara, nothing's the matter with you. You're terrific. You're probably too good for them, in fact, I'm sure you are—'

'Don't say a thing like that, it makes me sound worse. I'm not *good*—'

'What I meant was, you're too clever and successful and full of character. Actually you're quite good to people too but we'll let that pass.'

'You're saying I'm a paragon and men can't stand it.'

'More or less.'

'Why can't I meet another paragon, then, who can cope with me?'

'Give it time.'

'You're not right, you know. Gus is the paragon – he's got everything. Brains, good looks, charisma. And I was stupid enough to think he valued me – he – oh, God—' She collapses on to a chair and bursts into racking sobs. Her towel slips off, she slumps on to the table. I put the towel round her shoulders and hug her, waiting for the storm of crying to burn itself out.

'Oh, Nat, I thought he loved me. I thought we had the perfect open-ended modern relationship – he even said so – free but committed. All that jazz.' Tears start again, more gently.

'Perhaps you were asking too much of him.'

There's a longish pause while Sara gets into her night things – a T-shirt with HEAVEN on the front, and a man's plaid dressing gown which is probably Gus's.

'He always said that was how he liked it.'

'People don't always say what they mean. When's he off to Washington?'

'I don't bloody care. I ought to eat something. I didn't have any lunch either.' Sara gets out a yoghurt from the fridge, chops a banana into it, picks at it with a teaspoon. Then she looks up at me, her eyes intense. 'I had one of those moments today. You know, when the future opens in front of you like a great big hole and all you can see there is work, loneliness and death at the end of it.'

'Sara. You mustn't let Gus do this to you. He's not worth it.'

'No man's worth it.'

'No human's worth it. You're depressed, you need a holiday. You haven't been away for months.'

'Two weeks in North Cyprus last April. With Gus. Sod him.'

'Book yourself a break. A week in Egypt is terribly cheap at the moment – specially if you go at the last minute.'

'Who can I go with? I hate travelling alone.'

'Ask around. Or join a group – sometimes you can get lucky.'

'You're good for me, Nat. Most of the others just commiserate before they tell me their problems – the I-know-just-how-you-feel-now-listen-to-my-problems approach, which just makes me feel worse.'

'I saw an offer in yesterday's paper – yes, look, here it is – only £300 for a week in Luxor all found. It's a bargain. I feel like coming with you.'

'Why don't you?'

'I'm getting married, remember?'

'But that doesn't stop you taking breaks with your friends, does it?'

'Of course not. But Freddie and I are already taking a break in term time, and both of us feel one shouldn't do that too often. There's plenty of vacation to go away in.'

'When's the next vacation?'

'The week after Christmas.'

'Let's go away then.'

Sara's testing me. She pokes at her yoghurt, punishing her banana.

'The special offer won't be on. It's only for this month, look.'

'You wouldn't go anyway, would you?'

'Not so soon.'

'I knew it. You'll lose all your freedom. Freddie will have you tethered.'

'Balls. I can't go away in the next few months, and you can see exactly why. But you should have a break *now*.'

'I'll please myself.'

'Ask my sister. She's got nothing particular planned. She might leap at a cheap trip to Egypt.'

'We don't really know each other. Besides, you said she'll be off back to Australia soon.'

'She's decided to stay here.'

'Well, well. You sound over the moon.'

'I need some tea, not this wine.'

'Make a pot. I'll join you. So what is little sister going to do back in London?'

'Cramp my style.'

'London's a big place. You can avoid each other easily for as long as you want.'

'Not if she stays close to me, which she will. She will.'

'She didn't strike me as the clinging type.'

'Oh, no, she's certainly not clinging. She's the strong independent type, tough and pushy.'

'Why does she plague you so, Nat? Are you just imagining it?'

'I wish I was. Ever since she was born she's pushed at me, trying to do better, trying to beat me in everything. God, that sounds so childish.'

'I tell you, Nat, that most of the things that truly matter and truly hurt are childish. I sometimes think of it as the yah booh sucks syndrome. I'm stronger than you. No, you're not. Yes, I am. Prove it. OK. Tears, broken hearts. Do you get the feeling that life goes downhill? I do. We're conditioned from birth to think of life as a progress: upwards means success, downwards means failure. Personally I'm beginning to think it's an achievement to keep going at all, level if you're lucky.'

'Why has Gus moved? Is it promotion?'

'But naturally.'

'Then perhaps there's nothing personal in it—'

'Listen, Nat, give me a little credit. I'm not complaining about promotion, I'm complaining about the rat-like way Gus told me. In other words, not telling me, letting other people do his dirty work.'

It's funny how even intelligent people have to run over the same ground again and again. I used to be driven mad at college by the way the same topics would be shaken out, looked at, turned round, folded up, taken out, repeatedly. I do it myself when something's got to me. I think we do it for comfort, like sucking a dummy.

Sara went to bed at about midnight, seemingly cheered up. I was by then wide-awake, and the appalling sight of my bedroom galvanised me. I spent the next two hours putting my possessions into black plastic sacks: to keep, to wash, to give to the charity shops. The bulging black sacks settled against the wall like a row of crouching animals, rustling and breathing when I pushed past them.

The white wedding dress was in a sack of its own, with no label. I still hadn't decided what to do with it. Its successor hung on the back of the bedroom door, the last thing I saw as I finally fell asleep: a red banner against the white paintwork, flanked by those black sacks.

16

'Freddie, it's Meryl.'

'Good morning. You've just caught me. I was heading out of the door.'

'I hoped I would. How is that nice brother of yours? I was ringing to offer help if it was needed.'

'He slept well, and he will be tended later this morning by Ron of the splendidly named Zap Paramedicals. So all is under control, though it's very sweet of you to offer. I've given Tom your number in case he needs support.'

'Of course, Freddie, that's fine—'

'I must rush.'

Meryl put down the phone and looked at the messy remains of the family's breakfast. The boys had gone off to school with the usual Tuesday driver in the car pool, Sonia Tweedie. Normally there were predictable complaints from Piers and Harry about poor Sonia – her lateness, her bad driving, her silly comments. She was their least favourite of the mothers on the rota. This morning the boys, still annoyed with Meryl about their bus journey home, had departed with silent alacrity.

'Medium dudgeon.'

'What?' Dennis came back into the kitchen.

'Doesn't matter.'

'There's a meeting this evening that could run late, so don't wait supper for me.' Dennis kissed her cheek and left, banging the front door. Countless times she had asked him not to – plaster flaked down every time – but it seemed an ingrained gesture he could not stop. He said that he'd had heavy front doors all his life, he couldn't get the hang of this one at all, even after six years in what he still called the new house.

Meryl left the breakfast things to clear later, something she never normally did. She hated seeing unwashed dishes lying about. She went upstairs intending to get dressed but the phone rang before she reached the bedroom. Hoping it was Thomas Mentieth needing her services (why? never mind, she'd think about that later) she answered.

'Meryl Peak?'

'Yes. Who is it?'

'Ralph Mentieth here, Freddie's cousin.'

'Goodness.'

'I'm so sorry to bother you, but I need some information, and I can't bring myself to interrupt Freddie.'

Ralph. The unpredictable cousin, the black sheep. Dennis always said he was a rotter, but Meryl secretly found him attractive.

'How nice to hear from you. What can I do to help?'

'I've lost my invitation to the wedding. I'm not on speaking terms with most of the Mentieth family except for Freddie, so it's left me in an awkward position. I can't remember when, where, or at what time. All I know it, that it's soon.'

'Next Saturday in fact.'

'Tell me all.'

As Meryl told Ralph the relevant details she could hear the thump of reggae music in the background.

'Do you think he'd mind if I brought my partner?'

'I've no idea. Perhaps you ought to ask him. Numbers, seating—'

'Why do people bother to get married, Meryl? A wedding is always a pain.'

'I think they can be quite fun. You've had a few yourself.'

'Touché. I will admit, I'm curious to see what Freddie has snatched from her cradle. Do you approve?'

'I haven't met her yet. Her sister's—' Meryl suddenly couldn't use the word nice – Jane wasn't nice. 'Her sister's just arrived from Australia – I met her.'

'And?'

'Pretty.'

'Anthea was beautiful. She wanted me to paint her, but I couldn't make her see that my sort of portrait would not have pleased her.'

'You may have been wrong. Anthea was very artistic.'

'See you on Saturday, Meryl.'

Meryl opened the wardrobe and got out the black Issey Miyake suit she'd stolen. She often put it on and wore it round the house. The softness of the silk, the excellence of the cut, greatly cheered her. She longed to wear it outside the house so that others could see what it did for her, but she didn't dare. She held it up and stroked it, then put it back. Not today. It would distract her too much from what she had to do today. She had to decide what to wear on Saturday.

The choice was narrow and without surprise or pleasure – between her navy blue 'good suit' worn with the pink and white striped shirt, or the same suit with the emerald green shirt with a bow. Her flowery suit was far too summery. If only she could wear something of Anthea's – that cupboard was full of lovely possibilities. Perhaps she could ask Freddie—

Mad. Mad. He'd notice what was missing, he'd guess. She bundled the black suit to the back of the wardrobe out of sight, and laid the navy suit and the shirts on the bed. There was an oily stain on the jacket lapel, and neither shirt looked pristine. She'd take the lot to the cleaners, she'd try and find a new hat to match the outfit, she'd make do. When had she done anything else?

She went to the window and stared down at the dismal back garden. Rubbed patchy lawn, rusty swing, untended roses, tin junk that had once been shiny toys, a punctured football. Decaying garden furniture clustered on a small square of paving green with mould. It had stood there unmoved since the Hendersons had come for drinks in September and they'd all run inside when the rain poured down.

Tears started to run down Meryl's face. When Anthea was alive she'd tried a bit, she'd kept both house and garden under control, she'd done her best to reveal their few advantages. Not that Anthea had ever realised, or seen her sister's physical background as anything but a visual disaster. But Anthea had been Meryl's yardstick. Her sharp eyes had been watchful, her standards high. And now she was gone and the years stretched in front of Meryl full of mess, compromise, cheap clothes, chipped surfaces, muddle. And she would continue to put herself last and be kind, gush, flap, annoy her family and yet be unable to stop. Tears flowed.

That was, ironically, the morning Freddie had discovered the absence of the Issey Miyake outfit. He had unlocked the cupboard to get out his morning suit which he kept there, along with an eighteenth-century fancy dress costume complete with its wig Anthea had once bought for him at an auction of Covent Garden costumes. He looked wonderful in it on the one occasion he had worn it.

'Darling, you look like the most sizzling of Georgette Heyer's heroes. Every women will swoon.'

'Don't be ridiculous.'

'I wish you could have worn this wig when you took silk. Those dreadful grey full-bottomed doormats made you QCs all look like so many armadillos from the back.'

He fingered Anthea's clothes, her voice clear in his head. He knew the clothes so well, he could remember when she'd worn them – and of course he noticed at once that the black Issey Miyake wasn't there. Unexpectedly distressed, he went through the clothes several times with shaking hands before he relocked the cupboard and put the key back on its hook.

Mrs Wilks? Surely not. Natalie? Jane? It must have happened very recently. As he drove to court, he worried at the problem. Perhaps Natalie felt that, as his wife-to-be, she had a certain right to the clothes she found in the house. But it was unlikely, and she would have asked him anyway. She might have put it on unasked to show him how well it looked, but she wouldn't have simply taken it without a word.

Jane. She still hadn't appeared by morning. Perhaps she'd taken other things and done a bunk. He nearly drove into the lorry ahead when it stopped at a pedestrian crossing. He had to admit Jane's disappearance was distressing – he'd thought of her as a reliable person around the house during this busy and difficult week.

'Jane isn't back and she hasn't sent any message. I simply don't understand it. Here's your breakfast, Tom.' Freddie put the tray of food beside his brother.

'I don't understand the young either.'

'She's my guest – you'd have thought she'd make an effort to keep me informed of her whereabouts in case I got worried. Your egg should be soft boiled.'

'It all looks very good. I'm feeling extremely hungry.' Thomas was in his wheelchair, a rug over his knees. 'Don't forget to put the key out for Ron. I'm greatly looking forward to that bath.'

'Mrs Wilks will be here at midday, and get you your lunch.'

'What shall I do if anyone rings for you as a result of the publicity last night?'

'Put them on to Douglas. No one else. He'll deal with them. And if Jane reappears—' Freddie tailed off.

'I'm rather hoping she won't. She'll frighten the life out of me.'

'Do stop saying that.'

'It happens to be true.'

Freddie had to wait in a queue of cars to get into the court car park – security was particulary stringent that morning. Tippett's *Concerto on a Theme of Corelli* was on the radio, one of his favourite pieces of music, and his mind was far away when a voice said in his ear:

'Good morning, Your Honour.'

He swivelled round and saw a faintly familiar face bending down to his window. 'Good morning . . .' One of the new court officials, a jury officer? He didn't know her beyond this sense that he recognised her face.

'I had to talk to you, Your Honour, when I saw you there right near me. I saw the news, two attacks or is it three, terrible for you. That case has brought you a lot of trouble.'

'I'm sorry, but who are you?'

'I was on that jury, I was nervous myself in that jury room, I tell you. One of them was definitely nobbled by the police, Your Honour, it was clear as day—'

Freddie sat in horror. 'You mustn't tell me these things, you mustn't talk about the trial, it's contempt of court, you are solemnly bound as a juror never to discuss what happens in the jury room—'

'I've been so worried not speaking out, then I saw you there and I had to tell you—'

'You must talk to the jury officer, not to me. Go and ask his advice at once.'

'I got no evidence, only what I saw and heard—'

'Madam, please do as I say. Tell the jury officer, and *no one else.*'

'I thought you were the one to tell—' She looked very upset now; her face was flushed and shiny. Knitting needles stuck out of a large plastic bag she carried, two inches from Freddie's nose. The car behind honked at him for causing a delay.

'Please go away and act on my advice immediately. It's a serious matter and the right procedures must be followed.' His face was now as heated as hers, and he stalled the car as he tried to drive on. He knew he hadn't handled her well; she marched off towards the public entrance with her head bowed, her steps unsteady on her high heels. He had never been approached directly by a juror before, and the experience upset him. He told Mrs Frobisher to pass on what had happened to the jury officer immediately so that the woman could be helped. Then he sat in his room, aware that a curtain had been pulled briefly aside on an aspect of court life normally totally inaccessible to him – the mind of the juror.

Juries fascinated him. He knew that their presence on the seats was due to the shuffling of their cards by the jury officer and drawn at random; that those who weren't called were deeply disappointed and even experienced a sense of rejection; that the faces of those who settled themselves in the courtroom showed satisfaction and a sort of relief to be serving after days of waiting around in the jury assembly room and never hearing their names called. Freddie would watch them carefully as they settled down, aware that their silent, shadowy presence would grow less insubstantial if a trial lasted more than a few hours. In a long case, each face always in the same place gained such a distinct character that when someone was absent the gap was more than just an empty seat. Some jurors made furious notes, some sat placidly, some blankly, some watched the dock most of the time, some the barristers; all watched Freddie when he made any comment at all from the bench. Their receptiveness was unnerving in cases where the clarification of a complex web of uncertainties and discrepancies was the essence of his summing-up. He knew the danger of being biased, of the blotting-paper reception of his bias by the jury. He'd avoided it as best he could in the Poole trial; he'd given what seemed, in the circumstances, a masterly summing-up. He finished knowing that it could hardly have been bettered; as the jury retired he'd felt a buzz of satisfaction and pleasure.

And he remembered the woman who had accosted him; she'd stared at him fixedly throughout his speech from her corner in the second row, sitting behind a ginger-haired man whose bland sleepy expression made her alert one seem particularly vivid. That jury had obviously meshed together well in the three days of the trial – it showed as they filed in and out, smiling and making little gestures at their neighbours. Strangers had become allies in an extreme environment.

'Here's the list, Your Honour, three pleas first, then the Harrison case – just a straightforward possession of offensive weapons by the look of it. Assessed at half a day.'

'I saw a lot of press outside.'

'Don't worry about them, Your Honour, they're all here because of that dog case – you know, is it or isn't it a Rott-weiler? Before His Honour Judge Dalrymple. Are we ready, Your Honour?'

'More or less.' As Freddie spoke the internal phone went. It was Douglas.

'Your brother's just rung, sir, to say that some kind person has poured oil through your letter box. He says it looks like half a pint of diesel, but he can't get down to examine it.'

'This is getting a bit too much.'

'I just felt you should know as soon as possible, sir. Your brother's contacted the police, of course. They hadn't arrived yet when he spoke to me.'

'He's on his own, Douglas. How did he sound?'

'He sounded very cheerful, sir.'

'Tell him I'll ring him when I have a moment. It's already half past ten, Douglas, I'll have to go into court. Keep in touch with my brother, if you would, and warn him not to throw lighted matches around in his usual manner.'

'Sir—'

'It's all right, I'm teasing.'

Curiously, Freddie felt cheerful too. Oil through letter boxes was in the same league as a schoolboy trick. As he stood in court and received everyone's bows, he remembered a mad cousin of his mother's who used to pour condensed milk through the vicar's letter box when she didn't like the sermon.

Thomas found it difficult to let the police in without getting the wheelchair covered with oil: it made black tracks all the way to the sitting room. PC Partridge was most concerned and spread newspaper all over the hallway to help mop the oil up.

'It's diesel, ordinary diesel. They've chucked the empty can in the front garden. We'll test it for fingerprints but they'll have been wearing rubber gloves for sure.'

'I heard absolutely nothing after my brother left the house. I suppose oil is silent and viscous, but you'd have thought I'd have heard something. I only discovered it because I started to try and manoeuvre myself to the lavatory. Since I never got there, and it's not something a milk bottle could deal with, could you possibly give me a helping hand, Constable?'

The constable blushed but obliged, and when the two of them returned to the hall they saw a girl standing at the top of the basement stairs. She looked bedraggled and ill.

'Oh, hi. Is Freddie around? Or Natalie?'

'Neither. And you're?'

'Jane. Natalie's sister. You must be Freddie's brother.' She came further up the stairs, but not completely to the top, as if she wanted to make sure a speedy exit downwards remained an option. Then she saw the patch of oil by the front door.

'God. More trouble?'

'A minor hiccup. How do you do?' Thomas held his hand out until Jane came and shook it. This action dislodged the constable, who left, promising action.

'Would you like some coffee? That's what I came up to say.'

'Wonderful idea.'

Thomas watched the waif-like girl disappear downstairs; she

didn't look at all like her sister, which in his view was to her disadvantage. The coffee was some time in coming, and when it did arrive it was brought up by another young woman who was clearly also at home in the house. She didn't bother to introduce herself.

'Milk? I warmed it because I like it that way, but I'll fetch you cold if you prefer. Sugar?'

'Both, thank you, as they come.'

'I couldn't find any biscuits.'

'It doesn't matter. I had an excellent breakfast. I'm sorry, but I don't know who you are.'

The girl frowned. 'But I'm Jane.'

'You look quite different.'

Jane laughed, and looked fleetingly more like her sister. 'Everyone says I'm the master quick-change freak. All I did was get out of my jeans and sweatshirt, put on this dress, put my hair up, put on some make-up to hide the fact I feel knackered, and bingo.'

'I always look exactly the same. Have done for years.'

'Change your hair, that's the secret. In my case the student immediately becomes the businesswoman when I put my hair up.' Jane went and looked at herself in the overmantel mirror, pleased with what she saw. Thomas didn't much like her.

'This is excellent coffee.'

'Freddie has the best of everything. I used his Blue Mountain. But I can't find any aspirin or paracetamol – do you happen to have some?'

'I'm a veritable apothecary at the moment. There's a box on the dining-room table full of drugs. Help yourself.'

'Thanks. I've got the beginnings of something, I'm sure of it – it can't still be jet lag. Just my bloody luck to get flu this week of all weeks.'

She went off and within minutes stuck her head round the door to say: 'She'll be right now. See you later, then.' She disappeared, and before long Thomas heard the click of high heels going up the area steps and heading off down the street in the direction of the tube.

Pleased to be alone again, Thomas went into the dining room through the interconnecting doors and settled at his laptop which was installed at one end of the table. He called up the report he was halfway through, and stared at his words with the utmost pleasure. His work was the only passion of his life.

17

I suppose anyone making a big change in their lives feels as I do, but I've never been so tense. And I keep thinking of Jane and Dave Rosenberg, and those awful people who keep hounding Freddie. Oil through the front door. They're sick.

'Miss Harper – fancy a bit of crime?'

'Douglas, yes, I need to have my mind occupied.'

'There's a malicious wounding just come in – listed not before two at Southwark. Brief at court.'

'I'd better get myself down there then.'

'No hurry – straightforward section eighteen by the looks of it.'

'I'll be in my room for the next hour in that case.'

I find Patricia Saban on the phone, arguing about some ill-divided bill – a private call which continues acrimoniously for some time. I switch off and plough into a set of papers until my own phone rings. It's Jane.

'Nat, listen, I've just got back and there's a bloke upstairs who says he's Freddie's brother—'

'He is.'

'Strewth. He looks about ninety. I thought I'd better check. I said I'd make him some coffee.'

'Good on you.'

'You sound very edgy—'

'I'm working, Jane. What is this call about?'

'I thought you'd like to hear how I got on last night with Dave.'

'Not particularly and not now.'

'Miaow. Suit yourself. Anyway, Dave's fixed up an interview

for me with a film producer who wants a couple of weeks of research done. Good, isn't it.'

'Very. Mind you, anything Dave passes on rather than does himself needs careful inspection.'

'Have you got it in for Dave or something?' She says this without any undercurrents of meaning, so I begin to think maybe Dave hasn't given her the Don Giovanni treatment.

'No, Jane, I've just known him a long time.'

'I wish I felt a hundred per cent – think I'm about to get flu. Plus I've got a splitting headache—'

'Jane, you must stay well at least until Saturday. I have to have one member of my family around—' I stop, aware that Patricia is listening behind me. 'Anyway, are you busy this evening?'

'Why? What's on?'

'We're eating in – it would be nice if you were there.'

'Dine with the geriatric brigade – not very alluring.'

'Don't be so horrid.'

'Well, I might. There are a couple of people I said I'd contact but I could see them later on in the week – by the way, did you know someone had poured diesel oil through the letter box?'

'My clerk told me. Unbelievable, isn't it? I must go, Jane. I have to finish a set of papers and then I'm in court.'

As I get back to work I can see Patricia fiddling about at the window. She's clearly not in court today; she looks miserable. I deliberately blot her out; I haven't the time or the energy to listen to her problems at the moment. I'm not in the mood for female solidarity.

The riverside is magical in clear autumn light. I walk from London Bridge along the Thames towards Southwark Crown Court and watch gulls dive and wheel and boats pass; ahead is the blue and white tracery of Tower Bridge, its solid span lifted to allow the passage of a ship. I dwell on the vast grinding mechanism needed to achieve this delicate-looking effect. Dozens of children suddenly erupt out of HMS *Belfast* and scream and laugh their way towards Hay's Galleria; they play like dogs off the lead while their teachers amble behind them gossiping. A gust of wind brings a shower of sere leaves down onto the children as they run; a tug hoots as it passes.

I can't go and shut myself into the court yet – I decide to eat a sandwich outside rather than use the canteen. I buy what I need and sit mindlessly watching the fast-moving water. No wonder rivers are constantly used as images of life.

Samuel McKenzie is a West Indian in his late fifties; his hair is grizzled and his glasses need a good clean. They're probably also clouded by weeping – tears flow with great ease as he tells me his story. He's a security man in a big corporation, he had an argument with two of the male cleaners as he came off duty, he'd got angry and then was accused of attacking the two of them with a knife that happened to be lying around in the staff kitchenette. He said he was acting in self-defence – he wept again as he tried to tell me how big and aggressive the two men were.

I can see why the barrister who'd prepared the case initially had recommended that McKenzie was not called into the witness box. He would be incapable of coherent statements when under pressure; it would be much better if the jury saw him as the gentle-looking and confused man he undoubtedly was sitting silently in the dock. The cleaners had suffered very small injuries – certainly not serious enough to warrant the fact that they had insisted on being taken to hospital by ambulance.

'They're bad men, bad,' Mr McKenzie keeps repeating as we sit in the cells. 'And they hate black people.'

'I see your character witness has known you a long time and goes to the same church as you.'

'Yes, indeed, Mr Hanna is the best friend a man could have.' Tears threaten again, and I take McKenzie's hand.

'Have faith, Mr McKenzie. I feel this case shouldn't have been brought to court at all, the evidence is so conflicting and the wounds so trivial. Have faith that the jury will see it the same way.'

'I do have faith, miss.' He grips my hand convulsively. 'That's the one thing I do have.'

Faith. A woman sitting in the public gallery, clearly Mrs McKenzie, is wearing a crucifix on her bulging black woolly front. She keeps fingering it and tugging obsessively on the chain, an ingrained habit that shows she hasn't just put the cross on for today's hearing. She shuts her eyes when her husband is led into the dock, which in this box-like modern court is only a dozen feet away from her. His heavy stressed breathing is audible throughout the court. Mrs McKenzie's lips are moving as if in prayer.

Faith in God. It's not an emotion I have ever truly experienced, even as a child. The only faith I have is in my brain and my tongue.

Well-placed, as it turns out for my client. The prosecution witnesses – the two cleaners – are a pair of unsavoury South London wide boys, and their inconsistencies and their belligerence leave them wide open to an exhilarating cross-examination. I love it. I can feel the jury stirring in delight as I encourage the two of them to contradict one another, as I draw attention to their size in comparison with poor wizened Mr McKenzie. His plea of self-defence seems more and more justified. I stop before I completely destroy their credibility; it's never a good idea to do that: it can swing sympathy the wrong way.

The judge, an assistant recorder called Harry Swithin-Soames who seems pleased with the effect of my cross-examination, decides to rise early to deal with another matter and postpone final speeches until tomorrow. I'm extremely relieved; Douglas has slightly misled me about the apparent simplicity of this case. The barrister for the prosecution is a tough, rather fearsome woman called Janet Antrobus I haven't been against before, but I've heard a lot of talk about her. She's bulky with a heavy thatch of black hair cut in a monkish bob. She chain-smokes out of court, and enters with an almost visible – certainly pungent – aura of tobacco; her wig is yellowed by smoking with clients in the corridors of the court. She's unmarried – rumour has it she's a lesbian – and her plump white hands are remarkable for the unexpected length of her red nails. Francis Bates calls her Cruella Deville.

We happen to leave the court building together, and I remark that the case should have been thrown out by the CPS long before it got to this stage. She vehemently disagrees as she lights up a Gauloise and blows the smoke in my face.

'The defendant picked up a knife and cut two people with it. You can't ignore that sort of behaviour.'

As she mainly does prosecution work I could see the shadow of vested interest in her opinions.

'No, no, it's potentially a nasty little incident. But tell me, Nancy—'

'Natalie.'

'All this victimisation of your poor Head of Chambers – what on earth did he say in his judgment to cause all these attacks?'

'I don't know any details, I'm afraid. Of course it's been blown up by the press—'

'I realise that. But I have a lot of respect for Frederick Mentieth – he's one of the few recorders I like coming before – and I can't imagine him saying anything ill-considered in a sensitive civil rights case.' She started to cough, a deep raucous smoker's cough that came up from her pelvis.

'I'm sure he didn't.' I'm unwilling to discuss the case with Janet Antrobus – she's a famous gossip.

'Want a lift back to the Temple?' Smoke poured from her nostrils as she spoke. One eye was half-closed over her cigarette, the other flickered with an indefinable hidden invitation.

'I've got a return ticket on the riverbus.'

'How bold of you. I drive everywhere. Join me, be a devil and waste that ticket.'

'No, thanks, Janet. I love the river trip at sunset.'

'Goodbye then, Nancy. *À demain*.'

The tide has turned, the Thames is now choppy, and there's no sunset because a bank of cloud has moved up the sky. Spray dashes against the side of the riverbus, splashing on the windows. It's very snug away from the rough wet world outside; I feel lulled into sleepy abstraction by the contrast.

As I step, still abstracted, off the boat, I knock my left shoe and it jumps off my foot straight into the water. The conductor handing me ashore looks horrified as my shoe swirls away sinking fast.

'I'm very sorry, miss - how did that happen—'

'Don't worry, it was entirely my fault. I was in a dream.'

So there am I hopping up the long gangway to the Embankment, where I attract a certain amount of amused attention as I try to hail a taxi. You can't help feeling silly with only one shoe on, so I take it off and use it to wave down a cab.

'The nearest shoe shop. My other shoe is probably down by London Bridge by this time.'

The driver and I discuss possibilities and finally decide on Bond Street.

'Gives you a bit more choice, like. There's a shoe shop every inch of the way. You won't have to hop too far between them.'

'To Bond Street then.'

'Never had a barefoot fare before.'

'And I've never lost a shoe in the Thames before.'

'Bound to bring you luck.'

I feel quite light-headed by the time the cab drops me outside a Russell and Bromley. I could have avoided this by going back with Janet Antrobus, but I'm not sorry. I buy some plain black court shoes and a stunning pair of red suede mules to wear at my wedding.

PART TWO

18

A shoe dropping into the grey-brown river, dragged out of sight by the racing tide, dancing half-sunk through the turbulent murky water until it arrives alone on a sandbank perhaps, or is submerged in a pile of rubbish beached by an eddy in the prevailing current – I often thought about that shoe.

My life took a new turn the day I lost it. Changes which had begun slowly gathered speed and threatened to overwhelm me.

'Your sister just phoned. She wants you to ring her as soon as possible. And there are these two other messages.' Sharon the receptionist hands me a pair of slips as I pass her desk.

'Thanks. Did she say where she was?'

'No. She seemed to think you'd know, Miss Harper.'

What is Jane up to, pestering me in Chambers? It doesn't look good, and it isn't her style. She's too cool. I ring Freddie's house and of course get Thomas.

'Is Jane in?'

'I think she may be downstairs. Someone came in through the basement door not long ago.'

'Could you possibly shout for her, Thomas?'

'Well, it's a bit awkward actually. I'm not in the wheelchair at the moment, I'm in bed.'

'Sorry, sorry. I'll ring again, and just let it ring until she picks it up.'

'Apologies for my uselessness.'

'No problem.'

When Jane finally picks up the receiver, her voice is very quiet. 'I'm scared, Nat. I feel so ill.'

'Oh, Jane. Is it flu?'

'It doesn't really feel like flu. I've got funny cramps on and off, I feel sick, but the truly scary thing is my sight.'

'What do you mean?'

'I can't see properly.'

'Maybe you need new contact lenses—'

'Nat, I think I'm going blind. It's as if someone's squirted cloudy stuff in my eyes.' She starts to cry, but controls herself at once. She is panting.

'Jane, listen, take a deep breath and calm down. When did this blindness start?'

'Today. And I've got palpitations too. Oh, God.' Her crying starts again.

'I'm going to ring my doctor right now and get her to see you this evening. I'll ring you straight back. Chin up, Jane, and wait by the phone, otherwise Thomas will pick it up first.'

To my relief my doctor, Jenny Morton, is on duty and takes my call after I've hassled the receptionist.

'Jenny, it's Natalie Harper here. No, I'm fine, but my sister has arrived from Australia and promptly collapsed with some dreadful disease. Could you see her tonight?'

'Describe her symptoms.'

'Sickness, cramps, partial loss of sight, palpitations. And she says it all started today – though she has been complaining of jet lag for days, so she must have been feeling off-colour.'

'Did she mention any irregularities with her urine, by any chance?'

'No.'

'Let's hope it's just a very virulent flu virus she's picked up on the plane. Tell her to come here at six, I'll fit her in as surgery ends.'

'Thanks, Jenny, you're wonderful.'

So I ring Jane back, arrange for a taxi to take her straight to the surgery.

'Will you come there?'

'Promise. I'm leaving now. The surgery's only just round the corner from the flat.'

'Nat, I really am scared.'

This is so unlike Jane that I begin to feel frightened too. I rush upstairs and try to see Freddie but he's in consultation so I leave him a note about the latest of our problems. It's as if some cosmic joker is deliberately aiming at us.

I take another taxi as someone warns me there's another bomb scare on the tube. Luckily one has just delivered a solicitor to Chambers so I don't waste any more time. It's well after six when I get back to the flat. There's no one home yet, and the place stinks of dirty carpets, dust, stale food and cigarette smoke. It will be bliss to be out of it soon.

I go straight out again to the surgery; there's only one route Jane could take, and it passes a chemist. I pop my head in just in case she's in there collecting drugs, but there's no sign of her. When I turn the corner and arrive at the surgery I'm surprised to see it all dark and clearly shut. Puzzled, I run back to the flat in case Jane has taken a perverse route there. No one is there, and I discover that Sara has forgotten to switch on the answerphone. I try ringing the surgery but the call is diverted to a central receptionist and there is no message for me. There's nothing to do but wait. I pace around, utterly tense.

I try ringing Dave, but he's out. Perhaps that's lucky. I think of other friends, the old gang – Simon, Lucy, Sam, Nick, Amy, Charlie, Ginny – and I realise how difficult it is to ring friends for a casual chat if you've ignored them for ages. Freddie has taken up my life, and I haven't seen enough of my friends recently to know the gossip.

I look out of the window but there's no sign of anyone familiar in the street. I pop my head into Mark's room. It's bare and tidy, but dirty. His sheets and pillowcase are grey with use. I shut the door and decide to have a bath and get cleaned up ready for this evening. My hair needs washing; too late, dripping wet, I discover the hair-dryer's broken. I wrap my hair firmly in a towel and try on the red dress and the new shoes. I look as if I'm on my way to a nightclub. All my old fears of being wrongly dressed flood back – this outfit is even more inappropriate than the cream wedding dress.

I put a navy jacket over the dress, and search for a red cloche-shaped hat which I've had for ages but never worn. I bought it in a sale because it suited me so well. By a stroke of luck (the first today) it's the same red as the dress, and they all look good together. I'm flooded with a quite disproportionate relief – how silly I am to mind so much—

The phone rings. It's Doctor Morton, ringing from a noisy public place.

'Natalie Harper? Look, I'm at St Thomas's with your sister. We tried to ring you but got no answer. She's just been admitted—'

'Oh, God. What's the matter with her, Jenny?'

'Acute kidney failure.'

'*Kidney*—'

'When you told me the symptoms I was afraid it might be. Heart arrhythmia, loss of sight – hullo, are you there? Natalie?'

'Yes. I'll come at once. Oh, God.'

'She'll need her things. Could you bring her spongebag, nightdress, some underwear, all that stuff. She's menstruating at the moment, so a supply of tampons. Plus her contact lens kit – she's very worried she hasn't got her equipment with her.'

'Where shall I come?'

'Renal unit. She'll be on dialysis by the time you arrive, I hope. They're setting it up now. Take care, Natalie, this is a shock for you. See you soon.'

The call ends but I stand frozen, holding the receiver as it burrs in my ear. Then I drop it back with a clatter.

No worse, there is none. The half-forgotten words go round and round in my brain. *No worse, there is none*. I get dressed numbly, trying to remember where they come from because I can't cope with thinking about Jane.

I don't ring Freddie, I am too stunned. I simply get into yet another taxi and head for his house to collect Jane's things. I have to stop at a cash point to get money and my hands are shaking so much it takes me some time to key in the right number.

No worse, there is none. Black Tuesday. The fates, the furies, they're all after me. Toils, nets. No worse, there is none.

I let myself in and hurry past the mess of oil-soaked newspaper. I can see Freddie isn't back yet – the wrong lights are on. I call out to Thomas as I pass that it's only me, and rush downstairs.

It's difficult to find everything Jane needs in the mess. I know her lens kit is all in a small bag which she usually carries with her. At last I find it, half under the bed. There's a new box of Tampax, freshly opened, sitting beside her alarm clock. I put both in a carrier bag, and add the book she's reading (Freddie's precious hardback signed edition of Anthony Powell's *A Question of Upbringing* but never mind). A box of tissues – beside it is a worn brown object. I pick it up and memories return I didn't know I had. I'm holding Sid, the small teddy bear Jane was given one Christmas. I got one too, but mine is long gone and I no longer remember its name. Sid has lost an eye and his jersey is unravelling. He smells the same, though, that sweet teddy smell that comes from fake fur and sawdust. I put him in the bag too, along with the tissues.

I must leave a note for Freddie. No worse, there is none. I just can't write it, I can't tell him yet. Maybe there's been a misdiagnosis, maybe Jane has got some nasty tropical disease that's hit her kidneys which a dose of antibiotics will clear up. Maybe. I can't write the note. I try to creep out of the basement door but Jane has double-locked it and I have no key. I steal back upstairs but Thomas hears me and calls out.

'You couldn't just help me into my wheelchair, could you? Ron's shown me how to do it but I don't think I want to try it on my own.'

'Of course.'

Thomas is transformed. He's clean-shaven, his hair gleams, his clothes no longer stink.

'So Ron has done his stuff.'

'He is excellent. I've booked him to come every day. What about a drink with me, Natalie?'

'I've got to rush out, I'm really sorry. Tell Freddie – well, just tell him something urgent has cropped up and I won't be here for supper.'

'That's a pity.'

'I'll ring him later.'

'Family matters?'

'Yes.'

I help Thomas to settle himself in the sitting room and draw the curtains for him. My taxi is still waiting outside and I wave to reassure the driver that I'm coming soon.

'"No worse, there is none"' – do you happen to know where those words come from?'

Thomas is already reciting before I finish.

> *No worse, there is none. Pitched past pitch of grief,*
> *More pangs will, schooled at fore pangs, wilder wring . . .*

It's from the beginning of a sonnet by Gerard Manley Hopkins.'

'Of course. I did him for A level.'

'Wonderful poet.'

I leave him chanting the poem. As I shut the front door, he's got to:

> *O the mind, mind has mountains; cliffs of fall*
> *Frightful, sheer . . .*

I run down the steps to escape the rest.

Never in my life have I had so many taxi rides in one day. The diesel smell and rumble of the motor, the heavy clunk of the doors, the square space of a London taxi are now for ever welded into my consciousness as part of the unfolding of disaster.

'Jane has been functioning, unknown to anyone, on one kidney all her life; the other is vestigial and never developed properly. An infection appears to have destroyed her good kidney—'

'Oh, God.' Jenny Morton and I stand by the lifts which constantly fill with and disgorge taut-faced stressed people, whether patients, their families or hospital staff. 'How long will she be in here?'

My doctor hesitates, not quite meeting my eye. 'It's hard to say.'

'She came over specially for my wedding on Saturday.'

'She told me. She said she was determined to be there.'

'But she won't be, Jenny. I can see it in your face.'

'No. I haven't told her yet.'

I can feel tears gathering. Not just because of Jane, because of everything. I feel as if the turn of events is telling me not to get married.

'Don't cry, Natalie. We've caught her in time. If it had happened on her travels somewhere, she would have died.'

The lift doors open and shut, open and shut. There's a picture on the wall behind Jenny, a print of sheep crowded together in a field, all facing the viewer, staring out with impassive yellow eyes, woolly backs exaggerated into grey balloons. Amongst them is a goat, head turned, out of pattern. Scapegoat. I sob.

'Come on, Natalie. Let's go to the canteen and have a coffee.'

'I want to see Jane—'

'It won't do either of you any good if you go to her in this state. Come on, here's the lift.'

She bundles me in; we stand, surrounded by the heavy silence of strangers. No one's eyes meet except Jenny's and mine.

'Don't you have to get home to your family, Jenny?'

'My children are away this week with my mother – it's half-term. So I'm free to do as I please.' She leads me to a table, fetches two cups of coffee, sits down close to me.

'Jenny, you're being so kind.'

'This is what being a GP should be about. Being there in a crisis.'

I look at Jenny Morton with close attention for the first time. She's always so friendly and approachable as a doctor I haven't ever thought about her as a private person.

'How many children have you got?'

'Three. The oldest is seven. The last wasn't intended.' She grins at me. 'Doctors should be in control of their lives, I know, but there you are.'

'How comforting. What are they called?'

'Clara, Anna, and Jeremy.'

'So your mistake was your son?'

'It was a lovely surprise.'

'I can't imagine having my own children.'

'Does the man you're going to marry want them? Make sure he does.'

'Jenny, I've no idea. I'm feeling desperate about getting married, desperate about everything.'

'I can see that.'

'I love Freddie, I really do. More than anyone else I've ever met. But he's a lot older than me. Fourteen years older. He's a widower.'

'That's not too much. Does he already have children by his first wife?'

'No. I don't know why they didn't have any. I haven't asked. I don't want to know too much about his first marriage. He's said they were happy together.'

'Better that way. He'll be a good husband second time round as well.'

'I wish I didn't feel so uneasy.'

'Tell me why you are, if you like. It might help.'

'I can hardly articulate it.' The word articulate lands between us like a spiky object.

'Try.'

'My sister is so powerful. Her influence on my life has been – has been malign.' Another word that spins and lands, this time in leaden silence. Jenny Morton waits for me to go on.

'When I was very young, my sister threw a net over me while I was lying on the beach, dreaming with my eyes shut in the sun. A wet, old fishing net which stank of tar and awful rotting things. I couldn't get it off me. I was terrified. I could hear her laughing, mocking. It was one of the worst moments of my life, I can still feel that net and all this happened twenty years ago and more. I keep telling myself I shouldn't mind any more. I should forget it.'

'Better to look straight at it. It sounds an unpleasant experience.'

'I've had a thing about nets ever since.'

'I'm not surprised.'

'Jenny, I'm afraid she's going to net me again. All my life until she went to Australia she was there nudging at me, doing the same things only better, pushing at my standards by excelling at them herself. Now she's back, I'm afraid.' There is a long silence.

'You don't have to tell me any more if you can't.'

'I'm afraid she's going to take Freddie away from me. I don't want to marry him and then lose him to her. I'd rather not marry him in the first place.'

The words come out unplanned; I had not consciously thought

them. I stare at Jenny as she fingers her coffee cup. She doesn't see how surprised I am.

'Don't be defeatist, Natalie. You strike me as a positive person, you always have. Tell Jane to keep away from him. Tell Freddie about your fears. Warn him about her.'

'I tried but I found I couldn't. It sounds so petty. He sees Jane differently, and I can tell he finds her attractive.'

'It's common for men to be attracted to sisters. But it's you he's chosen. Hold on to that.'

'He didn't know her when he chose me. And now there's another fear I have to live with. I was thinking about it in the taxi on the way here. You know as well as I do that there's only one way out for Jane: a kidney transplant. And we both also know that the most suitable donor is likely to be a member of her family. My father is in Australia. That leaves me.'

'Natalie, you shouldn't assume any of this. I mean it. Yes, she'll need a transplant if she isn't to spend a lifetime on dialysis. But tissue-typing apart, you are clearly not the right person to give her a kidney if you feel like this, and no doctor would expect you to do it or even recommend it. The donor is much more likely to be the victim of a traffic accident than you. There's no need to worry about it, it's an absolute waste of your spirit.'

'You're probably right.'

'I know I'm right.'

'But you can surely understand that now the possibility is there, I can't just snuff it out. It's sitting in the corner of my mind like a toad.'

'Try not to think about it.'

'Perhaps I ought to find out if I am compatible.'

'I'm going to have another coffee.'

'How does one have one's tissue typed?'

'Do you want a coffee?'

'No thanks.'

'You have a blood test and go from there.' She fetches herself a coffee.

'It's funny, but I thought they needed a bit of your flesh. Tissue. Just blood. That simple.'

'I can get the process started any time you want if it will give you peace of mind.' Jenny stares rather intensely at me;

she has got very clear blue eyes with black flecks in them. I sometimes find them rather unsettling; they are at odds with her friendly relaxed manner. 'But there's no hurry, you know. It'll be several weeks before Jane stabilises enough to think about the next stage. Please don't worry about it. Where are you going on your honeymoon?'

'Budapest. Do you think we ought to cancel going abroad because of Jane?'

'Of course not.'

'People will think I'm heartless.'

'So let them. She's in very good hands.'

'Freddie might think I was heartless.'

'Let's go and see Jane.'

I wait in the reception area outside the Renal unit while Jenny finds the ward sister. Supper is being cleared away from the wards; the air is full of the sweetish smell of left-over hospital food. Above me on the wall is a strip cartoon of a little man lying in his underwear with a tube running into his stomach from a bag of liquid suspended above him. *CAPD – The New System that gives you Freedom* reads the caption. There's another drawing showing our hero's guts with tappets and tubes inserted. Finally the little man smiles as he runs off, now fully dressed and minus the tube.

I've always mistrusted any diagrams that resort to using cheerful cartoon figures to get a message across. Reality is banished; the Tom and Jerry syndrome operates. Appalling violence squashes flat the protagonists who then spring back into three-dimensional shape in the next frame. As a child I suffered with them and was never able to laugh at their unscathed resurrection.

'Come on, Natalie. Jane's in a side ward on her own. This is Sister Pennington.'

I follow Jenny Morton and the neat, rounded ward sister into a side room full of machinery. Jenny gently takes my arm.

Jane has a tube like an aerial sticking out of her neck. The tube is full of bloodstained liquid. More tubes enter her arms, bags of clear fluid are suspended in rows above her. She looks half-dead. I stop in the doorway, the world tilting.

I have to sit down to let my faintness subside. I hear Sister Pennington telling Jane quietly that her sister has arrived, but Jane doesn't move. The dialyser, the size of a juke box, whirrs behind her head. She is chained to it by those brutal tubes.

'She's feeling very woozy, poor thing. She'll be a lot better tomorrow.' Sister Pennington peers at dials; Jenny holds my hand.

'Nat.'

Jane's whisper comes from barely moving grey lips. I get up, free my hand to touch hers; tubes are bound into it inches away. Her fingers move under mine and I stroke them more firmly.

'I'm here.'

'Nat, tell Dave to ring that film producer.'

'Don't worry about it—'

'Tell Dave to explain why I've let him down. It looks bad.'

Her fingers are twitching, she hasn't opened her eyes.

'I'll talk to Dave and make sure he passes on the message.'

'Say I'll be in contact the moment I'm out of here.'

Sister Pennington is smiling a fixed smile, and does not meet my eyes. 'There, Jane, now you've passed on that message you must relax and stop worrying. Trust your sister to do everything that has to be done.'

'Jane, I've brought all your things. I've tried to think of everything you might need. I even put old Sid in.' My voice breaks.

But Jane doesn't answer. Her eyelids haven't even flickered. I've never seen anyone look so ill. Tears of pure fear collect in my eyes as I leave the ward; Jenny takes me to a row of chairs and sits me down, putting an arm around me.

'She doesn't understand how ill she is, Jenny.'

'They'll explain everything tomorrow, when she's feeling a bit stronger. When you're first dialysed it's always like this. Under the circumstances, she's doing fine.'

'There's no way out for her.'

'Well—'

'She'll die if she isn't given a transplant or if she stops dialysis.'

'She'll die, yes.'

'She thinks she's going to get better.'

'She is going to get better—'

'No, I mean she thinks this is a passing phase and she'll go back to how she was. Life as normal. Her life will never be normal again.'

'They are very good here at helping patients accept the inevitable.'

'Jane never accepts the inevitable – she thinks she can change it.'

'Not this time. Renal failure is renal failure.'

'No worse, there is none.'

'Sorry?'

A group of laughing, chatting visitors come out of the lift and go past us into the Renal unit. A girl of about twelve is holding a huge bunch of chrysanthemums swathed in creaking cellophane and mauve florist's ribbon.

'These are for Mum,' she says to Sister Pennington who appears at that moment from Jane's room. 'I chose them.'

'Wonderful! Let's go and surprise her then, Louise. She's been waiting all afternoon to see you.'

I watch the girl run ahead into the ward beyond, and then Jenny and I leave in silence. Outside it's viciously windy, and I get grit in my eyes as I look out for my last taxi of the day.

19 ∫

Freddie's consultation lasted until well after seven, and by the time he got home he was hungry and exhausted. He tripped over the oily newspapers and groaned at the damage to the carpet. The house was in semi-darkness; clearly Natalie had not come in yet.

'Tom?'

'Thought you were never coming home.' His brother's voice was slurred. 'Sorry, old chap, but I've been driven to drinking neat whisky because the soda ran out and I couldn't do anything about it.'

'Let me just get some more and I'll join you. Where is everyone?'

'No idea.'

Freddie fetched soda and looked in vain for a note from either Natalie or Jane; the flat was empty and still in chaos.

'Little bitches.' He didn't mean to say it, and he surely didn't mean it – he was just tired after his long and tricky consultation. He poured a packet of nuts into a bowl and went back to his brother.

'So what's been going on?'

'Ron came and did his stuff admirably.'

'I'm glad to hear you've had some attention today.'

'Mrs Wilks gave me lunch. And both Natalie and her sister have been here – the latter gave me coffee and Natalie set me up in here. I forgot to ask her for more soda.' Thomas ate nuts by the handful.

'Is Natalie coming back here for supper, did she say?'

'I honestly can't remember exactly what she said. Too much

whisky on an empty stomach. I think she won't be here to eat.'

'I'm going to ring up for a curry, which they will deliver soon with luck.'

'Good thought. Get a lot.'

'It's most unlike Natalie not to leave me a note. Are you sure she didn't?'

'I've remembered what she said – something urgent had cropped up and she would ring you.'

'No more details?'

'She was quoting Gerard Manley Hopkins.' Thomas hiccuped on the name.

'*Hopkins?*'

'No worse, there is none.'

'I've never heard her quote anything before.'

'Then she ran out.'

'I suddenly feel rather old.'

When Natalie walked in soon after nine, the two men had finished eating and were watching the news. She kissed Freddie's cheek.

'There's some curry in the kitchen for you.'

She warmed it up and rejoined them; Freddie squeezed her hand without taking his eyes off the screen. She sat quietly eating until he switched off the television and turned towards her.

'Excuse us, Tom, while we go and catch up on the day as we clear up and make coffee.'

'Sorry not to be of any help—'

'You never were, so what's the difference!'

Thomas laughed, a curious rusty sound, as they took the tray of empty plates and dishes downstairs.

'What's been going on, Natalie? I was quite worried. A note would have been helpful.'

'It's Jane. She's in hospital.'

'What's happened now?'

'She collapsed and my doctor was very quick to diagnose the problem – thank goodness she saw at once how serious it was—'

Freddie took Natalie by the shoulders and stopped her gabbling.

'Just tell me what has happened.'

'Jane has acute kidney failure. She's on dialysis.'

'Good God. This is dreadful news. But I find it hard to believe she's gone from apparent health to desperate sickness – are they sure of their diagnosis?'

'Dr Morton says there is no doubt. They wouldn't put her on a kidney machine if there was, would they.'

'Some hospitals are capable of anything in my long experience of PI.'

'They're sure. I saw her, Freddie. She looked terrible. And she had tubes jammed into her neck. Oh, Freddie, it was awful.'

'You poor thing. What a shock.'

'I feel as if we're living in a Greek tragedy, with new disasters coming at us one after another.'

Freddie put his arms round Natalie and they stood for some time in silence until her trembling calmed down.

'I'd like to stay here tonight, Freddie. I've had enough of my flat.'

'You can move in this moment. You know you can.'

'I felt superstitious about it—'

'Don't be silly. Move in. Give the flat up for ever. I'll go and get your stuff for you any time.'

'You're so good to me.' Natalie started to shake again, and then burst into racking sobs. Freddie sat her down at the kitchen table, fussed over her, hugged her.

'It's been such an awful day on all levels. I even lost my shoe in the Thames.'

'How on earth did you manage that! I didn't know walking on the water was one of your accomplishments.'

Natalie's sobs turned to giggles as she blew her nose. 'I was getting off the riverbus. Oh, Freddie, it is so wonderful to come here and pour everything out and know you're there.'

'Now tell me more about Jane. She didn't give us any warning of this, unless I was very unobservant.'

'She wasn't feeling well but she thought it was jet lag and kept going. Apparently she's been living on one kidney all her life without knowing it, and the second one developed some virulent infection and was knocked out of action. Badly scarred, is how Dr Morton put it. Finally it just gave up working at all, which is why Jane developed palpitations and lost some of her sight amongst other symptoms.'

'Poor little thing.'

Natalie shut her eyes; Freddie looked so concerned as he said this she had a hysterical desire to laugh. Jane could never be described as a poor little thing, never, never, but he clearly thought she was.

'So she will miss the wedding having come all the way specially.'

'Yes. They haven't told her yet what's wrong.'

'Oh, poor Jane, it's such bad luck. Just as she hoped to start a new life here.'

'Do you think we ought to postpone – postpone everything?' Natalie stared fixedly at Freddie. He took her hands; they were extremely cold.

'We can't. There are too many people involved.'

'I don't want to. I was just asking you.'

'I realise how difficult all this is for you, with your only sister seriously ill.'

'What about the honeymoon?'

'What do you mean?'

'Should we go?'

'Look, Natalie, what's got into you? Your sister is ill, but she's in an excellent hospital. Don't let's lose a sense of proportion. Our future is important too – we're going to Budapest as planned and that's it – unless things get much worse. I've wanted to see that city all my adult life and I want to see it now, with you. But if you honestly want to postpone the honeymoon, we will. I'd rather not.'

'I love you, Freddie, I love love *love* you!'

Natalie got up and hugged him so energetically they both fell over. They started to laugh, Freddie kissed Natalie hard and her gurgles of laughter turned into grunts of wild desire. Tongues tangled, teeth bit, as they rolled over and tore off clothing.

'What about your brother—'

'Bugger Tom. Oh, Natalie, I love it inside you. Hold me, hold me—'

'Freddie, Freddie—'

'Hurry, I'm coming—'

'Come, come—'

'What about you—'

'It doesn't matter, all I needed was for you to do this, go on, go on—'

The kitchen chair fell over as Freddie climaxed and they both started laughing again. By the time they went upstairs with the coffee their flushes had faded, and since Thomas had switched the television on and was sheepishly watching a Western they assumed he had heard nothing.

After a comfortable night in each other's arms, Freddie and Natalie decided to leave the house together to drive to Chambers before going to their separate courts. Natalie enjoyed the quiet bustle of preparation; the briefcases lined up in the hall, the last-minute domestic arrangements. Even the sight of the oil stain did not spoil her mood.

'I must just ring Mrs Wilks and tell her what to do about the carpet.' Freddie dialled as he opened his mail. 'Hullo, it's Freddie Mentieth speaking. Yes, I know. But we'll have it replaced, Mrs Wilks, and I'd like you to ring up the suppliers for me. All the details are in Anthea's household book, the one that lives in the kitchen. Type of carpet, colour, supplier, everything. Look it up under the section marked FLOORING. Just give them a ring and tell them to recarpet the hall a.s.a.p. It's unlikely the colour will be unattainable – it's a good Wilton, and Anthea always chose lines that had a long life.'

'Bless her.'

'I'm very grateful for this, Mrs Wilks. I'm in court all day, I haven't got time to do it myself.'

'It will be a pleasure. I'm glad you don't want to change her colours.'

'Of course not.'

'I think of Mrs Mentieth every time I clean that house, bless her.'

'Bless *you*, Mrs Wilks.'

Mrs Wilks's habit of blessing everyone constantly had irritated Anthea as much as it did him.

*   *   *

Freddie and Natalie sat in the thick rush-hour traffic chatting happily; the severe effect of their white shirts, dark suits, black shoes was undermined by the faint smell of the rose oil Natalie had rubbed on her skin after her shower, and the French baroque music, Lully or Rameau – delightful measured dances – pouring from the music system.

'I would never have believed it of George.'

'He's done worse things.'

'But to leave his junior in the lurch like that, just because he wanted to start another case.'

'He'd say it was good training. I told him the solicitor had complained and he just laughed and said it wouldn't stop them using him again.'

'How is he so successful?'

'Because he's a bloody good advocate. Unscrupulous. If you have scruples, you don't succeed at the Bar.'

'Freddie, you're not usually so cynical!'

'Yes, I am. I've hidden it from you, I've been shielding you from the real Frederick Mentieth. He's a cynical hard-bitten silk through and through.'

'But not unscrupulous?'

'I sometimes wonder. I'd like to think not.'

'You would never do what George Warne's just done.'

'I've been strongly tempted to. It's painful to see a case you regard as yours and have done a lot of work on going to someone else because you're stuck in another case that's overrun.'

'The big difference between you and George is that you possess the milk of human kindness; cliché, I know, but it's true, and George doesn't.'

'That and a few tens of thousands per annum. He's the highest earner in Chambers.'

'I thought you were about equal.'

'Not so at all. If you promise to be discreet I'll show you the next print-out of gross Chambers earnings.'

'Where does Colin come?'

'Low.'

'Sometimes I feel quite threatened by the lack of structure. Everything's so fluid and secretive. In other lines of business you know what people earn, where they are in the hierarchy. Barristers talk about good years and bad years but they never say how good or bad. Even Colin, who clearly has a cash flow problem which he constantly moans about, leaves everything vague.'

'He does too much crime. He should diversify.'

'I do quite a lot of crime—'

'You're developing a nicely mixed practice though. I'm proud of you, and so is Douglas.'

'It's a matter of luck—'

'Luck doesn't make you a good advocate.'

'But it gives you more chance to develop into one. Patricia Saban has no luck. She doesn't get enough court work. She'll lose her nerve.'

'Probably.'

'You don't sound too worried.'

'I think we made a mistake taking her on. She'd be better off using her law in the Serious Fraud Office or the Home Office – she's no advocate.'

'We all know Douglas doesn't like her. He's making sure she doesn't get a chance to show how good she is. Have you actually heard her in court?'

'I haven't, I admit.'

'But because of Douglas you think she's no advocate. That man can make or break us all at will and he's decided to break poor Patricia. I hate the power barristers' clerks have over people who are their superiors in training and intelligence.'

'I wouldn't underestimate Douglas's intelligence.'

'He hasn't sat and sweated through difficult exams.'

Freddie parked the car in the Temple without answering. Natalie wriggled her toes in the slightly tight new shoes.

'Well?'

'Well what?'

'Don't you agree in general about clerks?'

'I've been well served by them all my life. First by old Stan Bamford, and then by Douglas. I'm not complaining. Perhaps I've been lucky but there you are.'

Freddie got out of the car, leaving Natalie sitting there wanting to shout at him that he had no idea what it was like to be victimised in the way Patricia was. Yet she also knew it was a battle she wasn't going to fight any further. Patricia would have to sink or swim on her own.

She suddenly caught sight of Patricia herself in the distance, also coming into Chambers early. She swallowed, sure that her sense of confused guilt must be emanating from her like a ray.

After half an hour of administration, Freddie got back into the car and headed east to Snaresbrook and another day on the Bench. The sun shone, music (now Beethoven's first piano trio) filled his ears, and a sense of release, of letting go, flooded through him. Two women stood at a traffic light laughing delightedly at something; a beautiful ship was cruising level with him on the Thames as he drove in thick traffic down the Embankment towards the City.

I take the tube to Southwark Crown Court this time. It's a beautiful day and I don't think I can cope with the uplift that going by river gives me. I can feel my life closing in like a tunnel round me and I want to be in one. Freddie stands for all the light-filled stations: hang on to him, hang on to him, he may be a bit pompous sometimes, a bit stiff, a bit reactionary, but he's decent, he thinks straight and clear, and he loves me. I often wonder why, but he does.

It was obvious it never occurred to him that I might have to give Jane one of my kidneys. I didn't mention it at all even as a possibility; I watched him, to see if he was thinking things he wasn't saying. I can usually tell. But it never crossed his mind.

Dilemma. That Greek word originally meaning a form of argument choosing between two equally unpleasant alternatives. The horns of the dilemma. Bull's horns, hard and hurtful. The horns of my dilemma are subtly different from that ancient meaning: one alternative is deeply unpleasant to me, the other to Jane. One of us will suffer whatever is the final decision. Which means I will suffer anyway for both.

The train stops in a tunnel, the lights flick off briefly. Blackness. Anaesthetic. That'll be blackness of a new sort. Invasion of my body, removal of a vital organ. Cutting, blood, stitches—

'Natalie.'

'Ah—'

'Are you all right?'

'Yes. Yes, thanks. I'm fine.'

Janet Antrobus's bulk bends over me, breathing stale cigarette smoke and peppermints. A red-taloned hand is on my arm.

It is all I can do to stop myself shaking it off as if it's a reptile.

'You don't look it.'

'I really am fine.'

The train draws into London Bridge and she shepherds me off protectively, that hand still on my arm. I pull away as soon as I decently can.

'Come and have a quick coffee, you look as if you need one.'

'I've just got a headache.'

'I insist.'

So I find myself sitting knee to knee with Janet Antrobus in a busy little coffee bar. At least the coffee's good. She lights up and the smoke buries itself in her hair as if it's sucked in by nicotine-thirsty follicles.

'I thought you always took the riverbus. I was most surprised to see you on the tube.'

'I thought you always drove.'

'I do if I can. The car's being serviced. Are you going to call your defendant into the witness box, by the way?'

'No.'

'You should. Juries find it suspicious.'

'Too bad. I shall make sure they understand really clearly that it makes no difference either way.'

'It does to them. They long to hear the voice of the defendant. Very frustrating if he or she sits mute in the dock. I'm sure it affects the way they finally decide.'

'I don't agree. We must hurry, Janet.'

'Plenty of time. No need to get there yet.'

'I'm sorry, I like to be in court as early as possible.' I stand up. 'Thanks very much for the coffee.'

'We are the busy little advocate. Go on ahead, I intend to finish my fag.' Janet smiles her maddening heavy smile behind another smoke cloud. I run along Tooley Street, cross with myself for giving in and having a coffee I didn't want with a person I don't like.

My defence of Mr McKenzie goes very well. The character witness stands up strongly to Janet Antrobus's cross-examination;

Mrs McKenzie is watching him with her heart in her eyes. McKenzie himself is too distracted and stressed to take much in. I'm good with juries; this one is very attentive. Most of the twelve have their eyes fixed on me during my speech; most are listening very closely. Only one has her head bent, but that's because she's making copious notes.

The judge sums up – the woman who took all the notes looks rather disappointed because he underlines all the discrepancies in the prosecution witnesses' statements which she'd clearly noticed too – and the jury retires just before lunch. They obviously discuss the case throughout their lunch break of sandwiches in the jury room because they are ready with their verdict soon after two. The note-taking woman is the foreman, and gives a verdict of not guilty.

I don't think I'll ever tire of that moving moment when a client is found not guilty. Clients react in many different ways from the jubilant to the disbelieving. Mr McKenzie sits stunned, not taking it in at first. Then he rubs his cheeks and shakes his head. Mrs McKenzie stares at him with huge tears coursing down her fat cheeks. When he meets her eyes he starts weeping too. They are both blowing their noses by the time he's led from the dock.

When I meet them afterwards Mr McKenzie takes my right hand between his two hands: they are dry and papery, and quiver with the strain he's been through.

'I am so grateful to you, lady.'

'All part of the service.'

'It's been a nightmare all these months.'

'Are you still working in the same place as those two bullies?'

'No, lady, I left that job. I had to take early retirement.'

'So you can relax and enjoy not worrying about the future.'

'I'm afraid those two might come for me now.'

'I should doubt it. They'll be in dire trouble if they do. But they won't bother.'

'I hope not.'

'It's all over now, Mr McKenzie. Over now.' He's still holding my hand. His best shoes are worn and cracked but have been polished to a high shine. His 1960's tiepin with a shiny red sports car as its head was bought no doubt when he was young, in the hope that a similar car might one day be his.

'You must go and celebrate.' I start to pull my hand gently away.

'I wish you good fortune, lady. Happy life, many healthy children. A peaceful heart.' As he spoke he bowed over my hand. Now that the pressure had gone he could be himself again, a respected lay preacher.

'Thank you.'

Happy life, many healthy children, peaceful heart. As I hurry from the court building to avoid further contact with Janet Antrobus (excessively friendly as we left the courtroom) the words ring in my ears. I see Mr McKenzie in the distance walking stiffly, head high, arm in arm with his wife who is chattering and laughing. Happy life, many healthy children, peaceful heart.

I decide to go and see Jane now rather than later.

But then I procrastinate. First I buy her a book; she'll need lots of reading matter. I spend ages deciding between a Brian Moore and a Mary Wesley, both newly out in paperback. Finally I buy both, something I could have done in the first five minutes. Then I spend a long time buying some new tights for myself. Then I think perhaps Jane would like a treat of some sort to alleviate the boredom of hospital food, and choose some chocolates and some nuts; I'm about to pay for them when it occurs to me that Jane might not be allowed to eat them. Jenny mentioned something about a strict diet. I put them back.

Then I notice that a shoe shop is having a sale and find myself trying on some brown shoes – nothing special – and waste more time. But as I'm sitting pulling on another equally unremarkable pair I seem to hear Jane's voice calling me. I know it's only imaginary, but it gives me a shock. Having wasted half an hour I'm now in a desperate hurry and rush out. It's only in the tube I realise I've left the two books I bought in the shoe shop. Brilliant – I wasted all that time and now I've got nothing to show for it.

Jane's bed is screened off. Sister Pennington sees my face and leads me out of the ward.

'Don't worry, my dear. Your sister's much better today. She's just been having a little emotional crisis and we've been trying to calm her down. Nothing to worry about, and I'm sure she'll be pleased to see you.'

'What sort of emotional crisis?'

'Patients usually get upset when they begin to realise what's happened to them. Jane had her second session of haemodialysis late this morning and the trouble started after that.'

'She began to understand.'

'It is a terrible shock. We never underestimate it.'

'How upset was she?' Sister Pennington hesitates. 'Please tell me, Sister. I don't like things to be kept from me.'

'She did go over the top. We had to terminate dialysis a little early, she was so distressed.'

'Can't I go to her now?' I can see the curtains are still pulled around the bed area.

'In a moment. Nurse Rhona is helping Jane do her hair, put a bit of make-up on. Cheer her up.'

'I could do that.'

'There, they've finished.'

A plump black nurse with a big smile is pushing the curtains back. Jane is lying propped up by pillows. The dreadful blood-filled aerial is not there. Only a loose plaster covering the fistula shows where it springs when in use. The dialysis machine is silent, pushed back against the wall. Jane's eyes are shut, her face is deathly white with a gash of lipstick.

'Jane. It's me, Nat.'

Jane opens those bright beautiful blue eyes. They are filled with pure rage.

'Piss off.'

'Jane—'

'I can't bear to see you or anyone who's walking about leading a normal life. Piss off.'

'I can understand—'

'No, you can't. No one can unless they've been through the same torture. You've never had a hole made in your neck.' Her eyes burn with bitter, ice-cold fury. 'It's bloody agony, and now they tell me if I don't spend hours a day attached to that fucking machine I'll die. I think I'd rather die.'

'Jane—'

'You'll feel differently soon—' begins Sister Pennington in soothing tones.

'You piss off as well. Let me alone. I can't bear to see you being so cheerful.' Jane shuts those now frightening eyes. Her face is drawn, ill, exhausted. The lipstick looks awful, a mockery. Sister Pennington goes off, still serene. I stand by Jane in silence. Tears are running now out of the corners of her clamped eyes.

'Jane, my love. Do you really want me to go?'

'Yes. No. Oh, God, Nat. It's not fair.'

'It's not fair at all.'

'I really can't bear the thought of living like this.' She's whispering now. I sit beside her, but I don't touch her. In this mood, Jane would certainly snatch her hand away.

'It's appalling bad luck—'

'I can't accept it. Surely they've got the diagnosis wrong.'

'They seem sure, Jane.'

'You hear all the time about mistakes being made over what's wrong with people.'

I don't want to go on contradicting her. Perhaps she needs some false hopes to survive this stage. She runs a dry tongue over her red lips in the silence.

'Get me a drink, Nat. They won't give me anything, they take no notice when I say I'm dying of thirst.'

I look round. There are no jugs of water anywhere, no glasses.

'There isn't even a tap in here.'

'Ask those bloody nurses for a drink.' Jane's Australian accent has become more marked.

'I'll see what I can find.'

Sister Pennington is at the main desk scribbling into a file. She explains Jane has to restrict herself to a small amount of liquid per day.

'She says she's very thirsty.'

'I'm afraid there's nothing I can do for her. She can't have more than 500 millilitres a day, and she's almost had it already.'

'She usually drinks masses. It's hard for her.'

'They all get used to it eventually. I know it's hard to start with.'

'What other things can't she have? I thought of bringing her some chocolate or fruit—'

'No chocolate, I'm afraid. No high potassium foods – chocolate, bananas, oranges – no salty foods of course. Excuse me—' The phone has started ringing and she picks it up.

I go back to Jane, whose anger has faded and tears have dried. She's watching for me anxiously.

'No luck. She says you mustn't have more than 500 millilitres a day—'

'But that's half a litre only – I drink that and more some days for breakfast alone. You should have told her I drink a lot.'

'I did. I'm really sorry, Jane. I did my best.'

'It's going to drive me mad. And I have to eat such boring things as well. A bland diet – just those words are too much. They gave me some lunch which was so tasteless I nearly threw it at the wall.'

She goes on moaning and I listen. In her position I'd moan too, and often having a good moan can be therapeutic. Jane doesn't look any happier, though she eventually moves off food and drink.

'The tube they put in my neck – have you seen it?'

'Yes. It gave me a shock.'

'It's so horrid. It's the thing that upsets me the most. They've inserted this nozzle into my neck, like a bloody lilo. Only I'm not a lilo, I'm a human being and I HATE IT.'

'I can't imagine how awful it must be.' I take Jane's hand and she leaves her cool fingers in mine for a minute or two, then slides them away.

'I wish I hadn't come over. This might not have happened at all if I'd stayed in Sydney.'

'Jane, it was waiting to happen. Jenny Morton said it was not a question of if, but when. Maybe you're better off being treated here.'

'I don't know anyone here, I don't know the networks. Dad's a doctor now, he does, he could have helped me.'

'I don't expect homeopathy can do much for renal failure.'

'You don't realise how good he's got. He's really well known now in Sydney. He could have helped me gently without all this fucking invasion of my body. Oh, why did I come over, he told me not to; why, why, why!' Jane starts crying again; this time she lets me hold her hand, she doesn't pull away, though her fingers are limp. I stroke them while she sobs, painful racking sobs.

'I'll give Dad a ring tonight, Jane, and tell him what's happened if you want me to.'

'Dad's got no time for you, he says you're a stuck-up bitch.'

I know Jane's trying to hurt me because I'm sitting here well and whole, I know she's beyond controlling her emotions, but she certainly succeeds in putting the knife in. I force myself to keep hold of her hand. Her red nail varnish is chipped, her skin is as dry as Mr McKenzie's, her flesh is cold.

'I'll still give him a ring. He needs to know. He might come over.'

'No chance.' Her sobs are stopping, her voice has gone very quiet. Her whole face looks more relaxed and after a long pause I realise she's dropped off to sleep.

I stare at her recumbent body. It would be dead if it wasn't for the machine behind her. In her body are two useless organs, crucial to existence. I breathe deeply, try to sense my own kidneys, liver, lungs, heart, stomach, bowels. All so mysteriously efficient. I shut my eyes, feel my pulse, listen to my breathing, sense a tingle in my right foot, a tension above my shoulder blades. I clench and unclench my vaginal muscles. I move my ears. I feel as if I am in control, but I too could have a scarred kidney, or a growth deep inside me that gives no hint of its presence until—

'So she's asleep.'

I jump, as I jumped for Janet Antrobus. A thin Indian nurse with a beautiful profile is bending over Jane, checking her pulse.

'I'm Vera. Pat's gone off duty now.'

'She fell asleep about ten minutes ago.' I stand up shakily, and the nurse takes my arm. Her name badge says she is Sister Vera Akram. 'She was very upset earlier.'

'You look pretty upset yourself. Let me get you a cup of tea.' She leads me to a small sitting area and asks an auxiliary to get me some tea.

'My sister can't accept what's happened.'

'It's not surprising. She's very young. It's harder to accept if you're young and strong.' Sister Vera Akram is herself lithe, healthy, glowing, and stunningly good-looking.

'Jane's going to hate you.' The nurse stares blankly at me. 'She says she can't stand the sight of anyone looking fit and flourishing.'

She laughs. Even her teeth are perfect. 'I'll try to look my worst when I'm near her.'

'You couldn't look anything but beautiful.'

The nurse is shaking her head and continuing to laugh. She leaves me to drink my tea and returns to the wards.

I get into the lift; it's empty and without mirrors. I lean back against the anonymous blank walls and go up and down in it for a while. I find myself involuntarily tapping my head against the lift, like a small child rocking itself. Up and down I go in that lift, alone in my small square world, until at last a group of chatting nurses join me and we all go to the ground floor together.

I go out into London's rush hour. I ought to go to Chambers, I ought at least to ring in before six o'clock when the clerks leave. I make myself go to a phone booth; it stinks of vomit. Douglas is his usual brisk self.

'Right, Miss Harper. I heard you got a good win. What about a bit of GBH for tomorrow? Estimated one day?'

'Douglas, I know I told you I wanted to be busy this week but that was before my sister was taken ill.'

'I'm sorry to hear that. I didn't know she had been.'

'It happened last night. It's serious.'

'Oh dear, that's all you need this week of all weeks.'

'So give that case to Miss Saban if she's free. I really don't think I can cope with court tomorrow. All this has hit me rather with a sort of delayed reaction.'

'Miss Harper, go straight home and don't give Chambers another thought. Have a relaxing evening. You sound as if you need it.'

'Thank you, Douglas.'

I wander about on Westminster Bridge, staring at the brightly illuminated House of Commons and Big Ben. I can't face the thought of another evening in close proximity to Thomas Mentieth. I feel tense in his presence; he's so clever and his brusque way of talking and Freddie's habitual reactions to him are very excluding though neither of them realises it. They're on an old network of their own; outsiders have no place in it.

I don't want to go to the flat either, or talk to Sara or Mark. Dave? No, but I must ring him and tell him about Jane. I never passed on her message yesterday, I forgot all about it. Well, it's too late and I certainly don't want to speak to Dave yet.

I buy an *Evening Standard* and go into a pub. I sit in the corner and sip a lager, holding the paper up but not reading it. Then a headline catches my eye. 'University teacher says Government is mad.' University teacher – into my mind comes my own university tutor, Amanda Smallgood. So misnamed – she's six foot tall and does endless good. Dr Amanda Smallgood – she's the person I'd like to see right now. I've kept in touch with her since I left university because she was so special and did so much for me, but I haven't seen her for ages. Ever since Freddie came into my life I haven't given her a thought; I haven't even told her I'm going to be married. How could I have ignored her so – she's my guru figure, she's important to me. How could I.

I go to the phone in the corner of the noisy pub, thinking of her calm wry glance, of her warmth which has nothing sentimental about it, of her shrewdness and sense of humour. The number rings and rings. She's not in. I'm just about to put the receiver back when her voice answers.

'Amanda Smallgood.'

'Dr Smallgood, it's Natalie, Natalie Harper. It's been a long time—'

'Natalie. I was thinking about you the other day, wondering how you were getting on at the Bar.'

'It's going well, thank you. I'd love to come and see you.'

'I'd love you to come. Let's fix a time. I've got my diary right here by the phone.'

'Dr Smallgood, are you free now?'

'Now? Oh.'

'It doesn't matter.'

'I could be. I always have supper on Wednesdays with my neighbour, but I could go a little late. Come for a drink, then, as soon as you can.'

'I'm at Waterloo.'

'Very close.' She ends the call with her customary abruptness.

Another taxi, to Kennington. I can't face the Northern Line. Dr Smallgood lives in one of those surprising squares of neat eighteenth-century cottages off the Kennington Road. Not that her house is particulary neat any more – the paint is peeling and the front yard is full of paper rubbish jettisoned or blown in by the wind.

Dr Smallgood's smile is as welcoming as ever, and her house is unchanged inside. Books, books, books everywhere, in tottering piles on every surface. Wire trays full of theses. Worn rugs, battered chairs.

'I'll open a bottle of wine, unless you'd prefer gin or whisky—'

'Wine would be lovely. It's very good of you to see me at such short notice.'

As always, she disappears to the kitchen for some time; I hear glasses clinking, paper packets being ripped open. She never stops working on whatever is current – this time a huge tome on the special stand by her chair which she is clearly reviewing – until the doorbell rings. But I'm pleased to have the space – I wander round her study-cum-sitting room looking at her pictures. I'd never noticed them before; Freddie has certainly opened my eyes. I peer at the signatures with amazement – Duncan Grant, Gaudier-Brzeska, Wyndham Lewis, Vanessa Bell.

'Dr Smallgood, in my total ignorance I never realised before what a wonderful collection of pictures you have. All these famous names—'

'My mother was the collector. She knew a lot of those people.'

'How exciting.'

'I don't suppose they were – I've always thought the Bloomsbury group and its circle rather tiresome as people. But they produced splendid things. What gives me the greatest pleasure is in that bookcase. My mother's collection of all the early Hogarth Press first editions of Virginia Woolf, many of them signed.'

'My goodness.' I take out *Jacob's Room* with its lovely Vanessa Bell jacket. 'This is in such good condition too.'

'We weren't allowed to touch those books at all. My mother

bought us paperback editions to read so that they stayed pristine. I felt this was going too far, I used to argue with her about it. Books are to be read.'

'But now do you think she was right? These must be worth a lot of money.'

'I'd rather not know what they're worth.' Her voice is tart. 'But I get great pleasure from handling them and rereading them, and looking at the beautiful jackets and the standards of production, and thinking about Leonard and Virginia packing up parcels of books in brown paper and string.'

Dr Smallgood has put out crisps and little cheese biscuits, and opened a bottle of Spanish red wine. Her wine glasses don't match but each is beautiful.

'Well, it's extremely good to see you again, Natalie, so unexpectedly.'

'I'm sorry to spring myself on you.'

'I've never minded unexpected guests.' She smiles. 'If I did, none of you would ever visit me. The young don't seem to plan ahead.'

'I'm getting better at it.'

'You're less young.'

'I'm getting married on Saturday, Dr Smallgood.'

'My dear, what momentous news! Congratulations! Do tell me who to – and *please* call me Amanda.'

'To a barrister, Frederick Mentieth.'

'In your Chambers?'

'He's head of them, actually. He's also a QC.'

'How grand you'll be! Before you know where you are he'll be a High Court judge and you'll be Lady Mentieth.' Her tone was hard to read.

'Don't.' Jane's flat voice rings in my ears: he thinks you're a stuck-up bitch. 'I really and truly don't want that, Dr – Amanda.'

'I believe you. I don't hold with honours.'

We smile at each other and sip our wine.

'Natalie, can I be blunt?'

'Yes.'

'For someone about to be married, you don't look happy.'

'A dreadful thing has just happened. It's not to do with Freddie

at all. My sister—' I stare at Amanda, unable for the moment
to go on.

'In my ignorance, I didn't even know you had a sister.'

'She's been in Australia for years. She went to university there.
She came over for the wedding, and collapsed yesterday with
renal failure. I've just been visiting her in St Thomas's.'

'I am very sorry to hear this. I really am. How difficult for you.'
I know at once that Amanda has seen the full implications.

'She's on dialysis.'

'Poor thing. The implications are all grim, are they not?'

'I feel desperate. She's very bitter at the moment.'

'We all would be in her position. I suppose the only comfort is
that there are ways of making her life bearable on dialysis. One of
my students is on CAPD, which apparently stands for Continuous
Ambulatory Peritoneal Dialysis. No wonder they shorten it. It's a
big advance – you do it at home.'

'I saw some cartoon about it on the wall of the Renal unit.
How does it work?'

'As far as I could understand, several times a day you have
to hook up to a catheter and change the dialysing fluid in the
peritoneal cavity in your abdomen.'

'*Abdomen!* How disgusting.' I touch my stomach.

'A doctor told me the peritoneum is unique in that it allows
waste products and water to pass from your blood into the special
fluid, which you pour into yourself using a catheter. My student
says it's a bore but she can do it at home and it does allow her
a normal life in between the pouring sessions.'

Somehow this description of what is regarded as the easiest form of dialysis upsets me more than the big dialysis
machine did.

'It hardly sounds bearable, Amanda.'

'Quite.'

'You know what I'm thinking, don't you. It sits in my mind
all the time.'

'I can guess.'

'I'm terrified, literally terrified, of the idea of giving up a
kidney.'

'Then you shouldn't do it. Anyway, your tissues may not
match.'

'Oh, they will. They will. It's always been like that.' And I pour out the story of my childhood. Amanda listens, her eyes focused on the picture behind me. She used to listen to my essays like that, on the rare occasions I had a tutorial alone with her and she asked me to read them out.

When I finish she puts down her glass and leans forward. 'I had a sister, an older sister. Your story sends the strangest shivers through me. Excuse me a minute.' She leaves the room and I hear her use the telephone.

'There, I've told my friend Joan next door that I'm going to let her down this time. You and I are going to have some dinner together. We'll go to a little place round the corner I'm very fond of. That is, if you'd like to and you can. How awful of me, I'd assumed you were free this evening—'

'I haven't anything particular on. If I may just ring Freddie—' Freddie has left Chambers, and is not in yet. I leave a message with Thomas.

'Have some more wine before we leave. You're not driving, are you?'

'No.'

'I'm glad I don't. Joan next door reckons that in a lifetime's driving she's thrown away at least £100,000 on cars and that's before buying fuel for them. I take taxis, and spend an average of £1000 a year on them.'

'It makes sense if you live in London.'

'I'm a Londoner born and bred.'

As we casually chat Amanda is looking through a drawer, and finally pulls out a large photograph. She hands it to me.

'My sister Miranda.'

The black and white studio portrait shows a solemn girl in a gown and mortarboard. The girl's eyes are dark and rather sunken; she is staring to the left of the photographer at something that has given her food for thought.

'She looks very like you.'

'Different colouring entirely.'

'She seems slightly apprehensive.'

'She always said being landed with a sister like me was enough to make anyone nervous.'

I find myself staring at Amanda as if for the first time. Behind her neglected grey hair, her careworn unmade-up face, her glasses, I suddenly see her beauty. At twenty, tall, thin and fresh-skinned, she must have been stunning.

'We were misnamed. She should have been Amanda, meet-to-be-loved, and I should have been Miranda, meet-to-be-admired. I wasn't lovable, she was; I was a star at school, but she was popular. My parents made the mistake of sending us to the same boarding school. It wasn't a particularly academic school and I was the superbrain there all my school career. Worse, I was two years ahead of my age, in the same class as my sister.'

'How trying for her.'

'She always said she didn't mind. She laughed about it, she seemed very relaxed. And she wasn't stupid at all – very clever in fact. Just not in my league. The year I went to Cambridge she went to Oxford to read English. You'd have thought her troubles were over at last. I wasn't there to breathe down her neck any more, to get higher marks, to do better than her in everything.'

'I know the feeling.'

'But it didn't work out as we expected.'

'What happened?'

Amanda put the photo back into the drawer as she stood up. 'She committed suicide. Come on, let's go and have dinner.'

21 ∫

Freddie had only been home for five minutes when the doorbell rang. Cursing, he opened it to find Meryl on the doorstep, looking unexpectedly smart.

'Freddie, just passing, thought I'd drop in to see how your brother was doing – and deliver your wedding present.' She put an odd-shaped parcel carefully on the hall table.

'How kind of you. I won't open it until Natalie is here. Come and say hello to my brother – I'm sure he'll be pleased to see you.' Numb with tiredness, Freddie led her into the sitting room. 'You have a visitor, Tom.'

Thomas stared blankly at Meryl. She gave a laugh and clapped her hands together.

'You don't recognise me! It's Meryl.'

'You looked quite different. I am sorry. Of course I recognise you now.'

'It's because I'm all dressed up. Well, you seem very comfortable.'

'Everyone is spoiling me.'

Freddie handed Meryl a tonic water as asked, but did not sit down. He had no desire to encourage Meryl into making a long visit.

'Ralph rang me, Freddie. He'd lost the wedding invitation. He is so hopeless, isn't he?'

'Why did he bother you and not ring me direct? Is he coming?'

'Of course!'

'There's no of course about Ralph.'

'No. Well, he's a bit of a character, we all know that.

He said he'd like to bring his – his partner. I thought I'd warn you.'

'I expected him to, if he came himself.'

'Oh, good, I thought you might be annoyed. Isn't Natalie here? I'm so longing to meet her.'

'Not yet. She should be, I can't think where she is.'

'Freddie, I was going to tell you as the doorbell rang – she left a message to say she was tied up with her tutor.'

'Her *tutor*?'

'I'm sure that's what she said.'

'How very strange. She's never talked about a tutor.'

'Oh, the mysterious Natalie! What a pity, it looks as if I won't meet her until the great day now.'

'Did she say what he was called?'

'Just said her tutor.'

'The young like to have their secrets, don't they, even Piers is beginning to keep his activities dark—'

'How are Piers and Harry, Meryl?'

'Flourishing.' Meryl looked tired at the thought. 'Well, I'm very sorry to miss Natalie, but I must toddle off—'

'Sweet of you to drop in.' Freddie led her into the hall when she had finished her farewells to Thomas. 'I'll tell Natalie you called.'

'Is Natalie smart like Anthea? Always looking a million dollars?'

'She's got a completely different style. Completely.'

'So she may not appreciate all those wonderful clothes of Anthea's you've kept.'

Meryl and Freddie's eyes met briefly, hers full of instant regret she'd mentioned the clothes, his with an equally instant realisation.

'Goodbye, Meryl. Thank you for all you did for Tom the other day.'

'Any time. Well, see you all on Saturday. Goodness, how exciting it will be!'

Freddie shut the door as she drove jerkily away. He knew beyond doubt that she had taken the Issey Miyake outfit, and to his surprise he didn't mind.

Before he started to cook some food, he rang the hospital. He was told Jane was more comfortable, and that her sister had been to see her.

'This is Natalie Harper's fiancé – she isn't still there by any chance?'

'No, she left some time ago, just after I came on duty. She was quite upset. It's very hard on the relatives at the beginning.'

'But it's harder on the patient. Is Jane having dialysis every day?'

'Three hours each day at the moment. When she's stabilised she'll have it every other day.'

'We are all shattered at the suddenness of her collapse. There seemed to be no warning.'

'I think there were warnings, but she ignored them or interpreted them wrongly. Most people do.'

'Who am I speaking to?'

'Sister Vera Akram.'

'Sister, will you give Jane my special love? Tell her it's Freddie, and that I would have come to see her today but I had to hurry home to look after my brother. Tell her I promise I'll come and see her tomorrow.'

'She'll be pleased. She's feeling very isolated. No family except her sister here, all her close friends in Sydney. Poor girl. I'll give her your message right now.'

'Thank you, Sister.'

'My pleasure.'

Voices are strange things, thought Freddie as he chopped onions. You need never meet someone to know they are warm, open, generous, or closed, paranoid, cold. Thomas's voice on the phone is always dry – you can see it coming out of his craggy, academic face. Douglas Dean's voice is why he is such a good clerk: it sounds so dependable, efficient, utterly trustworthy. Natalie's voice – unexpectedly light and breathy, yet when she spoke in court she deepened her tone and projected her voice effectivly. Jane's voice – he didn't know what Jane's disembodied voice sounded like—

The phone rang. A male voice asked for Jane Harper. Freddie did not like the sound of the voice at all – a heavy nasal London accent overlying and almost obliterating middle-class tones.

'Who is it, please?'

'Tell her Dave. Dave Rosenberg.'

'Jane's not here actually.'

'She blew out a date she had. As she was dead keen to meet this guy, he got annoyed and I got worried. Is Nat there?'

'Natalie's not here either.'

'I don't seem to be having much luck.'

'I'll tell them you rang, Mr Rosenberg.'

'You do that. Thanks, squire.'

Freddie wondered why he hadn't told him about Jane. Jane needed visitors, she needed her friends. He hadn't taken his number. He'd been a bit chilly. He found the list of wedding guests and checked to see if Mr Rosenberg's name was amongst the few friends Nat had asked. It wasn't, so he put him out of his mind.

But Ralph was coming, Meryl said. Plus woman. His name was the only one without a tick or cross beside it, and it gave Freddie pleasure to tick it. The tick he made was quite the biggest on the page.

'We've never spent so much time together, never. Except for that weekend after Anthea died—'

'When we were boys—'

'No, Freddie. If you think back, we didn't do much together. Different schools, different friends. Did we ever go out together, spend an evening alone together? I can't recall one.'

'I remember going to the cinema in a gang and both of us trying to take Maureen Macdonald home. We nearly came to blows over her.'

'Maureen Macdonald. She was blonde, wasn't she, plump, with a mole on her cheek. A beauty spot. How I longed to kiss it.'

'I did kiss it.'

'You took her home, Freddie. You won.'

'I didn't kiss anything else. She wouldn't let me. Cheeks were permitted, no more.'

They both laughed at the memory of Maureen Macdonald and the passion she had aroused.

'We didn't get to know each other, did we, as boys? I've had a lot of time to reflect, sitting here alone in your house. I've realised how limited my relationships are. You've had a wife, you're committing yourself to another. You constantly cope with a group of people as Head of a set of Chambers, you probably develop bonds with some of your clients. I do a great deal of my work alone; I jet into a country, meet a group of people for a limited period, advise them, remain objective and disinterested, leave. I spend two-thirds of my time in hotels. I have no one close to me except you and my mother, and to a lesser degree the other Mentieths, Gittingses etc. And the dreaded figure of Elsie. The position is clear: you are the most important person in my life. I know I don't have that honour in yours.'

'Tom, you're very important to me. Good Lord. Don't underrate yourself.'

'I'm simply looking at the facts. That's why I'm so pleased to be here, so pleased you persuaded me. We've had time to chat. I find myself being thankful this happened.' He pointed to his leg. 'A week ago I regarded it as an unmitigated disaster.'

'You wouldn't have come to the wedding if it hadn't, would you?'

'Certainly not. When I'm on a UN assignment I never interrupt it if I can help it. Never. Unprofessional. Personal reasons shouldn't play a part in one's working life.'

The brothers smiled at each other as Freddie poured Tom another whisky.

'We're drinking too much, Freddie.'

'Not more than usual.'

'It's more than usual for me. I rarely drink on my own, though I have since the accident.'

'Alcohol's so much part of life I hardly think about it.' Freddie stretched out on the sofa. 'What does Ralph mean to you?'

'Cousin Ralph, the black sheep. No more than that. I hardly know him.'

Freddie was about to try and analyse Ralph's importance to him when he saw it was not the most sensitive way to return his brother's confidences. There was a silence.

'Why did you mention Ralph?'

'Oh, Meryl brought him to mind. I'm glad he's coming on Saturday, though why he couldn't answer through the normal channels I can't think.'

'Ralph would make a point of avoiding the normal channels. He's a self-conscious rebel. Usually it's a condition one grows out of – acceptable in the young, it becomes tiresome in middle age.'

'Tiresome. Yes.' Ralph was tiresome, but it didn't seem to matter when they met.

'What about Natalie's family? Who's coming?'

'No one. Not even Jane now.'

'How come there's no one else?'

'Mother dead, father in Australia too and unable to come over because of work commitments. No other close family exists – parents were only children on both sides, grandparents the only surviving children. So no cousins, aunts, etc.'

'Lucky Natalie is my first reaction, but no, I do see how alone she must feel. Particularly now, with her sister so seriously ill.' Thomas gazed sombrely at his brother. 'Is the father not going to make an effort to some over to see her?'

'I've no idea. I imagine Nat's spoken to him, but she didn't mention it. She said she wasn't close to him, but Jane is. I've no idea what's going on to be honest, and where she is tonight. Who is this tutor? Are you sure she didn't give a name?'

'I am sure.'

'I'm glad you're here, Tom. All this would be a bit nerve-racking without you. I do find Nat sometimes says and does things which are a touch alien. It doesn't affect my feelings for her, but it can be a strain.'

'I find everyone under thirty-five completely alien. I sometimes feel as a Roman senator must have felt when the Goths poured into Italy.'

'I'm just going to give Nat's flatmate Sara Reading a ring. She might know this tutor and where Nat is.'

But the answerphone was on and Freddie's pride stopped him from leaving a message.

Freddie retired to his study after supper and worked on an urgent opinion which needed to be typed up and sent tomorrow. He looked for his recorder when he was ready to dictate and found to his annoyance he'd left it in Chambers. He half contemplated fetching it, and then remembered that Anthea's old cassette recorder was still in a cupboard in the laundry room with a box full of tapes beside it. He'd meant to sort them all out and then done nothing. Anthea used to record radio programmes of some rare piece of music – it gave her pleasure to catch an off-beat performance which she wouldn't necessarily want or be able to buy.

He took the recorder and a couple of tapes upstairs; one had nothing written on it, the other had, pencilled lightly by Anthea: *Letter to S. B-J.* Freddie frowned; B-J could be a Belling-Johnson, but who was S? He couldn't think of an S. He put the tape in and switched on. His dead wife's voice said:

Dear Aunt Stella, you must think me awful not to have been in touch for so long and now it's nearly Christmas. Freddie went off to court this morning complaining we hadn't done our Christmas cards yet and so here's yours. Happy Christmas, dearest favourite Aunt – I wish you weren't so far away. But I promise that next year I *will* come and see you – and we can talk and laugh and be happy together and at least you won't be able to see the grey hairs that I'm afraid I now have . . .

Freddie switched off the machine with a desperate snatch of his hand. Anthea's easy tones, full of warmth if slightly self-consciously jolly, took his healed heart and ripped it open. The old pain of grief flooded him. He shut his eyes, back in the black free fall of that first day.

22 ∫

'So is Freddie very successful?'

'Yes, I suppose he is. He doesn't think so, but the rest of the world does.'

'We never know how lucky we are. If we did, there'd be little to live for, I sometimes think.' Amanda takes off her glasses and sits back. She's finished her food well before me; she says it's a vice in people who live alone. 'But enough facile philosophy. I was going to tell you about Miranda. Do you hate your younger sister?'

'Sometimes, I have to admit. I love her too.'

'What about liking her?'

'There's the rub.'

'I never really knew what Miranda felt about me, her awful younger sister. She always recoiled from any emotional interaction. If you asked her about her feelings she slipped away – it was like trying to pick up mercury. I used to send her cheerful postcards from Cambridge, but I never got one back. Not that I really minded – I was having such a wonderful time nothing could damp me down.' Amanda's surprisingly large yellow eyes are as usual staring unfocused over my shoulder. She could be beautiful now if she took more trouble with her hair and skin. 'Our first Christmas vac back at home, Miranda was even quieter than usual, more reserved. I should have paid more attention to this, and it ought to have alerted my parents too, but they were as usual too busy with their own lives and anyway she was now nearly twenty, old enough to be coping in their opinion. Miranda went back to Oxford and was found dead in her room at the end of the first week of term, wearing a gown and mortarboard.

Propped on the dressing table was that photo, which we didn't
know she'd had taken. Apparently she'd lined it up to be staring
at the window, where she hanged herself with a dressing gown
cord tied round the curtain rail. The rail had eventually given
way, too late to save Miranda.'

'How absolutely terrible.'

'She left no note, just the photograph. My parents never got
over the shock of it, and in a way, nor did I.'

'Did you blame yourself?'

'Who else was there to blame?'

'There may have been a dozen things – her work, her tutors,
a love affair gone wrong.'

'Her work was fine, her tutors were pleased with her. We
never knew if there was a boyfriend – if there was he never
came forward. There were no private letters, no diary, nothing.
My mother was sure she'd cleared the decks on purpose. It was
as if she wanted to expunge all evidence that she'd ever had a
private life. There was just the photograph.'

Our plates are cleared away, and coffee is ordered after we've
both decided against having a dessert.

'But there was another strange thing, Natalie. My parents
found that all the family photographs containing her had disappeared. She'd gone through the packets – my mother never
got round to sticking anything into albums – and removed every
one she was in, plus the negatives, and they were never found.
All she left for us to remember her by was that official image,
which she must have had done specially. Luckily relatives had
some snaps of us and made sure we had copies.'

'Your sister must have been quite ill to go that far.'

'It's haunted me all my life.'

'But it could have been a real illness, nothing to do with
you—'

'Maybe, but guilt is not a rational feeling, and I still feel guilt
over Miranda. So perhaps you can see why I have spent my life
teaching people of her age and being wholly available to them
if they were in trouble. It's a reparation of a sort.'

'You were the only one who cared about our problems
enough to put yourself out. Look how I've come to you now,
years later.'

'I'm glad. Not many keep in touch once they have graduated.'

'Are you free on Saturday?'

'Why? I thought you said that was when you were getting married.'

'I'd love you to come to the wedding. I should have asked you. I feel bad I didn't. It's a family affair with just a few of my friends, some you will remember from university—'

'You don't really want me to come, you know. I'd be the proverbial sore thumb.' Amanda gives me a quick smile, more a grin. 'I'm not good at social occasions like that. I'm a one-to-one person. And I've always preferred funerals to weddings. They're less uneasy.'

I don't know what to say. But Amanda has always been like that, prone to making remarks you can't deal with. And I can sense she's had enough of me from the way she calls for the bill (she won't let me contribute) and we part, briskly and affectionately, outside the restaurant.

We haven't talked any more about my dilemma, but I feel less anguished about it now anyway. There is no hurry after all. The hospital will no doubt try to put Jane on the CAPD method when she's stabilised, and she might do so well she won't need a kidney from anyone.

As I walk through the urban wasteland to the Elephant and Castle, I think about those two sisters, Miranda and Amanda. What a tragic mess. Their story is not ours, but Amanda Smallgood told it to me as if it was relevant, as if it might help me, might clarify and explain. Amanda doesn't seem comparable to Jane, and I feel no particular kinship with Miranda. I have never felt driven even to considering suicide because of what my sister is and has done to me. And Jane has none of Amanda's objective yet caring sympathy for others. Yet maybe—

A car honks with sudden shocking loudness as I step off the pavement to cross the street. Shaken, I make the crossing with more care and enter the neon-lit concrete and plastic squalor of the shopping centre to go down to catch the Northern Line. Taxis have passed me but I don't want to be whisked at speed back to Freddie's house. I need to reflect on my evening, which has been a rite of passage in its way, like a hen party. (Sara has threatened to organise an official party for all my girlfriends but I told her I'd much rather she did it in six months' time when there'd be more point in gathering the old gang together.)

I settle myself and as the doors are about to close a group of four teenagers carrying beer cans erupts into the carriage shouting. I get out my *Evening Standard* and hide behind it, but it's pulled forward and a flushed face says:

'Got a light?'

'Sorry. I don't smoke.' I'm about to say smoking is forbidden on the Underground when the man opposite lights up the boy's cigarette, clearly unwilling to cause friction by refusing him. A girl puts a ghetto blaster on and the group starts to dance. At Waterloo everyone gets out of their carriage and leaves them to their mayhem. As we settle down again and I'm reflecting on the cowardly ease with which we've banished the problem, the man with the lighter catches my eye and shrugs.

'Let them hang theirselves.'

The house is in darkness except for the hall and staircase lights. I creep up putting them off and pause outside Freddie's bedroom. His door is shut. I stand quietly on the landing, listening.

The silence is total, despite the fact something in the quality of it tells me he's awake. I'd been looking forward to a cosy chat before bed, or in bed, winding down on the day, and I'm clearly not going to get it. I'm unexpectedly upset. I must have offended him by staying out all evening. I stand there for ages, aware too that I ought to ring my father and now would be a good time, but I can't move.

At last I switch the spare room light on, and immediately see the cupboard doors are open wide. This is odd too; Freddie's not the sort of person to leave doors open which he usually locks.

I undress without looking inside the cupboard, and clean my teeth and skin with extra thoroughness as if the ritual will somehow wipe the image of those doors from my mind so that I can go to bed without thinking any more about them.

I must close them. As I move them chiffon of a magical colour flutters; it's so pretty I can't help touching it. My eye runs up the rest of the dress, hanging in the midst of a row of women's clothes, all expensive, subtle, soft. A faint scent emanates from them, a delicious, elusive perfume based on roses.

These are Anthea's clothes. They must be. This is how her skin smelt. There's a hair on that shoulder, a light brown hair. Her hair. Her clothes are ravishing.

I slam the cupboard shut and then freeze again. The noise is bound to have disturbed Freddie. But nothing happens and I stumble across to one of the twin beds and throw myself face downwards on it.

I will never be able to compete with Anthea. Her house is perfect, her clothes are perfect, she was perfect. What does Freddie want of me? He surely sees what a shabby freak I am. Rootless, chaotic, tasteless.

I'm awake most of the night.

23

What woke Freddie was the refuse collectors banging dustbins in the street, not the knocking in his dream – a dream of being interrupted while eating something vague and delicious with Natalie in a yellow room. He opened his eyes into the low morning sun streaming through his windows (he'd forgotten to pull down the blinds in his distress the night before). He lay feeling curiously relaxed and happy; the return of Anthea to his heart was no more substantial than the dream. He stretched his legs down the bed and then got up. Very quietly he opened Natalie's door and saw to his relief she was curled up in her usual dormouse position fast asleep. He was also relieved to see he'd shut the cupboard again after his crisis last night. He must give all those clothes to Natalie, today, to do what she liked with. If she didn't want them they could go to poor Meryl.

He went lightly downstairs and began to make breakfast for everyone. There were some croissants in the freezer which he popped into the oven. Soon the house was filled with their sweet buttery smell mingling with the scent of coffee. He prepared Thomas's tray and then laid the table with unusual care for Natalie and him. Thursday. Two days to go. This morning he felt so filled with nervous elation he might have been marrying for the first time.

He took his brother's tray up and dealt with the intimate morning rituals, then left Thomas in front of his breakfast with the *Financial Times* propped against a vase.

Natalie was still asleep. Freddie crept up to her and knelt beside the bed. She was hunched into the pillow and he bent closer. She smelt sweet, like a puppy. He pulled a strand of her hair aside and kissed her cheek, touching it with his tongue.

The effect was electric. She unwound with such ferocity she knocked him over backwards; she sat up in bed tense and wild-eyed. She seemed to cringe from him in fear.

'Nat, my love – whatever's the matter? Were you having a nightmare?'

She shut her eyes. He put his arm round her unresponsive shoulders and squeezed them; her eyes flew open and focused themselves on the cupboard behind him.

'Tell me what's the matter.'

She suddenly crumpled against him as if she'd been punctured.

'Oh, Freddie, I've had such an awful night.'

'When did you get in?'

'I wasn't late, but your door was shut—'

'I went to bed early.'

'Freddie, I'm not good enough for you. You're bound to be disappointed in me—'

'What is all this?'

'Jane is a disaster area and so am I. You should keep well away from us.'

'Natalie, Natalie. You're talking absolute drivel. Come downstairs and have a good breakfast and you'll feel much better. Come on. I insist. Where's your dressing gown?'

'Still packed up somewhere.'

'Then use Anthea's. I kept it because it was new and beautiful. You must have her things anyway now – I was going to give them to you today.' He led her over to the cupboard and opened the doors. From the back he pulled a blue velvet housecoat lined with emerald green silk which he held out.

'There you are. You are much the same height as she was. And go through this lot sometime and see what you want to keep.'

'Oh, Freddie, *Freddie!*' Natalie gripped his shoulders and pressed her forehead into his collarbone. 'Freddie.'

'I need my breakfast if you don't. Come on.'

Natalie followed him downstairs, the housecoat like a regal train behind her. It was long, but not too long. She caught sight of herself in the hall mirror and saw how well it became her.

'I wish we were getting married today, just us, with no fuss.'

'I agree. Croissant all hot from the oven?'

'You're too good for me, Freddie. I mean it.'

'Too good *to* you maybe, but I'm piling up credits so that you can spoil me later. Coffee?'

Natalie was still standing near the door. He stared at her, at the way the housecoat became her far more than it ever had Anthea, who had actually looked rather sallow in it. She stared fixedly back.

'Promise me, Freddie, if you change your mind about me that you will tell me and not pretend.'

'I won't change my mind.'

'Promise me anyway.'

'All right, I promise, but it's irrelevant. Now eat your croissant and drink your coffee but kiss me first.'

Freddie had to adjourn the case he was trying at lunchtime owing to the collapse from a minor stroke of the defendant, and since there was nothing else in the list for him he left court. As he drove back to London he realised it was an ideal opportunity to go and see Jane.

He bought a bunch of flowers at the hospital shop and made his way to the Renal unit. At the reception desk a beautiful Indian nurse was on the telephone; she acknowledged his presence with a quick smile as she finished her conversation. Her voice was familiar.

The ward behind was quiet; post-lunch torpor reigned. Perhaps Jane was asleep. He could leave the flowers and return to Chambers, honour satisfied—

'How can I help you?'

'I've come to see Jane Harper if possible. I think we spoke the other night – I'm her sister's fiancé.'

'Jane's receiving dialysis at the moment.'

'I should have rung first—'

'She's dialysing in the ward – you can go and see her if you like.' Sister Akram looked at him warningly. 'Some people find the first sight of a patient on dialysis a bit distressing.'

'I think I'll survive. You have to look at many unpleasant things in a life at the Bar.' Freddie smiled, Sister Akram smiled back and he followed her into the ward. Sun shone through the windows; the bunch of roses he was holding gave off a sweet scent.

He saw the whirring machine, he saw the movement of Jane's blood through the twin tubes like aerials which rose from the fistula inserted in her neck, he dropped the roses, he fell against the nurse, his knees loose.

'Steady.'

'Sorry. Give me a moment.' Freddie went to a window, leant against the sill. 'Sorry.'

'It's all right. Here's a chair when you're ready to sit by her.' Sister Akram took the flowers away to put them in a vase. Freddie made himself go and sit in the chair.

Jane's eyes remained shut; the tubes thrummed near her cheek. He stared at her, horrified by the change in her. Her skin was grey and puffy, her hair lank and greasy on the pillow, her chipped red nails were grubby on the white sheets.

'Jane.'

She moaned.

'Jane, it's Freddie.'

Jane opened her eyes just enough to see him through the slits.

'Freddie. Get me out of here.'

'Jane.' He took one of her cold hands.

'I'm terrified.'

'I can imagine—'

'You can't.' Her eyes were tight shut again. 'It's been awful beyond anything you can imagine.'

'My poor Jane.'

'This thing.' Eyes still shut, she moved a finger towards the machine, the tubes. 'They attacked me like vampires to put this thing in my neck. I thought I'd die when I came round. I thought they'd pushed the bloody thing into my heart and I was dying. It was indescribable. I can't open my eyes because I can't bear the sight of my own blood whirring past. Oh, God.'

Tears started running out of her closed eyes. Salt tracks showed it was not the first time she had cried that day. Freddie held her right hand between both of his, trying to warm it. He was wordless. After a pause she started whispering again.

'I thought my abortion was bad enough, but it was nothing, nothing, compared with this.'

Another silence fell; he had to find his voice.

'I wish I could help you, Jane.'

'Get me a drink of water. I'm dying of thirst. Those bitches won't give me anything to drink.'

'There's no glass here—'

'It's torture. I'm parched.'

'I'll go and ask the nurse.'

'Don't ask, just get me water.' As her tears flowed, her fingers caught them and put the moisture on her tongue. Freddie got up and tried to walk firmly back to the desk where Sister Akram was now filling in forms.

'Sister, that poor girl is dying of thirst.'

'I'm sorry, but she's already had almost her day's ration. She won't accept that she can only have two and a half glasses a day.'

'It's so little.'

The sister's shiny black eyes registered nothing. 'They all have to get used to it. I'll give her an ice cube, but she must begin to understand we are not doing this to torture her.' Her voice was stern, but when she arrived at the bedside with a small cube of ice on a saucer she spoke to Jane with warmth and gentleness.

'Suck this as slowly as you can.'

'It's bliss.'

'I'm sorry we have to be so hard on you. We have no choice.'

'I'm not helping you much.'

Sister Akram patted her shoulder. 'You're doing fine.' She walked away down the ward, her sensible flat shoes squeaking. Freddie noticed they needed reheeling. Life on a nurse's pay was unimaginable.

'I brought you some roses.'

'Thanks.' Jane's eyes were still shut; he could see the ice cube stored in her cheek. 'Freddie, I want to know the truth. I want to know the bottom line.'

'What have they told you?'

'I'm not clear.' She opened her eyes briefly, the fierce blue of her irises extraordinary against her deathly pale skin. 'Have I any chance of a normal life again?'

'Of course you have.'

Her blue eyes held his, her hand clung to his. 'I'm so terrified, Freddie. Why should this happen to me?'

'Oh, Jane.'

Her eyes flicked to the tubes bearing her blood and shut again. Her grip loosened, she seemed to go to sleep. He sat there unable to move, her fingers lying lightly in his. He made himself watch the dialysing process, despite his squeamishness. He could look at photographs of mutilated bodies in a murder case without too much of a twinge after the initial shock, why should he find this circulation of living blood so distressing? He stared at the red tubes doing the job of Jane's defunct kidneys. He felt faint again, and had to shut his eyes. Half an hour passed.

'She's asleep now. She won't notice if you leave.'

Freddie found Nurse Akram beside him; he followed her shakily out of the ward.

'She asked me to tell her the truth. Could you possibly fill me in with the full details and prognosis about my sister-in-law?'

'I'm afraid I can't. You'll have to talk to the consultant, or to her doctor. All I know is that her renal failure was total, and that she's got to be stabilised on dialysis.'

'Then what?'

'It's not for me to say.'

'There aren't many choices facing her, are there? Dialysis, transplant, or death.'

'It's the lack of choice they all find so hard, particularly the young ones like Jane. It's such a terrible, final thing to happen to anyone. There's nothing they can do about it. They do get bitter and depressed.'

'Lack of choice. I hadn't thought of that aspect.'

'They say to us, I don't want to have a fistula put permanently into my arm, or one in my stomach for CAPD, and we have to say, the only choice you have is either, not neither. It's very hard.'

'And a transplant is the best hope. What's the average length of time people have to wait for a kidney, Sister Akram?'

'It depends on a lot of things. Condition of patient, blood group, tissue type.' The phone had started to ring behind her, and she excused herself. But Freddie knew that she wouldn't say any more. It had also just come into his mind – how could he not have thought of it before? – that the first two obvious possible donors were Natalie and her father.

He had to hurry to find a lavatory before he was sick. It was years since he had retched like this, years since he had felt his body convulsed by the throes of vomiting. He washed his face when he had finished and sat for some time regaining his equilibrium. Perhaps he had eaten something that disagreed with him, but he doubted it.

A boy came into the gents, and Freddie stood and picked up his briefcase.

'Got the time, mister?'

'Just after three.'

'Only three.' The boy was perhaps ten or eleven, with a pale freckled face and crew-cut red hair. 'My dad had a heart attack this morning and we've been here all day.'

'I'm sorry to hear that.' Freddie heard his dark well-bred tones wrap themselves round the thin adenoidal South London voice.

'Yeah. And my nan only died a month ago and all.' The boy went to relieve himself and Freddie escaped. He'd had his fill of hospital. He rushed to the Saab, longing to sink into its luxurious comfort. A parking ticket was taped to his windscreen, but he was so intent on getting into his car and leaving the area he didn't notice. The heavy clunk of the door, the chocolatey smell of the interior, the gentle noise of the engine as he started it, all these were calming factors.

But not today. Even before he noticed and retrieved the parking ticket, he knew that the image of Jane chained to the large blue machine by blood-filled tubes was not going to go away.

And he had a sickening certainty that Natalie was going to be the best living person to free her.

24

I'd always planned to spend the last night, Friday night, at the flat and go to Temple Church from there for the wedding. My red outfit was still hanging on the back of the door of my old room, shoes and hat nearby.

'Sara, sorry to disturb you at work, but will you be free tomorrow evening?'

'I thought you didn't want to do anything – no hen party, you said.'

'I'd like us to do something together. Just the cinema, anything.'

'I'll have to unscramble plans. I really didn't expect you to be available the night before your wedding.'

'I told you I would be spending it at the flat.'

'I can't talk now, Nat. I'll ring you later.'

Why did I say no to a hen party? Now I feel it would be a wonderful way to spend my last bachelor evening. I even think of ringing Lucy, Amy and Ginny – but tomorrow's Friday night, they'll be busy. And they're all tied to their men – they might just as well be married, they're so immovable. The solidification of casual relationships—

'Miss Harper?'

'Come in, Douglas.'

'I just came to wish you the best for Saturday. No one in Chambers knows a thing – they all think it's just a holiday. So if it gets out, it's not through me.'

'You must be the most discreet clerk in the Temple, Douglas.'

'Most people talk too much, Miss Harper.' His neatly parted hair is expensively cut, his suit is handmade. He has a wife called Janice whom he has never produced at Chambers parties; perhaps she hasn't adapted so tastefully to a large income.

'I had a call from the police, and confirmed that the harassment appears to have ended.'

'You're right – I've been so knocked sideways by my sister's collapse I'd forgotten all about it. Is Mr Mentieth back from court yet?'

'Not yet. I'm not here tomorrow, I am going to Manchester with Mr Hardy, so I'll wish you the very best and bid you goodbye.' Douglas's stilted way of talking suited him. I tried to imagine him doing a messy job at home in old clothes and couldn't. Every inch of him was burnished, immaculate.

'The wedding will be announced in the papers on Monday so you can let it all out after that, Douglas.'

'It will be as big a surprise to me, Miss Harper, as to everyone else.' We both laugh, and Patricia Saban comes in at that moment. Douglas withdraws, eyes down.

'How's life, Patricia?'

'I hardly dare say it in case I tempt providence, but better. More work, and I seem to be getting over my broken heart.'

'Good. I'm really pleased for you. By the way, aren't you in Crashaw next week?'

'It's been the rounds and ended up with me. It's abominably prepared – a total dog's dinner. That solicitor should be struck off, Pritchett or whatever his name is. He's a little rat.'

'I did a preliminary hearing months ago.'

'I know – I saw your signature on the back sheet. I haven't had a chance to read the papers yet.'

'A delight in store for you. I was up most of the night trying to sort it all out.'

I can't actually warn her not to postpone preparing the case until the last minute. I leave the matter there while she unpacks her briefcase, and get back to my own work. I'm keen to finish all my papers before I go away – I'm neurotic about leaving a cleared desk. I settle pleadings for a couple of landlord and tenant actions, I write opinions for a contractual dispute between two sisters who have set up a catering business. They are no longer on speaking terms and communicate acidly through solicitors.

Jane. I'll have to go and see Jane today, I'm her lifeline. I have this sudden image of being bound to her by blood-filled tubes and get up and go to the window to banish it. Jane. I haven't rung Dave, and worse, I haven't rung our father. I'm letting her down badly already.

'I really hate winding up companies. All those tedious figures,' wails Patricia. 'I never expected to have to deal with so many columns of figures when I came to the Bar. I wish I'd done a course in book-keeping.'

'I did a weekend course – it was amazingly useful.'

'You're so organised, Natalie. I really hand it to you. You make me feel distinctly second class, particularly with that ring on!'

Flash flash goes Anthea's beautiful ring, emitting darts of blue fire. I put my hand in my pocket.

'Never say something like that about yourself. You're not second class, but if you say it people will believe it. See yourself to be as good as the next person.'

'It's called low self-esteem, and I've got a bad dose of it.'

'Cure it, Patricia. Change.'

The plane trees are bare against a grey sky, a grey river, grey buildings. Herring gulls are waddling on the lawn below until someone's dog disturbs them and they rise and flap through the lacy plane branches hung with their dangling spherical seeds. Gulls' cries. Lost souls.

'Cities should always be built on rivers. Budapest is on the Danube. I can't wait to see it.'

Patricia does not reply.

'Can you think of a single capital city that isn't on a river, Colin?'

'Rome, Paris, Prague, Cairo, Damascus, all on rivers. Athens? Madrid? Ankara?'

'We need a map. My geography is so hopeless.'

'Natalie, have you got a moment?' Freddie's body does not follow his head round the door.

'Of course – Colin and I are just playing at trivial pursuits.' I've finished my paperwork, Patricia is long gone, Colin and I are winding down together. I sometimes think he dreads going home. I give him a kiss on the cheek, and follow Freddie to his room. He's standing by his window when I arrive, staring out much as I did. I can see why cats position themselves at windows and gaze out; it gives them an illusion of control.

'I've got to go and collect my mother now; she wanted us all to go to her but it's too much of a problem for Tom. Will you come with me?'

'Of course, Freddie.' I've met Mrs Mentieth once only, and she'd patronised me. It was just after Freddie and I got engaged.

'Then we must leave. She hates eating late.'

'Wouldn't it be better if I went to the house and got the food ready?'

'Everything's in hand. Mrs Wilks has laid in supplies of M & S dinners, and prepared the soup and veg. Mother's very fond of Chicken à la King, thank goodness.' Freddie's voice is strained, and I put my arms round him from behind.

'You sound a bit low, Freddie.'

'I'm fine. Just tired.'

Jane. With all the pressure of finishing paperwork I'd completely forgotten I was going to visit her. 'Oh, Freddie, I'd forgotten Jane. I must go and see her. I can't possibly come with you now. And I must make some calls for her—'

'I saw Jane today.'

'You saw her? When?'

'Court rose early. I popped in on my way back.'

'She must have been thrilled to see you.'

Freddie goes to his desk and starts doing up his briefcase. 'Not noticeably.' He doesn't meet my eye. 'She was in the process of having dialysis.'

'I'm surprised they let you see her.'

'I wish they hadn't. I found it unexpectedly distressing.' He looks up at last. His eyes are stony.

'Was she – was she in a bad way?'

'She was dying of thirst.' The ill-chosen words hang between us. 'Desperate. It seemed so cruel to add that to her problems.' He snaps his case shut. 'So you won't come with me. But you'll join us later?'

'I'll only spend half an hour with Jane and be with you by seven thirty, I promise.'

'Mother is so obsessed by having punctual meals—'

'I know. I won't let you down. If there's a crisis I'll ring you.'

'Who was the tutor you dined with last night, by the way?'

'Dr Smallgood. You must meet her some day. You'd like her.'

London is clogged with traffic, it's drizzling, and by the time I get to the hospital it's a quarter to seven. I tell the taxi to wait for me; I can't risk not finding one later.

'I'll be fifteen, at most twenty minutes. Have a cup of tea on me.'

The driver grins at me, raises a thermos, and takes out the sports pages of the *Sun*. I run to the lift, rush to Jane's ward. She's sitting up in bed, the red of her lipstick echoing a big vase of roses on her bedside table. There's no machine beside her. She actually smiles at me. I go to hug her but she squeaks a warning.

'Mind my neck. That bloody tap thing is agony if you touch the tubes.' Plasters cover the base; a few inches of clear plastic tubing capped with yellow toggles lie on her nightdress.

'You're looking better.'

'I'm feeling a bit better. Not a lot.'

'The dialysis is clearly working.'

'I'd be dead if it didn't.' Jane and I stare at each other. 'That is the literal truth.'

'I know.'

'It's so unfair.'

'Lovely roses.'

'Your Freddie brought them apparently. I was so zonked out when he came I hardly registered. Tell him I'll be better company next time. What's the news from Dad?'

'I haven't been able to reach him yet. The number was on answerphone.'

'The clinic?'

'I rang his home number. It's all I've got.'

'Try the clinic. I'll give it to you – I know it by heart so start writing.'

'I'll ring when I go to bed.'

'There's a receptionist, Sandra, there all day. 'Tell him I saw the consultant today. He said both my kidneys were so badly scarred it wasn't worth doing a biopsy.'

'So how are they going to find out what happened?'

'They can't, but they can make a pretty accurate guess. What I find so awful is that I could lose a large part of my kidney function and not have a clue. I've had high blood pressure for some time – that's part of it but I thought it was just me. I'm anaemic, but lots of people are. I get headaches, but I always have. The blurred vision and the drop in my urine output only came at the end, with that ghastly nausea. But it could have been gastric flu and jet lag and you name it. How was I to know?'

'Thank God Jenny Morton knew what she was doing.'

'She's been in too.'

'You sound as if you've been flooded with visitors today.'

'It didn't feel like it. The day went on for ever.'

'I can't stay for long, Jane. I'm sorry, but Freddie's mother is coming to dinner and I've got to be there.'

Jane's brightness has already faded. Her red lipstick is a messy gash against her grey flaccid skin.

'Just speak to Dad for me. Get him to come over. Tell him I *need* him.'

'I'll go on and on trying tonight until I reach him. Promise.'

Jane runs her tongue over her lips. Her tongue looks shrunken, shrivelled.

'What I want more than anything at this time of day is a long cool tube of Foster's.'

'Poor Jane.'

'I lie here thinking about liquids for hours on end. Mineral water, Coke, orange juice, beer, wine, gin and tonic, vodka and tonic, ice in buckets, tea, coffee, water, water, water.' Her eyes close. I watch for tears, but none come.

'Don't torment yourself like that, Jane.'

'I'll do what I like.'

'You always do.'

'Fuck off.'

I'm annoyed with myself for reacting to her.

'Sorry.'

'Pee. That's what I think about too. Peeing with a full bladder, out in the bush after a good picnic. Letting pee flow out of you into the ocean while you're swimming far out. That feeling like an orgasm when you've been holding it in and at last you can let it go. Whoosh.' Her eyes open. 'Nat, I'll never pee again. Not while I'm like this.'

'I've got to go, Jane. I'm really sorry. I can't be late for Freddie's mum – she's a real gorgon. I'll come in for a long time tomorrow.'

'Who's going to visit me while you're away?'

'I'll ring round any people you know here. Just give me a list.'

'They're not the hospital-visiting type.'

'I'll ask Dave.'

'Can you see him coping with all this?'

'You never know.'

'Men are more squeamish than women. Don't kiss me. My breath smells like a sewer.'

I run down the stairs to use up my sense of misery and frustration. It's a great comfort to get into the large square taxi space and sink back as we move off. The diesel rumble, the sweet leatherette smell of the upholstery, the neat white hackney carriage number. So calming, the back of a London taxi. They ought to use them for therapy. I lie back with my eyes shut, picturing booths like the backs of taxis taking the place of analysts' couches.

If I'd met Freddie's mother before I met Freddie I'd have been tempted to give him a very wide berth. She is a monster. She doesn't look like one, she's far too clever; she's soft and feminine and wears pink cashmere and pearls. But her hair is fierce: it's been dyed so much and set into its style that it looks like stiff wire that would strip the skin off if you ran your hands through it. Her feet are small sharp darts at the end of her thin legs; she has those calves women develop when they wear high heels all their lives.

'Natalie my dear. How lovely to see you. Sit down here beside me while Freddie gets you a drink – you look as if you need it. So tired – they've been working you too hard, I can see.'

Everyone hates being told they look tired but from Mrs Mentieth it's a special insult. Women shouldn't be tired. I don't sit down, I hurry upstairs to try and make myself look better. High heels, pretty skirt, hair up; it takes a few minutes but it's worth it. The evening is going to be a battle and I don't intend to start it at too much of a disadvantage. I go down transformed; Mrs Mentieth praises the change but I can sense the poisoned arrows lurking.

'You've got good bones, my dear. Always such a blessing.'

'Mother, another G and T?'

'The tiniest little one, just to keep Natalie company. I'm sure she wants an aperitif.'

'Don't worry about me. If you want to eat straightaway please do – I know you like your dinner on the dot.'

Mrs Mentieth's smile is unchanged, but there's a shift behind it. 'Whoever said I did?'

'Mother, you did and do.'

'What absolute nonsense. Make mine a long drink. I'm in no hurry at all.'

Freddie winks at me when he gives me my glass of white wine. Thomas is sitting near us in his wheelchair but mentally he's far away. I suspect that's the way he deals with being in his mother's company; he's gazing over her head, his eyes totally blank.

'How are you getting on at the Bar, Natalie?'

'I love it.'

'You girls are so clever these days. How you all find time to work and run a house and care for a husband properly goodness knows—'

The 'properly' hangs around for a moment before Freddie volleys it.

'I don't need to be cared for, as you put it. Nat and I will care for each other. And as for the house, that's no problem – Nat needn't do anything if she doesn't want to.'

'Freddie runs everything so well I wouldn't dream of interfering.' I smile at Mrs Mentieth just as Mrs Wilks puts her head round the door.

'Shall I serve dinner now?' She looks only at Freddie, ignoring his mother. Mrs Wilks comes to dish up under sufferance; disapproval oozes from her.

'Ten minutes and we'll be ready.'

'I can't be too long, Mr Wilks will get concerned.'

'Ten minutes and no more, I promise.'

Before the door closes Mrs Mentieth has made a comment

sotto voce about tyrants in the kitchen. Thomas suddenly shakes his head and joins the conversation.

'Have you seen anything of Cousin Ralph lately, Mother?'

'Tom, you do ask the most ridiculous things. You know quite well that I never see Ralph Mentieth if I can help it. I think his way of life is utterly reprehensible. I hope he's not coming to the wedding.'

'I hope he is. He said he would.'

'Freddie, I can't understand why you have a soft spot for that rogue. I really can't.'

'Let's change the subject.'

'What about Henry and Isabel, then? Do you see them at all?' Thomas is now alert and watching his mother.

'We speak on the phone occasionally. I know they are coming on Saturday. It will be very nice to see them.'

'So who are your cronies?'

'What a horrid word, Tom. Do you have to use it! Cronies – it makes us all sound like witches.'

'Friends then.'

'I play bridge twice a week with Lorna and Frank Myers and Lady Atkins. You remember Ann Atkins. Her husband Reggie was knighted just before he so sadly had his heart attack.'

'Good timing. So you don't see our family at all?'

'What is this inquisition?'

'It's called conversation, Mother. I was wondering whether I got my total lack of familial duty from you. I probably have—'

'What nonsense you do talk, Tom. Look at all my work on the family tree.'

'Dead names.'

'You're being very insensitive.'

'Oh, I'd concur in preferring the family tree to the family. It's nice to find you do too, actually—'

Mrs Mentieth makes a gobbling noise and drinks her gin and tonic to hide it. Thomas is clearly winding up his mother with long-practised skill.

'Henry and Isabel are the distant ones I'll have you know, not me.'

'Ralph always says Henry has been frozen since birth. Deep frozen.'

'What does Ralph know about any of us?'

'I'm looking forward to meeting Ralph's new woman, aren't you, Freddie?'

'Mr Mentieth, it's nearly quarter to eight.'

'We're coming at once, Mrs Wilks. Drink up, everyone. And as soon as you've dished up the chicken, do feel free to go, Mrs Wilks. We can do the rest.' Freddie takes hold of the wheelchair and as they pass me I try to catch an eye, but both remain solemn. I follow the cortège – Mrs Mentieth, the wheelchair, then me – into the dining room. Mrs Wilks has put Thomas's suitcase on the bed and covered it all with a bedspread. The bed looks monstrously pregnant. Under it I spy two empty milk bottles.

We sit down round the candle-lit table and Mrs Wilks dumps soup in front of us – spinach soup.

'I hope there isn't any garlic in it, Freddie, dear. You know what garlic does to me.'

'Of course not, Mother. Have some bread.'

'My diet doesn't allow bread.'

'Ryvita? I think we've got some somewhere.'

Mrs Mentieth ignores this and turns to her eldest son. 'Tom, you didn't seriously mean that you expect Ralph to bring his mistress to the wedding?'

'Ask Freddie.'

'I invited him, so of course I do, Mother. She will add spice to the proceedings. On those lines, salt, anyone?'

The soup is completely tasteless and we busily add salt and pepper while Mrs Wilks is out of the room.

'I can't think why you ask that woman to cook when she's so useless at it. I use a girl called Caroline Pilling and she cooks divinely – I gave you her number once. Do you like cooking, Natalie?'

'Not much. Freddie's much better at it than me.'

'I must give you a lovely book I always give new brides about running a kitchen. It's American—'

'You gave that book to Anthea, Mother. It's sitting on the shelf downstairs. Oh, goodbye, Mrs Wilks. Thank you so much for all your help in getting dinner organised—'

'Mr Wilks will be wondering where I am.' Mrs Wilks is

in a purple coat and has a yellow scarf printed with grey poodles tied firmly over her perm. Freddie's mother stares at her smugly while murmuring 'delicious soup, so good', as Mrs Wilks departs.

There is a silence while Freddie doles out the next course; I decide to pour everyone more wine because I need it. When I get to Mrs Mentieth her varnished nails block off her glass.

'No, no, I've had quite enough. Well, perhaps a soupçon. That's lovely, no more. I've had an idea, Natalie. Perhaps instead of the book I could give you a cordon bleu cookery course—'

'How kind of you, but—'

'Mother, how on earth is Natalie going to find the time for some footling cookery course – she's a very successful junior barrister with a growing practice. Would you like some of this stuffing which Mrs Wilks has made – it looks suspiciously like packet stuffing.'

'I won't, thank you. Don't let him browbeat you, dear – my offer stands.'

'Paxo sage and onion stuffing. Give me a decent helping.' Thomas hands his plate back for more. 'I love Paxo stuffing, Bisto gravy, Bird's custard, Worcester sauce. I get very little chance to enjoy them in my peripatetic life. What a treat.'

'A weekend course might make you feel happier in the kitchen, dear. But if you haven't the time—'

'The other thing I really miss when I'm working abroad is Cheddar. Good old mousetrap. I could kill for it sometimes.'

'I'm surprised you notice you're not eating it.' Both brothers find this hilarious and laugh for some time. More wine is opened and the meal drags on. I'm getting drunk, I can hear it in my voice when I offer Mrs Mentieth some coffee. Her name comes out as Mish Smenthieth. We're sitting just the two of us in the dining room – Freddie has taken Thomas to the loo. Mrs Mentieth leans towards me, a little glassy herself.

'Call me Alice, dear, do. Now, while we girls are on our own, do let me ask you a question I've been dying to ask. Please don't be offended, but are you considering having a family one day?'

'I don't know.'

'It's none of my business, of course, but with Tom not married and none from Anthea, well, I really thought grandchildren would never come my way.' Tears start to flow without any warning. 'I've kept everything, you see, the family christening robe, the little bonnet, the shawl, everything. The bonnet's embroidered, so pretty, but both boys were too big for it. Such a pity, it's the sweetest little bonnet you ever saw. Victorian—'

'It sounds lovely.' I pass her a tissue; her mascara is running.

'I kept baby books for both of them, I wrote down every detail of their development until they went to boarding school. How tall, what weights, when they first crawled and walked, what they said, what diseases they got. When they went to school it all ended. They weren't my boys any more as they had been. They were only eight.'

'You could have kept them at home and sent them to a day school.'

'Their father wouldn't hear of it.'

'What wouldn't Father hear of?' Thomas propelled himself in.

'Just chatter, Tom. I must go home. Where's Freddie?'

'Calling you a taxi and bringing the coffee.'

'I thought he was going to take me home himself—' Her voice quavered.

'Don't be ridiculous, Mother. He's well over the odds. Can you imagine how the press would go to town if Freddie was booked for drunk driving.'

Mrs Mentieth dabs at her eyes while she gazes fixedly at her eldest son. Perhaps she's seeing the little boy whose every step and statement she charted so carefully.

She turns to me and whispers: 'That little bonnet would fit a baby girl.'

'Dave?'

'The ravishing Natalie. Or should I say ravished?'

'You're drunk.'

'Not very.'

'Have you heard about my sister?'

'The yet-to-be-ravished Jane. What a tricky lady. I gave her a bed for the night but it got me nowhere. By the way, she cut a meeting I set up for her. That annoyed me.'

'She cut it because she's in hospital.'

'Tell me more.'

'She collapsed on Tuesday. Her kidneys have completely failed.'

Silence.

'Dave? Are you there?'

'I don't know what to say, except how terrible.'

'She's in need of visitors, Dave. She'll be in hospital for weeks.' There's another silence. I can hear women talking in the room behind Dave. 'I'm going to be away for a week after the wedding, and there's no one to go and see her except my friends.'

'I'm not much good at sickbed visiting, Nat. Hospitals give me the creeps.'

'Try, please try. She's desperate. Please.'

'Can't they do anything? Like cure her?'

'It's a choice between a kidney machine for life or a transplant.'

'God.'

I tell him what ward Jane's in, I give him the telephone number so that he can check and go when she's not on dialysis. He resists all this information but I go on and on until he promises to visit Jane. Dave has many faults but he doesn't break a promise. Most of the time he never makes them.

'Don't take her the usual things, sweets, chocolates, fruit or anything.'

'What about a performing monkey?'

After speaking to Dave, I ring my father. It's over a year since I spoke to him. He'll be having breakfast – sitting in the summer sun in Sydney. As the phone rings I try to imagine him and can't. When the phone is answered he doesn't even sound familiar.

'Dick Harper.'

'Dad.'

'Jane?'

'No, it's Natalie.'

'*Nat!* Did you get my letter?'

'No.'

'I only wrote a few days ago. I really would love to have come to your wedding, Nat, but I am too busy – the practice has gone mad.'

'Don't worry about it, Dad, I understand. I wasn't ringing about that—'

'Why don't you come out with Jane when she comes back? Come and see your old dad?'

'Dad, Jane's sick.' I stop.

'How sick?'

I tell him and he's shattered.

'I should have guessed. She kept having those headaches. She was anaemic. I should have gone deeper into it, I should have guessed. Oh, my God.'

'She wants you to come over as soon as possible.'

'Oh, poor Jane. This is terrible news. Yes, tell her I'll do my best, tell her I'll try and get a locum set up – complete renal failure, they say?'

'The consultant said the kidneys were so damaged it wasn't worth even doing a biopsy.'

'My poor little girl. Turn that thing off, would you?' Someone in the background switches off a noisy radio.

'We can give you a bed any time, Dad. In fact if you come next week while Freddie and I are away, you can share the whole house with his brother Thomas.'

'You haven't changed your plans then?'

'No. Freddie – no, we decided against cancelling. Jane's in very good hands.'

I can sense my father's disapproval though he says nothing.

'Dad, it's difficult for us. This is my wedding after all. Jane understands.'

'I'll have to ring you back, Nat. I'll have to contact a few people, sort things out here. Where will you be for the next few hours?'

'Here, at Freddie's. I'll give you the number. It's midnight here but ring any time. I'll be here until you do, then I'll go straight to Jane in the morning and tell her. You've got to come, Dad. She's in despair.'

'I'm not surprised. Speak to you soon.'

At no point has my father actually committed himself and said: I'll come.

Freddie has a shower, standing for ages under the pressurised jets. He wraps himself up in the pale blue towels the house is full of (apparently Anthea always bought pale blue towels, she said they flattered the skin) and lies down beside me. I'm sitting staring at the phone, feeling brain dead.

'I'm shattered.'

'Have a shower.'

'A shower at night wakes me up too much. I'll have mine in the morning.' As I yawn, Freddie takes my hand.

'What did your father say?'

'He said he'd ring back when he's juggled things. I suppose he'll come over. Jane will be devastated if he doesn't.'

'Nat, I have something I must tell you. I went to see Jane today.'

'I know. You told me earlier.'

'It knocked me sideways. I didn't expect to be so affected. But to see her hooked up to that machine made me feel quite faint. I couldn't control my sense of shock. I was actually sick.'

'Oh, Freddie—'

'A hardened old barrister like me. Well, you never know exactly how you'll react in a crisis. I was a broken reed in this case.'

'I cried when I first saw her.'

'Get undressed and come and join me. Sleep here, from now on, in this bed. It's yours too. I need you here.' Freddie puts his free hand up to my face, strokes my chin. 'You look so white and drained.'

'I am. I've never felt so tired.'

'I'm exhausted too. I want you here for comfort, my darling, for your comfort and for mine.'

'I'll go and clean my teeth.'

When I come back five minutes later, wearing one of Freddie's old shirts as a nightdress, he's got his eyes shut. He's gone to sleep.

Then I notice – how could I have missed it earlier? – that all the photographs of Anthea have gone; faint empty squares on the walls mark where they've been.

'I'm not asleep. Not quite.'

'The photos have gone—'

'I took them down last night.' Freddie opens his eyes again.

'I had one of those moments of epiphany. The time had come to take them down.'

'Where have you put them?'

'In a drawer in my desk.'

'I think you should hang them again somewhere in the house – the stairs or the hall. Somewhere she can see us passing, and us her.'

'I was going to.'

'Good.'

'Nat, I haven't finished what I wanted to say about Jane. Come and cuddle up beside me.'

So I get in and switch the light off. Freddie wraps his arms tight around me.

'My experience at the hospital shook me so much it made me think the whole situation through. Nat, I realised I had the most intense physical revulsion to the possibility you might donate a kidney to Jane. You mustn't do it. I couldn't bear it.'

Freddie's cradling has become a crushing; there's a silence I can't break. He has more to say.

'I have to be honest with you. I couldn't bear you to scar your lovely body, I couldn't bear you to take the risk of your own single kidney failing and you too being hooked to that machine. I'd never stop worrying it might happen. I know it's ignoble and illogical but that's how I feel. I want you to be healthy and whole and bear our children. Natalie, *Natalie*.'

We cling to each other. We kiss the tears off each other's cheeks, we laugh a little as we do so. I can't speak. Freddie pulls away from me and says:

'Natalie, promise me you won't do it ever, promise me.'

We can just pick out each other's eyes in the dark. I touch his lips, his eyebrows, trying to find my voice.

'Promise me.'

'I can't. I have to leave it open, Freddie. Please understand. I can't.'

25

'Kerry Poole has gone back to America, sir. I think you'll get no further problems. Miss Poole's companion has also gone to New York. He, or someone very like him, was seen near your house when your first window was smashed. We questioned him but he had what seemed like a good alibi.'

'Good riddance to them. It's been a terrible week all round. Thank you for ringing, Inspector.'

'My pleasure.'

Freddie put the phone down and sat feeling deadened. His wedding tomorrow – he had to make some phone calls to check everything was properly organised at the Garrick and the church. That's surely Natalie's job, dear. He could hear his mother's voice.

There's nothing I wouldn't do for her, Mother. You'll never understand.

'My father finally rang.' Natalie came through the door of his room holding two cups of coffee. She'd waited back at the house for the call, and must have just arrived in Chambers. 'He's coming over.'

'That's excellent news. What's the matter?'

'I won't be able to see him. He's coming next Monday and returning by the weekend. I'm going to miss him completely.'

'And he you. Can't he stay a little longer?'

'He said it was the devil's own job to make even that short stay possible.' Natalie's pallor was accentuated by her black and white clothing. She slumped in an armchair and stared blankly at Freddie. 'I feel cheated. I really want to see him, Freddie. I'm surprised how cheated I feel, considering how little love there's been between us.'

'Darling Nat, if you want to come back early from Budapest let's change the return flight. It only takes a phone call.'

'Damn him. Why is everything so complex? We need our week away, we both need a proper break. I don't want to change our plans.'

'Did you ask him to delay his visit by a few days so that you could coincide?'

'How could I? He's coming here for Jane's sake. He's not coming for mine.'

There was a silence while they sipped their coffee.

'I've got a consultation booked in for eleven. We've got five minutes. Let's have lunch together in hall at half twelve.'

'Is there anything I can do for you this morning, Freddie? Arrangements for tomorrow?'

'You could check that the cars have the correct timings. I was just about to do it.' Freddie passed the number over. 'By the way, the police say that Kerry Poole has gone back to America.'

'Is Poole going to appeal against sentence?'

'I'm sure he is.'

'She'll be back when that starts. More charming reminders of her presence will come our way no doubt.'

'No doubt.'

They continued to talk gently until Paul announced that Freddie's client had arrived with his solicitor. Freddie was pleased to see Natalie looked less haunted when she left him, but when they met up again for lunch she was as tense as before. They walked through the Temple to Middle Temple Hall, Freddie's Inn. They helped themselves to food and swung their legs over the benches to join a group from Chambers. Natalie was at the end of the table with no one opposite her, much to her relief. She felt oppressed by the weight of history in this hall. The superb hammer-beam ceiling pressed down on her; the wooden floor, wooden walls, ornately carved minstrels' gallery, were all impregnated with the stuffy smell of hundreds of thousands of hot dinners; the empty suits of armour above the panelling seemed to lean over on her. She ate in silence.

'Natalie, you're stuck there at the end – why don't you move opposite me—'

'It's all right – I'm not in a chatty mood.'

'Let me get you some dessert or fruit or something?'

'No, thanks. Just coffee.'

Then George Warne noticed her isolation when Freddie went off for the coffee, and slid his bottom along the bench until his thigh touched hers. She edged away.

'Natalie, you're a bright young thing. I want to pick your brains. Tell me which night spot you all go to – I have to entertain some Americans tonight who are much nearer your age than mine. In fact, why don't you join us if you're free—'

'I'm not. Sorry.'

'Well, give me some advice instead. A gorgeous girl like you must have been taken everywhere—'

'I'll get cross with you, George.'

'Can't think why.'

'There's a place in Soho called Paradise which is very popular, or Griffin's in the King's Road is said to be good.'

'Which do you like best?'

'I haven't been to either, actually.'

'What a deprived life you're leading. Or perhaps you only go to Annabel's. I just wanted to take them somewhere different, but unless you know them I wouldn't like to risk it.' George chattered on. Freddie returned with the coffee and sat on the other side of Natalie. 'Freddie, persuade her for me – I want Natalie to come night-clubbing with some glamorous Americans—'

Freddie replied facetiously, and Natalie endured their barbed badinage in silence.

'I'm not surprised George's women walk out on him. I would regard it as hell on earth to be married to a chauvinist like him.'

'But, Natalie, he loves women—'

'No, he doesn't. We're just objects to him. Not full human beings, not of the same mental calibre as men. We are more or less attractive useful props to be used as he thinks fit, and discarded or ignored when life gets serious.'

'You're in a sour mood, I must say. Poor old George.'

'This place makes me sour. The whole hall gives off the same attitude to me – that women are here on sufferance. Even when *Twelfth Night* was played here the actors were all men. It's not used to having women around and I can almost feel its disapproval of women when I swing my legs over the benches. The suits of armour shudder in horror.'

'You have to admit you're very recent arrivals in its history. What a shock for the place to have attractive knees flashing at the ceiling every day. Mind you, I love the way you negotiate those benches—'

'You're as bad as George.'

'Never.'

They stood smiling at each other in Middle Temple Lane but had to move almost immediately to let a taxi past.

'Well, I'm off to drop this note in on the undertreasurer before I return to Chambers.'

'And I'm off to see Jane to tell her the good news.'

'And this evening you're going back to your flat? You're sure about that?'

'I've promised Sara. Besides, my wedding dress is there.'

'So it's goodbye until tomorrow, when we meet at the church door?'

'Yes.'

'Take care.'

'You too. You too.'

Freddie saw a tear collect at each corner of Natalie's eyes as she turned and hurried away up towards Fleet Street. His mind was full of that image of her dancing in the cream silk dress amongst the rubbish of a South London street.

'Mr Mentieth. I'd like a word if possible.'

'Douglas – I thought you were up north today.'

'Case folded, sir. Got back to find some good news for you.'

Douglas followed Freddie into his room, and then went on in his most unctuous voice:

'I am very pleased to tell you that the serious fraud involving a certain celebrated gentleman is yours, sir. John Ball of Green Target Finance. Estimated six months.'

'Well, well. You've pulled it in after all. Douglas, you are a very clever clerk.'

'Good news to get married on, sir.'

'When is it listed?'

'March. I suspect it will run longer than six months, sir.'

'So do I. Mind you, by then they may have reformed the system for these fraud trials. The Royal Commission is considering abandoning jury trials for this sort of case – look at that poor jury in the Blue Arrow case. Eighteen months. Do you know how much that trial cost the taxpayer?'

'I heard it was forty million.'

'At least. The prosecution wasted a lot of time on peripheral issues. It should have cost less. Mind you, the cost of unravelling Robert Maxwell's empire is going to make forty million look like holiday expenses. I'm sure the Treasury is shuddering at the prospect.'

'You sound as if you're in favour of reform, sir.'

'Of course I am, though I don't know what form it should take for this non-violent white-collar crime. Quasi-criminals is I believe the buzzword for people who indulge in improper enrichment.'

'Lovely phrases, sir. But they're still criminals, to be judged as such.'

'Quasi-criminals, please, Douglas. Get your jargon right. Since we're being pushed towards the American system, let's borrow their terminology. If we dealt with these quasi-criminals the American way, preliminary investigations would be carried out by the Serious Fraud Office, but once a prima facie case arose against an individual we'd do away with the set piece adversarial battle before a jury which we all enjoy and instead have a tribunal.'

Douglas shifted his neatly shod feet, uninterested in Freddie's speculations. Like most clerks he had no special legal training, and though he had a basic grasp of the nature of each case, his assessment of the fee was based simply on the given estimated length in court and the amount of papers. Tricky problems arising from two sheets of instructions causing a barrister hours of tough thinking had no place in Douglas's view of a case. To him, a long opinion equalled a bigger fee; a short opinion which had taken days of cogitation was never correctly assessed unless the barrister who wrote it took a hand. Freddie had often complained but realised that, short of clerks actually reading for the Bar, there was no remedy.

'Anyway, Douglas, let's talk about Chambers. How is Paul shaping up? He seems happy enough.'

'Very well, sir. Most of our solicitors like him, though one or two find him a little too confident. Let's call it cheeky.'

'A fault on the right side if put to good use. And Sharon? I'm conscious that I haven't had time for a chat with her for ages.'

'I think she's due a rise, sir. She's been with us for a year.'

'Has she really been with us so long? I can't believe it. Well, there's a provision in her contract for a rise after a year – give her whatever we agreed.'

'I can't seem to find the contract, sir. Nor can she. Do you have a copy?'

'No.'

'We'll have another look.'

When Douglas left Freddie took *Who's Who* off the shelf and turned to his own entry.

MENTIETH, Frederick Ashworth; QC 1990; a Recorder since 1989; b. 12 May 1950; s. of the late William Thomas Mentieth and Alice Margaret (née Gittings); m. 1976 Anthea Belling-Johnson; Stowe; Balliol College, Oxford; BCL; MA; called to the Bar, Middle Temple, 1974. Recreations: reading, listening to music. Clubs: Garrick, Reform.

He had debated for ages about what to put down as his recreations; though tempted to be witty, he had read another entry which said 'Learning less and less about more and more; trying to stem the progress of old age' and decided against it.

Anthea. He hadn't changed the entry, he hadn't recorded her death. Somehow he hadn't been able to bring himself to put it down in black and white as part of his life. Now he would have to; he would have to add m.1st and m.2nd: Natalie Harper. Freddie sat there staring at the two centimetres of print bestowed by the establishment as a seal of approval for getting silk. Then he turned to George Warne's entry: it was very short – no schooling listed, no wives. After recreations he had simply put 'Luxury'. His clubs were the RAC and the Royal Aeronautical. Freddie had heard rumours that George possessed a pilot's licence, but had never wanted to ask him about it.

He shut the heavy red-bound book and wondered how many other countries had such a convenient symbol with which to recognise a certain type of achievement and ability. He slipped it back into its accustomed slot beside Kobbé's *Complete Opera Book*. Almost everyone commented on the presence of Kobbé in his law library, but it was the sensible place to keep it – he could read the instantly forgettable summary of the libretto just before he left to hear the opera. So could Natalie. (In Anthea's day he'd kept it at home.)

Freddie sighed and turned his mind to the problem of swap deals between fixed interest ratepayers and floating ratepayers and whether they were wagering contracts as defined by the Gaming Acts of 1845 or 1892, and the afternoon passed.

26

Calamity Jane. Suddenly I can't get myself through the doors of the hospital and go off to walk by the river instead. Long lines of barges slide by; one has its cargo confined by netting.

Dad on the beach with that piece of net rolled up by his feet, his smile fading when he turned from Jane to me, convinced I'd overreacted with tooth and nail to Jane's harmless prank. The scene is as clear to me now as if it had happened yesterday.

Nets, toils, snares. I'm stupid to think I can ever escape them. My family is my family, and it won't change. My father didn't sound sad he'd miss me, even though it's possible we may never meet again after this. Jane, sick Jane, was his only concern. She always has been and she always will be. But will he go as far as being tissue-typed to see if he could give Jane a kidney – will he contemplate that ultimate bond? If he did, I'm sure she'd go to Australia for the operation—

But it's a pipe dream. My father will never give up part of himself, even for Jane. He's kept himself detached all his life, he won't take a risk like that now. Jane may be his favourite but his love for other human beings is a pale thing. Mum once said, after he'd left her, that you couldn't accuse him of being selfish because it implied he knew what unselfishness was. He didn't. He has, or had, no conception of denying himself for another's sake.

'I can't be angry with him, you know. He was born without altruism and can't learn it. Yet he can be very caring when it suits him and it fools you, it fools you.' Mum said this very near the end of her life, and the way she said it made me see how much she still loved him.

A small sailing boat passes me with a golden-haired boy at the helm. His instructor shouts something at him and the boat goes about, its sail flapping. I get up and run towards the hospital, eager now to tell Jane that Dad is coming over. She'll be so thrilled. I can see her eyes fill with delight.

'She's had a bad day, I'm afraid.' Sister Pennington passes me as I come out of the lift. She's carrying a huge pile of files.

'Oh dear.'

'The sinking-in process takes some time and goes through phases.' The nurse's brown eyes are fixed on the lift doors behind me.

'What do you mean?'

'Jane is fighting the treatment. She can't fight the disease so she's fighting everything peripheral. It always happens, and I don't blame her. It's hard to accept the finality of renal failure.' Her eyes move to mine. 'Anyway, I'm just warning you in case she gives you what she's been giving us. A hard time. She's just finished dialysing, which should have cheered her up.'

I stand in the ward doorway looking towards Jane's bed. The dialysis machine is still beside her bed, though not connected. Jane is lying with her head on one side, eyes shut; the tubes in her neck stick up at a cruel angle. Freddie's roses in their ugly glass vase are already looking rather wilted.

I sit quietly beside her and touch her hand. Her eyes fly open.

'Oh, it's you. I thought it was one of those fucking nurses again.'

'Hello, Jane.'

'Pass those tissues, would you. They've fallen on the floor.'

Her eyes are puffy and red, her blonde hair is oily and lifeless. The varnish on her nails is badly chipped; I feel compunction, I should have brought some nail varnish remover in for her.

'Jane, I've got some wonderful news.'

'No news could be wonderful.'

'Dad's coming over next week.'

'Oh, no!'

'But you desperately wanted him to come—'

'He'll hate all this as much as I do. It would be better if he didn't see me like this. He won't be able to accept it, it'll make him miserable.'

'Well, he's coming. While I'm away, so I'm going to miss him. Which I'm sad about.'

Jane is straightening herself in bed, her mouth pulled down in pain.

'This bloody thing in my neck is agony today. I jarred it when I was trying to brush my hair.'

'I thought the news about Dad would cheer you up.'

'Natalie, get it into your thick head that *nothing* today can cheer me up. Of course I'm pleased at the thought of seeing Dad, of course I want to see him even though I wish he wasn't coming. But you don't understand my situation, you've no idea what this is like.'

'How can I? I'm not going through it like you.'

'The nurses don't understand either. If they did, they'd make life easier.'

'I spoke to Dave too, by the way.'

She does not answer. She is in a coffin of private misery. We sit in silence for a few minutes, then she starts talking again with her eyes shut and her face turned away.

'They had a massive ward round today. Every consultant and doctor plus a thousand students. I was the special act laid on for them.'

'What was said about you?'

'Everything. I am a perfect case of advanced uremia. They lapped it all up. Platelet counts, creatinine counts, albumin, globulin, uric acid counts, on and on they went. How thrilled I was to hear my alkaline phosphatase at least was normal.' Her dry bitter voice stops for a moment. I say nothing.

'Those students were so eager, so fascinated. I just lay there waiting to scream. By the time they'd finished, if one of them had said "glomerulonephritis" once more I would have.'

'What on earth is that?'

'The nurse explained it to me afterwards. I wouldn't have known either. The students all kept saying it, like a bloody mantra they'd just learned. Nephritis is inflamation of the kidneys. The glommy whatsits are the tiny capillaries in the kidneys which filter the blood – apparently each kidney's got a million. Mine are all shrivelled up and useless. At least that's what they're telling me.' She pauses, her head still turned away. 'But what if they're wrong, Nat, what if I've just got some awful bug no one's ever heard of which I picked up on the plane? A fearsome new virus, not glomerulonephritis at all.'

'They must be sure, or they wouldn't have put you on dialysis, surely?'

'Doctors make mistakes. They haven't done a biopsy. My consultant was so pleased with himself I'd love him to be wrong in front of all his students. What a fart-arse.'

'Jane. Look at me.'

'He really got up my nose.'

'Jane.'

She turns her head slowly. I try to take her hand but she pulls it away.

'Don't try to give me a heartening chat, Natalie. I don't want it.'

'I wouldn't dream of it. I – I can't imagine the awfulness of what you're going through. I really can't. But I can say this – there is hope for you. A new kidney. You'd be back to normal with a new kidney.'

Jane's face goes weak, flaccid, and her lips tremble. This time she stays silent, so I plough on.

'So there is a solution, there is hope, there is something to be done that will give you back your life.'

'You sound like a missionary.'

'As soon as I come back from our honeymoon I'll go and get my tissues typed. Then if you and I match, we can – we can think about me giving you a kidney.'

I didn't mean to say this, I am not ready to. It all comes out because of Jane's terrible despair. My words hang in the air between us and Jane doesn't seem to take them in.

'Jane.'

'Why should you give me part of your body, and anyway I'm not sure I want you to.'

'It may not be a possibility, we may not match.'

'I don't want to be cut open and given a part of someone else. There must be a better way round it. They were talking about something called CAPD – maybe that'll work and I'll be fine.'

I sit by my sister and can't help feeling a surge of fury. I've just offered her my kidney, damn her, my kidney, I've made a huge leap into the unknown and all she can think about is herself. Then the fury dies away when I see her dry tongue go over her chapped lips. Her mouth is parched, her voice croaks. Her eyes are now on the ward clock. It's nearly six.

'Every evening I think of beer, big foaming pints of beer. Oh, God. I'd like to lie in a bathful of beer and drink until I'm dead.' She grins mirthlessly at me. 'What a wonderful end.'

'I can certainly think of worse.' I try to grin back, and suddenly we are both really smiling at each other.

'I'll tell you something, Nat. I never expected you even to offer me your kidney, ever.'

'Why not?'

'Why should you keep me alive at your expense? I've never done anything for you. Anything big.'

'I've never asked you to.'

'I didn't ask you, remember. You offered.'

'If I was in that bed and you were sitting here, wouldn't you?'

'Would I?' Again Jane runs a dry tongue over her poor lips. 'Would I consider cutting into my own body to give you a precious part of me? Would I? I don't think I would. I'm too like Dad. He won't.'

'Well, it's not something you and I will ever have a chance of putting to the test.' I reach out to tweak Freddie's roses, to remove the most wilted of them. This conversation is beginning to exhaust me; I feel consumed by Jane's disease, I feel her sucking out my strength as if it's the Foster's lagers she so longs for. Sister Pennington puts her head through the ward door, sees us together, goes away again. The other occupants of the ward are quiet; they have no visitors this evening. In the distance I can hear the rattle of the food trolleys, and the smell of warmed-up food filters through to us.

'Ah, my supper. My bland, boring supper. What a thrill. Along with Foster's I dream of oranges, of bananas, of grapes. They give me cooked fruit, cooked to buggery. To me, a fresh fruit freak. Pineapples, pawpaws all fresh and juicy is what I want—'

'Don't torture yourself, Jane. Look, I must go, leave you in peace to eat. Here's Dad's schedule, he faxed it through to Chambers. He's going to stay in a hotel, I don't know which one. He could have stayed at Freddie's place but he said he'd prefer a hotel.'

'When do you get back from Budapest?'

'Sunday week. I'll ring you during the week.'

'Ask the nurse for the ward number so that they can bring the phone over here.'

'I've got it. Dave and Sara have it too. They'll come in.' I stand up. We stare at each other, and the expression in Jane's eyes is impossible to read.

'Happy wedding day, big sister.'

'I'll be glad when it's over.'

'I'm sorry there won't be a Harper there.'

'Not as sorry as me.'

'I still haven't asked you what you'd like for a wedding present. How am I going to do anything about it now?'

'All I want is to see you looking better. I don't want any other present.'

The food trolley has reached her bed, and Jane is having to sit up. I kiss her on the cheek away from the fistula in her neck. The plastic tubes are transparent in the setting sun framed in the window behind her. They look almost comic. I lift a hand as I leave, and she lifts one. We freeze for a long moment.

Now I have my last evening as an officially unattached person ahead of me. My heart lifts as I hurry towards the tube station. I've made my offer to Jane and she's more or less refused it. 'I don't want you to give me part of your body.' My annoyance and frustration with her have faded, and all I feel is relief. It's the best possible outcome; my conscience is deliciously happy.

I take the stairs to the flat two at a time, and let myself in expecting the place to be empty. But Sara appears and bars the way.

'Into your bedroom, Natalie Harper. Just for five minutes.'

Her eyes are bright and full of hidden agenda. There's a suppressed silence from the rest of the flat. She slams the door on me and I find myself shut into my dirty derelict room. The bed's still unmade, the black plastic sacks still stand in a row.

I've got a new suitcase waiting under the bed, so I take it out and put the clothes I've left for Budapest into it. A suit, warm trousers, jerseys, silk trousers for evening. New underwear, still in its plastic wrappers. I free it, pack it. Quite a lot of stuff I need I've already taken over to Freddie's; we'll have to stop there on the way to the airport. But we were going to anyway.

I think of the usual bridal trappings and stroke the red silk dress. It's nice but it's highly unsuitable. So are the shoes. Oh, never mind, why should I worry, and at least I haven't got a backup of mother, sister, bridesmaids, all fussing and looking disapproving. But the dress isn't right; I can picture Freddie's face when he sees it.

'I'm going to be wrongly dressed and how.' I say this out loud as I search for the cream dress I left scrumpled up in a corner, in a plastic bag. But I can't find it, so perhaps I didn't leave it there; I can't think what I did with it. I bang on the door.

'What's going on? Can't I come out yet?'

'No. Two minutes.'

I can hear laughter from the sitting room, and the bumping sound of furniture being moved. I lie down to wait, and pick up my old battered Snoopy half-hidden under the bed. How I loved him once upon a time. I was given him when I was six, he was dressed in a cowboy outfit – a check shirt and jeans. His white stuffed head was pristine, his expression was jaunty yet resigned, his ears flopped entrancingly. How I loved him. The fact that Jane had an identical Snoopy mattered not at all. Mine had a different expression. I knew him in a crowd of Snoopies. To me he was unique, given an aura by my love. Jane didn't care much for hers. She loved her bear. She's kept Sid, I've kept Snoopy – what does this say about us?

I hold him above my head – his white head is a brownish grey, his cowboy outfit long gone. Love and age have battered him. He now wears a striped T-shirt that has seen better days, nothing else. His little legs hang sexless. I drop him back on the floor.

'Natalie Harper! You are summoned.' After a bang on the door, it is opened. Amy stands there solemnly.

'Amy! I didn't know you were here—'

'Follow me.' Not a sign of a smile, but Amy has always been able to look serious when the rest of us have collapsed completely. I follow her into the darkened sitting room. Candles burn on the coffee table and mantelpiece. There's a tableau at the end of the room: a bride stands there, with two attendants. They are dressed in shimmering cream silk, with coronets of leaves in their hair. I gasp, I can't help it. Everyone is as solemn as Amy. I shut my eyes and when I open them again grins are splitting faces and laughter bursts out.

'You devils!'

Sara is wearing the wedding dress, my discarded wedding dress. It's a bit long for her; she's standing on a box to compensate. On either side of her are Ginny and Lucy wearing cream silk straight dresses; all three have got strands of ivy and silver ribbon in their hair. We all stop laughing as I stare at them. I can't help being moved by the sight of them.

'You look beautiful.'

Amy bustles forward. 'Aren't I clever, Nat? I ran up these two dresses today. Just a plain straight shift really – Peter Jones happened to have such a good matching fabric in the furnishing department. We tossed up to see who'd be bridesmaids.'

All four are gazing at me. Sara, Ginny and Lucy are still frozen in their tableau.

'What a start to a hen party.' I don't know what else to say. I feel like crying.

'Nat.' Sara steps off the box carefully. 'I've had this dress cleaned and mended for you – I couldn't bear to see it lying chucked out in a heap. And I saw what you'd bought to get married in. You just can't wear that red dress.'

'Why not?'

'We forbid you.' Ginny and Lucy come forward and grab my arms. 'We absolutely forbid you. You've got to wear the proper dress. It's meant for you. You look marvellous in it.'

'It's over the top—'

'The red dress is even more so.' Amy is undoing the back of the wedding dress, and Sara steps carefully out of it, dressed only in knickers. She pulls on a sweatshirt.

'Sara rang me a couple of days ago and said we ought to get it all set up and hijack you. We decided you needed bridesmaids if you wore the dress so we've provided them.' Amy is looking dead pleased with herself.

Lucy kisses my cheek. 'Don't look so miserable. Trust us. Your sister's sick, you've got no one except us. You need us, Nat.'

'I never said I didn't, but not as bridesmaids—'

'We're not coming any other way, are we, Ginny?'

'I've never been a bridesmaid and now's my chance. Come on, Sara, where's the champagne?'

'In the fridge still. But get out of those dresses before you spill something down them.'

I'm silent while they take off the dresses and Amy carefully hangs them all from the picture rail. My three half-naked friends pass round glasses and fill them with champagne. Amy is still fiddling with hems and talking about shoes.

'Tomorrow Lucy and I will go to Anello and Davide to get some cream ballet shoes for all of you—'

'Leave those dresses alone and drink a toast to Nat.'

They raise their glasses; they wait for me to speak. I can't.

'Come on, Nat, you know this is a good idea—'

'I could improve on these wreaths—'

'I like them as they are.' I suddenly find I'm crying, hugging my friends, laughing, full of relief. 'So it will be a proper wedding after all.'

'Sort of proper. I've known more proper ones.' Amy's parents were married in Westminster Abbey with royalty present. 'You all need flowers to carry. I'll do three posies tomorrow. I bought this cream silk ribbon to tie round them.'

'You must have been very sure of me to spend all that time and money.'

'We made a pact to win you round come what may.' Amy is large, ginger-haired, endlessly energetic, naturally commanding. (Or bossy, depending how you took it.) She'll go far – she's already got a plum job in a publishing house. 'Anyway, come on, girls, drink up. There's another bottle in the fridge.'

I look at my bridesmaids. Lucy is fair with brown eyes, Ginny is fair with blue eyes in a face thick with freckles. Lucy is rounded and cuddly-looking, Ginny awkward and angular, but it's Ginny that has the sweet, easy-going nature – Lucy is a tough girl who'd break a man's jaw if he tried to cuddle her unasked.

'Sara, you must stand in for Jane. As my sister, she should have been part of this.'

'Undressed chief bridesmaid.'

'It's going to be fun, Nat. Cheer up.'

'I am cheered. Jane is the only sad thing.'

'How is she?'

We talk about Jane, we drink more champagne, Mark comes in and is thrown out again after one glass, then Sara tries to blindfold me.

'We're off. Another surprise.'

'I'm getting wary of all these surprises, and besides, if you're seriously thinking I'm going out with a blindfold on you can think again.'

They make me shut my eyes in the taxi, but I guess where we are going because nobody has dressed up. The Sanctuary.

'Brilliant choice for a hen night.' It's been years since we've been out as a group of women together to an all-female place like the Sanctuary, and by the time we are undressed we are whooping. (I'm sure the staff want us to leave long before we are ready to go, we behave so noisily all evening. But they don't show it.)

First we all leap into the swimming pool and commandeer the swing, from which most of us fall off. We go to the sauna, we go to the jacuzzi, we go to the steam bath, we behave like children. We all have a massage and meet back in the steam bath, our figures shadowy in the white swirling hot fog. There's just us in there now, lying on the benches head to foot, chatting comfortably, lapsing into silence. Then Lucy's voice comes out of the mist:

'How many of us here have been had by Dave Rosenberg?'

'Me.'

'Me.'

'Me!'

'Me, alas.'

'And you, Amy? Not you too?'

'I'm not so stupid, even though he keeps waving that dreadful book at me.'

'He said he'd never heard of Don Giovanni but I don't believe him.'

'He's mad.'

'He's crafty, not mad. That's one of the reasons I've held out.

He'll keep that book and one day when you're a QC, Natalie, or you, Sara, have been awarded the CBE, he'll pounce.'

'What do you mean?'

'I mean blackmail.'

'You're not serious.' Ginny sounds worried. She's sitting up, a ghost in the steam.

'I am. Why else would he keep a notebook?'

'To tick us all off. It's part of his thrill. I said I thought he was mad, and I mean it.' Lucy is sitting up too. 'You exaggerate, Amy. He's not wicked.'

'Just a bit twisted.'

'He's so hairy.'

'It's amazing.'

'His feet are like furry slippers.'

We all start laughing when I say this, and end up rolling off the benches. It's manic, uncontrolled laughter with an edge of fear behind it. Then there's a renewed burst of steam, our laughs simmer down, soon there's no sound except the hissing of vapour.

'Come on, gang. The jacuzzi.' Amy leads the way and we follow, all firmly wrapped in our white Sanctuary towels like a flock of classical statues.

'I think it's Dave's compensation,' whispers Ginny to my back.

'For what?'

'For not being very good at it. So by having the notebook ritual he twists sex into something else—'

'What was that, Ginny?'

'Dave's no good at fucking so he makes a drama of it—'

'*Shh!* Really, girls. What next.' Amy's pretend severe voice gets us all laughing again. Giggles continue to run between us as we lower ourselves into the jacuzzi. There are two other women in it already, quietly enjoying the pummelling of the water. I feel sorry for them as their peace is shattered by my hen party. One leaves immediately, her big loose thighs wobbling as she climbs out; the other hangs in there determined we won't dislodge her. Her face is blank, she doesn't return our smiles.

I can see from Ginny's face she hasn't finished on the topic of Dave. Her grin is just visible above water level, her eyes gleam.

'I think we ought to steal the book.'

Our eyes all link, and we wait.

'Amy is the one to do it. You must lead him on and then grab it.'

'I gave him such a brush-off – he'll be suspicious if I'm suddenly all keen.'

'Dave is never suspicious when people fancy him. He can't believe it isn't genuine.' Lucy is next to the unknown woman who's clearly listening to every word though her eyes are down. 'He's totally self-centred, don't forget.'

'Is he coming tomorrow, Nat?'

'He's not officially invited but he told my sister he was going to turn up at the service. Anyone can go to that, after all.'

'There's your chance, Amy. You're going to find Dave attractive in ways you never dreamed possible. When you get hold of the book you can give it to Nat as a wedding present.'

'I'll do nothing of the kind – if I get my hands on that book I'll burn it. It's lethal.'

'Simon would kill me. He can't stand Dave.' Lucy rolls her eyes.

'Are you sure Dave hasn't shown it to him already? He's the boasting type – just the sort of thing he'd do to raise his street cred.'

'Dave has always said he only shows the book to women he fancies. It's part of the fetishism.'

At this point the stranger leaves the jacuzzi, smiling to herself. We wait until she's gone before going on.

'Poor thing, we've driven her away.'

'She was gobbling up every word, she could have stayed for more.'

'I tell you something. Dave will be pathetic when he gets older.'

'I was thinking that myself the other day.'

'He might change.'

'Pigs might fly.'

We sit in the bubbling water, all very content with each other. Finally Ginny breaks the silence again.

'So tell us, Nat, about the lunch party tomorrow at the Garrick. Who's going to be there?'

'Some very boring members of Freddie's family, plus one or two he says are nice, and of our gang there's Simon, Charlie, Mark and Ben. That's it. And there would have been Jane.'

'I've been thinking about poor Jane all evening.' Sara is floating beside me now. 'She should have been here with us.'

'She'd have loved all this. But I don't want to talk about her tonight – this is my hen party and it's wonderful and I don't want to think about awful things. In fact I'm going to switch them all off until I come back at the end of the week and face grim reality again.'

My friends are all staring at me with different expressions, speculative sympathy uppermost.

'What's the actual prognosis?'

'I don't want to talk about any of it, Amy. I'm sorry. I've had a bucketful of my sister recently and I can't take any more.'

'I'm getting cold.' Lucy climbs out. 'Let's go and boil in the sauna.'

'You all think I'm heartless, don't you.'

'We don't. We really don't. To the sauna.'

We pack into the wooden cabin and lie two to a bunk. Amy spoons water over the hot coals and the heat hits us. I'm on the top bunk where it's hottest. I can feel sweat beginning to pour from my body.

'Tell us about the Garrick. Is it stuffy? Will we have to be on our best behaviour?'

'No, not at all, to both questions.'

'I've never been to a London club. Mystery world. Actually I can't see why men need them.' Ginny sounds disapproving. 'As far as I can find out they simply prop up the male establishment. Tories to the Carlton, grand fogies to the Athenaeum, all sorts to the Reform, toffs to Whites and Boodles, arty types and the Bar at the Garrick. And there are dozens more—'

'For someone who doesn't approve of them, you seem to know all about them.'

'Read about them in some magazine recently.'

'It's funny to think of you marrying someone who's a member of a London club, Nat.'

'Not as funny as it feels. And my eyelids are frying up here.'

'I'm really looking forward to seeing the Garrick. Do you think we can change out of those dresses before lunch?'

'No, Lucy, you can't. I'll feel a complete lemon if I'm in that wedding dress on my own. I'll feel like that anyway – oh, God.' Through my overheated body goes a wave of panic.

'What's the matter?'

'I'm not sure about the dress and the bridesmaids – Freddie will think it's too much—'

'Nat, stop it.' Sara is lying on the same ledge as me, facing the opposite way, and grabs my feet. 'Stop it. Everybody will look wonderful. You are going to wear that dress, Amy is going to make beautiful bouquets, brilliant old Amy, what would we do without her, and you-are-going-to-wear-that-DRESS.' She squeezes my feet with each word. 'So shut up. And Freddie will love it.'

'More heat.' Amy sloshes water on and we scream for mercy as the hot steam chokes us.

'I can't stand any more. I'm off to the pool again.' Ginny leaves, and one by one we follow. I'm last. I watch my friends leap into the pool ahead of me, yelping as the cool water hits their pink hot bodies. I love them all. This is the best possible hen party they could have chosen. I make a vow as I stand among the lush plants in the water garden. *I mustn't let my new life with Freddie push my friends out.*

I watch Lucy climb onto the swing while the others lark about. It comes to me then that the choice is not only mine: they could choose to disappear. They'll see the house, its size, its perfection, and they'll go silent. They'll see Freddie in his element at the Garrick, they'll see how different my life will be from theirs. They'll be uneasy, possibly envious. It's inevitable; I would feel the same if one of them married an older man, established, well-off, settled.

'Come on, Nat!'

An intense sadness fills me.

'Nat! Aren't you having a last swim?'

I move towards them. They're all grinning up at me, treading water.

'Come on!'

I run down the steps to the pool and fling myself in with a wild yell; as I go under my quick tears merge with the water.

27 ʃ

Freddie tried to calm himself by counting his blessings but the only one he could find at that moment was the weather. An intense blue sky arched over London: red brick, grey stone, dead leaves, green grass glowed in the clarity.

Everyone was sitting in Temple Church waiting and Natalie was half an hour late. So were most of her friends. The only ones to arrive so far were four young men, amongst whom was the sinister man with the pigtail he was fairly sure he had seen dancing in the street with Natalie that night.

Even Ralph had arrived on time, with his Nigerian girlfriend Lila on his arm. She was taller than him, and dressed in vivid traditional costume – the swathe of orange and black silk on her body and head eclipsed every other outfit in the church. Sitting in front of her was Meryl in muted navy and green, and between her and Dennis squirmed Piers and Harry.

For once Freddie was proud of his mother: she was dressed entirely in very dark blue, and her hat curved round her face framing it most becomingly. Aunt Isabel's hat on the other hand looked like something Napoleon would have been happy to wear. It kept knocking against Uncle Henry's ear.

Crawford and Zoe Gittings were mirror images of each other: tall, thin, cropped grey hair, tidy black, white and grey clothes. Their daughters Lalage and Esther were in direct contrast, with messy hair, rag-bag clothes, leggings. When Freddie kissed Esther she smelt strongly of tobacco, and he noticed her right finger was heavily stained.

'How are you, Esther?'

'Fine. I like Cousin Ralph's friend in aso-oke.'

'Sorry?'

'Her clothes. Buba, iro, gele. It's called aso-oke.' Esther touched her breast, hip, head as she stared aggressively at him.

'I agree, they're very handsome—'

'Freddie! Dear boy, you look very well!' Freddie was dragged away.

Now everyone had sat too long, they'd looked through the order of service several times, they'd stared at the church and at each other, they were now whispering speculations. The organist had given up for the moment. Freddie should have been at the front with Thomas but he hovered at the door of the church with the verger. His trepidation increased by the minute.

When Natalie at last appeared it was like a filmed dream-sequence. She was wearing the cream wedding dress, she had a wreath of leaves in her hair and a simple posy of creamy pink flowers and trailing leaves in her hand. On each side of her were two nymphs in silken shifts wearing wreaths and carrying posies that matched Natalie's. The three of them shone in the clear sunlight. Behind them were more friends in normal wedding finery.

Natalie froze when she saw Freddie, and her friends froze with her. Freddie stared in silence at them, and knew he would remember this moment for the rest of his life.

'Freddie, I'm so sorry we're late. Westminster Bridge is closed, there's a demonstration or something. We had to go all around it.'

'We're really sorry—'

But at his expression, Natalie, Lucy and Ginny smiled in relief.

'You look wonderful, all of you. You look as if you've stepped out of a Botticelli.'

Behind him the organist, tipped off that the bride had arrived, filled the church with a great fanfare.

'Will you take me up, Freddie? I know it shouldn't be you, but does it matter?'

'Nothing matters except you.'

Natalie put her cold hand through his arm and he covered it with his warm free hand. The dress she wore was so beautiful he wanted to stroke it. It was the same one he'd seen in the street, but it had looked white then in the neon lighting. Now he fixed his eyes on its subtle creamy-gold folds, on its voluminous skirts so sweetly nudging his leg.

He could sense the rapt attention in church. No one had expected a grand wedding dress and bridesmaids. He looked around as they walked slowly up the aisle towards the altar, and he caught the eye of the pigtailed man. Freddie half expected complicity, knowing smiles, some acknowledgement of the dress's earlier outing, but the man just looked distressed.

The wedding proceeded as weddings without sermons and communions always do, at a greater speed than seems fitting for the importance of the event. There was nothing to delay its progress except the signing of the register, and that did not take long. Christian rites of passage are brief when not plumped out with options. All pith, thought Freddie at the end, as he walked again down the aisle with Natalie, his second wife. All pith.

'Natalie and her nymphs. They look as if they belonged in that picture.' Above Ralph was a painting of a romantic actress – Mrs Siddons, perhaps – in floating draperies, playing Dido. 'But instead of Dido, Natalie is Flora.'

Esther stared stonily at her cousin. 'This place ought to be burned down.'

'Oh, come, Esther—'

'It's a total anachronism.' Esther's face was flushed. She swigged down her third glass of champagne and lit another cigarette.

'But I think it's beautiful. All these theatre people from the past.' Lila was staring about her at the ranks of paintings. Her black skin and aso-oke glowed against the real log fire behind her.

'You may think it is, but if you or Ralph tried to join you wouldn't have a chance. These clubs are so élitist.' Esther spat the last word out.

Lila looked unimpressed. Esther's cigarette smoke was getting in her eyes, and her enthusiasm for her clothes was irritating. Lila had worn them only to please Ralph; she had planned to wear her blue silk trouser suit, but Ralph had insisted.

'Shut up, my dear Esther. It's not good form to bite the hand that feeds you.'

'I didn't think you cared a toss for good form, Cousin Ralph.'

'Oh, my reputation, my reputation.' Ralph put his arm round Lila. 'Now if you'll excuse us, Esther, we must go and talk to the bride and bridegroom – there's a gap in the queue at last.' He steered Lila away from Esther, who went off to join her baleful sister on a sofa.

'Ralph. And Lila. I'm so glad you could both come.' Freddie grasped their hands.

'I was surprised to be asked, to be honest. I thought I was completely ostracised these days.' Ralph sounded quite pleased at this achievement. Alice Mentieth, standing on Freddie's left, was pointedly talking with her back to Ralph and Lila.

'What can you do about families?' muttered Freddie ruefully.

'Not a lot.'

'I needed you here. You're important to me. How's the painting going?'

Ralph shrugged. 'As usual.' Lila stood at his shoulder, a massive presence. 'I don't do enough, and I don't like what I do. Nothing's changed. And Lila hates my paintings, don't you, my love.'

Lila smiled but said nothing.

'What about an exhibition soon, Ralph?'

'Do me a favour, Freddie. Failures like me don't have such things as exhibitions. We flog our work to the odd fool we meet in the pub if we're lucky. I'm going to give you a picture for your wedding present, by the way.'

Natalie turned at that moment and joined Freddie.

'I'm going to give you both a picture.'

'Thank you, Ralph. Freddie will be thrilled – as for me, I don't know a thing about art.'

'Good.' Ralph's eyes were bloodshot, his skin was pleated with wrinkles, yet his hair was thick, black and young-looking. It was clearly not dyed. His hands were scarred, his nails battered and paint-ingrained. He was raffish. Natalie grinned at him and said:

'Raffish Ralph.'

He tipped back his head and laughed. 'Throw me out when I

get too drunk to behave.' He took Lila's arm and moved away as the solemn and sober figures of Crawford and Zoe Gittings came up to talk to Freddie and Natalie. Their skins were pale and somehow unmarked by life, they were neat, tidy, controlled and decorous. The spicy perfume left in the air by Lila seemed to evaporate at once in the icy calm of their aura. Platitudes poured forth. The stripy gele on Lila's head moved behind them, towering above the party. She and Ralph were now talking to Dave, who had expertly tagged along.

The Gittings pair were the last of the guests to arrive at the Garrick, and as they moved off (dandruff on Crawford's shoulder being the only sign of bodily decay), Natalie turned to Freddie. Much the same height, their eyes met and held.

'I'm sorry I was so late, my darling.'

'I was getting worried.'

'It wasn't only the bridge, it was me. I got in a panic about this dress.'

'Why? It's a divine dress.'

'It's too beautiful.'

Freddie stroked it. 'A wedding dress can't be too beautiful. Listen, Nat. I must tell you something. I've seen this dress before. I saw you dancing in the street in it.'

'Oh, no.'

'Don't look so horrified. Actually, I'll admit it upset me at the time, because it seemed so odd. You said nothing, so I said nothing. I put it behind me.'

'Oh, Freddie. And Dave's here too.'

'I recognised him in church.'

'He's upset that I'm wearing it.'

'I saw.' They continued to stare into each other's eyes as they talked. Their guests left them alone, seeing their absorption. 'But I'm not upset, Nat. I am thrilled. You looked lovely in the street, mysterious, magical – I confess I was sick with jealousy then. I couldn't think what you were up to and it looked like a wedding dress. I went home shattered.'

'You should have told me.'

'There was no point. You have your own life to lead.'

'And to leave.'

'That too.'

'I'm sorry Dave has gate-crashed.'

'I'm delighted. There's one absentee, so he can sit in their place, beside Aunt Isabel.'

'I'm going to break you two up.' Thomas surged forward in his wheelchair. 'I need to ask Freddie some boring family questions.'

'Your glass is empty, Thomas. Let me get you another. It's not champagne, is it?' Natalie took the empty tumbler from Thomas's lap.

'Champagne makes me ill, alas. Whisky, whisky and soda please. No ice. Now, Freddie, which is which of those two Gittings girls? Are they changelings? They don't look a bit like Crawford or Zoe.'

'Ssh, Tom. Esther is the one smoking.'

'I feared she might be.'

I give Thomas's glass to a waiter and hurry off to the cloakroom. It's not so much the lavatory I need but five minutes on my own. I sit in the peaceful little sitting room provided and stare at my reflection. I'm married. I wonder how many women have sat in the same chair and said the same thing. I touch my face, tweak Amy's leaves which still look good in my hair but have slipped forward slightly. I've no idea what has happened to my posy.

I try to keep these thoughts uppermost but the spectre of Dave keeps nudging them aside. I don't want him at our wedding feast, I don't want him to sit with us all, sit with people I'm going to have to live with in one way and another from now on. He's going to sit by that stately sister-in-law of Alice Mentieth's. It doesn't bear thinking about. Freddie'll have to change the seating plan and put Dave between the girls. I'll have to tell him now before they all sit down to eat. Damn Dave.

I hurry down the narrow, steep staircase which leads back into the main body of the club, my dress filling the treads behind and swishing against wall and banister rail, and there below me is Dave himself. He's pretending to look at pictures but I know he's lying in wait for me. Though I want to run back up, I make myself move slowly downwards towards him. His eyes are wild, his pupils dilated.

'Why did you wear it? Why did you wear that dress?'

'Why shouldn't I?'

'You told me, you told everyone at that party you'd never wear it again.'

'I changed my mind.'

'You shouldn't have worn it. It's against the pattern. Bad luck.'

'Dave, you're talking rubbish. Let me get past.'

'No, Natalie, you listen to me. There you were in the street in that dress, we danced, it was one of those acts you can never imagine, plan, recapture. We danced, we began the pattern, we made love. Perfect circle completed. You sacrificed that dress to me, to that moment, you know you did.'

'I did nothing of the kind.' I can feel I'm turning cold as I stare at Dave. His face is running with sweat, his hands are shaking. I do my best to keep control of my voice. 'What is this fantasy, Dave? What nonsense you're reading into that evening. I wore the dress almost by accident, because of a whim. I danced with you because you were there. I would have danced with a policeman or a dustman or Mickey Mouse if they'd popped up and suggested it. There was no significance, no pattern. You're mad if you think there was.'

'But you came to bed with me.'

'I wish with all my heart I hadn't.'

'But you did.'

'It meant nothing to you beyond another tick in that notebook. It meant nothing to me.'

'You're a cruel woman.'

'Oh, come on, Dave. What's all this tragic act about – where has your usual cynical sense of humour gone? This isn't like you at all.'

'That dress is sensational. Can I stroke it?'

'No!'

'Can I buy it off you at the end of this party, when you change out of it?'

'Dave, you are really off your trolley today.'

'I'm serious, Natalie.' His eyes are gleaming, his whole expression has suddenly changed and is now positive, cheerful. 'I'm dead serious. I'll forgive you everything, all your betrayals, if you sell me that dress.'

'You're a fetishist.'

'So what?'

'It's too expensive for you.'

'Don't make *any* assumptions about what I can afford. *Any*. I'll give you whatever you ask.'

'I don't want to sell it. That's final. And I'm going back to the party.' As I try to push past Dave puts his arms out.

'Let me pass, Dave.'

'Not till you promise me that dress.'

'I'll scream.'

'Go ahead.' Dave smiles his usual I-dare-you, cynical smile. 'It will liven up this morgue.'

'You are a total nightmare—'

'Dream me tonight.'

Again, I try to push past, hating the smell of Dave's sweat as he blocks my way. He puts his hands round my waist.

'What a dress. What a waist. What a waste.'

'Just take your hands off me, Dave Rosenberg.' Panic is rising but I'm not going to let it show. 'You've gate-crashed this party anyway and I want you to leave now.'

Dave starts to laugh and increases his grip. I can feel his erect penis.

'Your dear husband has invited me to lunch, don't forget—'

'Let go!'

Dave goes on laughing as I struggle. At that moment Lucy and Ginny appear at the top of the stairs behind us.

'Help me!' My voice releases the pressure of panic inside me. 'Help me!'

'What the hell is going on – leave her alone, Dave.' Lucy drags roughly at Dave's arms.

'Get him out of this building. He's mad.'

'Girls, girls—' Dave is still trying to laugh as Lucy gets him in a clinch.

'I'll go and get the doorman, I'm sure he's used to throwing out scumbags.' Ginny runs off.

'Relax, everyone. I'm going. I've no desire to stay at this party.'

'Look how you've upset Natalie, damn you. It's not on.'

'She's upset me. And take your bloody hands off me.'

'Leave him alone, Lucy.'

We all stand there breathing hard.

'I'm going but I meant what I said, Natalie. I want that dress. You'll change your mind, you'll see. I'm destined to have it.'

'It's going to cost you dear.'

'I told you I was willing to pay. Just give me a ring when you get back. Ah, here's my escort.' Ginny comes hurrying up with the doorman. 'You don't need to get heavy, I can't wait to leave.' He gives me an ironic little bow, and stalks off.

'Oh, God.' I cover my face with my hands. 'That wasn't fun.'

'He really is over the top. Now forget about him, Nat, and come back to the fun. They're waiting for you so that they can all go into lunch. Freddie sent us off as a search party.' Ginny arranges my wreath which Dave has knocked awry. I meet her eyes and put a hand on her arm.

'You know what I'm going to do?'

'You're coming straight through to lunch. Your gorgeous man will get very cross if we take much longer.'

'Do you really think he's gorgeous?'

'We're all envious as hell. Yes, he's a dream. Now come *on*, Nat.'

'Hang on, just let me tell you my idea. Listen. I am going to sell the dress to Dave, but guess what he's going to buy it with.'

Ginny and Lucy stare at me as I draw a small oblong in the air. We all start to laugh.

'We'll trap him.'

'Won't Amy be pleased when we tell her.'

'There's a bit of a gap beside you, Isabel—'

'Don't worry, Freddie, I'm deaf in that ear anyway, so it's a relief.'

Freddie moved to the end of the table and sat down with his mother on his right and Zoe Gittings on his left. The seating of the party had been tricky to resolve and Tom had been no help.

'Just don't put me beside Zoe. She's so bloody dull.'

So Tom was sitting between Amy Jenkins and Lila, and Freddie himself had the two women most of the men would have chosen to avoid. But all the men were moving before the dessert when Henry would take his place.

'At last I'm seeing the Garrick Club, Freddie. I've always longed to. It's a very handsome building.'

'I've invited you here several times, Mother. You've always refused.'

'Always in the evening. You know I don't go out in the dark.'

'You came to me the other night—'

'That's different. I know your house.'

'Crawford hates going out at night too. This idea of a late lunch is ideal.' Zoe smiled at Freddie, trying hard. 'And your wife Natalie is very beautiful.'

'Her dress transforms her.' Alice Mentieth broke up her roll though she had no intention of eating it. 'That dress would transform anyone. Where did it come from, Freddie?'

'I have no idea.'

'How strange she didn't tell you. It looks like a Hardy Amies to me.'

'Highly unlikely, Mother. Isn't he dead, anyway?'

The first course arrived, a delicate but tasty consommé, and conversation lapsed for a while. Freddie looked down the table and sipped the little glass of dry sherry which came with the soup. People looked happy enough, though there was still a palpable air of polite restraint. Freddie watched first Lalage and then Esther knock back their sherry in one gulp. They were sitting opposite each other, hemmed in by Natalie's friends.

Zoe tried to catch their attention as the waiter gave them more sherry, but they had no eyes for their mother.

'They're a bit silly about alcohol,' she whispered to Freddie.

'Who isn't, Zoe?' Freddie himself was trying to catch Nat's eye, but she was half-screened by flowers and candles, and talking busily with Ralph on her left and Henry Mentieth on her right. Someone gave a shout of laughter, others joined in. The noise level started to rise. The tension Freddie was feeling over this party began to ease. 'Who isn't? Have some more sherry yourself and forget about your girls. They'll cope.'

'They egg each other on, they are permanent rivals.'

'Like most siblings.'

'You and Tom weren't like that.'

'That was because we ignored each other.'

'Well, true or not, it made for a peaceful home.'

'Crawford has made himself a soundproof room in the basement.'

'I must say I always thanked God my two sons gave me so little trouble.'

'You packed us off to school to avoid it, Mother.'

'That's most unfair. We wanted the best for you. We did what everyone does.'

'Not any more, Alice. The girls refused to go to boarding school though Crawford and I would have preferred it.'

'Tell me about Crawford's soundproof room, Zoe.'

'He had to have it to get away from Esther and Lalage's music. He can't stand it. He goes in there and plays his Mozart.'

'Your girls seem to have the whiphand, Zoe. You shouldn't let them rule your lives like that.' Alice forgot herself enough to eat some bread.

'Oh, Freddie, they've taken more sherry. Can't you ask the waiter to avoid their glasses?'

'No. They would be mortified.'

Esther was laughing loudly at something Charlie was saying, her face very flushed. Alice Mentieth watched her for a moment and then turned to Freddie.

'I do think girls are a lot more trouble than boys.'

'Mother—' Freddie stopped. He looked at the frail bitter woman who had given him birth and his rising irritation melted. 'Mother, that's the last time in my life I'm going to call you Mother. It sounds ridiculous from a man my age. Alice. I'm going to call you Alice from now on. 'He picked up her hand and kissed it. 'Do you mind?'

'Not at all.'

'M – Alice, we should have done it years ago!'

'If you call me M – Alice it will sound like malice.'

Meryl, pink-faced from champagne and the relief of now being without her offspring, leans forward past Ralph to tell me how she likes my dress.

'Thank you.'

'It's the most beautiful wedding dress I've ever seen, even better than Anthea's—' She stops her pink turning bright red, and tries to laugh. 'Silly me. As Dennis says, I'm always opening my big mouth and putting my foot in it.'

'Lalage is drunk.' Ralph is staring down the table.

'That's Esther, Ralph.'

'She's just upset her soup all over herself, poor thing.' Esther is mopping at her clothes with Ginny's help.

'What do those girls do, Meryl?'

'I think they are at art school or something.'

'What bad luck. Art schools can be relied on to stifle any talent they possess.'

'Did you not go to one yourself?' I've finished my soup and feel better. I'd missed breakfast.

'I went to the Slade for two terms until they threw me out.' Ralph stares at me with his tired bloodshot eyes. 'Not for taking drugs, or for having sex with one of the models during a lunch break, both of which were true, but basically for being unteachable.'

'I can see why you don't like art schools.'

'I liked the place. It didn't teach me anything.'

I'm not sure I like Ralph, and look around. Meryl has turned away and is gushing at Charlie. Henry is deep in conversation with Lucy, who's flattering him by asking him the right questions about life at the top of the City tree. I say to Ralph:

'So you became the black sheep of the family quite young.'

'I didn't become it, I always was. My mother said I was visited by malign forces when I was in the cradle; I was disruptive from the word go. She hated me, you know. She only kissed me once that I remember, and that was when I fell off a high wall and woke up to find myself in hospital with a collection of broken bones. My mother was sitting beside the bed when I came round. She kissed me then. I was so surprised I passed right out again. When I next saw her she was her old self. Tense hard eyes, wary heart. Families are destructive things.'

'I agree.'

'You said that with great feeling.'

'But I only have a sister and a father, no other relations. We just don't have cousins and aunts and uncles – my two parents were single children and their parents came from small families too. I sometimes feel my branch of the Harpers has self-destructed.'

'Which is your father?'

'He couldn't make it. He lives in Australia.'

'And your sister? Meryl told me she'd met a sister. Is she one of the ravishing nymphs? Neither of them looks like you, but that doesn't mean anything. Siblings can be so different.' Ralph leans back as he is served a small dish of baked scallops. 'This smells excellent.'

'My sister isn't here either. She's in hospital.'

'I'm sorry to hear that. Let's tuck in – it's a pity to risk these getting cold. One should never wait until everyone is served – it's pointless when the food has to travel in the first place down long corridors.' Ralph begins to gobble up hot delicately cooked chunks of scallop, his head ducked to his food. 'Damn good. Have some bread to mop up the sauce.'

I watch white Burgundy being poured into one of my many glasses; as it fills the glass begins to frost. The water glass is already beaded with moisture which reflects and distorts the tiny rising bubbles. The biggest wine glass waits amply for the claret Freddie has carefully chosen, the smallest glass for the Sauternes to go with the dessert. I think of poor Jane and her dry mouth and her miserable allowance of liquid and bleed for her.

'I never thought Freddie would marry a girl like you.'

'Is that meant to be a compliment?'

'Of course. Would I have said it if it wasn't?'

'I don't know. You're famous for speaking your mind.'

'I expected a second version of Anthea.' He leans towards me, his scallops finished. 'Beautiful but cold. Cold like the rest of this family. At home at Glyndebourne, Ascot, Henley, all that nonsense. In *Tatler* now and again. Detached from ordinary life.'

'I've actually been to Glyndebourne. Careful.'

Ralph gives a noisy laugh causing half the table to look at him. 'You know what I mean.'

'I think my friends are afraid I'll get lost in the same social whirl.'

'Only too likely. It's all very seductive. Like this place. Wonderful, of course, I love the Garrick. Freddie invites me to dinner here once a year. Always has.' He accepts more white wine, scours his plate again with bread and chews it carelessly, dropping crumbs. At this moment Esther suddenly stands up, steps backwards, falls against the wall, and then supporting herself against it staggers to the door. Her eyes are glassy. Zoe leaps up and follows her out. Lalage announces smugly, 'She's pissed out of her tiny mind. This always happens. I've got a much better head for booze.'

'Lalage. Please mind your language.' Crawford's voice is sharp. His daughter doesn't look at him, but picks up her glass and drains it.

Luckily the waiters start to clear the fish course at this point, and Zoe returns smiling as if nothing has happened.

'Esther will be all right. Don't hold back the next course for her, Freddie.'

Lila stands up. She is staring at Zoe in amazement, eyes flashing, aso-oke even more dramatic in the dimly lit dining room.

'You aren't going to leave her alone in that state? Where is she?'

'In the ladies' cloakroom.'

Lila marches out leaving a total silence behind. It is broken by a giggle from Lalage and Ralph saying to the table at large, 'Leave Lila to it. She's a witch-doctor at heart. On with the feast! What delights have we next, Freddie? Your health, anyway. Cheers.' He lifts his glass and makes everyone else do the same despite the mutter from Meryl that it isn't the time yet for toasts. There is a lacklustre echo of 'Cheers' from the depleted company and the meal continues.

Lila and Esther return in time for the dessert, just as the men are milling about being reseated by Freddie. I end up with Dennis Peak on my right and Charlie on my left.

'Are you surviving?' I mutter at Charlie as Dennis goes off to retrieve his napkin.

'It's great. I've been talking to an old bird who has never to her knowledge watched television except by accident. And she says her husband farms ostriches. Is she serious?'

'Charlie, I don't know. I've never met these people before.'

'She says ostrich meat is delicious. Who's the man in a wheelchair?'

'Freddie's brother Thomas. He's terrifying – the brilliant bachelor brother.'

'I read a book on world demography by a Dr Thomas Mentieth in my final year.'

'Probably his. He works for the UN—'

'I seem to have lost my napkin but never mind.' Dennis Peak settles in beside me. He is fat and fair-haired, and his face is shining with enjoyment.

'Where are your boys? I saw them in church but they disappeared afterwards.'

'Gone to spend the rest of the day with friends, thank goodness.' Very briefly, his pale blue eyes catch mine. 'I'm continually surprised I should be the father of such thugs-in-the-making.' What he's really watching is every gesture made by the waitress serving the crème brûlée.

'I regard myself as a civilised man, I live in order to eat. Meryl interprets being civilised differently – food doesn't matter to her. This is a wonderful lunch. They have excelled themselves. Are you a good cook?'

'Useless. Freddie is the cook.'

'Lucky one of you can. Meryl can't and I can't either. I suppose it could explain why the boys are hyperactive – all that convenience food.'

'Was Anthea a good cook?'

Dennis gives me another quick look, wary this time. I don't know why I asked the question – it just floated unexpectedly from my subconscious.

'Anthea was very good at food for dinner parties.' Dennis has already finished his crème brûlée and is cradling his dessert wine. 'Château Climent. Sublime. I do like a good sweet wine.'

'Freddie introduced me to them. I always thought they were something you avoided.'

'Crème brûlée goes so well with it. People murder dessert wines by serving them with chocolate or fruit-based puds.'

'Freddie chose everything.' We sip in silence; Charlie is talking to Meryl who is telling him long stories about her sons.

'But I wouldn't have called Anthea a *good* cook, you know.' His glance is still wary, his pronunciation of the two pairs of oos is beautifully precise: each is subtly different. 'No good at the daily meal, just good at the set piece. I imagine that's why Freddie started to cook.'

'Well, he's brilliant at making a delicious dinner out of nothing. He and Anthea must have been a perfect culinary pair.' I find I'm longing to talk about Freddie and Anthea, and here is Dennis, an ideal source of information. I gaze at his red friendly face eagerly, wanting him to talk about them even if it hurts me.

'Everyone described it as the perfect marriage. Handsome, accomplished, successful, well-dressed, well-housed, well-fed. What more could a couple desire?' But his eyes are bleak.

'Children, I suppose.'

'Anthea didn't want children. She was a strange woman, Meryl's sister. Very closed. Not generous. Never gave her sister anything worth having for birthday or Christmas, or the boys. We're not well off, you know, and it used to upset Meryl. But jealousy between sisters is a common enough thing, and poor Meryl had everything to be jealous about.'

'Who was the oldest?'

'Anthea looked younger, but she wasn't.'

'I'm an elder sister too, so I just wondered. Tell me more about Anthea, Dennis. No one has told me anything much, and I'd really like to know more.'

'What fun this party is. I was dreading it, hate these family occasions normally, but this one is fun. To sit by a beautiful woman and be indiscreet about my ex-sister-in-law is extremely pleasant. While drinking this utterly divine wine – yes, do fill my glass up.'

'Not for me, thanks. No, give me some after all. I've taken it for you, Dennis.'

'My friend for life. Now, Anthea. Definitely a woman of secrets. Never let on what she was up to. Now keep this to yourself, but apparently she was an inveterate gambler, addicted to the horses. Extraordinary, absolutely the last thing you'd expect her to have a clue about, let alone be addicted to. Must have made a fortune out of it, too – must have, to dress as she did.'

'Does Freddie know this?'

''Course, my dear, he told Meryl. Told her to keep quiet about it but she did tell me. I don't think I should have told you but there you are, I have. You know, I love to think of Anthea slipping out to the betting shop. If you'd known her, you'd see how incongruous the idea is. But then life is incongruous, often.'

'Was Anthea easy to talk to, like Meryl?'

'Good God, no. No small talk at all. Fitted with her character, come to think of it: dinner-party food, studied effects, nothing spontaneous. I think the word stilted could have been coined for her. I sound catty, don't I? Yes, catty. I am being catty. She made us suffer quite a bit, did Anthea. Could have helped but didn't.'

His lips quiver. He is fairly drunk, but still speaks with his obvious customary precision. I put my hand on his for a moment.

'Now you're a completely different kettle of fish, I can see at a glance. You're going to have a wonderful effect on Freddie's cold, complicated family. New young blood. Good for the buggers.'

'You make me sound like one of Anthea's horses.'

'The Mentieths are all cold and intensely clever, the Gittingses are cold and very shrewd, the Peaks are neither so they treat me like a buffoon. I don't count and nor does Meryl. Anthea counted because she had such style. To be honest we're only here because Freddie is kind, and wanted us to represent Anthea, I suppose. I was surprised he asked us.'

'I am very glad he did. I feel I've found an ally.'

'At your service.'

'What about Ralph? He doesn't seem to fit the family mould at all.'

'Oh, yes he does. He just shows it differently. Totally self-centred. Lots of different women. Says he's a failure but don't you believe him. The Tate have been to see him, they want to buy his work.'

'He never mentioned that.'

'He's refusing to sell them anything, that's why. He says only dead artists should be hung in permanent collections. He's full of strange ideas, is Ralph. He likes us, he's the only Mentieth apart of course from Freddie to keep in touch with us, drop in sometimes. He couldn't stand Anthea, by the way. Chalk and cheese, those two. Talking of cheese, here it comes. I approve of it after the pud, in the English way – the continental habit of serving it in between doesn't appeal to me one bit. I like to finish a meal with a savoury taste in my mouth.'

As Dennis helps himself to large portions of cheese, I turn towards Charlie, who senses my movement and turns too. Our eyes join.

'Oh, Charlie, I feel such a fraud,' I whisper.

'Me too.' Charlie winks almost imperceptibly. 'By the way, what happened to Dave? One minute he was here, then he disappeared.'

'He's – he had to go.'

'Couldn't stand the scene?'

'It's too long a story.'

'He was on beam to make trouble, I thought. It's lucky he's gone.'

'He made trouble. For instance he wants to buy this dress.'

'He what?'

'My wedding dress. He wants to buy it.'

'He's mad.'

'He danced with me in it, remember?'

'Will I ever forget? Most extraordinary scene I've ever witnessed.'

We pause, our eyes still joined. I've always liked Charlie's face: his neat nose and chin, his high forehead (getting higher as his hair recedes), his deep-set black eyes surrounded with such thick black lashes he always looks as if he dyes them. Perhaps he does.

'You're not going to let him have it?'

'Probably.'

'Nat, don't. He's eccentric enough already. Don't encourage him. He'll start cross-dressing or something next.'

'Just look at Freddie.'

Freddie was sitting between Lucy and Ginny, holding both their hands in front of him on the table and laughing in delight.

'So you girls hijacked her and made her wear it. I love you all.'

'Freddie, you should have seen her face when she came into the sitting room. We made a sort of tableau at the end, with

Sara in The Dress, and us beside her – all solemn, candlelight, soft music. She was flabbergasted!'

'Dear girls.'

'Sara pinched the dress and paid a fortune to have it cleaned and mended after that party. Nat didn't notice a thing.'

'I'll pay Sara back—'

'No, no, she told Nat it was her wedding present.'

'I'm so glad you did what you did. I honestly am. Now, tell me how you all fit into Natalie's life, how you met in the first place.'

As he listened to them talk Freddie felt he was floating. He'd certainly drunk a little too much, but the sensation wasn't caused by alcohol but by his complete happiness. And the party was going well, amazingly well, the din in the room was deafening as people talked animatedly, often shouting across the table; his family had managed to keep existing tensions well below the surface for the first time he could remember. Ralph and Sara were deep in a discussion about shamanism, Esther was leaning back against Lila in obvious contentment as she sipped a glass of water, Zoe was actually laughing loudly at something Henry had said. His mother had stopped pursing her mouth in displeasure hours ago, and was swapping bridge stories with Crawford. Freddie felt he loved them all.

Natalie was looking at him, smiling. He raised his glass at her, and she picked hers up too. A lull descended in the noise around them as people noticed them both holding their glasses up high. Natalie's smile faded as she stared in concentration at her glass. Just as Freddie was about to toast his wife, her voice came low and clear:

'To Jane.'

'To Jane,' came the answering chorus with Lalage's voice asking 'Who's Jane?'

'Absent friends,' said another voice.

Freddie could not drink, nor say Jane's name. He had expected Natalie to say his name, just as he'd been about to say hers. His moment of delicious happiness, of content, of satisfaction, was gone. To Jane. Natalie had her eyes shut as she sipped from her glass. To Jane. Freddie touched his lips, but could not drink or speak. To Jane. He feared her.

28

I expected to be ecstatically happy.

I love Budapest, I love the fact the two halves of the city are divided much more dramatically by the Danube than the way the Thames divides London. Buda is hilly and historical, Pest is flat and sophisticated. We're staying in a lively small hotel near the castle in Buda, and the streets immediately around are like a set for an eighteenth-century film.

Budapest is a city that gives you a lift just to walk around – in fact the only aspect of Budapest I could have done without is the obligatory gipsy band that always plays in every restaurant while you eat. All very atmospheric but they come and stand close to the table and scrape their violins right into your ear. It's so deafening it puts me off my food. Chatting is impossible. But Freddie looks very pleased when they come up and gives them fat tips.

I should be ecstatically happy.

I stare out from our bedroom window at the Danube, at the handsome city reflected in its waters. It's early evening; the ferries are still busy on the river, circling its three islands in the fading light. Freddie's gone out to try and find a copy of *The Times* – he's looking for the law report of a case in the High Court on which some key judgment is due. I don't want to think about work.

I dial London, I dial the direct number of the hospital Renal unit. I've told Freddie I don't need to ring – I will be contacted if there's any problem – but I can't stop myself. Jane seems to pull at me. Her dreadful fate nags at me. I watch a ferry go by on the Danube as the line clicks and whirrs.

'Renal unit.'

It's Sister Vera Akram's voice. I tell her who I am and she smiles, I can feel it in her answer.

'You've rung at the right moment. Your father's here visiting Jane. I'll go and get him – Jane's on dialysis at the moment.'

My father. Then his voice is on the line.

'Hi there, Nat. How on earth did you know I was here?'

'I didn't. Just fluke.' I'm freshly surprised by how Australian he sounds, even more so than Jane. 'I felt a need to ring and here I am.'

'But where is here?'

'Budapest.'

'So you went after all.'

'It is my honeymoon, Dad.'

'I can't hear – the line's bad.'

'Honeymoon. I just got married, remember.'

'So you did, so you did – I'm so jet-lagged and pressed I could easily forget my name. Congratulations and all that. Hope it all went well.'

'I'm sorry to miss you, Dad. Your first visit after all this time.'

'First visit – oh, yes. Well, I'm sorry to miss you too.'

We are talking like strangers. I also get the distinct impression from his hesitation that this is not his first visit at all – that he's been over and not been in touch.

'How's Jane?'

'I'll take the phone over to her so you can speak to her yourself. Hang on.' There's silence while the phone is relocated, then I hear a noise like static. Jane's voice comes on and I realise the sound is the dialysing machine.

'You timed your call well.'

'Total coincidence. How are you?'

'I feel rotten. My neck's so sore I can never forget the fistula.'

'Oh, Jane, it sounds awful for you. I'm sorry.'

'Dad's got the doctors running round already.'

'Good.'

'He's even managed to see the consultant – winkled him out from somewhere.'

'Good for Dad.'

'He wanted to get at the full facts.'

'Did they tell him more than we all know?'

'He hasn't told me yet. You rang just as he began.'

'Ask him now.'

'He's over at the desk talking to Vera. Oh, God, how the vampire hurts today. I – hate – it.'

'I wish I could be with you both.'

'Don't be stupid, you're on honeymoon.'

'I still worry about you.'

'Well, don't. I've got Dad here. I feel so bad anyway I don't care who's around half the time. I'll have to stop, they're coming to unhook me.'

'Pass me back to Dad, Jane.'

'He's gone out of the ward.' I can hear voices beside Jane, and she says goodbye and cuts me off – or we're cut off – while I'm in mid-sentence. I sit there as it gets dark outside, blind to the beauty of the view. It's very difficult to be happy when you know life is so grim for your sister.

I'm still at the window when Freddie returns; he's rustling something when he comes up behind me.

'Did you get your paper?'

'No, instead I got this. Don't look yet.' The rustling goes on for a moment and then Freddie's hand touches my arm. On the bed is a black felt Hungarian jacket, covered in frogging and neat detail. It smells faintly of lavender and of camphor and it's clearly quite old.

'Do you like it?'

'It's lovely.'

'I couldn't resist the thought of you wearing it. I saw it in the shop window and went straight in to buy it. If it doesn't fit you there's a bigger one, but not so exquisitely worked.'

'Freddie, you're so sweet.'

'Put it on. Take your clothes off first. Just leave your black tights and your shirt. And those high heels.'

I laugh, he laughs too. I put on the little jacket and it looks wonderful. My legs seem to go on for ever under the peplum; I twirl, knocking the phone off its table.

'Leave it. I don't want the bloody thing to ring.' Freddie is undressing.

'Put the Don't Disturb notice out—'

'I have.'

I walk around, my arms outstretched. Freddie comes up behind me and puts his hands inside my shirt, kissing my neck, fingering my nipples. He presses his body against mine, rubbing his hard penis in the cleft between my buttocks. As he works on my nipples and moves his mouth over my skin, all thoughts of Jane are annihilated. I move my body against his, eyes shut. I do not touch him; my nipples sing under his hands, my knees become weak, my whole body begins to throb greedily for his. When he finally turns me round and we fall back onto the bed I am panting in frustration, pulling at him, biting at him to enter me. When he does we fuck each other with such fury that the sweat pours off us. The speed and pressure of our thrusting builds until I am ready to explode, to split apart.

'I'm coming, come, come, COME!' Bone to bone, our orgasms burst within us, we both shout as almost unbearable waves of pleasure pulse through us. My orgasm continues through several stages after Freddie's is over; he crushes me to him as my shudders slowly fade. We lie exhausted for a while, and then get in the bath together.

'We made such a noise, Freddie.'

'Who cares. These old walls are thick.'

Our glasses of wine are on the side of the bath. I lift mine.

'That was a brilliant fuck. I'll never wear that jacket without remembering.'

'What a good thing I bought it.'

Freddie sips from his wine. He's still flushed, and there are tiny burst veins in his cheeks. His hair has got two strands of grey above each ear in such neat sections they almost look false. There are grey hairs in his bushy eyebrows (he has to trim his eyebrows now and again or they would screen his eyes) and in his nostrils. I love his grey hairs. I love his firm white almost hairless body, with its neat appendectomy scar. I put my feet against his chest and he nibbles my toes.

'It's wonderful being here with you far away from home. No one to ring us or bother us, no appointments to keep. We must go away like this regularly, Natalie. Go to Amsterdam, Madrid, Berlin, Helsinki – have long weekends away.'

'I bet we don't. You don't like going away in term.'

'I'll make sure we do – my new resolution. Life's for living.'

'I'm getting cold.' As I stand up he presses his face against my stomach.

'You have such a beautiful body, Natalie. I can't tell you how much it delights me.' His voice is muffled. I look down on his head, a little thin on top but a long way from going bald. Baldness doesn't appear to be in his family. 'It's so smooth and perfect. I love all the lines and curves. It's a human body at its peak.'

'You talk as if it's separate from me.'

'In a way it is.' He slips back into the water as I get out. 'You will always be you whatever happens to your body of course – but what your body is *now* is a gift, a gift to us both.'

'I'll fetch the wine.' I retrieve the phone off the floor while I'm in there. As I replace the receiver I can hear the burring tone; illogically I listen for a moment, as if it's going to turn into Jane's voice. Freddie goes on when I'm back:

'Which is why, darling Nat, I can't bear the thought of a great long cut sliced through you.'

'I can't bear it either.'

'I wish you'd said that before.'

'The thing is, I don't know what I'd do if the worst comes to the worst and there's no alternative. I'm praying my father will offer, and be compatible. He's there with her now, I spoke to him while you were out. He's busy organising all the doctors.'

'How's Jane?'

'Low. Her fistula is very painful.'

'You said you didn't want to ring the hospital, you'd left them to ring you if necessary.'

'I couldn't help it. Jane – well, you'd do the same if it was Thomas in her place.'

'I'm not blaming you. I'm just sorry the news isn't better. Was your father in good heart?'

'I didn't talk to him for any length of time. Freddie, he and I are like strangers.'

'Come on, let's get dressed and go out to dinner. I've booked a table at Gundel's, remember.'

I put on my red dress since our guidebook tells us Gundel's is Budapest's top restaurant. Freddie insists I wear the Hungarian jacket, though it looks a bit odd over my red dress. As I look in the mirror I wonder briefly whether Anthea would have worn it like this, and decide probably not. Or perhaps Freddie never made suggestions about clothes to her.

I can see the musicians lying in wait for us in the corner of the grand, rather stuffy dining room, still silent but getting ready for an attack on the diners. Freddie and I are both a little drunk already, which helps us deal with the complexity of a Hungarian menu. I go for a completely unpronounceable hot appetiser which turns out to be trout stuffed with goose liver, Freddie has Serbian carp. We both choose goulash (gulyas) to follow, with the idea that surely a goulash at Gundel's will be the best you can get.

The food is good but heavy, as I find all the food here is. Everything is thickened with flour and cream, and cooked in lard: the Hungarians talk about the quality of the lard in the way foodies in London talk about olive oil. As for paprika, it comes in so many forms the head waiter is totally confusing me as he tries to explain just as the band strikes up and I can't hear him clearly anyway.

Freddie says they all serenade us because I'm beautiful and they think he's rich, but I know they sense, as everyone does, our aura of sexual fulfilment. The players come in close and scrape their violins right near my ears while staring at me with hot brown eyes. They always give our table a longer blast than anyone else gets and today is no different. Freddie is smiling happily; he has no idea I'm gritting my teeth. Luckily our food arrives and the men move on just when I think I might start screaming.

'What's the matter?' Freddie puts a hand over mine.

'Hungry. This looks good if unusual. Your carp looks fantastic – what is that curly thing on top?'

'Salt pork.'

'Odd mix.' I chatter on while the musicians go and deafen the next table.

The phone call comes two days later when Freddie's standing at the window using his shaver while staring at the view. I'm lying in bed reading a thriller, the remains of breakfast on a tray beside me. We've made love, it's getting pleasantly late, the day is ours.

'Natalie?'

'Hullo, Dad.' Contentment vanishes. He would only ring with bad news.

'Sorry to ring so early.'

'It's not early, we're a couple of hours ahead of you.'

'Jane's very crook, Nat. She very nearly died last night.'

'Oh, God.'

'I've been up all night with her. I'm bushed. I had to call you now before I get some rest. Jane's in intensive care, holding her own—'

'Is she out of danger?'

'With no kidneys, you're never out of danger.'

'I know that, Dad, give me some credit. I meant, over this particular crisis?'

'They said she'd begun to turn the corner, but it doesn't look good.'

'What caused it?'

'Septicaemia. Her wound developed an infection.'

'Should we come back now, Dad?'

'It's your choice.'

'But do you think we should?'

'Yes, I do. Straight answer to a straight question. She can easily have a relapse.'

'Give me your hotel number.'

'Don't ring me for at least six hours, I've really got to get some sleep.'

As I take down the details of his hotel I can hear the wail of a London siren – ambulance or police – in the background. As soon as the line is free I try to ring the hospital, but find all lines out of Budapest are busy.

'Jane nearly died last night.'

'We'll go straight back. I'll change our flight immediately.'

'Oh, Freddie, I'm so sorry.'

'Can't be helped. It's an emergency.'

Freddie takes the phone from me and dials reception while I lie on the bed curled up like a foetus. I can't move, I can't think,

I can't feel. Freddie does most of the packing and within two hours we are in a taxi on our way to the airport. The silence is heavy, and Freddie is sombre.

'I feel desperate about leaving like this.'

'Nat, don't worry. We'll come back another time.'

'Budapest is so beautiful.'

'You didn't like the food much, though, did you, in spite of what you said?'

I take his hand. 'It was the musicians I didn't like.'

'Really? I thought everyone liked being serenaded.'

'I was putting on an act.'

'I didn't enjoy them much either, to be honest.'

'You should have said. We are silly.'

Freddie hugs me fiercely, and the taxi driver starts to sing.

In the plane, Freddie becomes extraordinarily cheerful. We drink champagne and eat a rather better than usual aircraft lunch.

'We're going to lie low when we get back. We'll stay in a hotel, and only tell the hospital and your father where we are. I'm not going back home until the day we're expected. If we show our noses there, life will get back to normal and I don't want it to.'

'Brilliant. Where are we going to stay?'

'Surprise. Somewhere off the beaten track and special. So the honeymoon will continue.'

I catch Freddie's good cheer and find my depression, disappointment and flatness lifting. London no longer seems like second best, and when we arrive the sky is blue and the traffic abnormally light as we speed along in a new black taxi smelling sweetly of its pristine fittings. Freddie holds my hand; it's only four days since we made the journey in the other direction in our wedding limousine.

The taxi turns off the Cromwell Road and we are driving between tall stucco and brick houses which for me epitomise London.

'How I love London, Freddie. These classy houses, the squares.'

'Which is lucky, because we're unlikely to live anywhere else.'

'Don't you love it?'

'I thought I didn't. I bought the cottage as a first step to moving out, and then I realised I would never do more than weekend there. I love/hate London.'

'Did you say Roland Gardens, sir?'

'That's right.'

'Where are we going, Freddie?'

'Blakes.'

Before I can admit I've never heard of it, the taxi stops outside a typical row of houses. They've been turned into a stunning hotel: while Freddie checks in I gaze at the colour scheme of black, white, grey and occasional splashes of mossy green and then see a mountain of Victorian luggage with a pink and green parrot on top. As the parrot squawks and I realise the luggage is decor, I'm whisked into a lift. Our bedroom is full of period furniture including a four-poster bed; there's a palm tree in the corner, and beyond it is a cool white and grey bathroom.

'I've always wanted to stay at Blakes, and this seemed the ideal opportunity.'

'It's heaven.' The phone rings, and though it's reception asking when we'd like our tea brought up, I immediately freeze.

'I have to ring my father.'

'Where's he staying?'

'I've only got the number. He said it was a faceless place in Victoria.' My father has left a message at his hotel's reception for me that he has returned to the hospital, and when I ring the Renal unit I find Jane is still in intensive care.

'I must go.'

'I'm coming with you, but not until we've had some tea. Half an hour won't make any difference. Let's unpack too. It settles one.' Freddie has already started his methodical unpacking; all my travels have been lived out of suitcases gaping in confusion, but now I copy Freddie and hang up and stow away clothes and line up shoes. It's oddly therapeutic.

Tea comes and Freddie sits flicking through the newspaper while he pulls at his ear in between sipping from a cup; I haven't noticed this gesture before but it's obviously habitual. I stand at the window with my cup of tea watching him from behind, taking in his full human presence. The realisation that I have a companion for life if I wish it that way hits me as if for the first time.

* * *

When we arrive at St Thomas's I see a familiar back view along a walkway. Trim body, short grey hair, checked suit. The man is talking intensely to another man, in the way people do when they're making complex arrangements. Then they touch each other on the arm in a deliberate gesture full of private meaning and the man in a black leather coat heads past us away from the hospital. The man in the check suit walks on, and as soon as I see his movements I know why he's familiar. He's my father.

Why don't I run after him, shout at him to attract his attention? Freddie's paying the taxi as I stand frozen, hands shaking. I'm in shock. My father was clearly with a male partner; he's become a homosexual. Jane has said nothing about this, but she must know. If it was so obvious to me at first sight, she must have noticed too. I'm in shock because it's so unexpected. When did he come out? Did he leave Mum because he found he was? It was never mentioned by her; I'd stake my life she didn't know.

'Let's buy Jane some flowers.' Freddie steers me into the hospital shop; I'm silent, my hands are clammy and still shaking. Numbly, I help him choose, let him pay, let him hold my hand as he leads me to the lift. 'Come on, love. Don't be too upset. Jane needs you cheerful.'

I don't answer because I can't. Silently we take the lift to the Renal unit, come out into the lobby I am getting to know so well. My eyes dart everywhere, my pulse races, but I can't see my father. Perhaps I was mistaken—

'Hullo. You've come back already.' Sister Vera Akram stands smiling at us. 'I'll take you over to intensive care. How sad you've had to interrupt your honeymoon.'

'Is my father here, Sister?'

'I haven't seen him. Mind you, he knows his way around already – he would have gone straight there. This way.'

There's a row of hooks with gowns and masks for those entering the ward. On one hook hangs a checked jacket. He's here.

'Wait a moment, please. Your father's in there already. Gown up while we wait.' She taps on the glass viewing panel and another nurse, gowned and masked, pokes her head out.

'We are dialysing Jane at the moment.'

'Her sister's here.'

My father appears behind her. 'Nat! I didn't expect you until tomorrow!' He shuts the ward door behind him as he slips down his mask. I haven't put mine on yet, so gowned in white we kiss and hug.

'Dad, this is Freddie.'

'Good to meet you.'

'I'm very pleased you've been able to come over, Mr Harper. I know it's a desperately sad reason, but at least I have the pleasure of meeting you.'

'Call me Dick. Well, well, well, look at my little girl.'

My father's eyes are brown like mine, he's very tanned, his grey hair is beautifully cut. He's wearing a stud in his left ear. He looks different, smarter, more attractive, his tan thrown into relief by the tattered white hospital gown.

'Hardly little, Dad.'

'What a transformation. Our soignée barrister, successful and married.'

'You've changed too. It's been a long time since we've seen each other, lots of time for changing in.' I want to meet Dad's eye, but his gaze is sliding about. I can hear a clink as Freddie nervously fingers coins in his pocket.

'Beautiful ring.' Dad is still holding my hands, turning them over.

'It belonged to Freddie's first wife.' I don't have to tell him that, but I suppose I do because it makes me look less lucky.

'It's a family ring,' says Freddie. We stand there ill at ease in our threadbare gowns, and then all speak together:

'We're like a trio of druids—'

'Anthea didn't like it—'

'Only two of us can go into Jane at once—'

'You two go. Take as long as you like.' Freddie stands back as Sister Vera opens the door to call us in. We slide our masks up.

Jane is a frightening sight. She's on a ventilator as well as the dialyser; an unfamiliar nurse is in charge, checking readings, bending over Jane. Jane's face is white as milk, her eyes are shut.

'Jane, your sister's here too now, with your father.' Jane's eyes do not flicker; I touch her hand but there's no response. Yet I feel she's alert to us.

'Jane, it's Nat. You poor poor thing.'

She is silent – the only sound in the room apart from the swooshing of the dialyser is from my father as he rustles through Jane's notes. I feel I have to chatter to fill the gap.

'Budapest was lovely, and the Danube is quite something. Only it's not blue, can't think why it's known as the Blue Danube. Amazing art nouveau architecture everywhere. Amazing. Anyway.' I want to cry for my sister. I've never seen anyone so pierced with tubes. I try to hold her hand, the hand that is free of them, and she moves it ever so slightly. She's heard me, she's there but far away. 'It's good to be back, the weather's lovely outside.'

'Jane.' Dad comes up, takes my place. 'It's early evening now, Wednesday evening. Nat and I will be back tomorrow morning. We're going off now to catch up on news, years and years of news. You'll be out of this room in a couple of days, perhaps less, isn't that so, Nurse? The infection is responding well. She'll be right, girl, she'll be right.'

Dad sounds so bracing and hopeful I expect Jane's eyes to fly open. They don't, but her mouth tenses as Dad touches her forehead in farewell. I get the impression there is a miasma of anger being silently emitted by Jane's body, anger so intense it is shutting her off from us all as we leave her.

'She's so sedated she's barely conscious.' We take our gowns off and put our jackets back on – Freddie's looking very English in his tweed jacket and old corduroy trousers, Dad is natty in his checks. I turn to Sister Vera, who has followed us out.

'How did she develop this infection?'

'She got infected round the wound where the fistula enters the subclavian vein. There's always a risk of infection there, unfortunately, and her defences are very low, she can't fight back properly. It's very bad luck, because she was stabilising nicely.'

'How long will that fistula remain there?'

'Two or three weeks, then we put a permanent fistula in her arm for easier vascular access. I'm sorry, I have to rush back to the ward.' I stare at Sister Vera's retreating back, numb.

Freddie clears his throat, a mannerism he usually reserves for appearances in court.

'Now. I'm sure you two would like some time together. I've a variety of suggestions—'

'I've only got one – a drink. We need a drink.' My father takes my arm.

'I could leave you both to catch up on family news—'

'No need, is there, Nat? You're family too. Right on – let's head for the nearest pub.'

We get into a lift full of medical staff discussing some internal management edict. Crowded lifts always impose self-conscious behaviour on everyone in them: Freddie's staring at the ceiling as if it's a planetarium, Dad is fascinated by his shoes. Somebody has farted silently and the smell fills the lift as it creeps to a stop on the ground floor.

'Dutch ovens.' Dad waves his hand about to clear the air as we head for the exit. 'Silly game you can play in bed. You fart and pull the blankets over your partner's head. Crude Aussie stuff.'

'Dad.' I put my arm through his; Freddie drops behind us on the long corridor out of the hospital. 'Dad, I've noticed a change in you. You've come out, haven't you?'

'I thought you knew already. Didn't Jane tell you?'

'No. Not a whisper.'

'Odd.'

'Perhaps she thought I might be shocked.'

'And were you?'

'Yes, but only because it was so unexpected. I don't understand—'

'It's a long story. No it's not, it's a short story. I was bisexual when I married your mother and buried the other side of me. Now it's having its turn.'

'You look happy on it, Dad.'

'Not all of the time but who is? I do feel – well, adjusted.'

'Is this the reason you didn't want to come to the wedding?'

'Shit, no. I was too busy, like I told you. And now here I am anyway. So there you go. Freddie, what about this pub?'

Freddie was already poking his head in. 'It'll do. How about some champagne?'

'You're on.' My father's accent fluctuates a bit, but it's always

there. He and I sit down while Freddie deals with the barman.
'He's got style, your fella.'

'I know.'

'He seems a nice man.'

'He is. But Dad, let's talk about Jane for a moment. She looks terrifying. What is really going to happen?'

'Chronic renal failure is bloody terrifying whatever happens.'

'And a transplant is her only hope.'

'Don't forget even with a transplant you have to take drugs for the rest of your life in case your body rejects the kidney, so transplants aren't a bundle of fun either. You get fat, you get acne, you lose your hair. I can't see Jane liking the side effects.'

I stared at my father. I had only thought of the positive side of a transplant; it seemed simply like giving Jane a key to a locked door. Through it she'd go, good as new.

'Some people who've had transplants get so fed up with the drugs they stop taking them. The kidney collapses, they're back on dialysis, it's all been a big waste. Thanks, Freddie. This is very kind of you. Your health, both of you.'

'And yours.'

'It makes me sad that I'll never be able to drink Jane's health like this. The rest of her life will be a holding operation.' Dad takes a long pull at his champagne.

'It's tragic.' Freddie says this with such feeling we all fall silent for a while. Then my father goes on.

'I can't give her a kidney, either. Her blood group is B, mine's AB. That dose of A antigen would cause a violent reaction. If I remember rightly, Nat, you're O.'

'Am I? It's ridiculous, but I don't know. So I'm not the same as Jane either—'

'No, but Jane's blood won't quarrel with yours. Your blood is compatible. Other antigens in your tissues might not be, of course. Not that I'm in any way suggesting you should even consider giving her a kidney. As I said, it could be a waste. I wouldn't be sure that Jane would be a sensible recipient.'

Freddie is twiddling his champagne glass as we talk. 'I have to admit, Dick, I'm dead against Natalie giving up a kidney.'

'I am sure you are.' Freddie gazes at him as I refill our glasses.

'Nat's too young to have a scar like that. However neatly they do it, however well she heals, it's still a twelve-inch scar.'

I bang down the bottle. 'Let's talk about something else.'

But Freddie takes my hand. 'Listen to Dick, Natalie. He knows.'

'I know he knows, and I know a lot too. The only fact I hadn't fully appreciated was that the recipient of a kidney has to keep taking drugs. But please don't let's talk any more about it. Dad, tell us about your homeopathy practice in Sydney – it sounds as if it's going very well.'

'I seem to be good at healing people.' He puts his hands together in a gesture I remember from the past. But he would never have had such well-tended unblemished fingers then – his hands look quite different. We talk about his clinic, his clients, his lucky break when he successfully treated an up-and-coming politician he met on a beach and how his practice never looked back after that. He talks and talks: one thing that hasn't changed about Dad is his self-absorption. He doesn't ask Freddie a single question. Not that this bothers Freddie – he always finds it difficult to explain 'what he does' to people who know nothing about the workings of the Bar but think they do. His only contribution to the conversation is to suggest we either have another bottle of champagne or go out to dinner.

'No more champagne, thanks. And I'm afraid I can't join you for dinner. I've made other arrangements – I didn't expect you to come back from Budapest so promptly. In fact, if that's the time I'm late already.'

'Have dinner with us tomorrow, then.'

'I'll do my best. But I'll see you at the hospital anyway. I must fly, please forgive me, and thanks for the champers.'

Freddie and I sit on in the dimly lit pub after he's gone, finishing what is left in our glasses and being comfortably silent together. At last, I break the silence to ask Freddie what he thought of my father.

'I liked him. I found him a surprise, given the fact he's got two daughters yet he's obviously gay. You never mentioned that.'

'I didn't know. I'm annoyed with Jane for not telling me. She gave me no hint.'

'Your sister runs her life to rules of her own.'

'Right on, as Dad would say.'

'He has your eyes and much the same aura of energy.'

'He's still a selfish bastard. He put my mother through hell. He may be good at healing people but I'm sure he does it as much for the kick it gives him as the relief it gives them. I know that doesn't sound very kind, Freddie, but I had to live with Mum after he'd gone, and I learned too much about my father.'

We sit on absorbed in our thoughts. My diamond ring flashes blue, white, green, red, gold, as I lift my glass. Freddie holds my other hand.

29

Freddie walked through South Kensington towards the Victoria and Albert Museum humming to himself. Natalie had gone to St Thomas's on her own leaving him to his own devices, a phrase he'd always loved. To be walking through London midweek during term time on his way to a museum felt like truanting.

He hadn't visited the V&A for years, not since Anthea's death. She'd been so indefatigable about galleries and exhibitions she'd belonged to every art-connected society, with the result a constant flow of invitations to openings and previews had come through the door while she was alive and for months after her death until her subscriptions ran out. He'd reacted against them and attended none.

Natalie was by contrast markedly unaware of London's art scene. Or the literary or classical music scenes. She knew a great deal about films and jazz and the serious end of popular music. Freddie smiled as he looked up at the white stone crown that topped the great Victorian building. He had everything to learn and so had she. Fun.

He spent two happy hours in the V&A and then walked up Exhibition Road into Hyde Park towards the Serpentine. As he passed the gallery in the park, he noticed it was holding an exhibition called FLESH. It wasn't clear whether the painter was called Flesh or was depicting it. Anthea would have known, would have been already. He hesitated, then decided he would much prefer a sandwich and a brisk walk round Hyde Park to an exhibition that promised maximum obscurity and minimum attraction.

So he ate his sandwiches and drank his coffee and left the

cafeteria to begin his walk, but as if Anthea had her hand under his elbow he found himself going into the Serpentine Gallery to view FLESH instead.

The nightmare pounced. Huge smooth expanses of unbroken skin ended in red shreds, wounds split into swathes of viscous carmine, shards of bone and unidentifiable gristle, decayed stumps. Flesh damaged, flesh dissected, flesh crushed and pulped by metal, tyres, weapons. Close-ups of orifices: a toothless baby's mouth, tonsils, ears, a bloodshot eye, a clitoris, penis tips erect and flaccid, a rectum, an erupting boil. Flesh vulnerable, flesh ageing, flesh engorged, flesh cut open, flesh perfect, flesh rotted. Freddie stumbled through the rooms of mixed media constructions in a rising panic until he saw the exit and ran from the building through the bare autumn trees as his brain whirled.

He sat on a park bench and tried to calm himself. He stared at the flesh of his hands in his lap; his father's hands had been identical, and maybe back through the generations so were the hands of the seventeen-year-old Mentieth who joined Bonnie Prince Charlie's army . . .

The nightmare tried to creep back round these determined thoughts and with a gasp Freddie let it come. Tears ran down his face as he let his fears of Natalie's nephrectomy drown him. He dwelt on the images of knife, of long incision, of parting flesh, of the removal of a small dark wet kidney, of its transferral to another open wound, another set of blood vessels. He made himself stare inwardly at the empty hole in Natalie's body, at the neat sealing off of blood supplies, the closing, the sewing of flesh, the march of stitches round that slim, sweet waist.

What am I most afraid of? Of the danger to her life? Of the loss of a living part of her? Of the maiming of her body? Of the risk she takes of losing her own remaining kidney? What is worst? I don't know. And beneath them is another deeper murky thing. Jane has some power over Natalie I don't understand. Natalie seems diminished by her. Her lustre thickens when Jane is near and she knows it.

> *If thou dost play with him at any game*
> *Thou art sure to lose; and of that natural luck,*
> *He beats thee 'gainst the odds.*

Is that what I'm afraid of? That if Jane possesses part of Natalie's body, she'll somehow tarnish her permanently? Spoil our marriage, spoil our lives? It's a mad fear, but the worst fears are based in unreason.

Leaves whirled round Freddie's feet, even landing on his shoes. Two little boys on bikes whirled round his bench, then returned to their distant mothers. A dog sniffed his trousers but decided a nearby sapling was preferable. Freddie saw nothing.

Anthea. Behind Natalie was Anthea. Anthea crushed by a lorry, killed outright while popping out to buy some bread. Only her change purse, house keys and a basket with her. Taken to the morgue pending identification. Freddie returning home as usual, finding no Anthea, no note. Puzzled but not worried. Then the doorbell, and his new neighbour Madame Froissart standing there all eyes.

'I hope your wife is here.'

'She isn't at the moment, but I'm sure she'll be back soon—'

'Oh, Monsieur. I hope she is because they tell me in the baker's that a lady is in an accident just there outside. My friend says it's the lady who lives here, very chic all the time, Henriette says.'

'I'm sorry, I'm not quite with you—'

'It was an accident this afternoon. Just there, by the baker. I was not there, Monsieur, I am only telling you because of Henriette and she is perhaps wrong.' Madame Froissart's round grey eyes under plucked brows hold his; he smells her perspiration overlaid by the scent of her make-up, he notices a mole on her lip, he fixes on the minutiae to quell his rising panic.

'The police haven't contacted me.'

'Perhaps Henriette is all wrong. She doesn't speak English, she told me to tell you. But I am sure your wife will come up the steps just now. So goodbye, Monsieur. I am there if you need me.'

Freddie sees Anthea's handbag in the hall. He sees no preparations for supper. The answerphone is not on. As he stares at it the phone rings. He can hardly bring himself to pick it up.

'Hullo, Freddie, how are you? Anthea said that bout of flu really laid you low.'

'Meryl. Yes, I'm fine now, thanks.'

'Dreadful bugs around.'

'Is Anthea with you?'

'No, of course not. She never comes here if she can help it. Sorry, how mean of me. I was ringing up to speak to her. If she isn't there could you give her a message?'

'I don't know where she is.'

'On second thoughts, the message is too complicated, so tell her I'll ring again later. Stop that, Piers. Bye-bye, Freddie.' Piers's trumpet playing gets deafeningly louder as the line cuts off. Freddie was about to ask her what she thought he should do. He did it anyway. He rang the police.

Freddie could not bring himself to identify his wife. He had looked in the course of his work at many photographs of dead bodies in his time, but he knew this act was beyond him. He could not bear to see Anthea crushed and mutilated. He begged Meryl to come with him, just for the company, he said. She arrived by taxi in record time, red-eyed; she clung to him, sobbing. He could not cry yet.

'Darling Freddie, perhaps it's not her. Perhaps she went off on one of her trips to look at a country house and forgot to tell you.'

'It's her. I've just been given her basket.'

When they reached the morgue Freddie's mouth was so dry he could hardly get the words out when he asked the taxi driver to wait. Meryl held his hand as a policeman went through the formalities and then disappeared for a moment to make sure all was ready.

'Meryl, I can't go in. You'll have to do it for me.'

'Freddie—'

'I can't.'

Meryl shut her eyes. He thought she was going to faint.

'Freddie, together then.'

'I can't. It is beyond me.'

Frozen with emotions he could not begin to identify, he watched her stiff awkward figure follow the policeman through the morgue door. He could not breathe, had not breathed, before she was out again.

* * *

Why didn't I go in with her? Again, what was I afraid of? I failed Anthea, I failed her. I should have had the courage to see her mutilated body. All Meryl ever said afterwards was that she was glad she had done it, said goodbye. They do say you never fully grieve unless you see the dead face.

So I have a horror of damaged flesh. I can control this horror in the line of professional duty, just. Just. I don't look when unpleasant wounds or operations are shown in the media; I simply edit them out. I can't feel hardened to the results of physical violence or accident or operation. I can't bear any big invasion of the skin's containing surface.

I must ask my mother if anything happened to me when I was small. Perhaps I was born in the midst of haemorrhage and tearing flesh – she's never talked about my birth. Or perhaps I witnessed some terrible accident from my pram. I must ask her, ask Elsie.

That exhibition. Surely most people, like the couple wandering round behind me, can see it and not be thrown into a living nightmare?

Freddie sat in Hyde Park for a long time, long after the two little boys had been dragged home for tea. These hours of silence, of self-searching, were unique in his life; he had never spent so long doing nothing but think about himself. He had never used prayer or retreat. When alone in his house or at his cottage he gardened, he read, he thought about his cases, he worked on them. He did not think about himself. He suspected most of his relatives, friends and fellow barristers were the same.

Ralph was different. He had even undergone a couple of years of analysis, paid for by one of his richer women.

'You ought to do it, Freddie.'

'There's nothing I want to do less.'

'That's why you ought to do it.'

Ralph. Ralph had come up to him at the wedding and said Natalie was the best thing that had happened to him. 'Lucky bastard,' he said. He was drunk by this time, but he meant it. 'Fresh of breath air, ho ho ho.'

Ralph. He felt the most piercing need to talk to Ralph. He checked to see if Ralph's number was in his diary and then got up, completely stiff with cold. Once his joints were moving again he hurried back to Blakes, ordered tea and went straight up to the bedroom. Natalie had been back at lunchtime and gone again – a note on the bed said she'd bring her father back to Blakes that evening.

'Ralph? Freddie here.'

'That was a great party. Best family do I've ever been to.'

'Thank you. That wouldn't be difficult.'

'No, I mean it. Our family mostly self-destructs when it meets – for once it didn't.'

'There were a few hitches.'

'Minor.'

'Ralph, have you got a few minutes?'

'Time I have in abundance.'

'I need to talk through a problem, use your wise ears.'

'Not wise. Shrewd perhaps. What on earth are you doing ringing me from Budapest just to ask my advice?'

'I'm not in Budapest. We had to come back yesterday because Nat's sister Jane nearly died.'

'Sorry to hear about that.'

'The problem hinges on the sister.'

'Natalie mentioned she was in hospital. She didn't go into particular detail.'

As Freddie quickly described Jane's condition he could hear Lila shouting goodbye in the background. Ralph answered and a door slammed. There was a pause before Ralph said, to Freddie's surprise:

'You'd find all that particularly difficult.'

'What do you mean, Ralph?'

'You've always been famous in the family for your squeamishness.'

'Really?'

'I'm going back years, of course, but I distinctly remember a family picnic when I cut myself down to the bone and you were the one who threw a wobbly and nearly passed out.'

'I'd wholly forgotten that incident.'

'Your mother then blamed me for upsetting you. I remember thinking, right, that's it. Never trust Aunt Alice. We must have been about eight or thereabouts.'

'I am still squeamish. My first sight of Jane in hospital with tubes in her neck full of her own blood upset me far more than I expected. You'd think after a working life as a barrister I'd be immune by now.'

'Why worry about it, Freddie? You're made like that so accept it. We all have irrational fears. I can't bear touching felt or carpet underlay. I feel physically ill if I do. Hell to me would be to find myself wrapped inside a roll of underlay – I get shivers down my spine just thinking of it.'

'But it's all very well to say ignore my irrational fears when they don't affect others. In Jane's case my squeamishness could take hope away from her.'

'I don't follow.'

'Nat's probably the best person to give her a kidney.'

'Ah.'

'I can hardly bear to think of the physical implications, but quite soon the question will be asked – would Nat do it?'

'My answer – worth nothing – would be to say emphatically NO, she shouldn't.'

'Why not?'

'Nobody deserves to be given something so precious by another living being. There are plenty of accident victims – their kidneys should be used. I know they say there's a better chance with related donors, but there's a better chance of hidden agenda too. I've given you my kidney and look what you've done with your life since then – wasting my gift. Or: I feel so guilty taking your kidney I'll never do you justice. Or: I possess I part of you, you're in my power. Or—'

'You seem to have given it a lot of thought.'

'Not at all, Freddie. I'm just giving you reasons off the top of my head as they come. For instance, if the sisters are close the gift of a kidney could make them closer, or if there are tensions already it could lead to a very tense situation indeed.'

'There are tensions.'

'Don't touch it with a bargepole.'

'My feelings entirely.'

'Sounds as if you didn't need my advice.'

'My reasons aren't good ones.'

'Listen, Freddie, I believe in actions not motives. Motives

never affect events, actions do. What does Natalie feel about it?'

'She's confused.'

'Tell her from me that either way she'll live to regret it. It's a no-win situation. She loses more if she gives up a kidney and regrets it. So don't give one up. But I'm a selfish old sod, Freddie. No altruism in my make-up. Tell me about Budapest. I've always wanted to go there.'

30

'Where's Dad?'

'He'll be back soon.'

'I want him here.'

'He's been beside you for days, Jane. He had to pop out this afternoon.'

'He hasn't gone back to Sydney?'

'Relax, Jane. He's here, in London, and he'll be back at six.'

'What's the time?'

'Four o'clock.'

'It's nice to be back in the ward.'

'You've got some lovely flowers from Sara.'

But Jane has shut her eyes again, floated away. The ward is very quiet except for the shushing of a dialyser being used on the new patient in the other corner. I cradle myself, I can feel my pulse, my heart beating, my lungs filling and emptying. Inside my ribcage my kidneys are busy, invisibly busy.

At half past five Sister Pennington comes and checks Jane's pulse and temperature. Jane wakes up the moment she is touched.

'Good – everything's going well. Stabilising nicely. How are you feeling?'

'I need a drink.'

'With your supper.'

'I'm not hungry. I just need a drink.'

'I'll bring you something soon, Jane.' Sister goes on down the ward, ending at the new woman in the corner bed. But it's clearly someone who has been here before many times from the nature

of their conversation. How is. What's happened to. Has he had.
Did he reject.

'Nat.' Jane's eyes are much more alert.

'Yes?'

'Did Dad tell you he was gay?'

'He didn't have to. I guessed at once.'

'He didn't want you to know. He thought you'd be shocked.'

'I wasn't.'

'You're lying.'

'All right, I did feel shocked, but not for long. Don't let's
argue, Jane, even though if we do it must mean you're feeling
better.'

'Better. Bitter. I feel appalling. I'm just not dying at the
moment.'

'You gave us a terrible fright.'

'You shouldn't have come back.'

'Of course we had to. It was a crisis.'

'I wanted to die. As I got worse and worse I thought, good,
I'm going to die. I can't stand a lifetime of this. I'd rather die
than be trapped as I am. I pulled the tubes out of myself. All of
them. They didn't tell you that, did they?'

'Jane, *Jane*—'

'Killing yourself isn't easy in these places. When I came round
they were all back in. Everyone pretends nothing happened.'

'Don't ever think of doing that again.'

'And in a way nothing did happen. Just pulling them out
wouldn't kill me.'

'Please, Jane. Don't talk like this.'

'Who gave me those flowers?'

'Sara.'

'Thank her for me. And thank you for coming back, you and
Freddie.'

'It was the least we could do.'

'Not the least – the least would have been, oh, sod her, let her
get on with it.'

'How could we ever say that?'

'Easily, if you knew the truth about me.'

There is utter stillness in the ward, a freak stillness throughout
the building. I watch Jane and say nothing. I am so upset by

what she has just told me I feel I can hardly take in any more terrible revelations. Jane has shut her eyes again, is running a dry tongue over dry lips. Then the stillness is broken by a nurse dropping something metal with a crash in the corridor, and Jane's eyes flick open and fix on mine.

'Listen to me, Natalie, listen to me, though I can see you don't want to. Never trust your little sister Jane. Ever since I realised you were there in the nest with me, bigger, older, ahead in everything, I've wanted you out. Out of the nest, out of the way, out of my life. I was born a ruthless human cuckoo and I have stayed that way all my life. You bounced around always smiling, always friendly, one of life's winners, and I hated you. So I always had to go one better than you, to prove to myself as much as to everyone else that I was as good as you, better than you if possible. God alone knows what I'd have done if I hadn't succeeded.'

Numb, I watch her blank face, listen to her flat voice. My own voice is silent, frozen in my throat.

'If I hadn't been clever, been able to get as good if not better results than you, I think I'd have killed myself. It mattered that much to me. I remember when my GCSE results were due I was literally ill with tension. Desperate in case this first big testing was going to fail me against you. I remember telling Mum I had such bad period pains I had to go to bed, and then lying rolling on the floor biting my hairbrush handle until I broke it. Then the results came and it turned out I'd done even better than you. It was the best moment of my life. Pathetic, isn't it?'

Her eyes shut again. I stare at Jane, shattered at all she has said, unable to think, unable to utter. Unbidden, into my mind comes the story of Amanda and Miranda Smallgood. If I had been more like Miranda—

'In the end, I could see there was only one way out.' Jane's eyes are still shut, her voice is a whisper. 'One way out of the hell of family life. I used to dream you'd disappear, fall off a cliff by accident, run away because you couldn't stand me, but you didn't. You were too tough, too well-balanced, too lucky. So it had to be me that went. And when Dad left us, and emigrated to Australia, I knew I had to follow him as soon as I could afford it. Then Mum was ill and dying, and when that dreadful time was over and we both inherited a bit of money, off I went. Say something, Natalie. You look as if you've swallowed your tongue.'

What had Jane said? Too tough, too well-balanced, too lucky? Was that the main difference between me and Miranda? Was sibling pressure of this violence a common thing then, which I coped with because I was lucky, I had a tough mental constitution, and Miranda had failed through intrinsic weakness?

'I wish you'd say something, Nat.'

'It was awful for me too.' My voice emerges as a croak. 'You gave me freedom when you went away. It was like a new beginning.'

'So what I did for myself alone was also the first good thing I'd done for you?'

'Yes.'

'Life is so bloody ironic.'

'Yes.'

'Were you upset when Dad left us finally, left England?'

'Not really. I was too tied up with Mum, with what he'd done to her.'

'I was heartbroken, and neither of you saw it. It was him I loved, him I needed, him I wanted to live near.'

'We knew that. I thought that was the reason you went to Australia. To be near him.'

'It was one of the reasons, but not the main one. You were the main one. I hoped in Australia I'd have a new life away from you, and my father to myself in a new home. But life never works out the way you want it to. He didn't want me to live with him. He was making a new life too and being a father wasn't part of it. We could be friends, that's all. I'd have to find my own flat.'

'How did that work out?'

'Fine for him. For me – it was hard.'

Her lips are covered with cracked flakes of skin as she runs her tongue over them. There's no sign of saliva. 'But I'm tough too, I'm proud. I coped. I began to flourish.'

'So what was the real reason you came back?'

'You invited me.'

'I can't believe that was the only reason.'

'I was curious. I wanted to see where you'd got to. You'd been so cagey.'

'So had you.'

'It's a family characteristic. But you'd hidden more than me.'

Sister Pennington comes up with a small glass of water which Jane sips at in complete concentration. Sister fusses about for a few minutes. Jane keeps her eyes fixed on me, waiting for us to be on our own again, waiting to go on talking.

'Don't be under any illusions about me, Nat. One sight of you in court, of Freddie, of everything he was bringing into your life, and I was right back in the old nest determined to kick you out of it. When Freddie asked me to stay in his house I couldn't believe it, I just couldn't believe how easy he was making it for me.'

My silence is complete because if I open my mouth I feel I will scream.

'You'd done so well for yourself. I'd had a really hard time for a while, what with the abortion and breaking up with Jake, and there you were, my successful big sister, engaged to a gullible peach of a man loaded not only with money but taste and privilege, and about to marry into a style of life that made me feel like a sewer rat. It was almost too much to take in, but I took it in fast. When I left you both at the Garrick after that dinner – remember I went off early in a rush? – I walked for ages back to my awful hotel thinking, thinking, thinking. One thing was clear to me by then. If I was going to break you and Freddie up, there was no hurry. Freddie isn't the type to leave a girl in the lurch a week before the wedding. So I decided to take my time, go gently, get him in the end. And you are gullible, like him. It wouldn't be difficult, I thought. Not difficult.'

'I am not gullible! I knew exactly what you were doing!' My voice sounds as if I've borrowed it, I'm so angry.

'Judgment. That's what all this is. Judgment. I was out to destroy you and I've been stopped. Wham.'

We are interrupted by the arrival of the supper trolley. Jane is given some overcooked food and picks at it. I am so full of conflicting feelings small talk is beyond me. I can't move. I don't want to speak. I am shattered that my worst suspicions about Jane are being confirmed, even exceeded, by this cataract of confession. She's pouring it out as if she has to tell me, needs to tell me, is almost enjoying telling me. As if she's yearned for years to tell me.

Jane puts down her fork and touches her neck near the fistula, wincing as she does so. Then she takes a tiny sip from her miniature glass of water.

'Are you sitting there thinking why the fuck is she telling me all this? Are you?'

'Jane—'

'You've never had something like this happen to you, Nat. I've nearly died twice in one week. Life will never, never be the same again. I feel as if all my past has been wiped out. I'm tied to the disaster in my body for ever, and it seems a sort of judgment for being what I have been. But judgments are supposed to make you repent of your sins. I don't see my way of doing things as sinful. Life is what you make of it, given the starter pack you were born with. Or something. God, I could cry.'

'Jane—'

'Stop bleating Jane Jane like a sheep. Oh, where's Dad? I wish he'd come.'

'What can I say now to you? You have to believe that I knew what you were doing, in essence if not in detail. Get that, Jane. I knew what you were doing. Emotionally if not rationally. I'm not an idiot. I'd have fought you every inch of the way.'

'You wouldn't have won.'

Miranda Smallgood. Perhaps she knew she wouldn't have won. Poor Miranda.

'It's irrelevant now. Irrelevant. Chance has won the battle for me. You said I was lucky by nature, and perhaps I am. But I tell you something, I don't hold with your judgment theory – you're fooling yourself if you think life punishes you for doing wrong. Only your conscience does that.'

'You've always seen things differently from me.' She's tapping her fork on her plate. Her nails still bear traces of chipped varnish, the varnish she put on freshly while she was staying with us.

'Most people see things differently from each other.'

'Are you just trying to make what I've been telling you sound normal, just the ordinary way sisters behave?'

'No. What you've told me makes my blood run cold.' As soon as I've spoken these words I'm sorry I picked them, however heartfelt they were. Jane puts her head back and winces with pain as she laughs one of her unpleasant laughs.

'You'd never use a phrase like that if you were attached to that bloody machine every day watching your blood go round.'

'I'm very sorry.'

'It doesn't matter.' She shifts herself into a more comfortable position while an auxiliary nurse takes away her supper things. 'While I've been lying here day after day having blood pumped in and out I've been deciding many things. First, that when I'm stabilised and have got the physical side under control – perhaps being on CAPD, perhaps with a transplant – I'm going back to Australia. I haven't told Dad yet, I want to tell him now. It's become clearer and clearer that I should go back. There's nothing for me here. But the one thing you needn't worry about, Nat, is that I'll ever take a kidney from you. I wouldn't accept it. I couldn't bear to have part of the sister I've fought all my life sitting inside me keeping me alive. If I can't have a kidney from my father, and I can't, I'd rather have a perfect stranger's. If it doesn't work and goes bad on me, there's nothing personal in it. But if yours went bad on me I'd feel – I would feel poisoned.'

'And how the hell do you think I would feel?'

'Robbed.'

'You don't understand me at all. Not at all.'

'I understand you better than you think.'

'No, Jane.'

'You don't understand me and that's for sure.'

We stare at each other over the void. No, it's not a void any more. It's a space, a defined space, with perimeter and depth fairly clear. We've talked as we've never talked before and probably never will again; Jane at least knows now that I claim to have realised what she was doing, even if she doesn't believe that claim; I know that my fears and suspicions were real ones. One could call this progress of a sort.

'My two beautiful daughters.'

We have not heard him come in. There stands Dad in the doorway, and beside him is Freddie. They are smiling, they look as if they've spent some time together, perhaps chatting over a drink. Dad goes to one side of the bed and takes Jane's hand.

'Hallo, possum. How's tricks? You're looking so much better than you were this morning, believe me.'

'I'm tired, Dad. Natalie and I have been talking.'

'Do girls ever do anything else?'

'Chauvinist.'

Freddie stands back as if unwilling to intrude on a family scene. The sight of him there so unexpectedly has taken my breath away, has filled my heart with such delight and love and relief that I literally can't move or stand up.

Then I put out my hand and he comes over and holds it against his thigh. His shoes are caked with mud and flecks of rotten leaves.

'You look as if you've been for a walk.'

'Just to clear my head.'

'It's lovely you could come after all. You said you couldn't.'

He squeezes my hand hard.

'I sorted things out and here I am.'

Acknowledgements ∫

I would like to thank the following for the help and advice they gave me while I was writing this book: the staff and patients of Guy's Hospital Renal unit, in particular Lesley Kennedy and Helen Cancea (staff) and Sarah Agboola (patient); Primrose Retallack, who talked to me about being a kidney donor; and my husband, who put me right on all legal matters.

Walls of Glass

AMANDA BROOKFIELD

While many regard her marriage with admiration and a trace of envy, Jane Lytton quietly reaches the shocking conclusion that her relationship with Michael, a successful banker with little time for the nitty-gritty of family life, has failed.

Jane's decision to leave a man who does not love her, but who has shown no obvious signs of abuse or neglect of her or their children, is greeted with a mixture of vitriol and measured, uncomprehending sympathy by family and friends. Mattie, Jane's needy younger sister, is walking her own tightrope of depression. Even her oldest friend, while recognising the courage of Jane's action, becomes impatient with her difficulties in adjusting to a new life.

Sympathy and strength come from the most unlikely direction, but just as the seeds of trust have been sown, an unfortunate coincidence of events and human failing throws Jane off balance once more. When her vision at last clears to reveal her best chance of happiness, it seems she may have left it too late.

$\int$

SCEPTRE

The Marriage Bed
DIANA SAVILLE

It is high summer in Paradise. The smell of newly-mown grass and the scent of old blush roses mingle to form a fragrance warm and fresh as peaches; Laura Fenton feeds the black swans on the pond and watches her husband tidying up the lawn.

Geoffrey has given Laura everything she could possibly want: the mossy Elizabethan farmhouse that has been in his family for generations, the garden that is her greatest passion, the children whose children will inherit both.

There are times when her friends feel that just a tiny shudder to Laura's idyllic life wouldn't go amiss. But, unknown to anyone, the harsh real world of banks and business is already threatening the Fentons' perfect domesticity.

As Laura and her husband fight separately to save themselves, the net closes more tightly around them. Laura's former lover is ensnared; so are her daughter and her son-in-law, a City broker. And Laura wonders if love or money could be the answer to her problems.

SCEPTRE